FOREVER *Mine*

BOOK 2
THE TEMPTATION SERIES

ANNIE CHARME

First Published in 2022 by Chambre Rose Publishing

Forever Mine. The Temptation Series. (Book 2)

First Edition

ISBN: 978-1-7399906-3-3

Cover Designed by: Annie Charme

Formatted by: Chambre Rose Publishing

Annie Charme on Spotify

Contains:
This book contains infidelity and discussions on a past pregnancy loss, miscarriage and stillbirth.
For support visit…
www.babyloss-awareness.org/support

This book is for all my readers.

You pick me up after a hard day and remind me that my stories are worth being told.

Thank you for your continued support.

Forever grateful

Annie

PROLOGUE

CAL

"Is that your old work, Daddy?" Olivia asks as we drive by Browns Media.

"Yeah, that's the place." I always drive by here when I collect or drop off the girls. Each time I search the car park for her silver Suzuki, it makes me feel a little closer to her, but I haven't seen it this week. I've been off work for a few days over the Easter school holidays. Spending time with my girls has been a welcome distraction.

I pull up at their mum's two-bedroom townhouse. Priya is waiting and lights up the window with her beaming smile as she waves at the girls. They've been with me for the last week, so I know she'll have missed them terribly.

"Mummy!" Jumping out of the car, they run towards the house, leaving me to grab their bags. Priya opens the door and bends down to hug them both.

"Have you had fun with Daddy?" she asks.

"Mummy, we went to the seaside."

"I know you did. Your dad told me you were going for the day. Did you build a sandcastle?"

"It wasn't beach weather, but we won some toys at the arcade."

"Not more teddies?"

"Hey." I walk by Priya and drop the bags in her hall.

"Do you want a cup of tea?" Priya asks.

"No, I've some stuff to do. Another time."

"Sure. Everything all right? You haven't seemed yourself lately."

"I'm fine, just work stuff—new job and all that." I can't tell Priya about my fuck up with Steph. Although Priya would probably call Steph to discuss how much of a fuck up I am.

"Are they working you hard?"

"Nothing I can't handle."

She smiles at me. The girls have disappeared into the house.

"I'm gonna go. I'll pick them up Monday after work."

"All right. Girls," she shouts. "Come and say bye to your dad."

Olivia and Beth walk back into the hallway. Bethy hugs my waist, and I scoop her up in my arms to give her a big kiss on her cheek.

Olivia leans against the wall. "Bye, Dad."

"I'm not going without a hug," I say. She thinks she's too old for hugs from her dad, but these two will never be too old. I'll still cuddle them when they're thirty, forty even; hell, as long as I'm alive.

She reluctantly walks over, but hints at a smile in the corner of her mouth. Bethy's legs wrap around me as she rests on my hip. Olivia hugs my waist where Bethy's legs dangle, and I hold them both close before kissing them goodbye on their foreheads. "I love you. See you on Monday."

"Love you, Daddy," she says.

I bend down, letting Beth stand on the floor, and wrap both arms around Liv, kissing her forehead. "Love you, Liv."

"Bye, Dad."

She lets go of my waist and goes to stand near her mum.

"See ya soon." I nod at Priya, then head back to the car, rubbing my chest where the emptiness creeps in. I always feel like this when I drop the girls off, knowing I won't see them now for a few days. Steph was right. I wouldn't want this for her. It's hard being away from your kids and even harder being alone.

As I start the engine, I glance at the brown package in the footwell of the passenger seat, where it's been for about two weeks. Every time I finish work I drive home, contemplating dropping my journal in at Browns Media for her, and I chicken out every time. I know she won't be there unless she works late. Which is okay, I just want to drop it off for her. As much as I want to see her, I couldn't take her looking at me like she did that day. Not again. Watching the pink drain from her face and her vibrant eyes turn to a dull shade of sage.

I watched as she gasped for breath and the blood in my veins curdled. My stomach twisted, my heart strangled by the lasso that ties me to her as she walked away from me. I thought about jumping in my car and following her home, forcing her to listen to me, explain, apologise. But that would just piss her off even more.

I thought she would calm down eventually and forgive me as she always has. That was two months ago, and I haven't heard from her. I don't know how long I can live, knowing she's mad at me about those fucking photos. Yet I'm too much of a pussy to drop this damn package off, even though I've nothing to lose.

The worst that can happen is she bins it without reading and continues to hate me, in which case I'm no worse off. But the alternative—what I hope will happen, is that she'll read this and remember all the nice things I've done and somehow they'll outweigh the bad. Then she'll forgive me. That's all I hope for. I want her to know my feelings for her are real, back in our youth and now. I still love that girl, my woman, my Steph.

I know I don't deserve her. She was always too good for me. I knew it, her family knew it, her mates knew it. The only person who didn't know, was her. She always put me on a pedestal, ranked me high above everything and everyone else. I meant the world to her, and I tore her world apart when I left her at uni. And I've done it again. What the fuck is wrong with me? I want to be the man she deserves.

I drive by Browns again, searching for her car. Fuck it. I swerve my Audi onto the side of the road, then make a u-turn, heading for the entrance. The beats in my chest speed up, my ears muffle to the radio. All I can sense is the tightness in my lungs and the blood rushing to my head. What if she's here? I can just drop it off at reception with Sarah. I don't need to go into the office.

Why am I so fucking nervous? I blow out a huge sigh. Before my mind has other plans, I force my body to grab the parcel and get out of the damn car. Darting across the car park, I enter the glass doors of reception and see Sarah sitting at her desk. The bright office lighting bounces off her glossy hair, and she looks up at me, then spreads a smile on her face.

"Callum." She runs around the front desk with her arms out and throws her petite body at me, wrapping her wiry arms around my shoulders. I hug her, lifting her off the floor. She's so light. "It's great to see you. How are you?"

"I'm good. How's things with you?" Even though I'm not good. I haven't felt good in a while.

"I'm really good."

"How is everyone?"

"Same as always, really. Not much has changed since you left, apart from the new guy."

"How's Steph?" I glide my middle finger over my eyebrow, holding my breath.

She looks down at her feet and sighs. Her hesitance to answer tells me everything I need to know.

I rub the ache in my chest, hoping it will go away. "Is she here?"

"No, she's on holiday."

I let out a long breath, and I swallow the lump in my throat. "Good. Can I go through and see everyone?" This might be the last time I'm here.

"Sure."

I walk through the door to the large open plan office and see a bald bloke sitting in my old seat. I smile with relief when I see he's older. Steph won't be fantasising about him as she did me—I hope. A smile tugs at the corner of my mouth as I remember how she liked to fist my hair. Fuck, I loved that too.

Creeping over to Kelly's desk, I bring my finger to my mouth as Chris spots me, hoping he'll keep quiet so I can surprise Kelly. He smirks at me. The new guy gives Chris a quizzical look as I stand behind Kelly, tuck the journal under my arm and place my palms over her eyes, which makes her jump.

"Guess who?"

"Cal?" She spins her seat as I release her, then stands for a hug. "It's so good to see you."

"And you. Where's Steph?"

"She's on holiday?"

"Yeah, I know, Sarah said. Where's she gone? Do you know?"

"Some Greek island, I think."

I nod. That's typical of her to travel back to the same place she always visits.

"I have this for her." I lift my hand holding the brown parcel. "Would you make sure she gets it?"

"Leave it on her desk. She's back Monday."

I place it in front of her keyboard and grab a pen to write 'Stephanie' on the top in big letters. At least she'll be able to have a piece of me with her when I'm gone.

Kelly makes coffee while I chat with Chris. James comes over, then Jerry passes me, and we talk about my new job. Seeing everyone floods me with warmth. This is probably the last time I'll see them. I almost wish I hadn't left. I've spent half my working life here, even though the new job is more money, and bigger clients, I miss everyone. I miss my woman.

In my head, I know it's better this way. I can't be near her and not have her. I hope Steph can enjoy it here, as I did for the last ten years. If it means she can be happy, I'll gladly sacrifice my happiness for her. I fucking love that woman.

CHAPTER

STEPH

With blurry eyes, I stare at the leather book in my hand. The gaping hole in my heart overflows with sadness, and I'm drowning once more. After reading his letter, the thought of him sad and alone chokes me. I can't seem to take a deep breath. I'm a shipwreck, swallowed up by a sea of regret. Pulling a tissue from the box on my desk, I wipe my eyes so I can see a little clearer. I skim through the journal until I reach a new entry near the back dated the day I started working at Browns Media.

> *I dug this journal out after seeing you this week. I couldn't believe it was you. You were always stunning, but you are even more beautiful than I remember. I'd forgotten how I felt about you—really felt—until I saw you again sitting across from me.*
>
> *Honestly, I never thought I'd see you again, not in this life. I thought fate had given us another chance until I saw your wedding ring and you told me how happy you are. Why am I addressing this to you? I guess I'm just writing everything I want to say, even though I know you'll never read this.*

Watching you work, I couldn't help wonder if you still have your nipple pierced under that smart, sexy, sophisticated exterior. I thought about how I would take the ring between my teeth and tug at it, feeling the cool metal on my tongue.

Does your husband do that now? It drives me fucking crazy thinking of someone else touching you the way I used to. I know I deserve this torment for letting you go at uni. Seeing you again today has brought back all the feelings I had for you. They were never gone—just buried.

I close Cal's journal as I hear the guys coming back from lunch. My tears have dried, but I haven't eaten and my stomach rumbles. I hide the journal in the desk before anyone asks questions.

"Are you all right, Steph?" Kelly asks.

"Yes, I'm fine, thanks." Oh no, I bet my makeup has smudged. I pull out a little compact mirror and thankfully, I'm okay; my eyes are red but no makeup disasters.

"Did you eat anything?" she asks.

"There are two croissants left on the breakfast table; I'll polish those off."

"What was in the package?"

I can't stop the whimsical smile from spreading across my face. "It's his diary from university. He wrote things in it about me. I was just reading it."

She sucks in a breath, then squeals, "That's so romantic. You guys."

"Kelly, it's not romantic." But I know it is, and probably the most romantic thing anyone has ever done for me. That and his letter, and his playlist, and the fact he's left in the hope I can move on and be happy with my family. Even though I don't think I can ever move on, but I'm trying to focus on our happy times and allow myself to love him.

Even though we're not together, I am allowed to love him. That's something I never did before. Instead, I blocked him from my memory, and wouldn't allow him headspace. Now there's a little part of my mind where he lives rent free. *A little part? You mean the most part.* My subconscious is right. He takes up most of my mind, but I like him there.

Kelly pouts. "Well, I think it is. You're like two lost lovers rekindling their relationship."

"Not going to happen. That's why he left, remember?"

"What? Even now, do you not think you'll get together?"

"No, I can't leave my family, Kelly." She doesn't have kids, so it's hard for her to understand. I don't mention it again, hoping that she won't bring it up, so I can concentrate on my work. But with every passing minute, I just want to finish reading his journal. I've never known an afternoon to go so pissin' slow. The smile on my face just won't go,

Finally, it's 5pm. Everyone disappears, leaving me in the office alone. I open the journal again, knowing when I get home I won't get two minutes to read, not until the kids are in bed. Even then, I don't want to be pulling this out in front of Justin. Half an hour, then I'll head home. I open the journal at the beginning.

Mum got me this book at Christmas, said it would be good for me to write my memories at university so I can look back in years to come. Apparently writing's good for your mentality. If anyone knows how fucked up I am, it's my mother. Perhaps she's hoping this will help me with my relationships.

I split up with my girlfriend before Christmas. I knew she had to go when I was picturing Steph's face while pounding my cock into her. Stephanie Harrington does things to me she'll never know or understand. Fuck, I've

wanted her since we moved in together two months ago, maybe longer.

I've always found her attractive. She has this girl next door look about her, but I know she's an animal just like me. Hearing her in her room with some fucking shithead had me in a rage. I was with Stacey, my girlfriend at the time, but I wanted to be with her.

It's me she should be with, and my name she should be screaming. Fuck, I have it bad. I need to get laid to take my mind off her—I should just get laid by her—would she even have me? I can't go there. She's my best friend. What is wrong with me?

After reading, I lock Cal's journal away in my desk drawer. I can't have Justin finding this at home. My stomach tightens, and I rub the hollowness in my heart where his love should be. I never knew he felt that way about me before we got together. He was dead against us being boyfriend and girlfriend. I always felt like I had to talk him into being with me, even after we slept together. I never imagined he was shagging his girlfriend and picturing my face.

I can't stop thinking about what Kelly said. How Cal wasn't himself, acting like he was going somewhere. When we broke up before, I was in a dark place. It crushes me, thinking he's struggling. I need to check he's okay and see him with my own eyes.

With jittery hands, I start the engine and drive to his estate. I'm not ready to talk to him and open up old wounds. *You can't open up wounds that never healed,* my subconscious reminds me. I'll never get over him. It's always been him. Nobody else will ever compare to him, even when he's a dickhead. He's my dickhead, and I love him.

My pulse races as I pull onto his estate. I wait around for his car to make an appearance while I call Justin.

"Hi, sorry, I forgot to call. I got held up at work. I'm on my way home now."

"Don't worry, I'll put tea on simmer. It's nearly done."

"What we having?"

"I've done pasta."

"Okay, thanks. See you soon."

My head is all over the place. I wish Cal had given me his journal before now. I would've loved to read it when we were dating, although it would have probably only made the split harder, knowing how he really felt about me.

Somehow, I had convinced myself that he never really loved me. How could he have? He left me and still wanted to be friends. How could we be friends? Surely he never loved me as much as I did him, but reading things from his perspective has made me see him in a different light.

I blow out a puff of air through my lips. My chest caves as I turn on the engine and pull off his estate. I can't wait here indefinitely. Who knows when he'll be home? Plus, I don't want to run into the biker duo again.

INHALING a deep breath through my nostrils, I get a hint of the garlic bread and herby pasta sauce. "Justin, this smells delicious."

He turns away from the stove and smiles, wiping his hand on his grey joggers.

"Have you been to the gym again?"

"Yeah. I finished work a little early." He scratches the back of his neck, then runs a hand through his damp hair.

He's been going to the gym a lot lately, on some sort of health kick. At least he's stopped pestering me to go, and finally got the message that I'll never enjoy working out. Not with him, anyway.

"Cassie, come and set the table," he shouts, draining off the pasta. He places it back on the worktop, and I serve it onto the plates. His arm wraps around my waist, and he delicately presses a kiss to the side of my forehead. He's been very attentive these last few weeks, but after reading Cal's journal today, I can't stop thinking about Cal and how I wish it was him in my kitchen kissing my forehead.

I sit at the table with Cassie and Cairen while Justin slices the garlic baguette. I'm suddenly not hungry as the acid rises into my mouth.

"How was work today?"

"Good, same old." Although it has been anything but. I can't wait to get back there tomorrow to read more of his journal.

"Here, get some garlic bread." Justin hands me the plate, and I take several pieces. Another change in Justin I'm grateful for. After fifteen years of marriage, he's finally accepted me for me. Either that or he's just past caring.

"How was school, kids?"

"Mum, can Chloe come over at the weekend to play?" Cassie asks.

I roll my eyes. "I thought you hated her?"

"She's my best friend."

I can't keep up. "You hated her a few weeks ago." *You hated Cal a few weeks ago, and today you've been sitting outside his house like a stalker.* Fair enough.

"Can she come over, Mum, please?"

"All right." Oh crap, this means I'll have to speak to her bitch of a mother. Mrs head of the PTA and chair of the church fayre committee. She makes me sick. Her husband is an accountant and also on the board of governors. The opposite of Cal.

I wonder if this is how Cal's mum felt when talking to my mother when we were in junior school. He came to every one of my parties growing up. Mum would always throw something lavish and invite the whole class in an attempt to outdo everyone else.

I'm not complaining. What kid doesn't want a party with all those presents? Though Cal's gifts were never high on monetary value, they always meant the most to me. I still have the beaded bracelet he made me for my eighth birthday.

Cairen snaps me from my musings. "Mum, if she's having a friend over, I want a friend over too."

"You can have a friend over on Sunday." I can't deal with a house full of kids all at once.

"I'm not here Saturday," Justin says.

"Oh?"

"I'm going out with the lads from the building site. We're going to the races. I may not be home until late."

"Okay."

"Is that all right?" He smiles and takes hold of my hand, stroking his thumb against my palm.

"Of course it is." I don't mind him going out. I think about bringing Cal's journal home to read all day, but can't risk it being in the house.

"Which reminds me, will you iron my shirt and navy suit, love?"

"Yes, of course."

"Thanks." He leans over and kisses my cheek. I smile, though each time he's overly affectionate with me, it makes my skin crawl a little. I'm still not used to him being like this and can't help wonder what's come over him.

Maybe it's when he thought I was having an affair. *You were having an affair.* Yes, but he didn't know that. *Er, I think he had a pretty good idea.* Yes, well, whatever, it's made him realise he doesn't want to lose me, and he's been nice ever since. I'm not complaining, it's just odd.

CAL

AFTER PARKING on the roadside outside Dean's three-bed-semi, I walk through the metal gate at the front of his drive. I shake my head at the old VW camper parked on the grass next to another old banger with two wheels missing. He says he's doing them up, but there's been no improvement in three years.

"Hey," I shout, stepping through the front door.

"Did you get the beers?" Dean calls from wherever he is in the house.

"Yeah." I walk down the hall with the crate of Stella. As I walk through the kitchen door, I stop dead, eyeing Liz sitting on the worktop. "What the fuck are you doing here?"

Dean walks in, buttoning up his shirt. "She's just leaving."

"Are you two fucking now?" I glare at the two of them.

Dean shrugs and takes the crate from me. "I'll put these in the utility. There's no room in this fridge." He carries the crate through to the utility room at the side of the house.

Liz smirks, then runs her tongue along her top teeth. "Are you jealous?"

"Fuck, no." Although I am surprised Dean would go there after everything she did.

She opens her legs on the counter, and I glimpse her naked pussy underneath her short, black denim skirt. I dart my eyes away. "For fuck's sake, Liz."

She jumps off the worktop, her heels click against the tiled floor. "Chill, Cal. We had fun, didn't we?" Her hands glide up my chest. She smiles and moves closer.

I get a hint of alcohol on her breath, and she smells of strong perfume mixed with a brewery. She brushes her lips against mine, but I feel nothing. Her hand rubs my cock, and I take a step back before it gets any ideas.

"What's wrong, Cal? Has she sucked all the juice out of you?"

She's right. I don't have any juice left. Liz hasn't even got my cock's attention, and that lad's always up for whatever he can get.

I grab her wrists with both hands and remove them from my body. "Fuck off, Liz. I'm not interested."

"Why, because you're shagging big-tits-Bethanie or whatever she's called?" She sticks her small, perky tits out, and I can see she isn't wearing a bra. Her pert nipples are prominent underneath the red cotton of her tight vest top. Tapping her fingernails against the laminated work surface, she glares at me.

Dean walks back into the kitchen. "Are you still here?"

"Her name is Stephanie," I say through gritted teeth. "And I'm not with her. Thanks to you."

"You two sick fucks brought that on yourself." She points between me and Dean. "Don't shoot the messenger."

She laughs wildly, making me clench my fist. If she was a bloke, she'd be feeling my knuckles right about now, but I give her a glare instead.

"Come on, Liz, you've had your fun." Dean takes hold of her arm and ushers her towards the door.

"Okay, I'm going. I don't want to hang out with misery guts, anyway." She stares at me as she walks away, then shouts from the hallway, "You're no fun anymore, Cal."

They reach the front door, and Dean slaps her on the arse. She kisses his lips, staring at me the whole time.

"See-ya, suckers," she says, walking out the front door.

Dean walks back down the hall towards me. My eyes are like daggers firing at his chest. "What the fuck's going on with you two?"

"I figured you didn't want her." He walks past me, grabs the whiskey from the cupboard, and pours us both a drink.

I knock it back in one go, needing something to bring me down off the fucking ceiling before my clenched fist punches a wall. Or worse, Dean's face. "You're fucking?" I slam the glass down on the counter.

"She comes around sometimes, and I show her a good time. It's nothing serious." Dean pours me another whiskey. "Look, if you don't want me seeing Liz, I won't see her again. She's clearly still obsessed with you, anyhow."

"I don't give a shit who you fuck, just keep her out of my business."

"Liz is all right. She's fun."

"Yeah, she's great fun when she's blackmailing my girlfriend." I stop and realise I just called Steph, my girlfriend. I haven't called her that in twenty years. It felt so natural to think of her that way.

"Come through." Dean grabs a few cold cans from the kitchen fridge, and I follow him into the living room. I place my whiskey on the coffee table and sit on his leather sofa.

The dog, Buster, comes in, sniffing my legs. A big black German Shepherd. "Ay-up, mate." He rests his nose on my lap, and I gently stroke the silver fur on his head. "He's looking old now, and tired."

"Aren't we all?" Dean chuckles.

He's right. I spotted a few grey hairs the other day. Steph's probably the cause. I always said that woman would send me to an early grave. "What happened with that Daisy chick? She was hot."

"It didn't work out, mate. She was always fucking nagging. She was worse than my mother. I moved her out as fast as she moved in."

Dean opens a can of Stella and slides a can over to me. I

knock back the remaining whiskey, then grab the can from the table and crack it open.

"So have you seen Steph since all that shit went down?"

"Nah, I dropped a book in for her at work last week. I wrote her a letter, but I don't expect her to come running. Noughts changed, has it? She's still married, whether I'm a dick or not."

"Mate, I'm sorry."

"Fuck it. It is what it is. It's just my fucking luck, init?"

"Here, this'll make you feel better." He tosses me a pre-rolled joint. I pull a lighter from my jean pocket and slouch back on the sofa.

"How's Priya and the kids?"

"They're all right. She's moving." I light the joint and take a long drag, inhaling the sweet scent.

"Where to?" Dean holds his hand out for the lighter, and I throw it across the coffee table towards the leather armchair he's sitting in.

"Fucking Australia."

He lights up and leans back in the armchair after tossing the lighter back on the wooden coffee table. "How come?"

"Her dad's dying. They've given him a year to live. Nothing more they can do for him." I take another drag, trying to think what this tastes like. It's a different flavour to what Dean usually has. "Naturally, she wants to move back home and help take care of him and her mum and spend time with him while she can. The girls hardly know her parents, and she blames me for keeping her here the last ten years."

"I'm surprised you're letting her take the girls. Can't they stay here with you?"

"I suggested that after flipping my lid when she told me, said there's no fucking way you're taking my girls to the other side of the world." I lean towards the coffee table and flick the ash in the glass tray. "She begged me not to fight her. I wanted to ask the girls what they want to do, but she said *'don't make them choose between us or put any pressure or guilt on them,'* and she's right."

"I don't envy you, mate. What a fucked up situation." Dean takes a swig of the can in his hand.

"I apologised, but she knows I struggle to go a week without them, let alone fucking months at a time. She said *'I'm sorry my dad's dying.'* And I felt like a twat." I take another toke on the joint and lean my head back as I blow the smoke out.

Dean puffs on his spliff. "Mate, that's tough."

"She said, *'What option do I have? It's my duty. I'm their only daughter.'* That's why her parents hate my guts. They never forgave me for keeping her in the UK."

"I remember all the stress, mate."

"She said, *'You knew I wanted to move back to Australia years ago, and I stayed for you. I've missed so much time with my family, and now it's too late. Don't ask me to miss anymore time. The girls should know them.'* I get it. She needs them as much as I do. I won't fight her. I'm just gonna have to visit as often as I can, and she'll bring them back when she can."

"That's gonna cripple your bank account."

"Yeah, tell me about it." I take another drag of the joint. The room fills with the scent of blueberry muffins like Dean's just pulled a fresh batch from the oven. "That's what this is. Blueberry muffin."

"Right, it's good, init? I grew it myself."

"Nice. I'll have some from you." Steph would love this. She'd probably prefer a real blueberry muffin, but the smell of this is just as good without the carbs as she would say. I smile as I think about her always on a diet. Why can't she accept she's perfect just the way she is? She clearly doesn't believe a fucking thing I tell her anymore. Especially after all that photo shit.

Leaning forward, I flick the ash off into the ashtray. "You know what the worst thing is? She's taking Steve the fucking dweeb to Oz with her."

Dean pulls his bushy eyebrows together. "I thought you liked him."

"I do, even though I've never met the bloke, but the girls like him. I'm just fucked off that he'll be living with them on the other side of the fucking world, seeing my girls more than me, and I can't do a damn thing about it."

"Has he got a visa or green card or whatever, then?"

"Not yet. He's applied for one, but he's a fucking teacher, so they're not gonna deny him one, are they? And I'm glad Priya will have someone with her, but it just gets to me, you know."

"What's keeping you here? Go back to Australia. You lived there before. I bet you could get a job out there easy. Putting some distance between you and Steph may be good for you."

"I've applied for a working visa. So just gotta see if it gets approved."

"You were moping around after uni. Maybe the surfer chicks will get her out of your system again."

Maybe he's right. I'm constantly looking for her, waiting for her to call, hoping she'll come knocking on my door each night.

"I always thought you two would end up together. I've never known two people so different, yet so in love with each other. She was like the ying to your yang."

"Yeah, just keep rubbing that salt in."

"Soz, mate. We could always murder the husband. I reckon between us we could do it."

"Don't tempt me." The thought had already crossed my mind.

"Accidents must happen all the time on building sites." He chuckles and has another drag. "Why wouldn't she leave him?"

"She said it was her kids, but you should see their house; a fancy detached. It must be five or six bedrooms. If I had all that shit, it might tempt me to stay as well."

"So if she has money, why the fuck does she drive that old Suzuki?"

"She said she likes that little car. Stop fucking talking about her, anyway. You're supposed to be taking my mind off her. Some fucking mate you are."

"Come on, then. Let's get shitfaced. Do you want me to call Karla and her mate to show you a good time?"

"No way. I can't be doing with another bird. I'm going celibate. Women are too damn stressful."

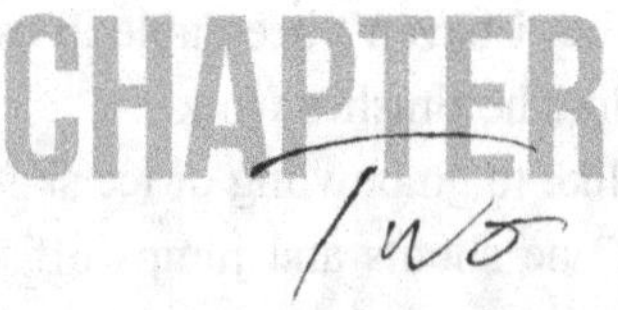

CHAPTER Two

STEPH

"I'm off then." Justin shouts over the sound of the hoover. I turn it off and look him up and down in his crisp white shirt and navy suit. I'm not used to seeing him dressed like this. The suit seems to fit him better than it ever has, especially as he's been working out a lot lately.

"Okay, see you later."

He walks over to me and lifts my chin, pecking my lips. "See you later. I'm not sure what time I'll be back. Don't wait up." His blue eyes twinkle as the sun shines through the window.

"Have a good time."

He nods, forcing a blonde strand of hair to flick over his forehead before he spins around and walks out the door.

"Mum, can we do something fun today?" Cairen slumps on the sofa, flicking his legs over the arm and points the remote at the TV. "I'm bored."

"Play with your sister and Chloe."

"I'm not playing with girls."

I wheel the hoover into the utility room and grab my phone from the worktop. Googling things to do, I check out what activities are near Callum's house. I'm verging on stalking now. *Not verging, you are stalking. You've been at his house every night this week.* I drove by to see if he was home, that's all, but I haven't been able to catch him. I'm not even sure what time he finishes work.

"Would you like to go bowling or ice skating?"

"Ice skating," he shouts and jumps off the sofa, running upstairs. "Cassie, do you and Chloe want to go ice skating?'

Within minutes, they're all downstairs getting their shoes on.

I lock the back door and grab the car keys and my purse. We all jump in my Suzuki. I still haven't upgraded. It's been all right since the battery died on me last winter, so I don't see any reason to spend money on a new car when this one is perfectly suitable. "Buckle up kids."

Turning on the radio, I listen to the latest chart music while I drive down the street, heading towards the leisure centre near Cal's house. The girls natter to each other in the back seat.

Cairen sits next to me in the front. "Are you ice skating with us, Mum?"

"No sweetheart."

"Mum, you never skate with us." His lips turn downwards and his eyes well up like a basin filling up with water.

"You'll be okay. You have Cassie and Chloe to skate with." I ruffle his hair.

"But I want to skate with you. Last time you watched while Dad took us on the ice."

The thought of skating terrifies me, making my palms clammy. I can't skate. The last time I skated, I was about nineteen. I was with Cal in London. There was a temporary ice rink set up near the tower for the winter period. It's only because I read about it in his journal this week that I remember it. I continue to drive and my mind drifts back to that time.

Cal kisses my cheek and nods towards the ice rink. "Fancy a skate?"

"You know I can't skate." I giggle.

"I'll hold you up, or I can get you one of those little penguins to hold on to." He chuckles and bumps my shoulder. His breath materialises in the cool crisp air, and he takes a drag on his cigarette before stubbing it out into an empty flower bed next to the wall we're sitting on.

"Come on" He stands and pulls me with him, interlacing his fingers with mine as he leads me towards the rink.

We've been together for almost a year, but I still get tingles when he holds my hand. I glance at his face and his rough unshaven jaw and can't stop my lips from pressing against his cheek; they have a mind of their own, wanting to kiss him all the time.

The bristles on his skin prickle against my lips and it sends a flicker straight to my centre. My hand squeezes his, and he smiles, turns his head and takes possession of my mouth as we wait in the queue for the skates.

Once on the rink, I daren't let go of his hand. He laughs as I cling to the railing, then he skates off doing a solo like Christopher Dean. Well, maybe not quite that good, but he skates effortlessly around the rink. He's fearless.

My bum was bruised after falling over a few times. He caressed each bruise with his mouth when we got back to the hotel. I would gladly bruise myself every day if I could feel his lips on me like that.

"We're here." Cairen's voice breaks me out of my memory, and we all make our way inside after I park the car.

I scan the leisure centre on the way through for any sign of Cal or his Audi. The boxing club membership we got him is for here. The gym is next door to the ice rink, but I don't see his car. I knew it was a long shot. What would I even do if I saw him? Probably nothing; especially with the kids here. I can't get into all that again. Not now Justin is actually trying to be a good man. Although it's too little too late as I think I just have the ick now. Every time he touches me my body shivers for all the wrong reasons.

Cairen's face lights up when I pay at the reception for one adult and three kids. The girls lace up and skate off doing their own thing. "Do you want a penguin, Cairen?"

"They're not penguins, Mum. They're polar bears."

"Oh, well, whatever. Grab one."

"They're babyish."

Dammit. I wanted one for myself. I slump over to the rink, knowing there won't be anyone around tonight to kiss my bruised arse better.

CAL

AFTER COLLECTING the girls from Priya's, I drive us to the gym. They're enjoying their self-defence classes, and I've even got used to the karate kicks the girls keep giving me. I pull up at the lights before I turn into the car park.

"Give it back," Bethy whines.

"You said I could have it," Liv says.

"Only to look at, not to keep." Beth wrestles with her sister over a stupid fidget toy.

"Hey, give it a rest. Nobody is having it if you're going to row over it." I snatch the plastic popping thing from them and as I face back out the front window, a silver Suzuki pulls out of the car park. I can't quite see the driver, but I notice two girls in the back. It couldn't have been her, could it? Fuck, I'm seeing her everywhere I go. I know it's just wishful thinking on my part.

A woman passed me in the city, causing me to do a double

take, thinking it was her. Another night out with Dean at our old haunt rock club, a woman caught my eye. The back of her long brown curly hair fell just above her perfect full round arse and those voluptuous hips.

I took in a breath, stopped what I was doing and wrapped my arm around her waist from behind, only to find it wasn't her, it wasn't my Steph. She didn't look at me with the same smile that Steph always had for me. Her eyes didn't sparkle when she looked at my face, and her body didn't react to mine the way Steph's always would; leaning in closer, pulse quickening and lips parting with a jagged breath. None of that happened. She pulled away, giving me a wary look, and I apologised before retreating to the bar.

Fuck, I miss her. I looked for that woman after a few drinks, but she left. I don't know why I looked for her; I knew it wasn't Steph, but I wanted to take her home and imagine it was her, feel those thick thighs wrapping around my waist, close my eyes and picture my woman. She would never come to the club. Rock music isn't her thing. She's more likely to be at the 80s bar down the road.

Bethy screams, snapping me out of my thoughts. I turn around to Liv, pulling on her sister's hair.

"Will you pack it in?" A car beeps and the lights are on green. "For fuck's sake. I'll drop you two back off at your mum's if you carry on." I pull into a parking bay. "Are you gonna apologise to your sister?"

Liv pouts, her big brown eyes looking up at me, and I can't stay mad for long. "Sorry Dad, but she started it."

"Bethy, say sorry."

"Sorry." She sticks her tongue out at Liv, and I chuckle under my breath. There's no wonder I'm seeing things and losing my mind. Them and Steph. My girls.

"Come on, let's go." We walk into the gym, a modern building, fairly new with big glass doors covered in vinyl graphics that we designed at Browns Media. The girls' skip down a corridor to their class. It's already full of the other students, and I blow them a kiss.

I walk into the gym, drop my bag in the locker room, and make my way to the punch bags for a warm-up. I have an hour to get some kickboxing in; something I used to do as a kid.

After Dad left, Mum thought it would be good to get all my anger out there instead of beating kids up at school for no reason. I think it worked to a certain extent. Now I just like to kick the shit out of the punchbag. It's either that or Justin. How I'd love to wipe the smirk off that smug bastard's face. I can never forget the glare he gave me when I picked Steph up for our London trip. I know it was a warning; the way he kissed her in front of me then walked away with a smile.

Argh. My foot collides with the bag again and again. He better treat her right. Does he deserve her? Do I? Probably not. I know I don't, but I don't know how anyone could love her more. The love I have for that woman is like nothing I've ever felt before.

I didn't think it was possible to love anyone more than my girls, but seeing her again and being with her has rekindled those feelings I had years ago. She makes me feel young again.

Fuck. If I was young again, I'd do things differently. The mental image I have of Justin morphs into my younger self. I loath that twat even more, and slam my fist into the padded leather bag, as if trying to knock some sense into my youth. If I wasn't so fucking selfish back then, I could be with her now. Our kids would be ours, and we'd be happy. I'd be a lot happier than I am now, that's for sure.

My fist hits the leather again and with each slam, a memory of how I treated her badly pops into my head. That little fucker never knew a good thing when he had it.

I was awful to her. I should have been there for her when she thought she was pregnant. Instead, I avoided her, shouted and treated her like shit. Bang. My hand aches from hitting the bag with all my strength.

We'd been together for about a year when Steph's period was late. That was the deciding factor for me. I knew then I had to end our relationship. My head fills with memories from our past.

She's on her knees, begging me to take her back. Her lifeless eyes are pleading with me while she unzips my jeans and pulls out my cock.

"Steph, what are you doing?"

"I'm showing you how much I want you." Her hand grips my soft dick, but within seconds, I'm hard as a rock.

Moving her hand up and down in swift motions, she licks the tip while gazing into my eyes. Fuck, it feels good, but wrong on so many levels. I won't go back with her. She thinks if she can convince my dick, my mind will follow.

"Steph—" I want to say stop, but the word won't come out because my dick's having too much of a good time.

She takes my now full erection into her mouth and teases the tip with her tongue. My head tilts back, and I close my eyes, running my fingers through her curls. I tug her hair, forcing her deeper. Her hand plays with my balls just the way I like. Fuck, how can something so wrong feel so right?

She stops and whips off her jeans along with her knickers. Her neatly shaven pussy is right before me. Normally, I wouldn't hesitate to kiss her sweet lips there, but I just stare. She straddles me, furling her fingers around my neck.

"Steph, I'm not fucking you."

"I'll get a condom." She bends to the side and opens the bedside drawer where I keep a stash. I've only started using them again recently, since we thought she was up the duff.

She opens the wrapper and positions the johnny. My mind

is saying no, but my cock has other ideas and stands proud as she slips the cover on.

After wiggling her bottom and grinding against me, I slip inside her. She rides my dick, looking into my eyes. Her lips brush against mine, but I can't kiss her. This isn't making love, it's just sex. We shouldn't even be doing this, but my dick wouldn't stay soft, so here we are.

Her eyes screw shut when she reaches her peak, just like they always do. When she tightens around me, that's my cue to follow suit, and shoot my load.

She pecks my lips and opens her eyes. "Kiss me, Cal," she whispers.

"I don't think that's a good idea."

"Please, just kiss me. I need you. I need to know you still love me." Her eyes bleed like sap seeping out of a luscious green leaf.

"I do still love you, Steph, as a friend."

She blinks and her tears drip onto my face.

"We shouldn't have done this."

She doesn't speak. Climbing off, she quickly pulls her knickers back on and picks her jeans up from the floor. She opens the door and storms through it, slamming it behind her.

I lie back on the bed. What the fuck just happened? Looking down at my dick shrinking back, I tell him it's all his fault. He needs to control himself in the future. I don't want to hurt her more than I already have, but I don't wan't to be trapped in a relationship. There's so much I want to do with my life. She knows I've always wanted to travel, yet she kept banging on about settling down and getting our own place. I'm not ready to play house and the pregnancy scare was a wake-up call.

Slamming my fist against the hard leather again, I'm jolted back to the present. That kid didn't know what he was throwing away. How could he know he would never find someone that loved him like she did? I punch the bag again. Sweat drips from my forehead, and I wipe my brow with my arm.

No girl or woman has ever looked at me the way she did, those big green eyes that buzz with electricity when she sees me. Her dimpled smile that brightens up my soul like stars brighten the night sky. Her touch was a rich silk swathing my skin in pure unconditional love like a mother swaddling her infant. That's how she loved me.

Nothing I've ever experienced comes close. She knows me better than anyone and still loves me despite all my flaws. Or she did until I hurt her again. I need to fix this, but I don't know how.

STEPH

Teddy rubs his wet nose against my face, waking me from a dream. Justin called last night to tell me he was staying at a mate's house after the races turned into a full session in the city. I check the time on the alarm on the bedside cabinet and roll over, pulling the duvet over my head, hoping Teddy will let me sleep in for a little longer.

I close my eyes again, thinking of the dream I just had. Callum was in bed next to me, moving the hair from my face. I bury my head into the pillow and imagine it's his chest. Teddy barks and scratches on the door, making me jump. I throw the duvet off and jump out of bed. I'm not a morning person. Justin usually gets up early and sees to the dog and kids on a weekend.

As I walk through the kitchen, I flick the kettle and open the back door to let Teddy out. Luckily, the kids are still asleep after watching a late night movie, so I can have my coffee in peace. I check my phone for any new notifications as I do every morning, hoping one might be from a certain person. My shoulders drop when there's nothing since the text I received last night from Justin telling me he's crashing at a friend's.

Teddy whines at the back door, so I let him in before settling down on the sofa. He cuddles up on my lap as I sip my coffee and pick up my book, a romance about a forbidden love. I huff to myself. Sounds familiar.

An hour later, I walk upstairs to get dressed and wake the kids. I shower, dress and do my hair and makeup. The kids are up now but still in their pyjamas. I hear the door go and the keys rattle. Teddy darts downstairs towards the front door and Justin shouts, "Where is everyone?"

Standing at the top of the stairs, I spot an enormous bouquet. "Who are those for?"

"Who do you think?"

The floral scent travels up the stairs. I try to think if I've missed someone's birthday or another occasion or worse, an anniversary of someone's death. But I can't think of anything happening in April.

"For you, silly."

"Me?" He never buys me flowers. Apart from the one time I asked him to buy me a chocolate egg at Easter, and he bought me a bouquet instead saying that chocolate wasn't good for my diet. I walk to the bottom of the stairs to get a better view of the colourful bouquet; lilies, roses, and carnations. "What's the occasion?"

"Can't I get my wife some flowers? Why does there have to be a reason?"

"They're beautiful, thank you."

I take them from him and walk into the kitchen, still baffled. What is he after? It can't be nookie. He hasn't tried to sleep with me since the beginning of our holiday several weeks ago—thank goodness. The drunken quickie we had in Greece seems a distant memory now, and thankfully, I could barely remember it after the wine.

Since reading Callum's journal again, I can't get Cal out

of my head. Once I know he's okay, I'll be able to move on. *Sure you will.*

I fill a vase with water and unwrap the flowers, breathing in the fresh floral scent as I snip the ends and arrange the flowers. Justin places both hands on my waist from behind and pecks my neck, sending a shudder down my spine.

I tilt my head and flash him a smile, but I want to remove myself from his hands. He's too close. I can smell the alcohol on his breath from the session he had last night, and his suit smells of cigarettes and musty aftershave—Justin doesn't even smoke. I know some of the lads do, but the stale smell paired with his hands on me and his lips on my neck makes me want to heave.

I turn around and take the vase to the dining table, placing it in the centre. It is beautiful and must have cost a pretty penny too. I don't mean to sound ungrateful. I know anyone would love a husband that cooks, worships their kids, and brings home flowers.

It's not him, it's me. I don't want to be with him. My mind is constantly elsewhere. I should never have married him. I guess I felt he was my only chance at happiness, the only one that would ever want me.

After Cal rejected me all those years ago, I felt worthless. The person I loved most in this world and the person I thought loved me unconditionally rejected me. I wasn't good enough for him. I felt I wasn't good enough for anyone. Justin was kind to me. He picked me up when I was down. Yes, he always had the odd jibe about my weight. He was just like my brother and my mum in that respect.

I was so used to taking their crap; it felt natural for Justin to bang on about it, too. It almost made me feel loved. I know that's messed up, but while they were going on about how I need to take care of myself and eat healthier, I always felt it came from a place of love like they cared and wanted me to be a healthier person. Now I know it's just another way of controlling. Maybe my brother says it from a health and fitness freak's point of view. But my mother certainly likes to be in control—always has. From the clothes I wore to the friends she would invite over for tea.

Justin also likes to be in control. It's just his nature and while I think he couldn't really care less about my weight, he likes to keep me in my place. I see that now. Maybe he's afraid of losing me. Hence the flowers and his entire attitude change since Christmas. It makes me feel guiltier, knowing he's putting in so much effort with me, and I still can't get my head away from Callum, even now when I haven't seen him in forever.

"I'm going to take a shower and get changed."

My head snaps back towards the kitchen door where Justin is standing with his arm leant against the doorjamb. "Okay. If you pop your suit on the side, I'll take it to the dry cleaners near work tomorrow."

"Thanks, love."

He disappears and I move the arrangement of flowers around until it's even on all sides. The bright pink roses and the yellow carnations stand out against my cream neutral home.

The front door rattles, and I look down the hall, wondering who this could be. "Mum."

"Morning Steph." She walks into my kitchen like she owns the place. "Put the kettle on, would you? I'm parched."

She takes a seat at the kitchen table.

"What are you doing here?" I flick the switch on the kettle.

"Just popped in. I was passing and thought I'd come and see you. I haven't seen much of you since you went on holiday."

I mash two tea bags in a teapot for her, as she won't have it any other way.

"I hope you've used Earl Grey and not that cheap nonsense you had last time."

"Yes Mum, I have Earl Grey. I buy it especially for you. Don't fret."

"Shall we retire into the dining room?"

Placing the teapot on a tray along with some custard creams, I carry the tray through to the dining room and set it on the table next to my huge flower arrangement.

Mum's mouth drops. "These are stunning. Did Justin buy you these?"

"Yes, they are beautiful, aren't they?"

Her face beams. "You're so lucky to have such an amazing man for a husband, aren't you?"

Am I? The way she dotes on him, you'd think she wants to marry the bloke herself. It's friggin' annoying. I smile and pour her tea into a china cup. She picks it up like she's the queen of England and has a dainty sip. *Queen of Sheba more like it*.

"You should thank your lucky stars. He's so generous and thoughtful."

He's bought me flowers twice the entire time I've known him. What is she pissin' talking about? I nod and shove a custard cream into my mouth, hearing the crunch as I chomp on the biscuit to drown out my mother's ramblings about Justin. "How's Samantha? I haven't seen her for a few weeks."

"Good. They've booked a holiday to the Bahamas."

"Nice. Well, they can go wherever they like with no kids, can't they?" I take another biscuit as she now brags about Sammy. When she comes up for air, I hold up the packet. "Biscuit?"

"No, and I think you've had enough, too."

I roll my eyes and take another just to piss her off.

"I really think you should re-join your slimming group. You're not getting any younger."

"What's that supposed to mean?"

"You want to keep your man happy, don't you?"

"What's me going to a slimming club or losing weight got anything to do with Justin's happiness? If he's not happy, I suggest he take up a hobby."

She shakes her head and sips on her tea, sticking her little finger out. She really thinks she is the queen bee.

"Hello, Nanna." Cassie walks into the kitchen wearing a floral summer dress, coincidentally one that my mother bought her.

"Hello, my little darling. What are you up to?"

Cassie looks at me. "What are we doing today?"

"Nothing. Cleaning and ironing,"

She huffs. "You're always cleaning and ironing on a weekend."

"Well, if you lot didn't make such a mess and have three outfit changes a day, I wouldn't have to, would I?"

She stomps her foot. "Nanny, can I come to your house?"

My mother smiles. "Ask your brother if he wants to come, too."

EACH MORNING IS like groundhog day. I force myself out of bed. Every fibre in my being craves him, his words, his touch, his warm embrace. I have to see him again, to check he's okay, at least. Since Kelly told me about him talking about leaving, I can't help but think he's spiralling into the darkness.

I remember the black thoughts I had in my teens when I felt alone. If anything happened to him, I'd never forgive myself. Perhaps he's just moving house, moving to the city to be close to his new office. Either way, I must see him again.

Checking my car doors are locked, I park up at the top of his estate, like I have done every other day since receiving his journal. His ground-floor apartment is in view, but his car isn't parked in his bay. I wonder if he's moved house already and I've been coming here after work for nothing. Kelly said when she saw him last, he sounded as though he was going somewhere, or he could just be working later these days. My hand grabs the pepper spray, remembering how things went down with the unsavoury duo. I'm determined to wait around this time so I can catch a glimpse of him. He must get home soon.

I text Justin while I wait. 'Running late x.'

Turning the key to start the engine, I contemplate leaving just as the heavens open. Rain hammers against my windshield and there's a flash of light in the grey clouds. I turn the engine off and wait out the downpour. Listening to the sound of rain on my tin roof soothes my mind, but the thundering sound from above sends a shudder through me and the crack of lightning spikes a bout of nausea.

This was a bad idea. What if I'm struck by lightning and die right here outside Callum's house? How would I explain why I'm here? *If you're dead, you won't be doing any explaining.*

My fingers tap against the dash as I stare out of the window through the veil of water pouring down, like I'm trapped in a car wash.

A black car pulls up at the side of me and my breathing halts. His window winds down, bringing his face into view. My heart thuds like the rain beating against my windshield.

He stares with a gaping mouth before shouting, "Steph."

His voice drowns out the rain with the jumping of my heart. I'm not ready to talk to him yet.

My Suzuki roars to life as I shift into gear to back up off the estate.

He manoeuvres his Audi behind me, blocking the road, then runs to my car door, tugging at the handle. "Steph, talk to me. Are you all right?"

I put the car into first gear. What was I thinking coming here?

He runs to the bonnet, trapping me between his body and his car behind. "Steph, please talk to me." His palms press down on my bonnet.

The rain drips off his nose, his wavy hair hangs limp and saturated. I daren't accelerate in fear I'll hurt him. Panicked, my foot presses hard against the break, I tense my body, not knowing what to say or do to get myself out of this situation.

A car pulls up behind Cal, pipping its hooter. "Oi, Cal, move your chuffin' car. What you playing at?"

"Gimmie a minute," he growls at his neighbour. The ink visible through his white shirt, sticking to his skin as the rain soaks into the fabric. "I'm not moving, Steph, until you get out of the car and talk to me. I'll get on my hands and knees if I have to." His powerful bicep flexes as he tenses against my bonnet and his inked sleeve ripples as his hands clench. "Please Steph, don't make me beg."

The guy honks his horn, getting more agitated by the second. "Callum, what the fuck?" he shouts through his window.

Cal turns his head with a scowl. "One fucking minute."

I can see this turning bad quickly, so I get out of the car. Typical April showers, glorious one minute and pouring it down the next, and I don't have a coat or a brolly.

Cal runs over to me, unclipping his house key from the

set. "Let yourself in while I move my car. Give me your keys and I'll move yours, too."

I hand them over and sprint down the small hill to his apartment at the bottom of the cul-de-sac.

I walk through the hallway, placing his key on the small table. Upon entering the kitchen, I notice my book on the worktop tucked behind the fruit bowl with various coloured sticky notes coming from the pages. Opening it, I see he's highlighted so many parts. I smile as I go through each marked up page; our first time, our first time again in this house, London, Christmas.

A photo falls out onto the worktop. Picking it up, I see myself asleep, my hair splayed over a white pillow. The image is cropped at the top of my breasts, showing my bare shoulders. My chest tightens thinking he took photos of me asleep, most likely naked. Oh no, please no. I gasp for breath. The door rattles as he enters, and I hear the key turn in the lock.

The hairs stiffen at the nape of my neck and the acid rises in my throat as I walk into the hall. "Have you just locked me in?"

"Yes, but you're free to go when we've talked." He holds the keys up and places them on the side, along with my car keys. Every inch of his white shirt has turned translucent, showcasing his magnificent torso with his black ink and the crows ascending from his pelvis onto his stomach.

"You're soaked." My voice breaks as I speak while gazing at his chest.

He runs his fingers through his dripping hair, leaving droplets along the tiled kitchen floor. "I'm glad you're here, Steph. How are you?"

I pull my eyes away from his body and gaze into his sunken sockets. "I'm okay, are you?"

"Yeah, better now I can talk to you." He unbuttons the top

of his shirt, then pulls it over his head. My eyes wander back to his inked chest. I've missed seeing him like this.

"When did you take this picture?" I hold up the photo of me sleeping.

"In London." He swallows, stepping towards me with a hand reaching out to take the photo.

"Is this it, or is there more? More of the photo, I mean." I dig my fist into my cocked hip and wave the photo in front of me. "Have you taken pictures of me naked?"

"Steph, I'm not a sick fucking perv," he growls, pulling his wet hair back from his face. "I wouldn't take photos of you like that."

I frown at him, knowing his track record with photographs. My stomach twists thinking of before. "You got Dean to take those other photos. I wouldn't put it past you."

He sighs, scrubbing a hand over his face. "I told you I was sorry about that."

"I want to see your phone." I hold my hand out for him to hand it over. "What other photos do you have of me?"

He steps closer. "Steph, you didn't come here to argue with me about photos." His fingers stroke my neck and his thumb brushes against my cheek, making my pulse quicken and my body tremble. "You're not going to begrudge me one fucking photo, are you?"

"If it is one photo and no naked ones, let me see your phone." My voice waivers as he continues to stroke my cheek, and I feel myself crumbling under his touch, as I always do, but I stand my ground and hold my hand out between us for his mobile and tap my foot while I wait.

"Fine." He pulls his phone from his pocket and unlocks the screen as he hands it to me in a huff.

My head throbs along with my heart at what I'll find on his gallery. As I scroll through his photographs, images of his gorgeous girls light up the screen; those big brown eyes and raven hair, olive skin, radiant smiles. Mostly candid shots, capturing them laughing and playing, unaware of the camera and then some posed with Cal taking funny selfies.

I smile inwardly at how adorable he is with his girls, but it's short-lived. Anxiety creeps up my throat, and I gulp down the prickling lump as I scroll past all the Christmas photographs, knowing the London trip will be up next.

My breath hitches when I see pictures of me at the work Christmas party. I'm smiling talking to Kelly, holding a glass of champagne. The next one of me is in London, walking around the art gallery. He's captured me from the side looking at a painting and another of me laughing and looking down, then there's the one of me sleeping. The duvet covers my breasts and thankfully you can't see anything, makeup is smeared around my eyes, and I look natural.

There are a few he took of me like this and then I see some from work, sat at my desk working and another reading my book. All natural unposed shots, then a few from the club event of me dancing with Kelly. I look ridiculously sweaty. My heart swells that he would take so many pictures of me, knowing that's all I'll ever be to him; a picture and a memory.

"I'm sorry." I hand him back his phone with a heavy heart. Why did I make such a big deal of the photo? Of course, I don't begrudge him photos of me.

He takes the phone from me and places it on the worktop. "Are you satisfied?"

My body tenses as I hold back my emotions and stop myself from throwing my arms around him to feel his body against mine. I want to kiss his lips and have his tongue slide into my mouth. I want him to make me feel all the things I haven't felt for so long since the last time I was here.

"I'm sorry. You're right. I didn't come here to argue with you. I wanted to check you were all right, and thank you for the journal."

He steps closer, his hands graze the thin fabric of my slightly damp navy blouse, running his fingers down my arms, awakening the goosebumps that have been dormant for so long. He never fails to elicit something deep within me, even when I'm still mad at him.

CHAPTER *four*

STEPH

His hands grip my arms, holding me in place. "Steph, I miss you. I love you. Please don't hate me. I can't bear you hating me for another twenty years."

Pain stabs me in the chest. "I don't hate you, Cal. Well, I do, but I still care about you."

He smiles as his hand goes to my cheek. "There's hope then."

I press my face against his palm, feeling the warmth from his hand. "There's no hope for us. I just wanted to make sure you were all right."

"The fact you're here tells me there's a glimmer of hope that you'll forgive me. I don't want to leave things like this between us. It's killing me. Tell me, Steph, tell me you'll try to forgive me." With his hand firmly on my neck, his thumb strokes my cheek with the gentlest, most delicate touch.

My heart already forgave him. It's my mind that's telling me not to, restraining me with every brain cell while my heart is pulling me closer with that invisible bungee cord that always bounces back into his arms.

I nod, lifting my face to gaze into his beautiful brown eyes that seem darker today, full of sorrow with a flicker of red; a hint of burning passion, love, and pain. It would be so easy to melt into his lips only inches away and let all my problems dissolve for a moment while I feel his love on me once more. I know he loves me in his own way. He just makes stupid choices that always result in hurting me one way or another.

I clear my throat as I resist the urge to kiss his lips. "You marked up my book?"

"Yeah, just some of my favourite parts I like to read. Did you read my letter? I'm guessing that's why you're here." Both hands caress my neck, his fingers tangle in my hair, and his thumbs stroke my skin.

"Yes, I read everything. Thank you." I look away, fighting the pull into his eyes.

He lifts my chin. "I meant every word. Nothing's changed for me, Steph. I still want you."

"Cal, please, not this again." But hearing him say those words sends a flicker in the pit of my stomach and I inch closer to him, resting my hands on his taut chest, feeling his heart beating as fast as mine. I bring my lips to his mouth ever so slightly, hoping he'll take the bait and kiss me voraciously as he would do before.

His warm breath with a hint of mint falls on my face, but he doesn't come closer. "Why are you here if nothing's changed for you?"

"I told you, I wanted to check you were all right."

His hands move to my shoulders, then grip the top of my arms, digging his fingers into my flesh. "Well, I'm not all right. I can't stop thinking about you and what our life could be like. I want you."

"Then kiss me," I beg.

He pulls me to his lips as they collide with mine, feverishly lapping his tongue around my mouth. I heat instantly as a light burns through my body, deep into my soul.

"Is this what you want?"

"Yes," I say.

Cal grips my arms tight as if he's never going to let me go. The water from his hair runs onto my forehead as his stiffened tongue darts into my mouth once more. Rough hands wander under the silky lining of my skirt and squeeze the top of my fleshy thighs. His ravenous lips suck along my neck before his teeth nip at my ear.

"Steph, baby, let me show you how sorry I am." His fingers dig into my outer thigh, and I want them between my legs.

"Show me, Cal." Leaning against the kitchen counter, I succumb to his will as he runs his tongue down my chest, popping open each button to my blouse as he goes. Roaming over my black skirt bunched around my waist, he reaches my full black satin knickers, and presses his lips against the fabric.

His hot breath seeps through, sending a wave of unquenchable lust through my centre. "Baby, I've missed you." He tugs at my knickers and pulls them down my thighs, then squeezing my cheeks, he buries his tongue between my folds and finds my bundle of nerves.

Tugging on his saturated hair, I rock my hips shamelessly into his lapping tongue. I wasn't exactly sure why I felt the urge to come here again—but now I know—this is what I came for, to feel his wicked tongue on me once more, those lips and his hungry mouth that never fails to bring out the sinner in me. I tug harder and moan as his stiff tongue licks in rhythm with my hips and everything tightens. The tenacious pressure builds, and I need to orgasm. I need it like I need to breathe.

Cal groans into me as he always does and the vibration from his mouth wrapped tightly around my swollen bud has my pleasure turned up another notch.

"Cal, I want you inside me." I beg. "I need to feel you, all of you, inside me, please."

"Not yet, baby. Not until I've shown you how sorry I am." He's on his knees, teasing, sucking, licking and nipping. The ache in me is desperate for something to fill the void, anything, him, his fingers. I need to come. I can't take much more of this. His tongue enters me, circling, pushing just inside my entrance, soft but firm strokes as his nose rubs against my sensitive spot, still fisting his hair I hold his head in place as I rock against him rubbing my slickness against his tongue and his nose, moaning and calling his name.

"That's it, baby, come for me." And I come like a bolt of lightning ripping through me just as the thunder rips through the heavens. My body trembles violently as the surge forks out into every limb, making them weak and pliable. I slide to the floor on my knees to meet Cal and wrap my arms around his shoulders. He holds me on his kitchen floor as I take a minute to come back to earth.

The downpour beats heavily on the kitchen window as I become aware of my surroundings again.

"Baby, I'm gonna make love to you now." His deep voice hints at a tremor. I lift my head to look into his eyes. Pools of desire swirl around his dark pupils. His lips trail my jaw, teeth nipping everything they come into contact with.

Using his large hand, he lowers me onto the floor. A shiver shoots down my spine as my heated body connects with the cool kitchen tiles. He untangles my knickers from my ankles, then slides his rough palms up the inside of my legs, forcing them wide open. The air hits my wet heat, causing another shiver of delight.

The sound of rain pelting hard against the glass fades as I lay quivering, watching him kneel between me. He unbuckles his belt and pulls down his trousers along with his boxers. Fisting his bulging erection in slow motions up and down, his eyes rake my body over my unbuttoned blouse, revealing my black lace bra. His tongue licks his bottom lip as his eyes roam between my disgracefully wide open legs, displaying my voracious, aching sex for him.

"So fucking sexy, Steph." His gruff voice causes my temperature to rise, and my panting breaths become more rapid as he continues to run his hand over his length. "I've dreamt about this, about having you one more time. You're always so hungry for me, so ready and willing, and I'm gonna show you how much I fucking love you and your dripping cunt. You won't be able to walk by the time I've finished showing you how much you mean to me."

"Cal," I pant. "Show me."

"Not until you tell me what I like to hear."

"What?" I move my hands down to circle my tender spot, desperate for him to touch me there again. Watching his grip tighten, his movements get faster, and it's so hot watching him stimulate himself.

"You know what I like to hear," he says in his gravelly voice, and it's like my vagina can hear the words as it pulses every time he speaks. "You want me?"

"Yes Cal," I cry. "I want you, I want you inside of me, please."

He leans over me, using his palms on either side of my head to support his weight. I run my hands over his body, scraping my nails down his back as he presses his erection against me, teasing, rolling his hips.

"You want this?"

"Yes, stop teasing me."

"Tell me you love me."

"What?"

"Tell me, Steph, I need to know you still love me."

"I never stopped, Cal, please."

He smothers my mouth with his lips and his full arousal

pushes into me. I'm lost in him once more, connected to him on a spiritual level. I see stars as he thrusts into me, stars brighter than anything I've ever witnessed, swirling in a vast galaxy of cosmic splendour, shimmering, glorious, sublime.

"Fuck, I've missed you. There's been nobody else, Steph, nobody since you."

"I love you, I love you, I love you." I chant as he pounds into me, hard and deep.

"Baby, I love you. I won't last. It's been so fucking long."

I run my fingers through his hair, still wet and silky, tugging and pulling him to my lips. His hard tongue darts in and out of my mouth in a passionate rage.

"Cal, just come into me. I want to feel you come inside me."

"Baby, I'm coming, I'm coming." And I feel the surge pulse through him as he spills inside of me, taking me over the edge with him. I feel myself tighten around him and he pulsates again, crying out my name. My eyes screw shut and all I see are stars bursting all around me into a glistening sky.

I needed this closure, or make-up sex or whatever this is. I needed it to help me move on with my life. Hopefully now we can both move on, no more worrying about the other half living, knowing the other is miserable.

"Steph, are you all right?"

"Yes." I exhale a breath. "I just need a minute." I can't think straight, I can't see straight. My bones are still weak, and he's right. I don't think I can walk or stand right now.

He collapses on top of me, and I hold him while we both breathe in sync, our hearts beating in rhythm with the rain thumping against the window.

He rolls to the side of me and lies flat on the kitchen floor. "Fuck, this is cold."

"I know. Why did we end up on the kitchen floor when

you have a comfy bed down the hall?" I smile, turning my head to meet his gaze.

"I didn't want to move to another location in case you changed your mind." He grins, then pulls my neck towards him, kissing my lips. "I miss you, baby."

I roll onto my side and take his face in my hands "I miss you, Cal." My lips press to his again in a slow and sensual kiss.

He stands, pulls his trousers up, then holds his hand out for me, helping me up. My skirt bunches around my waist, allowing the cool air to dampen the wet heat between my legs.

"I need to clean myself up."

"Here, let me." Pulling out a tea towel from a drawer, Cal runs it under the hot tap, then gets back down on his knees to wipe the warm, sticky liquid from my inner thigh. "Steph, seeing my cum all over you is making me hard again."

"Cal, as much as I would love to go again, I have to go."

He continues to wash me, running the wet towel over my slick, swollen pink lips.

"Make sure you wash that on a 90 degree wash before drying your dishes with it again."

He laughs, then stands and kisses me again. The rain has stopped, and the sun is now shining through the window. Everything seems lighter, most of all me. I'm weightless. The front door handle rattles and then a knock travels down the hall. I suck in a breath, wondering who it could be. My first thought is that it's the slut who took photos of us. Is he still seeing her? My chest tightens, and I quickly pull my skirt down and collect my underwear from the floor.

Cal smiles. "It's my kids. I forgot Priya said she was dropping them off."

I let out a sigh of relief and scurry to the bathroom to sort myself out. When I return to the kitchen, Cal is still topless, but he has his trousers back on at least and Bethy in his arms. A woman with bobbed black hair and olive skin is talking to Cal, but stops when she sees me. I swallow, unsure of what to say or do, while my feet itch to retreat back into the bathroom.

"Priya, this is my friend Stephanie."

Her kind smile reaches her light brown eyes, and I see her daughters in her face. "Hello Stephanie, nice to meet you," she says in an Australian accent but she doesn't look Australian, more of an Indian beauty, like a Bollywood actress. Of course, he would only date gorgeous women with model style features, making me question again what he sees in me.

"Hi, I've heard so much about you," I say.

"Oh dear," she says, smiling at Cal. "Whatever he's told you about me is a lie. I'm actually a really nice person."

"Fuck off," Cal says. "I've said nothing bad about you."

She smiles and raises her eyebrow as though she knows otherwise, and Cal laughs.

"So are you two…?" She waves a finger between the two of us.

"No, we're just friends. I'm just leaving, actually."

Cal looks at me with furrowed brows. "Not yet. Stay a while. I'll order us some food, or cook something." He lets Bethy go, and she skips into the living room, calling for her sister.

"I'll leave you to it. Don't forget Olivia's dance performance tomorrow. And don't forget the tickets for you and your mum."

Cal rolls his eyes. "I won't, 1pm, I got it. Tickets are in my wallet."

"Nice to meet you," I say.

"And you, bye."

Cal sees her out, and I grab my purse and car keys.

Following him into the hall, he closes the door after Priya and stands in front of it. "Don't go yet, please."

"I have to, Cal. Justin will wonder where I am."

He runs his hands along my arms. "Each time you run back to him, a piece of me dies inside."

I know that feeling. I know it all too well. Seeing Cal with someone else destroyed my soul. "Cal, you know why I can't be with you."

"I know."

"I loved your journal."

"I loved your book. Will I see you again?"

"I can't start this again, Cal. I just came here to make sure you were all right. It was tearing me apart, thinking you were miserable. Kelly said you looked like hell."

"I was in hell. Every day without you is hell."

"I'm sorry." I look down at my feet, tormented that I can't please everyone.

"No, I'm sorry. I know this is for the best, as much as I want to do this again, and believe me I want to do this again, over and over again, but I'm afraid there won't be anything left of me at the end of it."

His eyes are dull, like a withered tree in winter with no sun. I wrap my arms around him. His cheek presses against mine, the bristles scratch my soft skin, and I turn my face to kiss him there. "I will try and leave him. I promise."

He pulls away. His eyes are wide, hinting at a ray of sunshine seeping through thick clouds. "When?"

"I don't know. It's my son's birthday in two weeks. I have to get past that first and then I'll see."

He rolls his eyes. "Don't fucking bother."

"What's that supposed to mean?"

"There'll never be a good time for you, Steph."

"I promise, I will leave."

"When? After your son's birthday? Then it will be your

birthday, then your daughter's birthday, then the fucking dog's birthday, then Christmas again. Forget it."

"I'm sorry Cal." The tears threaten my eyes. I don't want things to end badly between us again. "Cal please."

"Fuck off, Steph. Run back to Justin, the jackass, like you always do."

"Fine. I will." I turn around, breathing heavily through my nostrils. Why does he always do this? I swing open my car door and Cal slams it shut. His firm hands push me back against the car and cage me in. Before I can speak, his hot lips smother mine. Our tongues twist in a frenzy of passion.

I close my eyes. The kiss slows, and his tongue gently flickers against mine. We finish with light pecks. If he wasn't pinning me against the car, my body would pool at his feet.

"I'm sorry," he whispers, then kisses my ear and my neck. "I just love you so fucking much it hurts."

My fingers entwine in his hair and, with my other hand, my nails dig into his shoulder as I pull him back to my lips.

"Daddy," Olivia shouts, making me break the kiss.

Cal tilts his head towards the doorway. "Just give me one minute, Liv." He kisses me again in front of his daughter.

"Cal," I pant, shocked that he's still kissing me in front of his kid.

"Steph." He gazes into my eyes as though nothing else exists.

"Dad, Beth pulled my hair. My plait has come out, and I need my hair plaited for the rehearsal in an hour," she cries.

Beth comes to the doorway shouting, "She started it, Daddy."

I giggle. It's nice to know they fight as well, just like my two.

Cal sighs. "Are you any good at plaits? Help me out here, Steph." He looks at me with his big brown eyes.

I fold my arms, but my lips curl in the corner. "I'm still mad at you."

He rests his forehead against mine. "You didn't seem mad a minute ago. Or fifteen minutes ago."

"My hands can't resist this body of yours."

He licks under my ear as he whispers, "Or this tongue, huh?"

Cal pulls me back into the house, holding my hand between his palms.

Liv cries, lifting her messy hair on one side. "Dad, what am I gonna do? Can you fix it?"

"Steph will sort it for you, don't worry."

"Sit down, sweetheart. Let me take a look."

She sits at the kitchen table, and I stand behind her, running my fingers through the left side of her hair that's come loose. Cal walks back into the kitchen with a pink hairbrush and hands it to me.

"I thought your dad would have learnt how to do plaits by now, having two girls." I glance at Cal and flash a smile.

"Dad can plait, but he has to put it in a bobble first."

"I can't do those French or Dutch things." He waves a hand towards Liv's hair and leans back against the worktop as I drag the brush through her hair.

"So what's happening tonight?"

"It's my rehearsal. It's the show tomorrow."

"I see. Is it a dance show?"

"Yes, I'm a butterfly."

"Lovely. Does Beth dance too?"

Cal laughs. "She isn't into dance. She'd sooner go to karate."

I smile and plait Liv's hair.

Cal puts the kettle on.

"Are you and Dad boyfriend and girlfriend now?" Liv asks.

"No, sweetheart."

"But I saw Dad kiss you."

I don't know how to respond. Cal stirs the coffee, flashing me a smile, then takes two steps towards me. He wraps his arms around my waist from behind and kisses my cheek. "I want her to be my girlfriend, but she won't."

My skin tingles where the bristles on his jaw rub against my neck.

"Dad, that's gross."

He chuckles and moves back to the coffee while I finish the braid.

"All done, sweetheart. It's as good as new."

"Thank you." She takes herself off to her room, and Cal hands me a coffee.

"What time's the rehearsal?"

Cal looks at his watch. "In about thirty minutes. Do you wanna come?"

"I really have to get back." I sip on my hot drink, wanting to stay, but my time is limited.

"So this is it, then?"

I take a deep breath and exhale into my drink, watching the ripples in the mug. "I hate goodbyes, you know that."

Cal places his empty cup in the sink. "Let's not say goodbye then."

I look into his desperate eyes, pleading with me. "But I can't see you again."

He leans back against the counter and looks down at his feet. "I know. If you're not gonna leave him, I don't want to see you again either. I can't take you leaving me for him time after time."

I step closer and slide my arms around his waist, feeling the warmth of his body. "Let's just say I love you and leave it at that."

He cups my cheeks in his hands and lifts my face to his. "I do love you, Steph."

"Cal." My words come out choked as the lump rises in my throat. Moisture gathers in the corners of my eyes. I wrap my arms around his shoulders and nuzzle my face into his neck, soaking up his aftershave mixed with the sweet smell of him. The rough stubble that runs onto his neck scratches my cheek and I kiss him there, feeling the hairs on my lips.

"I love you more than you'll ever know. There are no words to describe how much I love you, Cal."

He pulls away, holding me at arm's length to look into my eyes. "I know Steph. I know exactly how you feel because I feel the same about you." He rests his forehead against mine and kisses my nose. "Take care of yourself."

"You too, Cal." I kiss his lips and walk out the door, not looking back. If I look back, I'll cry, not knowing when I will see him again, and once I let the tears out, I don't think I'll be able to stop. I've been here so many times. How many times can two people say goodbye? This is the last time. I can't take anymore. It's all or nothing.

CHAPTER *five*

STEPH

Jerry corners my desk with urgency. "Steph, I have a client coming in half an hour, but I have to go out. Can you see him?"

"Yes, of course. What is he after?"

He waves a hand in the air. "New logo, website, the works. He does spiritual healing or some reiki nonsense. I'll let you get the details. Must dash." He taps a portfolio in his hand and exits the office.

He walks out the building with his briefcase in one hand and umbrella in the other. The weather has been awful lately. I finish the menu I'm working on and wait for my client to turn up.

Sarah shows a middle-aged man through to the office and brings him over to my desk. His bright patterned trousers catch my eyes first, covered by a cream kaftan. I stand and shake his hand, then pull up a seat for him. "What can we do for you?"

"I need a logo, graphics for my vehicle, a website and leaflets."

"Wow, the full works, then?" Jerry wasn't kidding. I grab

a notepad and pen. "Tell me all about your business and any ideas you have."

"Reiki is a form of complementary therapy that works with the energy fields around the body and involves the transfer of universal energy from my palms to the client."

"And what does it do? Like, what are the benefits?"

"Lots of health benefits, including harmony and balance, as well as relaxes and releases tension from the body, helping you sleep better."

I can get all that from sex, and I don't have to pay for it.

"Balances the mind, body, and spirit."

Oh, he's still going. I nod along, listening and making notes.

"Clears the mind and improves focus. Cleanses the body of toxins and supports the immune system and can accelerate the body's self-healing ability."

Can it stop you from wanting something you can't have? *That's hypnotherapy.* "It sounds fantastic. I'll have to try it someday." I humour him, knowing there's only one thing in the world that can help me, and he's the one thing I can't have.

"Your voice sounds hoarse. Are you not well?"

"I'm run down, that's all." I have been ever since…ever since I started working here. "Just a scratchy, sore throat. I don't sleep well, but I'm okay."

"I can help you with that." He claps his hands together and rubs them in fast motions.

"Oh, do you have some throat soothers or something?"

"I can heal it by re-aligning your chakra."

"My what?" Before I can say anything else, he's standing in front of me, waving his hands in my face, then wafts at the side of my head. I glance at Kelly, widening my eyes as if to say, 'help.'

She shrugs her shoulders, curling her lip in the corner.

His hands move in quick motions in front of my forehead. "I'm just cleansing your crown."

"Okay." I close my eyes so I can't see Kelly smiling, as I'll burst into a fit of giggles.

His hands move in front of my throat. "I'm just moving down to your third eye."

"My third eye?" I didn't know I had one.

His hands move in rotation in front of my neck as if he's doing the Agadoo dance. He's currently pushing the pineapple before shaking the tree. Heat rises from my throat, spreading to my cheeks. Is it actually working? *No, that's just the embarrassment colouring your face.*

With my eyes closed, I let him do his thing, but he's not cleansing my mind. I'm still thinking about Callum. However, things are becoming clear. It suddenly dawns on me. I'm making myself ill. I need to take control of my life. Youth is no longer on my side, and I want to make the most of what life I have left. I love my kids, but I need to love myself too. Why can't I be happy? Surely a happy mum is better for them.

I don't know how much longer I can live like this. *You're not living.* I thought if I saw Cal again, I could get some closure, but I can never escape that boy, or man. My man. Every part of me wants to be near him, to see his eyes crease in the corners as he smiles at me, to feel the hairs prick up on the back of my neck when he touches me.

"How does that feel? Better?" The healer asks, snapping me back to reality.

I open my eyes. "Yes, I feel lighter." Has it worked? It's like the weight of the world has lifted from my shoulders. I've made up my mind. I choose myself.

CAL

"DADDY," Bethy shouts after opening the door, and jumps up, wrapping her arms around me.

I carry her through the hallway into the kitchen, where Priya is cooking one of her amazing Indian dishes. "Something smells good."

"Hi Cal." She turns and smiles while stirring the food on the hob.

"Hey. What's all this for?"

"Steve's coming round," Bethy says.

"Is he, now?" I smirk. "Is he bringing his entire family, too?" I look at the variety of food Priya has prepared. She always went to town with her meals.

"It's just Steve. I've made enough for me and the girls tomorrow. I'll save you some if you like."

"Maybe I should hang around and finally meet this Steve. What time is he coming?"

"He'll be here around six, and no, you're not." She swats my arm, shooing me away. "Liv, are you ready to go? Your dad's here," she shouts into the living room.

"If he's gonna be spending more time with my girls and moving to Australia, I need to meet him and vet him for myself."

"Cal, please, I actually like him. You're just going to intimidate him."

"Intimidate him?" I laugh. "Is he a man or a mouse?"

Bethy laughs. "Daddy, you and Steve could be friends. Why don't you invite him to your house?"

I smile and raise an eyebrow. "Maybe I will."

Priya swats my arm. "Clear off and let me finish preparing dinner. I need to change before he comes."

"Go and change. I'll keep an eye on the curry. It's just

simmering, right?" I drop Bethy down on the floor and turn to the hob.

"Thanks Cal. You're not going to poison him, are you?" She titters.

"Don't give me ideas."

She trots off upstairs while I stir her keema, sneaking a spoonful of the hot minced lamb. Fucking delicious.

Liv comes into the kitchen. "Hi Dad."

"Hey lollipop. How's school?"

She shrugs "Okay. Where's Mum?"

"Getting changed. Steve's coming round."

She rolls her eyes. "Great."

"I thought you liked him?"

"He's annoying and so embarrassing. It's bad enough having your mum work at school, but now everyone knows she's dating the ICT teacher. It's not cool. He does talks about being safe on the internet and stuff. He's lame."

"I like him even more." I sneak another spoonful of keema.

Priya comes back into the kitchen wearing a little black dress. I haven't seen her dressed like this in a long time. The fabric clings to her slender frame, showing off her feminine shape.

"You look nice." I wipe my mouth, erasing any evidence of me eating her meal.

"Thanks." She wraps an apron around her and takes over the dinner, putting the saag dish in the oven to keep warm. There's a knock at the door. She glances at the clock. "He's early. Liv, Beth, are you ready? Your dad's waiting to go."

I chuckle. "No, I'm not."

She tilts her head at me and glares.

I step towards the hallway. "I'll get the door for you."

"No, I'll get it." She follows my steps, but I beat her to it and open the door to a beefy bloke.

"Hello hon—" His smile turns to a frown when he realises I'm not Priya.

"You must be Steve. I'm Cal, Livvie and Bethy's dad."

He balances the bottle of red he's holding and a bunch of tulips in one arm and shakes my hand. "Great to finally meet you. The girls don't stop talking about you."

"And you, mate. Come on in." I hold the door open and close it behind him.

He walks into the kitchen. His eyes widen when he sees Priya and kisses her on the cheek, handing her the flowers and placing the wine on the worktop. "Honey, this is amazing. You didn't have to go to all this trouble."

"It's no trouble, really." She pulls a vase out of a cupboard. "These are beautiful, thank you."

She always puts on a good spread. It's one of the things I liked about her. She was always an amazing cook, taught me a thing or two. I'd love to cook one of her recipes for Steph. She'd love my aloo gobi potato cauliflower dish.

"Are you staying for dinner, Callum?" Steve asks, pushing his glasses up above his nose.

Priya waves the oven gloves at me. "He was just collecting the girls."

Bethy's brown eyes gaze up at Priya. "Can Dad stay for dinner, Mum?"

"Yeah, Mum let Dad stay. There's plenty of food," Liv says.

I chuckle. "It's fine girls. We can order pizza when we get home."

Priya looks at Steve in defeat and deflates her shoulders.

Steve shrugs, giving her a kind smile that reaches his blue eyes. "I don't mind, honey."

Priya shoves a plate of roti's at me. "Fine. Take those to the dining room."

The girls and Steve help carry everything through, and we

all sit down to eat. Priya places the keema in the middle of the table along with the saag, dahl, and cool yoghurt. "Dig in, everyone."

I can't remember the last time I had a proper Indian meal, other than a takeaway. "This is nice, Priya."

She glares at me. "Yes it is, and not awkward at all."

I chuckle and feel bad that I ruined her date, but I could never resist her cooking.

"So what is it you do, Cal?" Steve asks as he places a napkin on his lap.

"I work in marketing."

He nods, and there's an awkward silence.

"I hear you're the ICT teacher at school." I tear off my chapati and dip it in the sauce.

"Yes, it's how we met, actually." He takes hold of Priya's hand and smiles. It's nice to see how much he adores her and treats her better than I ever did.

Priya looks at me. "Have you heard anything about your visa, Cal? Steve got his through last week."

A thump hits me in the stomach, so this is really happening. He's really going to be living with my girls. I'm actually looking at the guy that will take my place as their dad. While I couldn't have handpicked a better man myself, my lungs cave as the weight of resentment lays heavy on my chest.

"I've not heard anything yet, but as soon as I do, I'll be joining you. You can put me up until I find somewhere to live, can't you?" I smirk at Steve, then at Priya. Her eyes are wide at the thought of awkward dinners like this, and I put her out of her misery. "I'm just kidding."

They both laugh, but the girls don't get the humour.

"Daddy can live with us, can't he Mum?" Bethy says.

"Sure he can, boo," Steve says, using mine and Priya's nickname for our Bethy-boo. I loosen the collar of my shirt, wishing I'd worn something more casual, but I came here straight from work. I flash a fake grin at Steve as he scoops up the curry onto a folded roti.

The brown curry drips from the flatbread onto his pristine white shirt, leaving a trail of sauce.

My fake grin turns into a genuine smile. "That's gonna stain."

Priya jumps to her feet. "Take it off. I'll put it in the wash."

He whispers to Priya, "I can't sit here in nothing."

"Yeah Priya. He can't sit here in nothing." I bite back a laugh.

"I'll get you a top. I'm sure I have something to fit you."

"Thanks honey." Steve sighs heavily, glancing down at the stain over his beefy chest, then runs both hands over his short brown hair.

"I wouldn't worry, mate. We've got kids. She's used to cleaning up spills. Especially from this one." I tickle Beth at the side of me to ease the awkward silence.

Priya comes down with a large oversized t-shirt of hers from her campaigning days that says 'End period poverty' with a tampon graphic. I quirk a grin and remember her feminist views which I share, of course.

Steve takes one look at the t-shirt with wide eyes. "Don't you have anything else?"

Please say no. I can't wait to see him sporting this.

Priya crumples the top up in her hands. "Not in your size. I'm sorry." She hands it over gingerly with a wince.

Steve takes it into the utility with Priya and returns minutes later, like a good sport, wearing the ensemble. A smile spreads across my face as he slumps into the seat and the t-shirt clings to his body, stretching the tampon over the expanse of his chest.

"Dad, what are you laughing at?"

"Nothing, Beth. Eat your chapati." I chuckle to myself again and dip the bread in the sauce. "So, when are you moving to Australia, Steve?"

He pushes his glasses up and clears his throat. "I'm applying for jobs at the moment. I have a few interviews lined up on Zoom next week. Hopefully, I'll be able to secure a job soon, then hand my notice in."

"So you're not moving out next week with Priya?" I'm kinda glad, but I also wish she had someone with her.

"Not right away. I also have my house to sell. It's all happened rather fast."

Liv reaches over my plate for the yoghurt and knocks Priya's glass of red wine over in my direction.

"Liv," I shout. "Why didn't you just ask me to pass it over?"

She sits back down with the pot of yoghurt in her hand. "Sorry, Dad."

Priya bursts out laughing, pointing at my shirt. "That's gonna stain."

"No shit." I mop it up with a napkin, but the red has splattered everywhere.

"Let me get you a t-shirt." She sits up and smiles at Steve, who looks rather smug.

Priya comes down with an old faded 'I love Hanson' t-shirt.

I take one look at it. "Really?"

She smirks. "It's all I could find."

"Don't you have another period shirt for me?"

"Just put it on and stop being a baby."

Liv giggles as I reluctantly pull it over my head, and Priya smiles. "Suits you."

I glance at Steve, still wearing his smug grin, then carry on eating my dinner.

Priya sways to her own hums and clicks her fingers, singing the words, "MMMBop."

Livvie rolls her eyes. "Mum, that's so cringe." But Priya giggles and knocks my arm with her shoulder, making me chuckle along with her until Steve joins in.

After filling up on her delicious food, I stand and carry my plate to the sink. "Thanks for dinner."

"Do you want to stay for dessert?"

"Nah, I think I've tormented you enough for one night. Come on, girls. I'll call and get us an ice cream on the way home."

"Yay." Beth runs to grab her bag and shoes.

"Good to meet you, mate." I hold out my hand to Steve and stifle the laugh as he stands in his tampon t-shirt.

"And you, Cal. I hope to see you in Australia."

Priya walks out to the car with us and kisses the girls as she buckles Beth's seatbelt. "What do you think of him?"

"He seems decent enough. Look, I'm happy if he makes you happy and treats the girls with respect."

"Thank you." She throws her arms around me and kisses my cheek. I haven't hugged her in a long time. It feels strange hugging her after all this time, and I feel nothing but love for her. Not the same love as I have for Steph, but more of the love you have for a sister or friend. I'd do anything for Priya, but I couldn't stay with her. We're better apart than we ever were together.

CHAPTER Six

STEPH

Walking into the kitchen, the half eaten cake from Cairen's party yesterday sits on the side in a container. Justin hands me a coffee and tells the kids to clean their teeth before school.

The balloon in the shape of a figure eight wafts from side to side and I stare, mesmerised, thinking of Callum and how I need to be with him. I want to marry him. I will marry him. The next time he asks me, I will say yes. I've made up my mind. Whatever it takes, I'll make it work.

"I want a divorce." My throat closes up after spitting out the words and I hold my breath, waiting for Justin to speak.

He slams his empty cup on the worktop. "Not a chance in hell."

"We'll share the kids. Lots of people make it work." I thought I could live a happy life knowing my family is happy, but my misery has been rubbing off on everyone lately. I put on a brave face each morning, cover myself in makeup and apply my red lipstick, but underneath it all, I'm torn between two worlds. The man I love, the other half of my soul, the one that makes me feel at home, and the life I have where I try to keep everyone happy except myself.

"You ungrateful bitch. I've tried my damned hardest to make you happy. What more do you want from me?"

"I'm sorry. I just don't think it's working out. We only get one life, Justin."

Cassie walks down the stairs and rummages through the shoe box in the hall.

Justin walks around the breakfast bar to the kitchen table where I'm sitting. "You should've thought about that before we started a family. We'll talk about this later." His jaw clenches and his eyes are like shards of ice piercing my soul.

"I'll be late home." If I make it home. I could stay at my sister's house tonight or Claire's. The thought of coming home and him manipulating me into staying again makes my stomach twist. I won't stay. Not this time. It took every ounce of strength I have to say those words and I'm not backing down now.

The coffee tastes stale like my marriage. I leave it on the table, grab my bag, kiss Cassie goodbye and Cairen as he comes down the stairs, knowing I may not see them again tonight.

Will Cal still want me? It's been a few weeks. What if he's seeing someone new? I have to tell Cal how I feel and hope he still feels the same. I'll go after work today and tell him. My heart pounds and my stomach flips, but I can't stop smiling at the thought of seeing Callum's face when I tell him, YES, YES, YES to each time he's asked me to leave Justin. It's never too late. I hope I'm not too late.

I DRIVE by his house after work, as I have done many times over the last few weeks, hoping to see him. Hoping I won't change my mind. Hoping he still wants me. I could just call him, but I can't seem to tap his name, afraid that he won't answer, afraid that he's changed his mind. I need to see him, so I can make a judgement call before spilling out my heart to him.

As I drive onto his estate, my breath hitches, seeing his Audi parked in his allocated parking bay. My heart races, and my stomach flips like I'm about to jump on a rollercoaster.

With clammy hands, I grip the steering wheel and manoeuvre the car into the next bay, taking deep breaths to calm my nerves and stop the twitch in my lip. I'm still undecided to go in or not. Justin will expect me home soon to talk me into staying with him. Bile rises in my throat.

If I go into Cal's house, I'm pretty sure of what's going to happen—if he still wants me. There'll be no going back.

I wind the window down, letting the cool breeze hit my clammy skin. The evening sun pokes out from behind a cloud, causing me to blink and pull the visor down. The longer I sit in the car, the more I sweat and not because of the weather.

Sod it. I grab my bag, climb out of my car, checking my surroundings as I grip my pepper spray. Closing my eyes, I knock on his door and wait with bated breath. What if he has his girls? I should turn around. No, I should knock again. No, turn around. I force myself to spin on my heel and step towards the car.

The door clicks. "Steph?"

I pivot on the spot. My mouth open and dry, preventing me from speaking. I can barely breathe as I scan his body in the doorway in nothing but a pair of black jogging style shorts with a drawstring waist. The sun shines on his inked torso, making the phoenix on his chest glisten with sweat like he's just been working out.

I suck in a breath. Who is he working out with? Does he have a woman in there and has just chucked the shorts on for quickness?

"Are you all right, Steph?"

I nod with eyes wide, wiping my clammy palms on my skirt and doing all I can to keep my heart and lungs functioning.

"Come in." He turns sideways, making space in the doorway for me to enter. I take a step forward, then another. With each step, my heart stutters. The door clicks behind me, making me jump. There's no going back now.

My foot collides with a stack of boxes in the hallway, and I place my hands on them to stop the wobble. "Sorry. What are these?"

He smoothes a finger over his eyebrow. "Just packing up some stuff."

Everything in his kitchen is packed up, too. Only a single mug and plate sit on the draining board. "Are you moving?"

"Yeah, I'm just packing the rest of my stuff. I was just moving these boxes into the hallway when you knocked."

That explains the sweat on his body. Plus, the weather is hot today, really hot. It seems ten times hotter now than it did earlier, but maybe that's just me.

"Where are you moving to?"

"Sydney."

I pinch my eyebrows. "I haven't heard of Sydney. Where's that? Is it a village near your work?"

He clears his throat. "Australia."

"What?" I flinch my head back, but I heard him. My entire body heard him as a numbness creeps up my spine and spreads over my skin like ice, freezing everything in its wake.

"My girls have moved back there with their mother. Priya's father's dying. He has about a year to live, so she's gone to take care of him and her mother. I'm moving back there to be with my girls."

I can't speak, everything rushes through my mind, and I

can't form a sentence. Willing my tears at bay, I stare blankly into his eyes, wondering if he's back with his ex.

He steps close. "Why did you come here?"

"I…I… don't know." What's the point in telling him now? He's moving to the other side of the world. My chest crushes that this really is the last time I will see him.

"Steph." One simple word, but the way he says it as a gravelly whisper, encompasses all the love he has for me. He places his hand on my arm, and I close my eyes, soaking his touch into my memory. I take in a deep breath and sigh before opening my eyes to find his lips inches away. His other hand brushes my cheek, and I lean my face into his palm.

"I had to see you. I hope it's okay."

He bites his lip, inching closer to my face. I lift my head to meet his lips as they hover over mine. His fingers wrap around the back of my neck while his other hand presses against my back, thrusting into my body with his.

I suck in a breath, feeling his erection dig into my belly. "Is this what you came for?"

I gulp. Is it? My lips brush against his, hoping I can entice him to part his mouth, but he stands still and doesn't falter.

"I can't kiss you, Steph. I fucking want to believe me, but a kiss isn't enough. If I kiss you, I won't be able to stop myself."

"Then don't."

He pulls away, letting me go as he takes a step back. The phoenix on his chest sinks as his shoulders curl inwards.

I step forward with him, resting my hands on his bare chest. "I mean, don't stop."

His eyes meet mine, and he inches closer once more. His heart beats faster against my palms and the phoenix comes alive beneath my touch. I push on my toes to meet his lips, and he hesitates again.

"Cal, please, I need you." My words come out like a

breathy whisper. *If this is the last time I'll see him, I need to feel him, just once more.*

Our noses kiss and our lips brush. His tongue runs along the seam of my mouth, the signature move I've missed so much. Our lips lock as our tongues entwine with a promise. He pulls me into him so I can feel his erection again, and I'm breathless. My skin tingles where his hands roam like flames licking my skin. The heat rises from my core and spreads over my chest and up my neck, painting my cheeks.

He tugs at my top, pulling it out of my skirt so he can run his hands underneath the fabric, against the bare skin around my back. Pulling away, he unbuttons my shirt while looking into my eyes. The only sound is our heavy breathing as his intense brown eyes peer into my soul.

My shirt falls to the floor, and he wraps his arms around me, kissing my neck and the top of my breasts. I run my fingers through his hair, pulling out the black elastic band. His hair falls, tickling my skin as he nibbles at my chest.

Coming back to my neck, he takes my hand and leads me out of the kitchen. "I'm not fucking you on the tiles again."

I laugh. "At least it would cool us down this time."

He opens the door to the living room. "I told you I didn't want to see you again unless you were leaving him. You've just come to torment me, haven't you?"

My teeth bite down on my bottom lip. *I can't tell him I'm leaving Justin now. I won't make him choose.*

"You know what happens to naughty girls, Steph." With rough hands, he hikes my skirt up and cocks an eyebrow. "No tights, too. You came prepared."

When he speaks to me in that deep tone, my ovaries explode.

A deep rumble leaves his lips as his eyes rake over my breasts in my satin bra. "Do you remember what happens?"

"Yes," I pant.

"You want me to spank you, don't you?"

My walls clench at the thought. "Yes"

He chuckles. "Is that what you came for, Steph? A good spanking?"

"No, but if it will make you feel better, do it." I lean in to kiss him.

He pulls back. "You're gonna have to get yourself a vibrator when I'm gone if Justin's not doing it for you. Or do you already have one?"

"No, I don't."

"Bend over, baby." He pushes me over the arm of his black leather couch and spreads my legs. His fingers hook under the elastic and slide along my slit.

This is what I came for. I knew…I hoped this would happen, this intense ecstatic euphoric high, raw, animalistic passion that only Cal can conjure in me.

"So fucking sexy, Steph. So fucking sweet and soft."

"Cal, I want you inside of me." I pant.

"Your so fucking dirty, that's what I love about you, how you're always desperate for my cock or my tongue or my hand. Tell me, Steph, how much you want me." He grinds himself into my fleshy, plump skin.

"I want you, Cal. Please, I need you inside of me."

"All in good time." He yanks my knickers down and bites my bottom, sinking his teeth into my fleshy cheeks. A jolt of ecstasy bolts through my core. He sucks and licks at the sting and spreads my cheeks. His tongue slides down between my arse, and I tense, squirming as he presses down on my back with the palm of his hand.

I turn my head to gaze into his hooded eyes as he focuses on my arse. "Callum. Not there." I squeeze my cheeks together.

"You're not still hung up about me seeing your arse, are you? I thought we were past all that."

"We are. It's not that."

He teases a finger between my tensed cheeks. "Shh, baby. Let me take care of you."

I squeeze my eyes shut and cringe as I blurt out, "I've been hot and sticky at work today."

With a gruff voice, he says, "Even better. I like you sticky."

"Cal, please."

He chuckles, shaking his head. "Is that what you're worried about?"

I nod and bury my face in a scatter cushion.

"Don't move." He disappears, leaving me bent over the arm of his sofa, with shaky legs. The light shines through his living room window, even through the grey blinds. It wouldn't be so bad if it was evening, but knowing him, he'd insist on leaving the light on.

He returns with a warm wet tea-towel.

"What is it with you and tea-towels? Remind me never to eat or drink anything here."

He chuckles before swiping between my cheeks.

I suck in a breath as he rubs the rosette there and the unfamiliar pressure sends a wave of pleasure through my core. "What are you doing?"

He huffs out a laugh. "I'm washing my salad before I toss it."

My eyes bug out of my head, seeing his gaze fixed on my rear, and I cover my burning face with the cushion again. "I knew I was sweaty and gross."

"There's nothing gross about you, Steph. I just thought it would make you comfortable." He drops the cloth to the floor, spreads my cheeks and, with his tongue, glides down the valley. "Just relax."

"Callum." I screw my face up as the heat bubbles under

my skin and as the pleasure takes over, I shamefully hide my flushed face in the cushion.

"Shh." He continues to spread my cheeks and his stiff tongue circles my rosette.

"Cal. Oh gosh." Feeling his tongue there makes me forget everything, and I don't want him to stop.

"There's nothing I won't do for you, baby."

I'm going to come, and he hasn't even entered me yet. His finger slips into my wet heat and my walls clamp down around him.

"Fuck, Steph."

He flutters his fingers inside me and rims my rosette as I ride the pulsing wave of my orgasm.

"I wish you'd told me you were coming. I need to feel you come around my cock."

"Don't worry. I'm sure you can make me come again." I'm breathless and turn my head to see the fire in his eyes.

"Oh, I will. Don't move." He pulls off his shorts in one swift motion and his erection springs free. I couldn't move if he wanted me to. My centre is still firing as I lay limp over the edge of the sofa. He positions his length at my opening, then slides it between my cheeks, coating us both with my cum.

His skilful fingers massage the tight rosette as he slides his throbbing length into my slick opening. Every inch of him fills me, hitting all the right spots as he withdraws slowly and then rams into me at full force. The velvet material of the cushion grazes my face as he pushes my body further up the sofa.

His finger massages my tight entrance. "Relax."

I breathe out slowly and then inhale deeply, shuddering with desire.

"That's it, baby." A finger coaxes through my tight entrance and my muscles tense again. "Relax, baby." He's still pounding me at a steady pace, hitting all the right spots. His finger pushes in deeper, with each wiggle, my core thrums.

"Callum, stop or I'm going to come again."

He huffs, pulling on my hair with his other hand. "That is the idea." He rams in hard again and faster this time. "I haven't spanked you yet."

I whip my head around to see the smirk on his face, then a crack. The force sends my body jolting forward.

"That's for tormenting me."

My walls tighten around him and his finger crooked inside of me. I screw my eyes shut, knowing another slap of ecstasy is imminent.

His hand smacks against my flesh. "That's for making me want you."

Orgasmic waves crash over me with each sting of his hand. He owns me completely like this. I'm at his mercy, submissive in every way. He can do whatever he likes to me, and I will just roll over and take what he has to give. And I want everything he gives. All that delicious alpha hotness that he demonstrates in our most intimate moments.

Another slap as he ploughs hard. "That's for all the times you ran back to him, leaving me alone."

My eyes water. The crashing waves subside to a gentle pulse, and I don't know why I'm crying. Is it from the overwhelming euphoria he's giving me or the fact that I have to leave him alone again? I bury my head in the sofa cushion and wipe the tears before he notices.

Catching my breath, I hum into the pillow that covers my flushed face.

He slips out of me then, using my cum, he coats my arse, rubbing my entrance. "I haven't finished with you yet."

My body tenses when I feel the head of his erection

pushing into the tight rosette of my arse. "Callum, I can't take anymore."

"You're gonna take it. It's my leaving gift to you. You're gonna feel me inside you for the next week." He works the head into me. "Breathe, baby. Just relax."

I pant into the cushion. "Cal. I'm not gonna be able to sit down."

He huffs a laugh. "Good. I want you to feel me every time you sit down. I'm gonna give you a leaving gift to remember."

He pushes in deeper. I clench my fists around the cushion as the pinch burns, but sets my core on fire.

Moans escape my lips, and he grunts as he thrusts into me more, filling me up to the hilt. My legs vibrate. His palm glides up and down my spine, soothing me.

"That feels so fucking good," he growls, then digs his fingers into my fleshy hips. "Are you all right? You're doing so good, baby."

I hum into the pillow. Having him inside me so tight like this is pain and pleasure rolled into one.

He pulls out slowly, then back in again. "Fuuuck, Steph. I wish you could see what I see."

"What is it?" I pant, resting my head against the cushion.

"My dick filling up your tight ass. I'm gonna fucking explode any minute."

"Don't come yet. I want both holes filled. I want all of you inside me." My head may explode along with his dick as the euphoric pressure builds again.

His fingers find my slick folds and work their way into me. "Like this, baby? You like it like this?"

"Hmm." I can't speak, only moans and pants leave my lips as he pumps both entrances. Everything is tighter. A gratifying stretch as he fills me with love, working me into another frenzy. My hands grip the cushion in front of my face as Callum's pace picks up, and his balls smack against my arse with every thrust.

He leans over and fists my curls, forcing my head back slightly as he comes with a low guttural growl, pulling taut on my hair, and my walls pulsate around his fingers. "That's it. You did so good, baby, taking all of me like that."

His rhythm slows. The grip on my hair loosens, allowing my head to drop forward onto the pillow.

He leans over, planting soft kisses along my back before pulling out of me, leaving my body limp and shaking. "Don't move. I'll clean you up."

I can't move, even if I wanted to. I'm breathless, boneless. The waves are still lapping around my toes. I've never experienced anything like that before, only in my books.

Cal collects the wet cloth from the floor and wipes between my folds, then up between my cheeks. His soft lips press against my back and move down to the sting on my bottom.

I turn my head so I can see his glorious face. "I love you."

His arms wrap around my waist, and he turns me over. My breasts smash against his chest, and he kisses my nose. "I love you."

Pulling myself up, I perch on the arm of the sofa, not quite able to stand. His lips press against mine, and I giggle, turning my face to the side.

"What's wrong?"

"I know where that tongue's been."

He chuckles. "You liked it, though."

The heat from my centre rises to my cheeks. "Yes. Do you want me to do that to you?"

He smirks.

"I want to be inside you, like you are me."

"Maybe one day I'll let you." He holds me tight against him. "Now give us a kiss."

"Not until you wash your mouth out."

He takes my face in his hands and slips his tongue between my lips. I can't help but kiss him back.

"How long do you have?"

"However long you want me."

"Forever, Steph. I want you forever."

I lift the hair from his face, and he presses his lips to mine once more.

"Do you want a drink? I'm gasping after that."

"I'm pretty thirsty." My vagina still pulsates along with my arse with the imprint of him, and my mind is still dazed from my high. After a moment, I pull my knickers up and adjust my skirt before wandering into the kitchen to find my blouse.

Cal pours a glass of water. "Who said you could get dressed?"

"What?"

"I only got up for a drink," he smiles.

I freeze.

"I'm teasing. You can get dressed, but I want to fuck you again before you go."

"Okay." Gosh, I won't be able to walk after tonight. My knees already feel like they could buckle under me at any moment, but I don't care.

"What do you want to drink?"

"A water, please."

Cal drapes my blouse over the dining table chair. I wrap my arms around him from behind. He has his shorts on now, but he's still topless. I run my lips along his lower back where there's no ink. He turns, handing me a flavoured water, what I like.

"Thank you." I take a gulp. "When do you leave?"

"Two days."

My heart breaks a little more. "Are you taking all this stuff with you?"

"I'm putting most of it in my mum's attic. The apartment is gonna be rented out fully furnished. I'm only taking my clothes and stuff I need. I'd tell you to come with me, but I know the answer."

I grip my water tight in my hand and stare into the glass. "I guess I won't see you after today, then."

Cal's hand strokes my arm. "Call in sick tomorrow and spend the day with me."

My head tilts, and I gaze into his eyes. "I want to, I really do."

He places his drink down on the counter and grips both my arms. "Then do it," he demands. "We can stay here all day, or we can go somewhere. I don't care what we do as long as we're together."

I take in a deep breath. "Okay, seeing as it's the last time I will see you."

His face lifts and brightens as if the sun's rays shine down on him. "What would you like to do?"

"I'm not sure. Surprise me." My smile widens, matching his, and although I have an emptiness creeping into my heart, a bubble of excitement rises in my stomach.

He rests his arm around my shoulder and brings me close to his chest. "All right, I'll have a think. Do you want to get dinner tonight? Do you have time?"

The musky scent of him catches in my nose, and I want to stay with him all night. I'll deal with the wrath of Justin tomorrow. "Yes, what do you fancy?"

"Do you want to order or go out?"

"Order take out." I don't want to share him with anyone else, not tonight. I want to kiss him whenever the mood takes me. *And ogle his bare chest.* Hmm.

Cal pulls some menus from the kitchen drawer. "There's a good pizza place down the road or a Chinese."

"Pizza is fine."

"Do you want to share a bbq chicken and chips?"

"Yes, that sounds good."

Cal pulls a chair out for me at the kitchen table as he dials the number to order the food.

Sitting on the hard leather chair, my bottom pinches a little as the ghost of him inside me still lingers, sending a twinge of the ecstasy he gave me straight to my centre.

"When did Priya and the girls move?"

He sits opposite, placing the phone on the table. "Two weeks ago now. It's been planned for three months. I've been sorting everything out and trying to get a job over there."

"I hope you'll be happy, Cal."

"I'll be happy when I get to Australia, and I can hold my girls again."

"It might be a fresh start for us."

"I want you to be happy, Steph. That's why I left work, but I know you're not happy, or you wouldn't keep showing up here."

"I've spent a lifetime with Justin. We've shared things, a lifetime of things, since we married fifteen years ago. I do care about him, but I'm so tied to you, even though we only knew each other intimately for a year."

"We've known each other for 35 years, Steph. Since we were five. We shared a lot of moments, not just when we were together."

"You'd think I would have moved on. Why can't I move on, Cal?"

"Perhaps you can when I go to Sydney."

"Perhaps." I slump on the table, letting my shoulders drop.

"I got you something. I was gonna hand it into work for you tomorrow before I left."

"What is it?"

He disappears into the living room and returns with a gift. "It's for your birthday next month."

STEPH

I stare at the wrapped present. "Oh, can I open it or—"

"Save it for your actual birthday."

I pop the gift to one side.

"Fuck it. Unwrap it now. I want to see your face."

"Okay." I smile like a kid. "It feels like a book."

Cal beams as I tear off the wrapping.

"It is a book, Secrets of the Renaissance. I love it, thank you."

"I wasn't sure if you had read it already. You knew a lot about Botticelli."

"I haven't read it, thank you."

Underneath the book is another gift, a thin beautiful scarf with the Birth of Venus printed on the fabric. "This is beautiful."

The sheer fabric slips through my fingers, and I wrap it around my neck and lean over the table to kiss his lips.

"I went to London for a work meeting recently, and I visited the National Gallery."

"It's beautiful. Thank you so much."

The doorbell rings. "That was quick."

Cal returns from the hall and places the box on the table and gets me a plate.

The smell fills the kitchen when I lift the lid. "This pizza looks delicious. I haven't eaten pizza in a while."

Cal sits opposite me at the table. "You look like you've lost weight since Christmas."

"I wouldn't know. I stopped going to my slimming group."

"I'm glad. You know you're beautiful, whatever size you are, right?"

"Thank you, Cal. You always say the nicest things."

"It's true. You don't see me weighing myself every week. The scales don't measure the size of your heart, Steph."

"Or the size of your dick, huh?" A giggle bursts from my lips.

He smirks, chewing down his pizza.

"So, do you have a job?"

"I'm gonna move in with Priya while I look for one. Hopefully, something will turn up. Sydney's a big place. I just need to be near my girls."

I nod, biting into the greasy pizza and the strings of melted cheese drip down my chin. "So good," I mumble with my mouthful.

"I'm gonna make you say that next time you have a mouthful of my dick." Cal chuckles, watching me wipe the grease from my lips and chin.

Numbness claims my skin as if I'm turning to stone. There won't be a next time. He won't be here after tomorrow. Weight presses down on my shoulders, and I slump back in the chair.

"What's that noise?" Cal mumbles.

Straightening my back, I train my ears to the buzzing from the hall where I left my bag. "It must be my phone. I have it on silent at work."

Pulling the phone from my bag, I notice the late hour on the screen and several missed calls from Justin.

"Hello."

"Where have you been? I've been ringing you. I even called the office, and no one answered."

"I said everything I needed to say this morning." I stand in the hallway and hope Callum doesn't hear our conversation.

"So you're divorcing the kids as well, are you? I'll tell that to your sick son, shall I?"

My throat closes as my body goes rigid. "What's wrong?"

"Cairen's not well. But you'd know that if you cared to come home. Where are you, anyway?"

There's no point in dragging Cal into this mess. "I'm at a friend's house. I'll come home now. What's wrong with him?"

"He has a temperature and tummy ache and has been drowsy since I collected him from your mum's. He's been asking for you."

My chest burns with guilt. I close my eyes and swallow the prickling lump in my throat.

"I've run out of medicine. Can you pick some up? If it's not too much trouble for you." The anger and resentment in his voice is deafening, causing the burn to rise into my mouth.

"I'll come home now." I end the call and look up at Cal leaning against the doorjamb.

"Everything all right?"

"I have to go. Cairen isn't well."

He strides over to comfort me. My arms slip around his waist, and he lifts my chin to press his lips against mine. His tongue flickers in my mouth, and I wish I had more time with him, but my kids come first.

"I'll call in sick tomorrow. I'll call you when I'm setting

off." The words choke up in my throat as the lump rises again. I grab my belongings and step into the dark night.

My car clicks when I press the button on my key. Cal stands in the doorway with his hands in his pockets, watching me buckle up and start the engine. The light from his hall illuminates him in a soft glow. A yellow aura radiates his body just like the sun radiates heat and light.

I back out of the parking bay and spin the car around. His light fades the further up his street I get as I drive into the setting sun.

"Mummy. Where have you been?" Cassie asks as she walks through the hall in her pyjamas with a glass of milk.

She walks by, and I kiss her forehead. "Just working late and then called at a friend's house. I'm sorry I'm late home, sweetheart. I'll come up and tuck you in soon."

What was I thinking? As if I could have stayed out and not come home. Not told the kids where I was. The guilt weighs heavily on my shoulders, to think my son's been ill while I've been enjoying myself, and I should have been here.

I take my shoes off. Justin walks into the hallway and glares at me. "Did you forget you were a mother? Or do you just not care about them, either?"

"Justin, please. Not now." I'm not interested in what he has to say. All I want is to comfort Cairen. Avoiding his gaze, I walk by, but he drags me back, digging his fingers into my arm.

"You're going to have to deal with me at some point. I'm not going anywhere, and I'm certainly not giving up this house. Or giving you a divorce, for that matter." He spits in my face as he speaks, and I turn my cheek. "If you think you're screwing me for half my business and this house, you have another thing coming."

"Mum." Cairen stands in the living room doorway, looking small and frail with a teddy in one hand and a bottle of water in the other. "My belly hurts." His voice is weak. Grey clouds mask his sky-blue eyes, making them dull and lifeless.

Justin lets me go. I kneel in front of Cairen and give him a hug. "I know, sweetheart. I've got you some medicine."

I walk into the kitchen, place my bag on the worktop, and look for the medicine.

Justin picks Cairen up, sitting him next to my bag.

"Have you and Dad fallen out?" His eyes fill with water like a paddling pool about to overflow.

I glance at Justin, clenching his jaw. "No, sweetheart, we haven't fallen out. Dad was upset that I didn't come home, nothing to worry about."

I give him his medicine. "Let's lie down. I'll rub your tummy and make it better."

Justin picks him up and carries him through to the living room. Cairen and I cuddle up on the couch. I can feel Justin's eyes on me as if laser beams are burning into my head, giving me a headache from hell. I shoot a glare back, but his stare just intensifies.

FIRST THING IN THE MORNING, I call the office, telling them I won't be at work today. Justin takes Cassie to school, and the house is at rest. I shower to erase the sickly smell from my hair and body, then check on Cairen again. His small weak frame lays limp in my bed. A layer of moisture covers his forehead, and I brush my palm there, moving back his blonde hair, checking for a temperature. To my relief, he's still cool and seems to have a bit of colour back in his cheeks.

Picking my phone from the set of drawers, I make my way into the bathroom to call Cal. My heart aches knowing he's going to the other side of the world, and I'll never see him again. I was ready to give myself to him fully and deal with whatever the consequences were. I always said I'd follow him to the ends of the earth. If it was just me, I'd go with him in a heartbeat, but I have two children.

I couldn't tell him last night that I wanted to leave Justin. I'd be asking him to choose between me and his girls. Even if he came home for the holidays, it would never work. I couldn't live with myself knowing I stopped those girls from having their dad in Australia with them. They'd end up resenting me. I have to let him go as he let me go.

With a tightening in my throat, I tap his name on my phone.

"Steph?"

"Hi." My eyes screw shut as I lean my head back against the bathroom door.

"Hey, did you call in sick?"

"Yes." The word comes out as a squeak as I try to hold back the wobble in my voice.

"What time are you coming?"

"I'm not. Cairen's poorly." I hear a heavy sigh and then a pause. "Cal, are you still there?"

"Yeah, I'm here, baby."

I slide down the bathroom door and crumple into a pile on the cool white tiled floor. "I'm sorry." My voice breaks as I speak the words and wipe away a tear with my shaky hand.

"You've nothing to be sorry for, Steph. It's just…"

I cut him off. "Don't say it's for the best."

"I wasn't gonna say that. I was gonna say, it's just these things happen."

My head rests against my hand, and I rub my fingers over the throb in my temple. "I've been up with him all night. He's been vomiting."

"Poor kid. How is he now?"

I sniffle into the handset. "He's sleeping now in my bed. I've had to strip his bedding down."

"Are you crying?"

I wipe my cheeks again and grab the tissues to blow my nose. "Yes, you always have that effect on me."

"Where's Justin?"

Just the mention of Justin makes me nauseous. He slept in the spare room last night, but only because Cairen was in my bed. "He's at work."

"I'm coming over."

My head snaps up. "No, Cal, you can't. You'll get sick. You don't want to be throwing up on your flight tomorrow."

"Baby, I won't have you crying on your own. I'm coming."

"Cal, no. I've been cleaning sick up all night, I could have it. I don't want to pass it on to you."

"I'm already in the car. I've put you on speaker."

"Cal," I cry down the handset.

"Steph, don't cry, baby." His voice is soothing.

"I was looking forward to spending the day with you. Your last day as well."

"I know, so was I. I had a full day planned for us."

I suck in a breath. "You did?"

"Yeah, I spent all night packing the rest of my shit so I could see you today."

I twirl my hair around my finger and smile at the thought of him doing that for me. "What did you have planned?"

"It doesn't matter now."

"It does. Please tell me."

"I can't." He sighs down the phone.

I pinch my eyebrows. "Why not?"

"Because you'll start crying again."

"Why, was it that bad?" I snort.

I hear a smile playing in his voice. "Was that a hint of laughter there?"

"Maybe." I puff out a small laugh.

"I was gonna take you on a proper date."

"Cal." My hand rubs my chest as my shoulders curl inwards.

"It occurred to me I've never taken you on a date, not since our teens, anyway."

"Where were you going to take me?"

"The beach."

I take in a breath. He was right. The tears build again, and my shoulders rock as I silently cry into the handset.

He lets out a breath. "You're crying again, aren't you?"

"I can't help it. I love the beach." With a sniffle, I dab my eyes with a tissue.

"I know you do, baby."

I swallow and press my cheek against the handset, wishing he was here to hold me. There's a long pause as I close my eyes, willing the time to go faster so I can wrap my arms around him.

"Cal."

"Yeah, I'm here."

"I really do love you." My head leans back against the door and I close my eyes again, forcing another droplet to roll down the side of my face. I listen to his ragged breaths, waiting for him to say the words I long to hear.

"I love you more than you'll ever know, baby."

"I do know, Cal. I read your journal."

"I hoped you would see things differently after you read that."

"What do you mean?"

"I hoped you would forgive me."

I sigh. "Cal, I forgave you a long time ago."

"You don't know what it means to me to hear you say that. Don't cry. I'll be there soon."

"Okay." I wipe my cheeks again with the crumpled wet tissue. "I'm going to check on Cairen."

"All right, see you soon."

"Bye."

I splash my puffy cheeks with cold water and pat with a hand towel. Walking into the bedroom, I brush my hand against Cairen's forehead once more, then lightly feel his cheeks with the back of my hand. I watch his eyebrows move, but he doesn't wake and continues to snore ever so gently. Hopefully a good rest will do him good, he didn't sleep last night.

Knowing Cal is on his way, I rustle through my makeup bag for my concealer, eyeliner, and lipstick. I need to make myself look presentable.

As I put the mascara away, a car engine comes within earshot. Looking through the bedroom window, his black Audi parks on the side of the road. I check Cairen one more time before tiptoeing downstairs to open the door.

Cal walks straight in, and I close the door. Before I can speak, his lips press against mine, darting his tongue into my mouth in a frenzy of want and need. Pinning me against the door, his hands roam my body, squeezing my breast, then my arse, anything he can fist. My arms wrap around his neck, and I keep him locked in our passionate state for some time. Our tongues slow to a flickering waltz before he pulls away to look into my eyes, cupping my face in his hands. I kiss his palm and his thumb runs along my lips.

"Are you all right?" he asks.

"I am now."

"Where's Cairen?"

"In my bed. His bedding is in the washer."

"You look tired." His thumb runs under my eye and delicately kisses my nose.

"I haven't slept."

He wraps his arms tight around me, pressing my head into the nook of his neck and shoulder. I can't help but kiss him there, then rub my cheek against the stubble on his jaw that never fails to elicit the fire in me.

"Do you want to get your head down for an hour? I can listen out for your son."

"No, come through. Do you want a coffee?" He nods and I take his hand, leading him into the kitchen. As I fill the kettle, he wraps his arms around me from behind and nuzzles into my neck, gently sucking and licking the flesh there under my ear.

My heart races as my head spins and the heat between my thighs spreads throughout my body. I turn to him and kiss him again, knowing this will be the last time we're together. He knows it too. I can see it written in his eyes; dark eyes that burn with possession and hunger. With his hands wrapped around my waist, he pulls me with him to the kitchen table, forcing the wood into the back of my thighs as he unbuttons my shirt.

"When did you last check on your boy?"

"Just before you came."

"Do you think he'll stay asleep?"

I nod, knowing what he's thinking, and I want it too. I need this. Just one more time. His lips steer down my body, navigating over the soft rounds of my breast as he pulls the cups of my bra down, catching my nipple between his teeth, tugging and groaning.

I watch his eyes flicker as his hard tongue grazes and flicks around my stiff peaks before trailing kisses of desire down to my plump stomach. My leggings are yanked down with his rough hands, but his mouth tenderly kisses over the thin pink stretched skin left from pregnancy.

My legs grow weak the farther down he goes, and I wish I had put some sexy underwear on this morning instead of my comfortable big knickers. I screw my eyes shut as he peels away my leggings, thinking I am going to have a Bridget Jones moment right about now, but he doesn't seem bothered; more interested in what's underneath and pulls my big plain cotton pants down. They fall to the floor.

My whole body trembles. I only had him yesterday, but each time I'm with him, it's like the first. He presses his lips against my folds and finds my bundle of nerves with his wicked tongue. His hands grip my thighs tight and his fingers dig into the chunky flesh there as he licks further down around my entrance. Then he draws his tongue back up to engulf me with his mouth, groaning into me, sending a vibration through my centre that radiates my entire body.

"Cal," I cry, fisting his hair. It's the only thing I can clench as I pant his name, trying to be quiet, still listening out for Cairen.

"Ah, baby," he groans into me again, and the vibration from his words rock through my core.

"Cal, I want you inside of me." I pant the words in utter desperation and whimper as his lips leave my bud, making their way to my face. I open my eyes to see his mouth slick from me, and then his fingers are sliding down my seam, entering and withdrawing at a steady pace.

"Are you ready for me, baby?"

"Always." I pant and kiss his wet lips, tasting myself on his tongue, and he groans into my mouth.

"I love your pussy, Steph; always soaked for me." He removes his fingers to unbuckle his belt and unzip his jeans, pulling his boxers down just enough to free his erection. Taking in a breath, I prepare myself for the full length of him.

He grips his erection and I rest my bottom on the edge of the kitchen table, wrapping my legs around his waist as he guides himself into me.

My bottom aches with the memory of him from yesterday, and every time I sit down, I feel him there. Relaxing into him, all thoughts disappear; he's all I see, hear, and feel. His large, rough hands roam under my shirt around my back, leaving a trail of flames in their wake.

With his hot mouth sucking my neck, he groans, pushing into me. Each time deeper than the last. His lips lock onto mine and our tongues entwine around each other. His lips turn upwards against mine and small huffs of laughter breathe into my mouth.

"What is it?" I say against his lips, trying not to break the kiss but wonder what's making him laugh at a time like this. Is it my big knickers? Has he just realised how big they actually are? Now they're strewn somewhere on the floor.

He laughs again into my mouth, but continues with his tender assault.

"What's funny?" I say again, slightly pulling away from his lips this time.

"Your fucking dog is humping my leg."

I look down to see Teddy's paws clinging onto Callum, wrapping himself tightly around his knee while his back end moves in swift motions and a laugh rocks through my body.

"He wants a piece of the action," I say, laughing wildly as Teddy's eyes bulge, and his motions get swifter as his grip around Callum tightens.

"He wants a piece of me," Cal says. "He thinks I'm his bitch." Cal shakes his leg, trying to free himself of Teddy's claws, but he clings on for dear life, dry humping, making us both laugh even more.

"Let me put him outside," I say.

"No, let me." Callum buttons the top button on his jeans

to hold them up while he attempts to walk to the back door. The dog hangs on to his calf, sliding along the high gloss tiled floor as Callum pulls himself out of the kitchen. I listen out for Cairen, who seems to still be asleep.

Callum returns, unbuttoning his jeans. "Where were we?" His hands slide back under my opened shirt to caress the skin on my back once more with his rough hands.

Taking my lip between his teeth, he takes full possession of my mouth, consuming my senses. I gasp as his erection fills me, and I melt into him. Everything blurs. I'm ascending into the clouds. Light and colour swirl around me. The only sound is our hearts beating as one.

I taste him mixed with my flavour and feel every inch of him. Not just between my thighs, I feel his soul ripping through me, infiltrating every cell as he courses through my blood.

He bites down on my shoulder. "I won't last much longer, baby. Come for me."

"I won't be long. You know what I like to hear." I pant.

He wraps his fingers around my curls, tugging my head back as he nips my lips. "You're mine, Steph."

And with those words, I'm taken over the edge. Flashes of white brighter than the sun fill my mind. My body stiffens, my toes curl, and I fist his hair.

"That's it, baby." He rests his forehead against my shoulder as he comes down from his high, steadying his breathing.

He kisses me again as tenderly as our first time. The dog barks and scratches at the back door.

"I'll let the dog in before he wakes your boy," he says, zipping himself up, walking out of the kitchen.

He returns with a calmer Teddy, who thankfully has put his lipstick away.

"Shall I make us that coffee now?"

"Yeah, I'm parched." He grins, kissing my nose. "Do you want me to get you some tissue or a flannel or something?"

"No, I'm going upstairs to clean myself up." I slide my bottom off the kitchen table, looking on the floor for my clothes. "Where are my knickers?"

Callum glances around, and I look again, but all I see are my leggings.

My fingers fiddle with the buttons on my shirt, trying to button myself up as I scour the kitchen, under the table, behind the bin. "That's odd. Have you taken them?"

I look at Callum, knowing it wouldn't be the first time he has stuffed my underwear in his pocket, though I doubt my big cotton knickers would actually fit in his pocket.

He lifts his hands up, breaking into a laugh. "Don't look at me. I'm not guilty this time." Callum nods towards the living room and when I turn around, the bloody dog is standing in the lounge with my big knickers hanging from his jaw.

STEPH

My hands slap against my face as I gasp in horror. A tingle sweeps up the back of my neck and moves over my cheeks, making them excessively hot under my palm. "Teddy," I shout, then pat my legs to beckon him to me.

"Is your dog always this randy?"

"Yes, he's as bad as you." I let out a puff of laughter. Teddy ignores my pleas and continues to rag them around like he would play with his blanket, swishing them from side to side while making a playful growl.

"Teddy, here," I command, walking towards him, but he runs around the coffee table as if it's a game. Please let me just teleport now. I cover my face with my hands. Luckily, my shirt covers my arse, so I'm not running around the living room with everything on display. Callum hasn't stopped laughing, and his usual chuckle has turned into a high pitch squawk as he tries to corner the dog to rescue my embarrassingly big knickers, but Teddy is playing chase.

"Leave them. He'll get bored soon enough. I'm going to clean up," I say, grabbing my leggings and running upstairs to get some fresh underwear. After sorting myself out and checking on Cairen, I return to the kitchen, hoping I can retrieve my garment only to find Cal and Teddy now playing tug of war. Standing in the kitchen doorway, I cover my face with my hands again, feeling the heat emanating from my cheeks. Please floor, just swallow me, please.

Eventually, Callum wins the battle of the drawers and holds up my big knickers with a cheeky grin. "These are different."

"Piss off." I snatch them from his hands and take them to the laundry room. I catch my face reflected in the glass cupboard and my cheeks have turned a bright shade of purple.

"I like them," he says, smirking when I return.

"Sure you do." I swat his chest, and he catches my wrist, pulling me close to him, wrapping his arms around me.

"I like that you wear them at home, for *him*. I can sleep easier knowing you don't wear sexy knickers for him."

"Only for you, Cal." I kiss his lips again.

"What have you got on now?" He tugs at my leggings.

"Cal." I squirm, thinking I wouldn't be sleeping with him again today. I put on some more comfortable underwear, equally as big and embarrassing.

"Let me see," he says, grinning, tugging at the elastic of my leggings.

"No." I swat at his chest again, but he pulls me in for a kiss. His fingers tease my waist, tickling my skin. I squirm as his digits dig into my ribs, making me convulse uncontrollably by his tantalising torture. He pins me against the fridge, feverishly lapping his tongue around my mouth, and his hands wander underneath the elastic as he catches me off guard, distracting me with his greedy mouth.

Squeezing my cotton covered cheeks, a smile plays on his lips against mine, and he seems satisfied that Justin won't be seeing me in any lace underwear later. Justin will never see my underwear again. Unless he rifles through my drawers.

"Let me make us that drink now," I say, and he releases me so I can flick the switch on the kettle again.

"How is Cairen doing?"

"He seems to have some colour back in his cheeks, but he'll most likely be asleep for the next few hours. If he wakes up, you must leave. I can't have Justin knowing you were here."

I don't want Cairen knowing that Cal is the reason I want a divorce. The kids would resent him and me for breaking the family up. There's no point bringing Cal into the equation when he won't even be here. I pull out two mugs from the cupboard and scoop the coffee from the jar with a teaspoon.

"Why, he knew I worked with you. I've met him before. He thinks we're friends, doesn't he?"

"No, he'll go ballistic if he finds out you've been here."

"Why?"

"Because someone he knows saw you kissing my neck in Maccy's." I pour the water into the mugs.

"Fuck Steph, I'm sorry. I wasn't thinking. What did he say?"

"He went mad. I had to convince him she was confused about what she saw, but he still didn't want me seeing you again out of work and was relieved when I told him you had another job." I stir the drinks.

"Did he hurt you?" Cal holds my arms, gripping tight, anxiously waiting for my response.

"Do you think if he'd hurt me, I would still be with him?"

"No, cos I would have wrung his fucking neck."

"Not if I got there first, but he isn't violent."

Cal lets out a breath. "I hope he's good to you, even if it makes me fucking crazy to think of you with him."

"He treats me well. You don't need to worry. He only has one flaw."

"What's that?"

"He's not you."

"Steph." His hands cup my cheeks as his lips touch mine, sucking and nipping at my bottom lip.

"Here, get your coffee." I hand him a mug.

"Thanks."

"So, where are you flying from?"

"Heathrow, London."

"I know where Heathrow is." I smile, rolling my eyes.

"You didn't know where Sydney was."

"Well, I didn't imagine you'd move to the other side of the pissin' world."

"I'm getting the 6am train tomorrow morning. My flight is at 11am. I've sold my car. They're picking it up from my mum's tomorrow."

"I can't imagine you without your car."

"I'll get another in Australia." He sips on his hot drink as we both stand in the kitchen leaning against the worktop facing each other.

"I'm still gutted that we didn't get to go on that date, but I'm glad you came over." I blow into my mug to cool the contents.

"Me too."

"What did you have planned at the beach?"

"I don't know." He sighs and takes another sip. "Probably not as much fun as we just had. The dog was enough entertainment, not to mention your knickers. I can't remember the last time I laughed so much."

I place my coffee on the worktop and swat his chest. He pulls me in for a kiss, placing his mug down so he can wrap his arms around my waist and under my shirt to feel my bare back.

Looking into my eyes, he says, "We would have bought fish and chips and ate them on the beach, fighting off the seagulls."

I smile at the thought. Sounds about right.

"Then we would walk barefoot on the sand trying not to tread in dog mess."

I giggle. He paints such a realistic picture of the East coast.

"Then we would have had a paddle in the murky sea water where your feet end up muckier than they were before you went in."

"You're really selling this date to me."

He laughs. "Yeah, I bet you will be in tears all night that you didn't get to go."

I smile. "Yes, I will."

"After the paddle we would get an ice cream, but it would be so windy on the seafront, blowing your hair in your cornet."

"I've had stickier things in my hair," I say with a smile.

Callum kisses my nose, tucking a loose curl behind my ear before he continues. "We would go on all the rides. After the fifth time on the waltzer, you'd throw up all over me. Then I would spend all my money on the arcade trying to win you a teddy that you can't even keep in case Justin asks where it came from."

"Sounds like the perfect date." A whimsical smile is etched on my face.

Cal grins, rubbing his thumb against my cheek. "I booked a nice hotel."

"What?" I hold my breath. Did I hear that right?

"I booked a hotel on the seafront."

"Cal, you didn't?" My chest caves.

"I booked us a room and lunch. They have a balcony terrace overlooking the beach and served nice food, according to Trip Advisor."

My mouth opens, but I have no words. Tears threaten my eyes again, only this time, overwhelming tears of joy that he would do that, and an overwhelming sadness that it will never come to pass.

"I was going to wine and dine you, then take you to the room and seduce you. We would have made love all afternoon, then we would have walked along the beach hand in hand with an ice cream. You would get some on your nose, and I'd lick it off, telling you how much I love you. You'd tell me you love me, and that you're going to leave Justin the jerk, and we would watch the sunset together. I'd cancel my flight, and you'd move in with me and we'd live happily ever after."

I taste the salty tears as I lick my lips. Cal wipes his thumb over my stained cheeks and kisses my nose. "Cal, that's a lovely dream."

"It doesn't have to be a dream."

"But Cal, your girls."

"I would sort something out, go over when I can, have them for the holidays. I would make it work, Steph."

"I wouldn't let you do that for me."

"I would be doing it for me, too. I want to be with you."

"Your girls would resent me for keeping you here, and you would come to hate me for making you choose. It's better this way." Isn't it?

"If you say so." He looks deflated.

I press my swollen lips to his warm mouth. The feel of his soft lips, the stubble on his chin, his wet tongue against mine are all I ever want to feel. I want no one else to touch my mouth, fearing they will erase his kiss, his scent, and his memory.

"Cal, I would have loved that date."

"I know baby, so would I." I can see the sadness in his eyes. They're not a lustrous brown anymore, but a dull sepia with a hint of grey.

"You needn't have gone to all that expense, though. I would have loved the first date you described."

A laugh escapes him. "You were always a cheap date." My heart aches knowing I will never get to live out either date.

"Do you want anything to eat?"

"No, I'm good." He wraps his arms around me, nibbling my ear and licking at the spot below my jaw, before sucking my neck lightly, not strong enough to mark my skin. His treacherous lips trail along my shoulder and each kiss, nip and lick, tingles between my legs, and I never want him to stop with his tender assault. I pull his hair, bringing his lips to mine, our tongues flicking against each other in waves, our breathing in sync as we settle into each other's embrace.

"Come through into the living room." I lead the way and sit on the light grey fabric of our corner suite, fluffing up a furry mustard cushion as Callum sits next to me, taking in his surroundings.

"You have a beautiful house, Steph."

"Thanks," I say, house proud of my decorating skills and meticulously hand picked accessories and soft furnishings.

"I didn't realise how big your house actually is."

"Justin bought it for us. He re-modelled most of it."

"Wow, being a builder must pay well." He scans the room again. I watch his eyes rest on the walnut drinks cabinet and the tall French bookcase.

"He earns a decent wage, but he had a large inheritance from his Nan. Most of this antique furniture was hers."

"I get now why you don't want to leave him."

I look at him, squeezing my eyebrows together. Is he serious? "Was that supposed to be a joke?"

"No, I get it. I wouldn't want to leave all this either." His hand waves in the air around my living room. "I can't exactly compete, can I? Fuck knows what you must have thought when you stayed over at my place."

"You think I give a toss about Justin's money and this house? If you believe that, then you don't know me at all."

His words hurt more than any physical wound I have ever had, and his harsh statement from our teens rings through my head when he called me a materialistic bitch.

"I don't know what to believe, Steph, I still don't understand what's tying you to him. People get divorced all the time, and the kids are fine. Happier even. I just wonder why you came back to me yesterday if you're still not willing to leave Justin."

If only he knew I was going to leave him. I was ready to give myself to him fully, for him to have me, all of me to do as he pleases—mind, body, and soul—to be his woman every minute of every day, to wake up in his arms and be able to kiss him goodnight. I never want my soul to be parted from him. I never want a day to pass where I don't feel his skin on mine, his lips on my mouth, and his gaze on me.

How could I be so foolish? The first time I slept with Cal in the snow, I should have left Justin. I knew then, deep down, there was no going back. I was kidding myself, pretending, living a lie.

But how can I tell Callum this now? He's leaving tomorrow. I won't make his life more complicated than it already is. He's been doing fine without me all these months. He'll be okay. I can't tear him away from his daughters.

"I told you why I came. I wanted to see you, then I found out you were leaving and…" I sigh. "You told me before I was a materialistic bitch. If you really think that about me, I think you should go. You clearly don't know me at all."

"I told you I didn't mean that, and I'm not going anywhere."

"You just basically said that I'm only staying with Justin because of his money."

"Tell me, Steph, why are you staying with him? It doesn't do the kids any good to grow up seeing their parents miserable." He looks at the family portraits on the wall. "But looking around your house at all your family photos, you don't even look miserable. Why the fuck do you keep coming back to me? I finally feel like I can breathe again, then you show up on my doorstep to torment me. Each time I think you're gonna tell me you've left him, yet you go back to him. Like you're using me."

"How can you say that I'm using you? I don't hear you complaining when you're screwing me." I hear a whimper from the top of the stairs. "It's Cairen. I don't have time to argue with you, Cal."

He rolls his eyes before I run up the stairs to check on Cairen. He is disorientated and drowsy. "Hi sweetie, how are you feeling now?" I ask, running my hand under the blonde hair on his forehead.

"Mummy, my head hurts." Scooping him in my arms, I place him on my lap as I sit on the bed. I pass him a drink of water from the bedside table that I poured this morning and stroke the top of his head as he takes a few sips. The front door slams. I look out of the window to see Cal get in his car. He doesn't see me, he doesn't look back, just drives.

My chest tightens, making it difficult to breathe as an ache settles in my heart. I don't have the energy to think about this right now. I'm all out of tears. How could he think I'm staying with Justin for the money, to be kept in a life of luxury? Of course, we're comfortable financially, but we're not millionaires. We have nice holidays, and the kids want for nothing, but I'm not filthy rich.

I grew up comfortable. My mum never worked and

reaped the rewards of my dad's business, part owner of a small pine manufacturing business, which was very lucrative.

Cal always said I was spoilt, unlike him. Growing up, his mum worked two jobs to support him and his sister, but it still wasn't enough. They never had the luxuries of holidays abroad like I had or the latest trends, high end clothing, or new toys.

Perhaps he's right, I am a spoilt brat. I've certainly taken what I wanted from him, chewed him up and spat him out, all the while deceiving Justin. I am a terrible person and don't deserve either man in my life.

I carry Cairen downstairs, laying him on the sofa with a blanket. "Do you want to eat something? I can make you some toast."

He nods at me and asks, "Can I watch TV?"

"Of course." I hand him the remote and go to make lunch, trying to focus on my son, but Cal keeps coming into my mind.

Later, I will deal with him. I'll call him. No, he should call me. He was the one in the wrong. *What's the point in anyone calling anyone anymore?* My subconscious says, that annoying cow. *It's not like you're gonna see each other again.*

He didn't even say goodbye. The last time we parted at university, we never said goodbye. I can't bear the thought of going another twenty years or longer without at least saying goodbye. I've never been one for big farewells, but I can't leave things like this with this animosity between us.

I take Cairen his toast and a drink, sitting with him as he takes small bites and reluctantly chews and swallows. He still hasn't got his appetite back. I attempt to clean the house, keeping myself busy, but every half an hour I check my phone. I thought he would have called to apologise by now, friggin' arsehole.

Mum collects Cassie from school, telling me to get some

sleep. She sits with Cairen while I go to bed, but I can't sleep. I stare at my phone, waiting for a text, a call, anything. By the time Justin comes home, I can't stay awake. My eyelids grow heavy, my throat is sore, and my body is weak. I give in and let the blackness take me. I haven't even got the energy to think, just nothing. An emptiness fills my mind.

I wake up to the sound of birds chirping through the open bedroom window. Reaching for my phone, it's 5am and still no missed call, voicemail, not even a text.

His train is at 6am. I could meet him at the train station. The scenario plays out in my head, and my heart accelerates as I jump from the bed. I'm still in my clothes from yesterday, which is a bonus. Creeping in the bathroom, I clean my teeth and wash my face. I don't bother to change. There isn't time.

In full stealth mode, I turn the key in the front door as delicately as possible. I don't want to wake Justin asleep in the spare room. I hope the car engine won't wake him as I pull off the drive. Please let me make it to the train station on time. Please, please, please let me see him before he goes.

His face, eyes, and his smile are all I need to see. To have those warm lips on me just one more time and say goodbye. I can't leave things like this. I need some sort of closure. Can I ever get closure from that man?

I turn on the radio to calm my nerves. Dido. I listen to her words and have to turn it off. Any more of that, and I fear I'll spiral into a deep depression in a bottomless pit of never ending sorrow. I should just tell him I want him. We could have a long distance relationship. I could see him on holidays and take the kids to Australia twice a year. It would be an experience.

He could come back to the UK at Christmas and summer. I could visit him there at Easter and October. We could make it work. Anything has to be better than this misery I'm in. But would he stay here? I won't take him away from his girls. I couldn't look them in the eye, knowing I was the reason they had to grow up without their dad. They're only young for a few more years. I'm not going anywhere. When they're older, he can come back to me. I won't let him choose.

I park at the station with ten minutes to spare. My heart beats as if I have run here, not driven. I'm still undecided about what I will say to him, but I have to see him. Scanning the board for the correct platform, I notice the train to London is on the other side of the tracks. Spotting the bridge, I run up the steps as fast as my legs can take me and search the platform for him as I fly down the steps on the other side. He must already be on the train.

STEPH

I board the carriage and make my way down the aisle, moving past seat after seat with no Cal. My hands are sticky. Beads of moisture surface on my skin. I'm out of breath after my brief run across the bridge. I'm so unfit.

You should have kept that gym subscription, you lazy sod. My subconscious is right again. If I had gone to the gym, perhaps I wouldn't be sweating right now like a roast chicken on a spit. Thinking of roast chicken makes my stomach growl.

Moving swiftly through several carriages, I wonder how many more. I've walked through at least three so far. Suddenly, the train comes to life. The floor creaks, and a high pitch squeal pierces my ears as the metal runs along the rail. A low hum spreads down the line and the floor moves beneath me.

As I look out of the window, the platform pulls away. An alarm rings through me, buzzing in my temple as panic sets in. The platform fades into the distance, and I realise I never even put a parking ticket on the car. Justin is going to wake up and wonder where I am. I stand in the middle of the aisle and take in a deep breath, trying to compose myself and think.

I can go to the next stop and catch the next train back to my car. Frantically unzipping my bag, I pray my purse is in there. I let out a breath, when I see my credit card, even though I don't have any cash. At least something has gone right this morning.

I wipe my forehead before my fringe sticks there and continue with my search for Cal. It would be just my luck if he's not even on this pissin' train. I imagine he missed the train and is on the platform now, waiting for the next one. Or he told me the wrong time, or maybe I misheard him.

Stepping into the fifth carriage, I continue to walk down the aisle, still hopeful. I hear that gravelly voice that I love, and my body stops functioning for a moment as I hold my breath. I'm sure my heart skipped a beat.

His dark hair is visible over the top of the seat. A woman sits opposite him on the other side of the table. As I approach, he's deep in conversation. I slip into the seat diagonally behind him and wait for him to stop talking so I can get his attention.

"What do you do, Callum?" she asks in a sultry tone.

"I work in marketing."

"Interesting. My company is looking to market our next product. Maybe we should get our heads together."

I stare at her as she bats her eyelashes and pouts her lips. She wants to get more than her head together with him.

"What product? What business are you in?" Callum says with a smile in his voice, even though I can't see his face.

"I'm a sales representative for a high-end beauty range."

Of course, she works in beauty with her airbrushed skin and glossy black hair.

"Ah, that makes sense," Callum says.

What the heck is he getting at? *Probably the same conclusion as you.*

"Why's that?" She gives him a coy smile, showing her perfect teeth.

Callum huffs out a laugh. "I think you know why."

Is he for real? He came to my house yesterday saying all that crap and now he's flirting with some other woman, acting as if I don't even exist.

She circles her middle finger on the table with her polished red nail. "I don't know what you're saying. Spell it out for me."

Oh, please, lady. Could you be any more obvious? Talk about fishing for compliments. I settle back in the chair, waiting for Cal to shoot this kitty-slinger down.

He laughs under his breath. "Let's just say you don't need all those beauty products."

She smiles and looks down at her nails, batting her eyelashes.

I glance down at my clothes. What was I thinking coming here like this? I haven't even showered. Lifting yesterday's shirt over my nose, I check myself, then pull the bobble from my hair and smooth out the bumps, styling it up in a messy bun.

I must have a lipstick in this bag somewhere, gloss anything to paint some life onto my face. Though, whatever I do, this woman is in another league. Even if I had the best makeover from that show, 'Ten Years Younger', it wouldn't be enough.

I can't let him see me like this and embarrass myself. He would take one look at me, then look back at her and wonder what he ever saw in me. I need to go, but my body won't move out of this seat, and my ears won't stop listening to their conversation, torturing me with every flirty word that leaves his lips. Words that only yesterday would have been meant for me.

"I like a man that appreciates the finer things in life." She pouts.

"I certainly know how to appreciate a beautiful woman."

My body collapses onto the table in front of me, burying my head into my folded arms. Closing my eyes, I'm back at uni again, watching him flirt with his new girlfriend at a bar. I heard his voice behind the partition while sitting in a booth. Every word he uttered made me gag, just like now. If I'd eaten anything this morning, I'm sure I would have spewed by now.

"Are you single, Callum?"

"Yeah." He says it so matter-of-factly, with no hesitation.

"Why don't we get our heads together in London tonight? We can discuss the marketing, and you can show me exactly how you appreciate a woman."

I can't help but stare at her, my eyes now torturing me along with my ears. She bites her red bottom lip, waiting for his response.

He clears his throat. "I'm sure I can show you a thing or two."

Her mouth parts and her eyes sparkle, mirroring my own glistening eyes, but for very different reasons. I'm sure she could show him a thing or two as well.

"Like what?"

A huff escapes Cal's lips. If I could see his face, I'm sure he would have his head tilted, stroking his stubbly jaw with a sinister but sexy-ass grin plastered all over his face.

"Do I have to spell that out to you, too?"

Her red nails circle the table. "I like to know what I'm getting myself into."

If he says he's going to spank her arse, I'll rip his friggin' head off.

"I bet you like it rough."

She continues to bat her lashes and bite her full lip. "Is that how you like it, Callum?"

"Maybe."

Oh my gosh, get a friggin' room. If this conversation continues, they'll join the train equivalent of the mile high club. Is that even a thing? I wouldn't know, I haven't done either. The high-speed club, getting railed? The whistle stop? Why am I thinking of this nonsense? Although anything is better than listening to these two. The acidity burns my throat. I would cry, but my tears have all evaporated when my blood reached boiling point several minutes ago.

"I'll let you be rough with me if you make it worth my while."

Callum clears his throat and chuckles. I bet he's hard, watching her lick her lips and finger shapes on the table with her long nails.

"I'm staying at the Hilton."

He stretches out an arm. "Pity I won't be there."

Her face drops. "Oh? Are you only in London for the day?"

"Morning, actually."

"Another time then?" She's desperate now.

His hand smooths over the top of his hair. "Yeah, if you're ever in Sydney, look me up."

"You live in Australia?"

"I'm flying over there at midday. I'm not sure when I'll be back."

She slumps her shoulders, waving her hand in the air. "That's just typical. I meet the man of my dreams, and he's moving to the other side of the world."

No sweetheart, he's the man of my dreams, even if he is a dick most of the time. A big friggin' dick, too, in every way.

Callum huffs out a laugh. "The man of your dreams, aye?"

She bites her lip, then reaches in her bag and pulls out a business card. "Here, next time you're in the UK, call me."

He takes the card, grazing her fingers. "I will."

My temple throbs as my eyes strain, and my ears scream. What a stupid idea this was. Why didn't I let things lie, let him leave thinking I'm a gold-digger, and me thinking he's an arsehole instead of a player?

Even if I told him I wanted to be with him now, I couldn't stand the thought of him in Australia, away from me, flirting with every girl that flashes him a smile. He'd soon forget about me and break my heart again. I don't think I could take it a second time, to be cast aside for a younger or slimmer model.

With heavy limbs, I stand to make my way to another carriage to wait for the next stop. I just want to crawl back into bed and never get up.

As I put one foot in front of the other, the woman shouts, "Excuse me!"

I freeze. Is she talking to me? A lump replaces the bile in my throat.

"You dropped something."

My eyes dart to the floor as my lipstick rolls along the carriage.

I think about leaving it, ignoring the woman and making a run for it, but my body reacts first and bends down to retrieve the stick. My hand collides with Callum's as he stops the lipstick with his boot and reaches for it before it rolls under the table. A surge of electricity courses through my veins.

He retrieves the gold casing. His gaze meets mine as he hands it back to me. "Steph?"

My lungs can only take in short shallow breaths. His mouth opens, and he stares at me as we both stand. He won't let go of the lipstick. I try to pull it from his grasp before I make a run for it, but he grips my wrist with his other hand.

"What are you doing on this train?"

"I…" I can't speak. The words won't come out, blocked by the overpowering lump in my dry throat.

"Are you all right?"

A watery film covers my eyes, and tears prickle at the back of my throat. "I…I wanted to see you before you left." My voice is barely a whisper.

He frees my hand, and I turn to escape. My shaky legs carry me into the next carriage, with his footsteps following swiftly behind me.

"Steph, where are you going?"

"Home."

"But you said you wanted to see me."

"I've seen you now, so you can go back and appreciate Miss-Fucking-World back there." I continue walking into the next carriage to put some distance between us, but he closes the gap.

"How long were you there?"

"Long enough." My feet pick up the pace, but I won't outrun him. *Again—shouldn't have cancelled that gym subscription,* my subconscious says. Why can't she ever be helpful? Give me a friggin' bone here. I'm breaking. Talk about kicking a dog when it's down.

"Steph, stop running away from me," Cal growls. He grips my arm, pulling me back to him, and I snatch it from his grasp.

"Don't touch me."

I step over the connection into another carriage.

"Steph, stop. You can't escape me. You're on a fucking train. Talk to me."

I spin around to face him. "Like you talked to me? I can't

believe you left without so much as a goodbye, knowing we'd never see each other again."

"You told me to go."

"I thought you would have at least called me."

"It works both ways. I thought you would have called me to apologise."

"You think I should apologise? For what? You were the one implying that I was a gold-digger. How dare—"

He holds onto my shoulders and crashes his lips to mine. Electricity surges through my bones, giving my limbs the energy I need to lift my arm and slap his face with the palm of my hand, breaking the kiss.

My hand stings, and he rubs the red mark on his cheek while moving his jaw from side to side. As I step backwards, a woman stares and a teenager smirks.

"Are you all right, love? Is this man bothering you?" A man close by asks.

Callum glares at him and, not wanting to cause any more of a scene, I nod and move into the next carriage.

Cal follows. "Steph, sit down. You can't go anywhere else, unless you're going to sit with the driver." He slides into an empty seat with a table. "Please, sit with me."

I sigh heavily and drop into a seat opposite. I don't have the energy to fight him anymore. My chest burns. Every bone in my body is shaking, though I can't decide if it's rage, hurt, or a need for him.

He chews on his bottom lip in silence. I barely have the energy to feel, let alone speak.

"Sorry, Steph. You're not a gold-digger. I was hurt. I am hurt. For fuck's sake, I love you. Each time you're with me, I hope you'll stay, but each time you choose him, and it fucking riles me."

I huff. "Save it for someone who gives a shit."

He takes my hand in his, stroking his thumb against my skin. "You give a shit, Steph, or you wouldn't be here."

"Well, that was before I heard you flirting with that… that…kitty-slinger."

"Fuck's sake, Steph."

"What?"

"You don't want me, but you begrudge anyone else having me."

I do want him though, that's the problem.

"I've told you, you can have me. All of me. I'll fucking marry you, just say YES."

CHAPTER 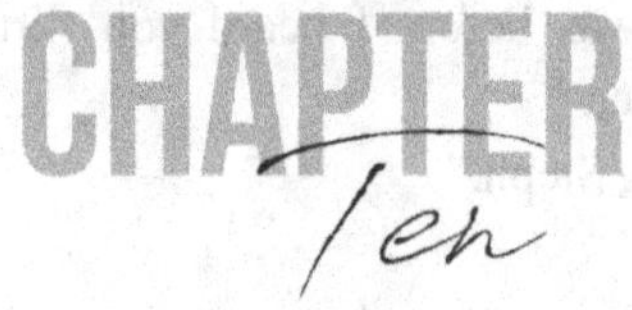
Ten

STEPH

I glance up at him with sad eyes, but don't speak. What is there to say? He's moving to Australia to be with his girls. My kids are here. I chew on my fingernail. How can we have a relationship on two continents? I know how much a flight to Australia costs, and neither of us has that sort of money to sustain a relationship. He's not good at long distance. I'd end up hurt again, I just know it. I can't return to that dark place. My heart just can't take another rejection from him.

"Thought so." He runs his hands through his hair and fists it in frustration. "I doubt I'll ever meet anyone I love as much as you, Steph, but don't deny me going on a fucking date once in a while when you're playing happy families with golden balls."

I cover my face with my hands, so he doesn't see me ugly cry. My shoulders shake as emotion rocks through me. He moves around the table and slides in beside me, and his hand runs down my spine before pulling me into his chest.

His other hand caresses my cheek. "Baby, don't cry." His lips press against the top of my head, and I sob into his t-shirt.

With a muffled voice, I say, "I know it's unfair of me to

expect you not to date. I want you to be happy. I just hate seeing you with anyone else."

"Welcome to the fucking club."

"I'm so sorry, Cal."

He kisses my forehead, then lifts my chin to gaze into my eyes. "Are you gonna let me kiss you properly now, without getting another slap?" He lets out a puff of laughter, and I smile along with him. "Was that a smile?" He pecks my nose, then moves away, wary of my hand. "I want to kiss you, Steph."

"You can."

"Are you sure? I don't want to walk through customs with a black eye."

I wrap my fingers around his neck and press my lips to his. My tongue glides into his mouth in a swirling motion, full of love and sadness from my heart.

His hands move to my cheeks, continuing the caress of his tongue. As he pulls away with small pecks of adoration, he wipes my stained cheeks with his thumb. "This is becoming a habit, isn't it?"

"What?"

"Me, wiping away tears that I've caused." He presses his warm lips against my cheek, then my nose and my forehead, as if trying to kiss away all my sorrow. "When I saw you on the train. I thought… hoped…maybe you'd left Justin and come to tell me you wanted to be with me."

"I would never ask you to choose between me or your girls."

"Why are you here, Steph? I'm glad you are, but what are you doing on the train?"

"I only came to say goodbye, then the train set off. I didn't mean to stay on, but it was too late."

He laughs. "That's so typical of you. Why didn't you just call me? I would've got off the train and caught the next one."

"You don't want to risk being late for your flight."

"But what about you? You're halfway to London."

"I know. I'm so stupid. I didn't even put a parking ticket on the car. I'm gonna get a fine."

He presses his lips to mine in a slow and tender kiss and with every stroke of his tongue and brush of his lips; I feel all the love this man carries for me.

"Tickets please."

I pull away from Cal's embrace as the conductor approaches.

Cal pulls his wallet from his jeans. "I take it you don't have a ticket either?"

I shake my head. "I was hoping I could get off at the next stop and miss the whole ticket thing."

Cal hands the conductor his ticket, and with his gift of the gab, explains my situation. The elderly man takes one look at my stained cheeks, sad eyes and general dishevelled appearance and, with pity, lets me off on the understanding I get off at the next stop.

"He must have felt sorry for me. I look so pathetic."

Cal strokes my cheek with the back of his hand. "Not pathetic, but you do look like a homeless person."

I suck in a breath. "Do I look that bad?"

"You look tired, and I know you had these clothes on yesterday because I remember peeling them off." His lips inch closer as he speaks, and his breath finds my neck, sending tingles down to my core as he sucks at my flesh, trailing kisses along my jaw. His stubble grazes my skin, and I relive the memory of yesterday.

"Do you still have your big knickers on?" he whispers, then licks below my ear.

I giggle, and before I can confirm or deny, his fingers tease their way under the elastic of my leggings, and he roams the cotton fabric of my underwear with a big cheesy grin on his face.

"Go on, say what you want to say?"

"I'm not saying anything."

"I know you're dying to say something about my big knickers."

"Me?" He laughs. "I wouldn't."

"Just tell me what's funny?"

"Okay. It just reminds me of that phrase you always said, something about food pickers and big knickers."

I smile. "Fridge pickers wear big knickers."

"There it is."

I swat his chest. "You weren't complaining yesterday when you took them off. If you don't like them, go back to Miss World. You could probably floss your teeth with hers." I fold my arms over my chest, stick my chin out, and turn my head in a huff. "That's if she's even wearing any underwear."

He nuzzles into the crevice of my neck, his hands still under the fabric of my leggings, and he squeezes my arse cheeks. "I'm not going anywhere. Don't get your knickers in a twist." His hot breath swathes my skin as he laughs and continues to nip and suck my neck, making me giggle. "I still have your red lace ones," he whispers.

"Please tell me you washed them."

He lifts his head and grins.

"You washed them, didn't you?" My brow wrinkles, waiting for him to respond.

He laughs.

"You sicko."

He laughs harder. "Course I fucking washed 'em. I was gonna give 'em back, but I forgot. I was only teasing you about keeping them."

"Oh. Where are they now?"

"I packed them with the rest of my stuff that reminds me of you."

"In your mum's attic?"

"No. They're in a suitcase with your book and photo, coming to Australia with me. I like to have them to hand when I think about you."

"When you?" I cough and my eyes widen.

He nuzzles my neck and whispers, "Yes, Steph. When I fuck myself, I rub them against my cock and think about you in your stockings and imagine your wet pussy wrapped around me and your big tits bouncing in my face."

My eyes are as wide as the O on my mouth. His words are making my temperature rise. It's already way too stifling on this train.

"Tell me, Steph. What do you think about when you touch yourself?"

I swallow the lump, but it won't budge. Glancing around the carriage, I check for other passengers. A man sits a few seats down with headphones on, his baggy joggers wafting as his leg taps to the music.

"Tell me, baby." His stubble grazes against my shoulder as his lips brush my neck, and his words are like a symphony to my ears, stimulating every cell in my body.

I tug his hair, bringing him back to my lips. "I think about you."

His brown eyes are like the inside of a volcano ready to erupt. "What am I doing?"

"Kissing me," I say between panting breaths.

"Where?"

"Down there."

"Baby, I wish I could taste you now."

"Cal."

His lips crash against mine, and he takes possession of my

mouth. I'm so hot and sticky. I need to stop this before I'm begging him to take me right here.

"Don't forget to put your train ticket back in your pocket."

He picks the ticket from the table and opens his wallet. The business card from earlier is on display, covering the picture of his girls in the clear window.

Victoria Pimperton, Beauty Sales Representative.

Even her name oozes sex appeal. I must stare at the card for a beat too long as Cal pulls it out and tears it up into little pieces, then slides open the top window, releasing the tiny bits of card.

I watch as they scatter to the wind, much like our fleeting relationship. "You didn't have to do that."

"I wasn't gonna call her, so it makes no difference to me. And now you won't picture us together."

"Cal. You can go with her. I'm not blind. I could see how attractive she was. If not her, then it will be someone else. Even if I wasn't married, I can't compete."

"It's them who can't compete with you. Nobody can replace you, Steph. Nobody knew me when I was five years old, only you. The stuff we shared is only with you. Nobody else can compete with that. I've heard you talk some shit before, but if you think I prefer anyone over you because you think they're better looking or slimmer, you must think I'm really shallow."

"I just know that you can have any girl or woman you want, so obviously you're going to choose to be with someone equally attractive."

"You're wrong again. I can't have any woman I want. If I could, I'd already have you."

"Cal."

His tongue darts between my lips, filling the void, dancing and swelling in a tangle of love and need.

The tannoy dings, announcing the next stop.

"I guess I best get off here."

He kisses me again with urgency, his tongue stiff, rough, and intoxicating. I drink him in, knowing I'll never feel this much passion in a man for the rest of my life. His arms tighten around my body, crushing my breath against his chest as he takes what belongs to him and I take what's mine.

The tannoy dings again, and I know our time is limited as the train slows to a halt.

He tears himself away, pulling my lip with him between his teeth. Holding my face in his hands, he gazes into my eyes. "I love you, baby."

"I love you, Cal."

"Do you have any money to get home?"

"No, but I have my credit card."

He opens his wallet again, flicking through a wad of notes, some Australian money and some English. He separates the two and hands me a wad of twenties. "Get a taxi back to your car."

"It's fine. I have my credit card."

"Take the money. You don't want Justin seeing a credit card statement with a taxi or train fare bill. Just take the money. I can't spend it where I'm going, anyway. And I'm not spending my last minute with you arguing again."

I take the money and shove it in my bag. "I'm sorry I couldn't give you all of me, but know you have my soul and you're always on my mind."

He follows me to the doors, and I wrap my arms around him. His warm breath falls onto my neck as he exhales deeply. I kiss his cheek, rubbing against his stubbly jaw, closing my eyes tight, imprinting this moment into a memory. We stay like this until the doors fly open.

"I can't let go, Cal."

He squeezes me tighter. "Baby, call me when you get back to your car, so I know you're safe."

I nod. "I will."

"If you need anything, just call me, yeah?"

"Are you getting off, miss?" the conductor asks.

Cal pulls me close. With a jagged breath and a tremble in his lip, he kisses me one last time. The morning sun reflects in his eyes as I step off the train onto the platform. The doors close in front of me, closing our relationship. He leans his forehead against the glass and presses his palm flat. I walk along the platform as the train sets off again with a screeching against the metal rails.

He fades into the distance and something inside me fades with him. Hope, maybe, or my heart, as if it's being ripped from me. The screeching sound rings in my ears as my body cries out. I'm standing on the platform in the morning summer sun, but my spirit is showered in darkness. Collapsing onto a bench behind me, I let my head fall into my hands, my elbows dig into my knees. I'm numb. No tears, just emptiness, nothing where my soul once lived.

A buzz and vibration from my bag brings me back to consciousness. I don't know how much time has passed, but the sun hides behind a cloud, turning everything dull. Looking at my phone, I notice it's 8.21am before I swipe right against Justin's name.

"Steph, where the hell are you?"

"I'm sorry. I'll be home soon."

"What are you doing leaving in the middle of the night? I woke up to you gone with no explanation. I know we need to talk, but you could have at least left a note. The kids, Steph. The kids are asking for you."

"I'm sorry. I just went for a drive early this morning to think. How's Cairen?"

"He must be better. He's asking for pancakes. Where are you? You're scaring me. You don't sound right."

"I'm about an hour away. I'll come home now."

"Steph. You're not doing anything stupid, are you?"

I close my eyes and bang my head against the brick wall. "Justin, I wouldn't do that. I'll see you soon, and we can talk."

"Hurry home."

The phone slips from my hand onto my lap, and I take in several deep breaths. After a few minutes gathering my thoughts, I walk into the station looking for a local taxi company on the pin board.

The ride is a blur. I stare out the window, but nothing registers. Once back at my car, I pay the driver and let out a long breath when there's no parking ticket, unless they just send a letter these days with no warning.

I sit in my car, and call Cal like he asked.

"Hey."

I close my eyes. Hearing his voice sends a spark to my heart, as if bringing it back to life for a moment. "Hi."

"Everything okay? Did you get to your car all right?"

"I got a taxi."

"It's taken you a long time to get back. I was getting worried."

"I'm sorry. I didn't want to worry anyone. I must have sat at the station for a while. What are you doing?"

"I'm sitting in the departure lounge with a coffee."

My fingers tremble as they fiddle with the hem of my shirt. "So this is it, then?"

"If you say so, Steph."

I exhale into the handset. "What's that supposed to mean?"

"It means that you call the shots. You always say I'm the

dominant one, but you have the last say here. The only time I have the upper hand is in the bedroom, and you know it."

"I'm sorry. I'll be here waiting for you when…if you ever come back to the UK."

"And I'll be here waiting for you when you decide to leave that jerk."

"Take care of yourself, Cal."

"And you, baby."

The dial tone plays, and the handset slips from my fingers. I rest my head against the steering wheel and cry like I've never cried before. Not since I miscarried and not since he told me he didn't want me all those years ago. The tears won't stop dripping over my swollen, quivering lips. I glance in the rearview mirror at a washed-out face, lifeless eyes like a frozen river that's stopped flowing. Who is this person? It's not me. There isn't even a glimmer of hope in her eyes. No longer the optimist.

Once home, I toss the keys on the side and climb the stairs. Each step feels like a mountain. I'm hiking, fighting against the wind. My feet are like lead weights pulling me down, and every bone in my body roars with pain.

I hear Justin at the bottom of the stairs. "We need to talk."

"I'm too exhausted, Justin. Not now, please." I haven't even got the energy to turn and face him. I can't think straight, but I know I can't stay with him.

I crawl back into bed and curl up beneath the covers, where I stay for the rest of the day in my drained state. The emotional pain has materialised into a physical ache that lives in my chest. I know that familiar emptiness. I've felt it before. The first time he left me. It doesn't get easier. Each time he leaves, it only gets harder.

STEPH

It's been a week since Callum left. Justin and I still haven't spoken. I avoid him at all costs. I need to look for a place to live, but I'm so exhausted lately. All I do is work and sleep. I picked up some sort of bug too, as I keep feeling sick. Mainly every time I look at Justin. *Nothing new there then*. He sleeps in the spare room, but we put a front on when the kids are around.

After reading Cairen a story, I curl up in bed. My book of Botticelli is in my bedside cabinet, and once settled under the duvet, I read.

At the beginning of the book, Cal's scribed a note.

I read this, curious to know what you love about it.
Now I know.

Cal highlighted some things in the book and made notes about Venus.

Venus is the Roman goddess of love, beauty, sex, fertility, prosperity, and desire.
In Latin, the noun Venus means 'sexual desire'.

*Botticelli was in love with Simonetta Vespucci, who was
already married to someone else. Simonetta was known as
the greatest beauty of her time.*
As a result, Botticelli never married.
*According to his wish, Botticelli was buried at the feet of
Simonetta Vespucci.*

As I turn the page, a postcard falls out. An image of the
painting Venus and Mars. On the back, Cal has written, '*You
are my Venus.*'

Goosebumps coat my flesh, and tears prickle at the back
of my throat. I hold the card close to my chest and close my
eyes, imagining he's with me now, holding me against his
warm body.

I grab my phone from the nightstand and scroll for his
number.

I strain my ear, listening for anyone outside the bedroom
door, but if Justin hears me, so be it. Excitement ripples
through me at the thought of talking to him. I should have
called him before, but I thought, what's the point in torturing
ourselves? I have to hear his voice and tell him how much I
love this gift.

The dial tone is flat. I cancel the call and try again, but
nothing.

I Google the guidelines for calling Australia and try again
adding the correct prefix, but all I get is a flat dial tone.

———

PARKING AT THE NOOK & Cranny for our usual catch up and
coffee, I bounce out of the car, excited to spend some time
with Claire. I haven't seen her in like forever.

As I walk into our favourite jaunt, scanning the room, her
hand waves me over to our usual window seat. Her hair glows

under the basking of the sunlight pouring through and her skin radiates life. Unlike mine, I had to apply several layers of makeup this morning so I wouldn't look half dead.

She stands as I approach and gives me a tight squeeze. "Happy Birthday."

"It's not my birthday yet," I remind her, not wanting to turn another year older before I have to.

"Not long, a few more days," she sings.

"Thanks for reminding me."

"Here." She thrusts a gift bag under my nose. "No peeking."

"Thank you." I can't stop the smile from spreading across my face. Even if I don't want to turn another year older, who doesn't love a gift?

I slip into the comfy chair and the waiter comes over to take our usual order of cream scones and large cappuccinos.

Claire's smile pushes her glowing cheeks up. "What have you been up to? It's been so long. Did you have a good Easter? Greece wasn't it?"

I sigh and lean back in my chair as I take in the scene out the window of two students holding hands, reminding me of Cal and I. "Not a lot. The holiday was okay. What about you? Are you still seeing what's-his-face?"

She rolls her eyes. "He got boring. He was too clingy and started talking about moving in together, so I had to cut loose."

I smile, thinking she is the female version of a teenage Callum and I can't help feeling for the bloke. "He liked you. What's wrong with that?"

She glowers at me. "You're not serious?"

I shake my head and smile, knowing I can't convince her otherwise.

The cappuccinos arrive with a little biscuit. "The scones will be out shortly."

"Thank you," Claire says. "So, how's things with Justin? Last time I saw you, things were fraught."

I let out a long breath, contemplating how much I should reveal. I want to tell her everything, but I can't seem to speak the words. Like having someone else know my sins is like making them real, and I'm trying to move on.

"The holiday was good. We were both ready for some rest and relaxation." I take the biscuit from the wrapper and bite into the crunchy texture, tasting the burnt caramel on my tongue. It's the simple things in life. Then I wash it down with a sip of my hot drink.

My nose scrunches as I slide the cup away. "That drink's not right. The milk must be off."

Claire looks puzzled, pulling her eyebrows together and takes a sip of hers. "Mine tastes fine." She picks up my drink and has a sip to compare the two. Licking the froth from her lips, she places the cup back on the table. "They're exactly the same."

I take the cup and have another try, but the taste makes me want to hurl. "No way. I can't stomach that. Can't you taste it?" My head shakes as a shiver takes over my body, and I stick my tongue out as if the air can evaporate the flavour residing there.

Claire laughs at my expression. "You're not pregnant, are you? Last time you were expecting, you went off coffee."

I laugh at the ridiculous thought. "Justin had a vasectomy before Easter. Plus, it would be a miracle to get pregnant from the two drunken times we actually did *it* on holiday." My nose wrinkles thinking about it. I was trying to rekindle something between us before seeing Cal again, but it was like trying to light damp wood.

She laughs and speaks, but all I hear is a muffled sound. My body stills as panic claws up my chest when I realise I came off the pill at Easter. What was the point in taking it now since Justin had a vasectomy?

The cafe blurs all around me, and time slows down. My head swirls, making me light and dizzy. The blood drains from my face and an icy chill follows, but I'm sweating on my top lip. The sudden urge to expel my breakfast comes over me as my mouth waters, and not in a good way. I can't have his baby, I'm leaving him, as soon as I get my arse in gear and find somewhere else to live. *And pluck up the courage to explain the situation to the kids.*

I cover my mouth. My body reacts while my mind tries to unscramble my thoughts, and I'm stumbling towards the bathroom. Bursting into the cubicle, the biscuit and this morning's cereal come up. I retch into the porcelain bowl again.

No, no, no, please. I can't be pregnant. Not now. I lift my head and wheeze. Callum. All those times with Callum, I was so used to sleeping with him without a condom. It never crossed my mind to put a cover on it. That I could...he could...I retch again, but there's nothing left.

Sweat drips from me profusely. I've done it now. I wipe my mouth with a tissue. My brain thinking a little clearer. I could just have a stomach bug. *Yeah right...a stomach bug that discriminates against coffee. You had no problem eating that biscuit.* Breathe, just breathe. I blow out and in again like I'm practising my birthing pants.

I rinse my mouth under the tap and feel better. I pat my mouth dry, making sure I don't upset the makeup I caked on this morning and reapply more lippy. If I didn't have a fake face on, my skin would be as lifeless as the corpse bride, confirming that I surely can't be pregnant? Pregnancy makes you glow.

It took me years of trying to get caught with Cassie and Cairen. Surely one time with Cal won't do it. *It wasn't one time though, was it?* I take several deep breaths in an attempt to pull myself together before I return to my seat. Feeling perfectly fine now, I wonder what came over me. Was it the biscuit that made me ill? *Not likely.* Oh, shut up.

I slide into the seat across from Claire and my scone has arrived, looking divine with lashings of red jam and clotted cream. It's warm too, and my tummy grumbles as if it's saying feed me.

"Are you all right?" Claire asks.

"I am now."

"Do you want your drink?"

"Gosh, no." I slide that as far away from me as possible. The memory of it lingers and I can taste it still. I catch the waiter's attention. "Excuse me, can I order a chocolate milkshake, please?"

He writes it down, and I hand him the cappuccino to take away.

Claire has already devoured half of her scone, and sod it. I'm going in… if I throw this up after, so be it; at least I'll get to taste it on my tongue.

The homemade strawberry jam is sickly sweet and melted into the warm, crumbly, buttery scone. The clotted cream fills my mouth, the sweetness kissing my tongue. *You're not moaning now, are you?* My subconscious pipes up, and funnily enough, I agree with her as a hum escapes my lips.

My milkshake arrives, and it's filled with ice-cream and chocolate sauce. A deluxe indulgent perfect for my birthday. I should have ordered it from the beginning.

"You never said Justin was getting a vasectomy," Claire says, wiping her mouth with a napkin.

I shrug. "Since I stopped going to the slimming group. Justin said he would do that so I could come off the pill. I'm sure it wasn't helping with my weight."

"You can still get caught up to three months after a vasectomy, though. That's what happened with my sister."

My heart flutters with panic again, and I wipe my brow before my fringe sticks to my forehead. "Yeah, I doubt it, though. I mean, we had two drunken quickies when the kids were asleep. I doubt his swimmers are even capable of impregnating me. We tried for years before. I just can't see it, Claire."

But Callum's swimmers are probably gold Olympians. Have you thought of that? I take another large bite of the scone to shut up the annoying voice in my head.

A shiver claws up my spine and the hairs prick up on my neck. "I had an affair," I mumble with a mouthful of scone.

Claire's lips part and her silvery-blue eyes stare at me as she leans over the table and places her hand on mine. "I know, hun."

I pull my hand away and wipe the crumbs from my mouth as I gulp. "How do you know?"

"When you were upset at Christmas, I guessed. But he left work right, it was over?"

"I slept with him again. After my holiday."

Claire's eyes widen. "So the baby could be Callum's?"

I suck in a breath and cover my mouth with my hand. This baby *could* be his. "Wait. I don't even know if I'm pregnant. It could just be a bug, Couldn't it?" *Right. Keep telling yourself that.*

"Look, don't do anything drastic just yet until you know for certain. There's no point in telling Justin about the affair if the baby turns out to be his. Especially now you're getting on again."

"I told Justin I wanted a divorce the other week. He's been sleeping in the spare room ever since." I rub my hands over my face. "Everything is such a mess."

"Hun, is that what you want?" Her head tilts, and she gives me a sympathetic look.

"I think so. I did. I was looking for somewhere to live, but I think Justin's hoping I'll change my mind. Deep down, I wonder what his motives are. I'm certain it's because he doesn't want to sell the house or give me any money."

"You're entitled to half of everything. You realise that, don't you? If you want to leave, I think you should."

"What if I'm pregnant? I don't think I could be a single mum."

"Lots of people manage, and you will too. You're an amazing mum." She smiles and rubs my hands as it rests on the table.

I don't feel like an amazing mum. I'm certainly not going to win any awards for mother of the year any time soon.

I AVOID coffee for the rest of the day. My outburst in the cafe had left a bitter taste in my mouth. Come to think of it, I can't remember the last time I drank coffee. I've been opting for tea.

Pulling out my diary, I work backwards trying to think when my last period was. I can't even remember. It must have been before the holiday about seven weeks ago now. I definitely had a period before the holiday as I remember being thankful that I wouldn't have to deal with it abroad. Although, since I came off the pill, they have been irregular.

My palms sweat as I realise there's a good probability that I could be pregnant. If I'm carrying another life, I need to stop freaking out and stay calm.

I lean back in the office swivel chair in the study at home and rest my hand over my soft round stomach, feeling a bubbling sensation, and I wonder. Could it be? *No, that's the scone.* I ignore the annoying voice and smile as the possibility of another baby sets in.

As old as I am, and while it's the last thing I would expect or plan at this stage of my life, the thought that I could be carrying *his* child fills me with overwhelming joy and protection. A motherly instinct takes over. This is the push I need to come clean and leave Justin for good.

How will I contact Cal? My shoulders slump, as I have no idea of how to contact him since he changed his number. If he even changed his number or just blocked me? I need to do a test. Maybe a scan too, to check the dates.

I imagine a dark-haired little girl like his daughters. He'll be torn between two worlds. I'll practically be a single mum, but I can't stop smiling, thinking of him kissing my stomach and reading to our unborn child as he used to read to me. His hands placed there while our baby kicks and an arm resting on my heavily pregnant belly as he snuggles me from behind. All things I imagined him doing before when I thought I was pregnant in our teens.

———

Monday morning comes around all too quickly. The dreaded birthday, where I'm officially another year older. I walk into the kitchen, and Justin hands me a tea, noting that I don't drink coffee anymore. He thinks I'm on some detox health kick, cutting down on caffeine.

I haven't been sick since Saturday at the cafe, but cleaning my teeth this morning made me gag. I tried to forget about the possibility of a baby this weekend, so I can celebrate my birthday. Justin gets top marks for effort. He's planned an evening meal with my family, even though I'd much rather spend it on the sofa with a takeaway, bottle of wine, and a good book.

"Mummy, open your presents." Cassie drags me by the hand, leading me into the lounge where two helium balloons waft and entwine. A number one and a four. It would be much simpler if I were fourteen.

Cairen hands me a gift bag. I open it to find my favourite chocolates and a bottle of gin. Holding up the bottle, I wonder if I'll even get to drink it this year. Cassie's gift bag contains a book by my favourite author and a candle that smells of the beach.

"Thank you. I love my gifts." I hug them both as they squirm from my arms and wipe their cheeks where I planted a kiss. A tear forms in the corner of my eye, knowing this will probably be the last birthday I have where we're all together.

The cuckoo clock sounds out, signalling it's time to get to work. Justin hands me a large bouquet that he kept hidden until now.

I flinch, but let him kiss me on the cheek as he hands me the flowers. "I didn't expect anything." He's making an effort tonight with a birthday meal, but Mum will have been behind it as well.

"Look, I know things aren't right between us, and we're just going along with this charade for the kids' sake, but I want us to try again. We can do marriage counselling or whatever you want."

The thought of being a single parent fills me with dread. The night feeds alone are exhausting. I don't know if I could do it alone. If this baby is Callum's, I have to, but if it's Justin's, should I at least try to work things out? I smile at Justin. "We'll see. Let's get today over with, shall we? I'm just tired, Justin."

He takes the flowers from me. "I'll put them in a vase. Have a good day at work, sweetheart."

Each time he calls me that, guilt rises in my throat. "Thanks. I'll see you tonight."

AT LUNCH, I read Cal's journal, something I do most days now.

25th June. Steph's Birthday.

Today was a good day. She loved her ring. I made sure she didn't get the wrong idea. I'm not ready to marry. But I thought if I were to propose one day, I'd bring her back here on the big wheel at sunset. She seemed to like it. In fact, the reward she gave me at the hotel told me she loved it.

A whimsical smile forms on my face, thinking about that day.

My nineteenth birthday was magical. We spent the day at Blackpool Pleasure Beach. The summer sun was setting, and the warm air had changed to a welcomed breeze.

"Shall we go back to the hotel?" I say with a glint in my eye, desperate to have him inside me as I did this morning.

"One more ride." He winks, squeezing my hand.

I giggle. "We can make our own ride at the hotel."

A puff of laughter leaves his lips, and he drags me towards the big wheel. "I have another present for you."

"You keep saying that, so let's go back to the room, and you can give it to me."

He laughs again. We show the attendant our wrists and board a carriage. I sit next to Cal and he wraps his arms around me, kissing the side of my face. "I have an actual gift for you. As well as a good seeing to later."

"What, another?" I don't know what I'm more excited about, the gift or the seeing to. My tummy vibrates just thinking about it.

"Yeah." He smirks, and the wheel moves us to the next

position and stops, allowing another couple to jump on the next carriage.

"What is it?" I hold my breath as he pulls out a small box and smiles. My heart races. Is he? No, he wouldn't. It's too soon. Although I would say yes. There's nobody else I want to spend the rest of my life with.

Tears well up in the corner of my eyes and I take the box from him with a trembling hand. "Cal."

"Wait. Don't get excited, it's not what you think it is." He rubs the back of his neck and shuffles in his seat.

My heart sinks, but I keep the smile on my face. "Whatever it is, it's beautiful."

He twists the metal in his eyebrow, and his tongue darts out to wet his lips. "It's earrings."

I smile and nod, wondering if he's just teasing me? There's a little part of me that hoped he would propose.

"It's not earrings, it's a ring." My chest flutters and my throat closes up. Tears drip down my cheeks. Is this really happening?

"For your middle finger." He quickly adds before swallowing hard and pinching his eyebrow.

I open the box and see the amethyst flower glistening in the setting sun.

Cal takes it out of the box and slides it on my middle finger. "I hope I got the right size."

It fits perfectly. The shiny jewels match my eyes as they glisten at Cal with blurred vision. "I love it."

Our carriage halts at the top of the wheel, allowing people on or off below. The view up here is sublime, but it's nothing compared to him and the way he's looking at me. He takes my face between his palms and brushes his lips against me. His tongue slips in as he takes possession of my mouth. I melt into him like I always do and place my hand on his cheek. The jewels catch my eye once again. This boy has my heart, and I can't imagine a life without him in it. I don't know what the future holds for us, but as long as we're together, I'll be happy.

His chest rocks against me as he chuckles. "I saw that playing out differently in my head."

"Oh?"

"It only just occurred to me you might think I was gonna propose when I pulled out a ring box." He knocks my shoulder with a grin.

"I…I didn't think that." I lie. I was slightly disappointed.

"I'm sorry. The next time I bring you here, maybe I will propose."

He kisses me again and everything blurs.

CHAPTER *Twelve*

STEPH

Now the birthday celebrations are over, I take the pregnancy test out of my bag when everyone goes to lunch. Nobody asks me to go to the pub anymore, as I usually say no and eat a sandwich at my desk while I read Cal's journal.

Walking to the toilets with my bag on my shoulder, my stomach flips like I have triplets in there jumping on a trampoline. I lock myself in a cubicle and hang my bag on the back of the door. I still can't decide how I feel about it and what I want the result to be.

It would be much easier to keep my betrayal a secret and carry on as I am on this treadmill I can't seem to get off. But each time I think of being with Cal and having his child, my stomach flutters and my heart is ready to burst like a party popper full of confetti.

I haven't stopped thinking about the possibility all weekend. I imagine calling him. He'd get on the first plane and come home to me. We'll make things work somehow.

After peeing on the test, I place it on top of the loo roll holder, waiting for it to change. My chest tightens, and my leg won't stop shaking. I shouldn't be doing this alone. Cal should be here with me, although the last time we did this ended in heartbreak for me as he didn't take it too well.

I almost daren't look at the small window on the stick. Even if I'm positive, I need to book a scan and get a date of conception. The scan can calculate the baby's growth and give me an exact date. I can't have Cal flying halfway around the world to find out it's Justin's.

The thought of it being Justin's makes me heave. I don't want anymore ties to him than I already have.

A faint line appears on the test. With my fuzzy brain, I double check the stick, is it one line, two, or a cross? It's been so long since I did one of these things, I can't even remember what I'm looking for.

One line equals not pregnant and two lines equals pregnant.

A second faint line appears. The lines blur to spots in my vision and I lean back on the toilet as everything turns hazy.

Dread claws at my throat, making it difficult to breathe. My shoulders curl inwards and I hold my neck, then my hand moves to my stomach.

I hug myself, knowing there's the miracle of life inside me. Taking deep, controlled breaths, I stand and carry the stick to the sink. The lines grow darker with every passing second, and there's no doubt I'm pregnant.

The door bursts open, making me jump. "Steph?"

My head snaps to the side as Kelly walks in.

"Are you all right? You look as if you've seen a ghost."

With a trembling hand, I show her the stick.

Her hands cover her face as she forms an O with her mouth. "Did you plan this?"

I huff. "No." Heat swathes my skin and the toilets close in on me. "I need some air."

"Come on, let's sit down." She holds the door open, and I float back to my desk, still dazed.

Plopping down in my chair, Kelly sits next to me. "Do you want me to cover for you? Take the rest of the day off. Go home to Justin."

"No. Please don't tell anyone yet. I need to sort things out."

"My lips are sealed." She moves her fingers over mouth, zipping them shut.

"I need to make an appointment with the midwife. Have you heard from Cal since he moved to Australia?"

"No, have you?"

I shake my head. "I think he's blocked me. Would you call him?"

"What, now? Isn't it around midnight over there?"

"I just want to know if it's me he's blocked, or if he's changed his number. If it rings, I know it's me. I just need to know why."

She pulls her phone out and taps the green icon next to his name. "There's a flat tone. Nothing."

I let out a breath, happy that he hasn't blocked me. "Do you know how I can contact him?"

Her hand covers her mouth as she gasps. "It's his, isn't it?"

"Keep your voice down. I don't know, but I need to get in touch with him."

"Do you have his personal email?"

"No, I only ever had his work email on the company server. Do you know his personal one?" My stomach flutters with hope.

She scrolls through her phone. "I'm sure it was something like Gandalf82@gmail."

"That makes sense." I smile, remembering his map of Middle Earth.

She searches her email list. "Or maybe that other geezer? What's his name?"

"Precious? Gollum?"

She shakes her head. "It's not that."

"Bilbo Baggins."

"Nope. It could still be one of those. I just don't have it in my contacts. I've probably never emailed his personal address."

I slump back in my chair. I thought we were onto something there.

"HR should have his next of kin details. Although if it's Priya, you're probably screwed, seeing as she's no longer here either. I can ask for you."

"Kelly, thank you so much."

She disappears, leaving me to call the doctors for an appointment with the midwife and book an early scan.

Kelly returns with a sheet of paper in her hand. "His next of kin is his mother. I have her address and phone number." She hands it to me, and I relax my shoulders.

"That's great. I really appreciate that."

"No worries, just don't tell anyone I gave it to you, as it's confidential. They have an old email too, but I'm sure he doesn't use this one anymore. I don't even think this company is still going."

I try the email address, but get a bounce back. He's worked here for so long he probably hasn't updated his details since he started. I fire off a few more emails using characters from his favourite book. With each new address I try, I get a bounce back. Will I ever be able to reach him?

WHEN I LEAVE WORK, I drive to the address Kelly gave me. A modest home, but the front garden is beautiful with pink roses in full bloom. I knock on the door before wringing my sweaty hands together as I wait.

The door opens, and I'm met with a much older woman than I remember.

"Can I help you, dear?"

"Hi, Mrs Richards. It's me, Stephanie."

She pushes her glasses up with a furrowed brow. "Steph? What are you doing here?"

"I need to contact Cal."

"He doesn't live here. He's moved to Australia with his family."

"I know. I just need his number." While chewing on the inside of my cheek, I pick at my purple nail varnish. This woman makes me feel like I'm a teenager again, calling for her boy, although she was more friendly back then.

"I can't give out his details willy-nilly. You're practically a stranger. What do you want him for?"

"It's private. Please, I need to talk to him. It's important." I don't understand why she's being so difficult.

"You know he's settled over there, don't you?"

"Settled?" My throat closes up and I curl my arms around my waist.

"With Priya and his girls."

I nod. "Right." My shoulders cave inwards, and I look down at my shuffling feet. "I still need to speak to him."

"I'll tell him to call you." She smiles and closes the door, but I jam my foot over the threshold.

"Wait. Let me write my number down. He may not have it." I rummage in my bag, looking for a pen.

She hands me a notepad and pencil from the old telephone table positioned in her hallway. "Write it on this, dear."

"Thank you." I jot my number down and hand it over. She smiles and closes the door. The encounter leaves me with a sour taste in my mouth. Even walking by her beautiful rose garden can't lift my spirits. I sigh heavily and slip back into my car, though I can't blame him for giving things another go with Priya. If not her, it would have been someone else. He's not the sort of person who would go celibate.

———————

SITTING in the waiting room at the private hospital, my bladder is ready to burst. I glance at the clock and know my appointment is imminent, thank goodness.

This scan is costing me a pretty penny, but I couldn't wait for the NHS appointment to come through. I need to know whose baby I'm carrying, and if it's his, I'll be making another trip to his mother's. Priya or no Priya. He needs to know he's going to be a father again.

A sharp pain stabs me in the chest when I think of him seeing another woman. Although I'll have to get used to it. I'm thankful now he's in Australia, and I don't have to see him around the street like I did in our teens.

"Mrs Bailey," the sonographer calls, snapping me from my depressing thoughts. I put on a fake smile and clutch my bag as I follow her into the small room. "Make yourself comfortable on the bed and lift your top."

I do as she asks, although it's hard to make yourself comfortable with a pint of water in your bladder. I can already feel a dribble in my knickers as it seeps out. After my last two kids, I've never been able to hold my bladder. They destroyed my pelvic floor. I haven't been able to go on a trampoline since. *You never went on one before?*

"Right, Mrs Bailey, how many weeks do you think you are?"

"I'm hoping you will tell me." I flash her a fake smile and hope she hurries up so I can relieve myself.

She pushes up her black-framed glasses and tucks her dark bobbed hair behind her ears. "Let's have a look, shall we?"

My stomach tightens at the cool sensation when she squeezes half a tube of lube onto my belly. The screen comes alive, lighting up the dim room. I tilt my head to see the black and white images as she moves the doppler around my skin.

The screen displays an odd-looking bean and I let out a sigh of relief that there's just the one. The sonographer turns the volume up, and I hear the heartbeat pulsing from the machine. Water pools in the corners of my eyes and rolls down the side of my face when I blink. It's such a special moment the first time you hear that, especially after suffering from miscarriage.

Cal should be here with me. We should experience this together. If only he hadn't been so difficult. He hasn't been in touch with me yet. I find it hard to be mad at him, though. We'd be together if I hadn't denied him. I'm going to make things right. As soon as this woman stops pressing on my bladder, and I've had a pee, I'm going to make this right.

"From these calculations, you're nine weeks pregnant," the woman says, adjusting her glasses as she examines a chart.

I hold my breath as the small, dark room closes in on me. "Can you check again, please?"

"I've done the calculations based on the baby's measurements, seeing as you can't actually be sure of your last period." She writes some dates on my notes. "Would you like a picture to take away?"

I nod, unable to speak. If the lights were on, she'd see the colour drain from my face as I lay numb.

I hear the printer behind me fire up and the lights flicker back on. Using the blue paper roll, she wipes the lube from my stomach, and I pull my top down.

"All looks well." She hands me a strip of photographs. "I've estimated the due date to 20th January."

My mouth drops open. Callum's birthday too. What a coincidence.

"You'll be happy to know you can go to the toilet now," she says with a hint of laughter in her voice.

I had forgotten all about the need to relieve myself.

"Are you all right?"

I nod. "Thank you. I'm fine." Still dazed, I walk out of the room and blink at the bright light of the waiting area. I place the photos in my bag while I go to the loo and tears of joy fall down my face.

The baby is healthy. It's all any mother wishes for, but knowing it's Cal's and I have a piece of him inside me floods me with warmth.

Is it selfish of me to want a piece of him? Even if he doesn't want me anymore and is working things out with Priya. I will have a piece of him forever that will never stop loving me.

A knock at the door snaps me from my thoughts. "Hey, can you hurry please, pregnant lady here, needing to pee."

I pull a wad of tissue from the roll and pat my cheeks.

I unlock the door to a heavily pregnant woman, tapping her foot. "Sorry."

She darts past me into the cubicle, and I wash my hands, glancing in the mirror to check my eye makeup, which is intact thanks to the waterproof mascara I invested in.

At least now Justin will let me go. He definitely won't want to make things work, knowing I'm carrying another man's child. I sigh, thinking of Justin. I still have to tell him I'm pregnant. This is the push we both need. I'm going to take the rest of the day off to sort things out.

It's lunchtime when I pull up at the building site; a new development on the edge of town. Hopefully, I'll be able to catch Justin on a break. I park in front of the sales office and wave at Linda through the large glass window as I walk around the side to the construction container that Justin uses as an on-site office.

I open the door and step inside the container. His head snaps to the side, and he whips his hand from underneath Maxine's skirt. Her little bottom perches on the edge of his desk with her legs open, resting on either side of his waist. "Steph," he says before clearing his throat and sliding his chair back slightly so Maxine can close her legs.

My mouth gapes, and my bag falls from my shoulder, landing on the floor with a thud.

Maxine jumps off his desk, adjusting her skirt. "We were just having lunch."

"Clearly," I say, staring at Justin. My body tenses. My heart pounds against my ribs, and I ball my fists. Although I'm only mad because this whole time I could have been with the man I love and now it's too late. "How long has this been going on?"

"Steph. It's not what you think. We were just getting some lunch."

"What were you eating? Because this whole container reeks of deceit…and tuna."

Maxine smoothes a hand over curly red hair and collects her cardigan and bag from the floor. I step aside to let her scurry away with her head down, hiding her freckled face in shame.

"Don't lie to me, Justin. I think there's been too much lying on both our parts. Don't you?"

"What about you? How long were you shagging what's-his-name?"

"Is this what this is? Are you trying to get me back? Or do you actually like her?" I sit in the chair on the opposite side of his desk.

Justin sits down. "It just happened. After I found out about you and that bloke from work."

"Since Christmas? This whole time, you've been manipulating me and trying to salvage our relationship while screwing your little whore on the side."

"If she's a whore what does that make you? You started this. If you'd been faithful, I'd never have gone elsewhere." He leans over the desk. His icy blue eyes send a chill through me. "And don't say you were, because I know you weren't. I went through the damn washing Steph. I saw your stockings and new underwear, and you certainly weren't wearing them for me."

"Is that where you went when you disappeared? You were with her?"

"I needed someone to talk to. Maxine actually listens to me. She actually wants to know about my day and doesn't glaze over when I talk."

I rub my temples and breathe in and out, trying to keep calm. He's right, I do glaze over, though not on purpose. I've just had a lot on my mind. "I want a divorce."

"Not this again. Is that so you can go back to your fuck boy?"

"He's in Australia. I'll probably never see him again. He's nothing to do with this. I want a divorce. I'm moving out or you can move out. Whatever, but you're going to help me financially."

He laughs. "Like hell I will. We're not getting divorced. We can sort this out. If I can forgive you, I'm sure you can forgive me."

"I forgive you. I don't even care. What does that tell you?"

"You can't even cook, Steph. Our kids will starve."

"I'll learn. I'll manage. Anything has to be better than putting our kids through this misery. It must rub off on them, seeing me miserable all the time."

"Is that why you're miserable cos lover boy moved to Australia?"

"No, I think I'm miserable because every day I have to put on a fake smile and pretend I'm happy to be your wife. I'd sooner be alone even if that means cooking my own meals, putting the bin out and picking up the dog mess and all those other jobs that you brag about like you deserve a friggin' medal."

He huffs. "I'd love to see you cope without me."

I lean forward in the seat, gripping the armrest. "What about all the jobs I do? Is that why you don't want a divorce? Are you worried about who's going to iron and wash your clothes and do the pots? I'm sure Maxine will be happy to clean up after you."

He taps his fingers on the desk. "What are you doing here, anyway? Shouldn't you be at work?"

I slump in the chair and drop my head back, closing my eyes as I let out a long breath. "I'm pregnant." My eyes open, and I lift my head to get his reaction.

He leans forward, resting his elbows on the desk, and runs a hand over his face. "How far?"

"Nine weeks."

He stares at the desk calendar right in front of him while he does the math. "Greece?" His eyebrows pinch. "I knew we should have used something."

He thinks it's his. "Yes, we should. Especially as you'd been shagging mingy Maxine."

"Don't call her that," he snaps with slanted eyes and stands from the chair as he paces the room, stroking his clean-shaven jaw.

"She's the reason you wanted a vasectomy, isn't she?"

He stops and looks at me. "One reason. I didn't want any more kids, Steph."

"Neither did I, but it's too late now."

"We can't get a divorce. I'll do better. I'm a good father, you know that, and I'll do better for this one, I promise."

His words crush my chest. Even after everything he still wants to do right by this baby. "You don't have to worry. It's not yours."

"What?" His eyes flit back to mine.

"It's Callum's. The dates point to after Greece."

His fingers rub his temples. "You're sure?"

I swallow and nod. My heart beats in my throat. "With our past track record and the vasectomy, it's obvious it's his."

He wipes his hand over his face and lets out a long sigh. "Jeez, I have to admit, Steph. I'm sort of relieved. I really didn't want to have to go through all that again, with the nighttime feeds and nappy changing and everything else."

I screw my face up. "Since when did you do the night time feeds? And I think you only ever changed the odd nappy."

"You know what I mean. It's hard to sleep when you have a newborn crying every two hours." He bends into the chair and swings back with a slight smile on his face. "It's lover boys, then? But how if he's in Australia?"

"I saw him before he went." A dull ache grows in my stomach like a weed zapping all my energy when I think of him in Australia.

Justin stares blankly at me with a tense jaw. He cracks his knuckles and twists the wedding band on his finger.

"I asked you for a divorce a few weeks ago and you manipulated me back when Cairen was ill. You're not doing the same again. The best thing we can do is divorce. If you care for me at all, you will support me and help me. If you want to be with Maxine, go for it. I won't stand in the way of two people that love each other."

He stares at me for a while, bouncing back on his office chair. "You're right. Maybe I could have got past the infidelity, but this pregnancy changes everything. There's no way I can stand by while you have another man's kid."

"I never expected you to."

"Don't ask me to sell the house."

"I don't want you to sell it. You bought it with your nan's inheritance. But I want you to help me get my own place. All my money is tied up in the joint account. If you cooperate, I don't think we need to get lawyers involved. I just want my money and some support to help with the kids."

He strokes his chin. "Fair enough. As long as I keep the house. I've put too much work and money into that place and it's the kids' home."

My eyes well up. "Of course. I don't want to upset the kids any more than we have to." I inhale a deep breath. "We can share them. I'll find somewhere close by."

"There's no rush to sort anything today. We can look at other places on the weekend. I'll carry on sleeping in the spare room. There's no rush for you to move out."

"Thank you."

He stands and corners the desk with his arms out. I take a step back, knowing where his hand was.

"You can come near me when you've showered." A shudder rocks through me.

He wipes his hand on his jeans and opens the door. "I'll see you later, and we can tell the kids together."

I nod and step out into the afternoon sun, feeling lighter than I've felt in a long time. My head is weightless, like stepping out of a salon after a drastic cut.

CAL

"Hello," Priya calls from the porch.

"In here." I shout as I unpack the last of my crockery in the kitchen. Finally, I've got the keys to my own place. A small two-bed apartment, but it's no different from what I'm used to.

"Daddy, I want mummy to see my bedroom," Bethy says, dragging Priya through the kitchen.

"All right, boo."

Priya places a large dish on the worktop and continues through into the bedrooms. The aroma of one of her curry dishes fills the kitchen, and I lift the lid and take a peek at the aloo gobi potato dish.

Liv follows with her phone in her hand. "Hey lollipop. How was school?"

She shrugs but doesn't look up from her screen. "Okay, I guess."

"Are you gonna show your mum your room?"

She walks into the bedroom, and I hear Priya say how nice it is. The girls picked out some colours, and they helped paint it at the weekend. I've tried to make it as nice as their old room. Beth was upset about her doll's house, but I told her we can make a new one here and the old one will stay at nanny's house in England.

Priya walks back into the kitchen. "You've done a lovely job, Cal. I like the turquoise."

"I picked that colour, Mum," Liv says.

"I got you a ticket for Olivia's dance show. It's not for a few months, so don't lose it." She places an envelope on the counter. "Your ticket is for the Friday, and I'm going on the Saturday, so she has someone at both performances."

"Thanks. What's this?" I point to the dish on the worktop.

Priya waves a hand in the air. "It's nothing. I made a curry and did extra for everyone. I know you've been busy lately."

I've been busy? She's the one that hasn't stopped; securing herself a part time teaching job while still being a mum and taking care of her folks. And she still finds time to make me dinner. "Thanks. It's my favourite."

"I know." She tilts her head and smiles. "I always think of you when I make it. Usually wanting to tip it over your head." She covers her mouth as she giggles, and I let out a puff of laughter.

"Funny how I have that effect on people."

She narrows her eyes, rubbing her chin. "Hmm, I wonder why?"

"Are you staying? I'll warm it up. There's plenty for all of us."

"Stay, Mummy, please." Bethy looks up at Priya with her big brown eyes. She's so damn hard to say no to.

Priya smiles. "Oh, go on then. Cal, just pop it in the oven for twenty minutes."

"I know how to cook." I roll my eyes as I take the lid off and place it in the middle of the oven.

"Only because I taught you." She has a smile playing on her lips, trying to get a reaction out of me.

"Fair enough. You taught me how to cook a good curry,

but I taught you how to cook a roast dinner." I lift the new dinner plates I just bought from the cupboard and set them on the worktop. "We'll have to rough it. I don't have any furniture yet, other than a coffee table and a small two-seater sofa."

"That's okay." Priya leans on the worktop and taps her fingernails against the laminate. "Did you hear anything back from that interview you had?"

"Nah, but I picked up some freelance work." I pull out a packet of rice from the cupboard, glad I bought some essentials.

She pulls her head back. "Freelance?"

"Yeah, I can work from home. It'll do until I can get a full time marketing job. Plus I can help out with the girls more."

She yawns and her tired eyes weep in the corner. "Can you keep the girls until Sunday night? I'm taking care of Dad all weekend to give Mum a rest."

"Sure. You know I will. How's he doing today?"

"He's had better days, but it's taking its toll on Mum. She's so tired and drained, I worry she's going to make herself ill, too."

"I'm glad you're here for them." I wish I could do more for her. Having our girls just doesn't seem enough. Maybe I should have stayed living at her place until Steve gets here. I could help with the kids, dinner, and other household chores. It was uncomfortable sleeping on her couch, though.

"You should find your dad, Cal." Priya sighs and draws circles on the mottled laminate worktop.

My eyebrows gather inwards, and the mention of my father makes me lose my appetite. "What for? I don't need that drunk in my life."

"You said he was always kind to you, just not your mother. He obviously cared for you, Cal."

"How can I forgive what he did, though?" A dull ache

travels through my body, hardening my stomach, remembering how he treated my mother.

"He left, didn't he? Maybe that was his way of doing the right thing."

I think about what she's saying, and I realise I've done exactly the same thing with Steph. She said I always leave, but in my mind it's always been for the best. Am I a chip off the old block?

"I just don't want you to be in my position and your dad is dying or worse, dead, and it's too late to reconnect. If you just spoke and allowed yourself to forgive him, it wouldn't weigh so heavy on your heart."

Priya knows my demons. She knows that's the reason I was in Australia when we met the first time around. I came looking for my dad. I found him too, living in Sydney with his new family. Nothing hurts more than rejection and after seeing him with his new life, I wasn't about to let him reject me for a second time.

He passed me in the street a few times and never recognised me. Why would he when he'd not seen me since I was about seven? Then I saw him playing happy families with his wife and her son. It should have been me he was taking to the football. *You hate football.* I huff out a breath. That's not the point.

The timer dings, and I open the oven and pull out the bubbling dish. The spices carry through the air and fill the apartment with the familiar scent of home that Priya's cooking always gives me.

"I always wondered if it wasn't for your dad. Maybe we would have worked out."

"We didn't work out, Priya, because your family wouldn't stop interfering." I serve the curry onto the new plates.

Priya drains the rice. "They wanted me to be married. Was that too much to ask?"

"Yeah, and I fucking proposed, didn't I?"

She turns to me with the pan of rice in her hand. "I would hardly call that a proposal. *'We'll fucking get engaged to shut them fuckers up.'* I think were your exact words." She mocks them in a deep gruff voice and acts all macho, swinging her arms, pretending to be me.

"I'm sorry, but never do that terrible impression again." I chuckle at her attempt to mock me.

"If you think that was bad, you should see yourself." She giggles and serves up the rice.

"Girls, dinner," I shout, not really sure if they're in the bedroom or living room.

Livvie comes into the kitchen. "Where are we eating, Dad?"

"The living room. Carry your plates to the coffee table."

Priya carries her plate through behind the girls and sits on the sofa. I join her, resting the plate on my lap. "This is cosy."

A little more cosy than I would have liked, but Priya has a way of making the most awkward of situations comfortable. It's also nice to just be myself with someone who isn't trying to flirt with me.

"Have you heard from Steve?" The potatoes melt in my mouth and I moan and point to the food in my lap, mumbling, "So good."

"He's secured a job at an IT consultancy. He's working his notice and selling the house. By the end of the month, he should be here."

"Good. I'm happy for you." I scoop up another forkful and wish I'd got a spoon.

"Thanks Cal. I have missed him. I was worried that he'd change his mind about coming over. It's a monumental move, and it's not for everyone."

"I've only met the bloke once, but it was clear he dotes on you."

"Steve's bringing his dog, Buddy, to live with us, isn't he, Mum?" Bethy says.

Priya sighs. "That was another thing I feel terrible about. He loves that dog of his, and it's costing him three grand to bring him over."

I suck in a breath and almost choke on the cauliflower. Coughing, I hit my chest with my fist as my eyes water. "Three grand?" I wheeze.

Priya gets up and disappears for a minute, returning with a glass of water.

"Thanks," I say with a hoarse voice.

"It made my eyes water too, when he told me. But it's just been him and Buddy for years, so I understand why he wants to bring him over. Even if it is costing an arm and a leg."

"I've had enough. Can I play in my room?" Bethy asks.

"Sure, scrape the rest of your curry onto my plate." I'm not having that go to waste.

"Why didn't you and that Steph girl work out? I know you liked her as you took the girls to meet her."

"I liked her, Dad. She was nice."

"Me too, Lollipop." Heat rises from my knotted stomach at the mention of my Steph. I run a hand over my face. Fuck, I miss her. I haven't even got her number anymore since I threw my phone at the wall one night, sick of staring at her name, waiting for her to call me or itching to call her. It was driving me insane.

Liv gets up and carries her empty plate into the kitchen, then pops her head back in the living room. "Have you seen my phone?"

I look up. "You mean it's been surgically removed from your hand?"

"Haha. Dad, you're hilarious." She gives me a sarcastic smile and goes to her room.

"She's more and more like you every day," I smile at

Priya.

She knocks my shoulder. "Me? It's *you* she takes after."

I snort as I laugh through my nose. Maybe she's right.

"So tell me more about this Steph. Did you ruin things with her?"

"She wouldn't have me." I place my empty plate on the coffee table and lean back, rubbing my full stomach that's hardening every time I think of Steph.

Priya's eyebrows pinch. "Really, why not?"

"She's married."

Priya's pretty face wrinkles as she cringes. "Cal, you didn't go with a married woman?"

"Yep." I let out a long breath. "It's not like that, though. She belongs to me. She's mine. Since we were kids, she's been mine. I love her. Like really love her. You know, the kind of love where you don't feel complete without the other."

"Yes, Cal. I know what you mean. That's how I felt about you once."

"Ah shit. Priya, I'm sorry. I love you. You know that."

"You just couldn't marry me." She rolls her eyes and places her plate on the coffee table on top of mine.

"I'm sorry."

"It's fine. I think I had a lucky escape." She giggles again. "So, if she's the love of your life, why aren't you together?"

"She's married. I asked her to leave. I even proposed."

She raises her brow, and her brown eyes bore into me. "Did you propose, though? Your proposals leave a lot to be desired."

"I said, 'I'll marry you if that's what it'll take.'"

She covers her mouth either in horror or amusement. It's hard to tell. "Cal, you're the worst at proposals. You need to stop. The next time you feel the urge to mention marriage, please consult someone first. And by someone, I mean me."

I lift my feet on the coffee table and wave my hand. "Yeah, yeah."

"Cal, I know being married resembles abuse and control for you. It's understandable that you wouldn't want that, but you're not your father."

"That's what Steph would say."

"I think we'd get along."

"You would."

PRIYA SETTLES the girls in their beds before she leaves. The house is still and resting. I sit on the porch with a can, enjoying the coolness the night air brings, listening to the crickets chirp.

Everything seems peaceful at this late hour, but my mind is restless. It's in the still of the night when my brain is most active; when nothing but *her* fills my thoughts. I lean back against the wooden frame of the porch and swig my beer, closing my eyes to imagine her here.

The breeze brushes the hair from my face like her fingers have swept down from the heavens to brush my skin as she always does. Is she thinking of me now? Is she imagining my touch as I am hers? As nice as I've made this place. It'll never be home without my Steph.

STEPH

"STEPH." Justin's voice makes me jump and the ladder wobbles. His large hands grip my waist, and he helps me down the two steps. "What do you think you're doing?"

"I thought I'd make a start with the decorating."

"I told you I'd sort it. You shouldn't be up a ladder in your condition. Good thing I came round when I did."

"I'm fine. Are the kids here?" I look behind him but don't see them.

"Your mum's taken them out for lunch. They picked out some paint, though, for their new bedrooms." He points to two tins on the floor. One a bright green and the other a purple glitter.

"No prizes for guessing who's picked what." I giggle. "At least it isn't bright red after his favourite football team."

Justin looks around. "What shall I start on first, your living room or the bedrooms?"

"How about you help me with the living room, seeing as I've already started? I'll paint the bottom, and you do the top."

He picks a paintbrush up and dips it in the cream paint. "I don't know why you wanted to move so quickly. You could have stayed at the house while we decorated this place for you."

"It's already been long enough. I'm grateful for all you've done. Your team has transformed this place already with the new bathroom and new kitchen. I didn't want to leave it any longer. We both needed our space."

"I still wish you'd bought the bigger place I showed you."

"I didn't want the extra expense of that other house."

"Where's the baby gonna sleep?"

"She can have the box room. It's big enough for a cot and when she's older, she can share with Cassie."

"She?" He raises an eyebrow.

I shrug. I don't know why I keep thinking she's a girl. My hand glides over my stomach. I'm not really showing yet and just look fat, but I can feel her in there. "I was thinking if it's a girl, I'd call her Caitlin. You know, keep with the 'C' theme, if you don't mind."

"Why would I mind?"

I shrug a shoulder. "Just because *our* kids begin with C." I shouldn't be here discussing names with Justin. It should be Cal here with me, helping me decorate my new place. Instead, he's blanked me.

He huffs, climbing up the ladder. "What you gonna call it if it's a boy? Let me guess. Callum?" He says his name like he's the antichrist.

"No. He's due on his birthday. Calling him the same name would just be weird. I do like Caleb, though."

"Yeah, I actually like that." Justin pulls his phone from the back pocket of his jeans. Placing the brush between his teeth, he types into the phone. "How ironic."

"What?"

"Caleb means faithful." He quirks an eyebrow, making me smile.

"What does Caitlin mean?"

He types in his phone again. "Pure."

"That's nice." It kind of resembles a fresh start. A new baby that won't be tainted by our toxic relationship. We've been getting on so much better as roommates these last few weeks. We're verging on friends, which is something I haven't felt around him for a long time.

My face brightens. I dip the brush in the paint and shuffle along the floor to the next bit of wall. "Do you remember, it took us ages to agree on names for Cassie and Cairen? I guess that's one benefit of going it alone."

"You're not alone, Steph." He gives me a sympathetic smile with a pained look in his eyes. "You still not heard from *him*?" The pained expression turns to an icy stare at the mention of *him*.

"No. I guess the apple doesn't fall far from the tree."

"How so?"

"His dad left when we were kids. He abandoned him. It

was a difficult time for Cal."

"Hang on. You knew him then?"

"I've known him my whole life."

"It makes sense now. Your mum said he was your ex, but I didn't know how far back your history went." The pained look in his eyes returns. "Is he the wanker you were crying over when I called for your brother all those years ago?"

I smile, thinking about all the crying I did over him. "Probably."

"So he left you then, and he's left you again." Justin shakes his head. "And I'm here picking up the pieces. Again."

"I'm sorry. I don't expect you to help when the baby comes, but I appreciate you helping me with my house." My bum shuffles along the floor to applying more paint.

"Yeah, well, I'm not just doing this for you, Steph. My kids gotta live here, haven't they? Even if it is half the week, I won't have them living in squaller."

"Before I forget, my friend Amy has asked if I can meet her in London for a weekend."

"When?"

"Next month. Is that okay? I'll write the dates down for you."

"Sure. I'm out this weekend with the lads. Don't forget."

I roll my eyes. He's always out on the razz lately, like he's just got out of prison and making the most of life. I can't blame him. Our marriage felt like a prison sentence sometimes; for me anyway.

After painting the bottom half of the walls, I leave the rest for Justin to finish while I tidy up the dining room. "Do you want to stay for dinner, Justin? It's the least I can do to say thank you for all your help."

He twists on the ladder and stares at me with pinched eyebrows. "You're cooking?"

I huff and rest my fist on my hip. "I have learned to cook a few things this last week while I've been living on my own."

"Oh? So, what are you cooking?"

"Well, I was going to order a Chinese."

He chuckles, shaking his head. "I hate to turn it down, but I have this thing that Maxine invited me to."

I smile and grit my teeth. The mention of her name still grinds on me. It's not that I'm jealous, but if I'd known, I would have left him a long time ago and maybe Callum and I would be together now.

He's in Australia. My shoulders sag, knowing he's over there with Priya. He should be happy. I just wish I was the one making him happy, but if there's a chance for those girls to have both their parents living together and be a family, I won't upset that. *You couldn't if you wanted to. You don't have his number, remember?*

"So, what meals have you been cooking?" Justin asks, snapping me from my musings.

"Erm…" I think back to what I've cooked this week. "Beans on toast."

Justin smirks. "What else?"

I tap my chin. "I did jacket potatoes."

He nods with a smile. "Anything else?"

"Pasta Bolognese."

His lips curl downwards as he nods, looking a little impressed.

"Okay, that one I bought pre-made. I just had to warm it up, but I made scrambled egg with smoked salmon one morning."

"Maybe our kids won't actually starve when they're here." He turns and winks, and I shake my head. I'll learn to cook a proper meal one day and tell him to shove it up his arse.

"We're back," Mum calls as she enters. Cassie and Cairen wander into the room.

"Don't come in here. Everything is wet, and you have your best clothes on." I usher them out into the kitchen, and Mum pops her head in to see our handiwork.

"Looks nice and fresh. Hello Justin."

"Hey, Sue."

"Come through, let me show you my new curtains?" I lead Mum into the dining room, where the curtains drape over a chair.

Mum rubs the fabric between her fingers, inspecting the quality. "A little modern for my taste, but they'll do, I suppose." She looks around my dining room with distaste.

"Shall I make you a pot of tea?"

"No, I'm not stopping. You should make Justin one, though. You're so lucky to have him helping you."

Ugh. Here we go again. I walk into the kitchen to boil the kettle, and Mum follows.

"I worry about you, Stephanie. You had that beautiful home, and now you've been reduced to this." She waves her hand around my tiny kitchen, screwing her face up like there's a foul smell in the air.

"This kitchen is brand new. What's wrong with it?"

"Well, there isn't enough room to swing a cat."

"I don't have a cat, Mother." The water in the kettle bubbles just like my blood.

"Why don't you stop being so stubborn and work things out with your husband?"

"We're never getting back together. Justin has accepted that. Why can't you?" I open the cupboard and reach for a box of tea, then throw two tea bags into the pot before slamming the cupboard door shut.

Mum folds her arms. "You'll never get another man like him."

I huff. "Good."

Steam billows from the spout as the kettle reaches boiling point. I clench my jaw and grip the handle as I pour it into the teapot, imagining I'm pouring it over her head and watching her melt like the Wicked Witch of the West.

"What makes you think I want another relationship? I'm perfectly happy on my own." I've accepted I'll be alone for the rest of my life. I can't think of anything worse than dating. It sounded horrendous when Kelly told me all her dating stories accompanied by dick pics.

Is that what the lads do nowadays? If a guy ever sent me a dick pic, I'd send one back of my vibrator. *You don't own one.* Well, I'd buy one just for a photo. I make a mental note that I'll have to invest at some point.

"I don't know any man that would decorate his ex's house. He clearly still loves you, even with the devil's spawn in your belly. I think you're being so unreasonable, Stephanie."

"Are you serious? You know he was screwing Maxine."

"Stephanie," she scolds, then looks around to check the children aren't in earshot.

"In fact. He's still screwing her. Seeing her tonight. That's how much he misses me." I have to laugh, or I'll scream.

"If you'd been a proper wife, he wouldn't have strayed." She juts her chin out and runs a hand over her perfectly styled burgundy hair.

My eyes bulge. Crescents imprint on the palm of my hands as my fingernails dig deep in my clenched fists. "I thought you were going."

"I am. It's obvious you're still not ready to come to your senses." She struts back into the living room to say bye to Justin. I'm sure she fancies him herself. If she wasn't with Dad… Ew… I shudder at the thought.

CHAPTER
fourteen

CAL

I arrive at the theatre early for Liv's show and after finding my seat, I call Mum. She's been struggling lately.

"Hello, love." She sounds cheerful this morning.

"How you doing, Mum? Feeling better?"

"A little. I have good days and bad days. I'm seeing the doctor next week. Hopefully, he can change my tablets. I've been ever so forgetful lately. Your sister, Cheryl thinks it's the pills they gave me for my heart."

"Yeah, I've heard those pills can have that effect. Are you still tired all the time?" I wish I was over there, but my sister has been visiting more.

"Don't worry about me, love. I'll be all right. How are the girls?"

"Everybody's all right, I'm just at the theatre, waiting for the show to start." More people enter the auditorium, filling it with a din of chatter and rustling.

"Oh, I won't keep you, then. You enjoy the show and give her my love."

"Will do. Love you, Mum."

"Oh, Callum, before I go, I almost forgot to tell you. I saw Stephanie the other day."

Her name wraps around my heart as if squeezing the life from me. "Is she all right?" My voice croaks. I hold my breath, feeling the pulse in my neck.

"Yes, love. Shall I pass on your new number if I see her again?"

I sigh heavily into the handset. "She's the reason I got rid of my old one." I run a hand through my hair. I can't go there again. Things were just getting easier. As much as I'd love to talk to her, what's the point? She's married, I'm here. We're worlds apart.

"Say no more." Mum chimes. "I'll talk to you tomorrow, love."

"Bye, Mum." I cancel the call and relax back in my seat.

The theatre fills, and a dark-haired woman catches my eye. She steps sideways down the row of seats, her low cut top reveals her bouncy tits. Her bright smile makes me sit up straight, or is it her chest?

"Hi." She pulls the seat down next to me and parks her perfectly round bottom covered in tight denim.

I clear my throat and shift in the seat to give her some arm room. "Hey."

"I think our daughters are in the same class. I've seen you around the dance school."

"Are they?" I've never seen this woman before. I'm sure I'd remember her. *You haven't exactly had your head in the game.*

Her long dark hair falls over the curve of her breast and a loose strand rests in the deep valley between her tits. I pull my eyes away. For fuck's sake, I shouldn't be looking down her top, but my eyes can't stop following the loose strand of hair that's lost down there.

Fuck, it's been too long since I buried my face between a pair of knockers. She does have nice tits, though. The lad twitches, and I have to adjust my jeans.

"I'm Danni." She holds a box of popcorn out to me. "Popcorn?"

"Cheers. I'm Cal." I take a handful; anything to distract me from her chest.

"Your girl's the British one, correct?"

"Girls? Oh yeah, Olivia. What are your girls called?" My eyes wander downwards again. They're just so big.

"My daughter's Harper."

I snap my head up and nod while chewing on the salty popcorn. *Just focus on her eyes. Focus on her eyes.*

"They're friends. I've been meaning to catch her mother to arrange a get-together."

"I can arrange a get-together." I smile. *What the fuck was that?*

She turns towards me, thrusting her knockers over the armrest. "We should totally do that. I'm free after the show if you want to grab some food with the girls?"

My eyes wander back to her girls, making my mouth water. "I could eat with the girls. Sure." My voice is a little high.

Fuck no. I force my eyes back to hers and notice they're sparkling green under the bright lights of the theatre, reminding me of my Steph. Maybe a date with this woman will help me move on. My dick's certainly up for it.

Shuffling in my seat, I adjust my jeans again and glance at my watch, hoping the lights will go dim soon so I won't keep getting distracted. *Or so you can look at her tits with no one noticing.*

More people enter and fill the row behind me. A couple take the seats next to Danni. "We're not late, are we?"

"Hi Dad. You're fine. They haven't started yet."

I glance at the man next to her. Then do a double take. The air is sucked from my lungs and a chill courses through my veins. "Dad?"

Danni turns to me. "Yeah, this is my Dad, Bill. Dad, this is Cal."

The colour drains from my dad's face. He's frozen apart from his rapid blinking. My pulse quickens, throbbing in my neck, and my entire body vibrates. I don't know whether to punch him in the face or shake his hand.

Danni looks between the two of us, staring each other out over the top of her heaving chest. "Do you two know each other?"

I can't speak. I thought about this moment for so long and all the things I want to say to this man, but I can't seem to form any words.

He breaks the deafening silence with a croak in his voice. "Son."

The word travels through the thick air prickling my skin. Every muscle in my body burns. How dare he call me son? He lost that right when he left me. I crack my neck along with my knuckles.

"Son, what are you doing here?" His deep brown eyes droop, and he runs a hand through his grey hair that was once jet black.

"I—"

"Wait." Danni leans forward, looking between the two of us. "This is your Dad?" She turns to Dad. "Dad, this is Callum, your son Callum?"

He nods.

She looks back at me. "Does this mean you're my…" Her face screws, and she shivers. "Ew."

Acid rises in my throat, and I swallow hard before puking all over my sister's tits. "Please tell me we're not blood related."

I wipe the sweat from my forehead. To think I was getting hard at the prospect of a tit-job. The popcorn regurgitates in my mouth, and I force it back down.

"Danni is my stepdaughter. Callum, it's so good to see you. This is my wife, Helen."

I relax my shoulders.

Helen reaches across Bill and Danni and takes hold of my hand. "It's so nice to finally meet you. Bill's told us all about you."

I remove my hand from under hers and pinch my eyebrows together. "He doesn't even know me."

Dad's sad eyes shine under the theatre lights. "I'm sorry, son. I'd like to change that. If you'll let me."

The lights dim and the opening music plays out through the auditorium. "Maybe you can start by watching your granddaughter." I whisper-yell the words and accidentally throw spittle over Danni's chest. "Sorry."

She wipes her face and breasts, then pulls the show programme from her bag.

"You have a daughter?" Dad chokes up, dabbing his eyes.

"I have two, but you'd know that if you bothered to keep in touch." I lean back in my chair and fold my arms.

Danni opens the show programme to the cast list and shows her parents Livvie's picture.

"Hey, be quiet," a woman says behind us. I glare at her, then face back to the stage, waiting for my girl.

My foot taps uncontrollably, and I catch Dad looking at me out of the corner of my eye. I sink further into my seat, hiding behind Danni's chest. This has to be the most awkward two hours of my life.

Finally, my girl graces the stage. Danni whispers to Bill, pointing out Livvie in her blue floaty dress and leggings, the same as the other backing dancers performing the chorus for Swan Lake. She didn't get a main part due to joining the dance school halfway through the season. But she still steals the show in my eyes and her footwork is on point, as Priya would say.

Sitting only three rows back, she spots me and beams. Her eyes fix on me each time she pirouettes, and I wave and beam back at her, expanding my lungs till they're bursting with pride.

Now the show has finished, the lights flick on. Everyone stands and makes their way to the exit. Dad blocks the row and turns to me. "Callum, would you like to come back with us?"

"I have to collect Liv from the stage doors and take her home. Her mum's expecting her back."

"Another time then?" He dips his head.

Helen interrupts. "How about Sunday? Bring the girls too and your wife. We'll have a barbecue. Danni will be there, won't you, with Harper? So the girls have a familiar face."

Danni nods. "Sure."

I rub my eyebrow, pinching it where the piercing used to be. "I'll think about it."

Helen rummages in her bag, pulling out a pen, and writes her address on the back of the ticket. "This is us. You're welcome anytime, day or night."

I take the ticket and shove it in my back pocket. "I'll see, yeah."

Dad sulks away, rubbing his brow, looking frail compared to the last time I saw him.

Danni and I walk out the side door to wait for the girls to change backstage. She clutches her bag and chews on her lip.

I stuff my hands in my pocket and rock back on my heels. "I guess that get-togethers out of the window now, huh?"

She covers her face with her hands. Her shoulders rock, and I can't tell if it's a sob or a laugh. I was only trying to lighten the mood.

"Is that a laugh?"

She snorts. "Yes." A giggle escaping her. "Can you

imagine if we had actually got together? Like together, together."

I huff. "Yeah, how weird would that have been?"

She snorts again, making me chuckle. "Imagine if I'd taken you home to meet the family. It would have been so awkward."

I laugh along with her. "Yeah, probably just as awkward as tonight."

She stops laughing and smiles. "Dad's always talked about you. I think he's always wanted to get in touch, but guilt and shame were always in his way."

I rock back on my heels and nod. Not really sure what to say. He has a lot to feel guilty for and a lot to be ashamed about. He seems to be doing all right now, though.

"Please come on Sunday. I think it would mean the world to him. Even if you never see him again, just come on Sunday."

I rub my eyebrow, thinking about what to do. I have so much anger bubbling under the surface.

Livvie comes through the doors, and I wave. She makes her way through the sea of girls, and I lift her into my arms and kiss her cheek. "Lollipop, you were amazing."

She wipes her cheek and kicks her legs. "Da—ad," she whines.

I let her feet hit the ground, but she'll never be too big for a hug from me. I glance at Danni. "I'll see you Sunday."

Her bright smile widens, and I salute her as I leave, wrapping my arm around Liv's shoulders.

STEPH

STILL NO CONTACT with Cal after several weeks. It's time to try a different tactic. Searching my friends list on social media, I stop at Dean's name. If I can even call him a friend after the photograph fiasco.

Thinking of him watching us still makes my skin crawl as icy fingers with sharp cold nails scrape over my skin. The logo 'Dean's Auto's' sits as a header on his profile. I copy the address and make my way over on my lunch break.

Parking the car in his yard in front of an MOT testing sign, I get out with unsteady legs. The September sun shines on my face and I squint my eyes as a shadow appears.

"Steph." Dean's face comes into view as the sun fades behind a cloud.

I jump at the sound of a clatter coming from the garage. Gosh, I'm a bag of nerves. My hand tightens around the strap of my bag. "I need to get hold of Cal."

"He moved to Oz." He rubs his hands on his overalls.

"I know that, or I wouldn't be here, would I?" Another clatter makes me jump.

"It's okay, it's just the guys working. Come into the office." He leads me to a small room on the side of the garage with a desk and computer. "I'll get his mobile number for you."

Hope blossoms in my chest and I relax a little.

He pulls his mobile from his pocket. "I'm sorry about all that business with Liz and the photo's."

I stick out my chin and tap my foot. The sooner I can leave, the better.

"Do you want to add it to your phone?"

"Yes, but can you call him? He might answer if he knows it's you. I think it's the least you can do for me, don't you?"

He nods and presses the green button at the side of his name. Dean holds the handset to his ear, then flinches his head back to look at the screen. "That's odd." He taps it again.

"What is it?"

"There's no dial tone."

I check the numbers. It's his old number. "Have you not spoken to him since he moved to Australia?"

"No, why would I? He's not exactly gonna call to say he's coming round for a beer, is he? When he moved there before, I didn't hear from him again until he moved back. You know what he's like."

"Do you know how I can contact him? An address, anything?"

"I ain't a clue. His mum will know. She'll be in touch with him and the girls."

Inhaling a breath, I walk to the car with tears prickling my eyes. I hope his mother will help me this time.

Back at work, I hand write a letter. If his mum is unwilling to give me his new number still, she can pass on a letter at least.

The rose bushes on her front lawn have filled out since I was here last, like my middle area, although I still don't look pregnant—just fatter.

I knock on the door and wait with bated breath. She answers with a frown. "Stephanie. I told you he's in Australia."

"I know. Did you ask him to call me?" I twist the strap on my bag as I shuffle on my feet.

"I can't make him call you if he doesn't want to. He's doing what's best for him and his family. I think you should do the same." She goes to close the door but I place my hand on the glass.

"Please. It's important. Can you pass on this letter? He's going to want to read it."

She takes the letter from me and looks at the white envelope with Cal written on the front. "What is it, dear?"

"It's private, but if you can post the letter or give me an address or some form of contacting him." I'm not about to have her give me a lecture by telling her the truth. My own mother has lectured me enough these last few weeks. I don't need her making me feel worse than I already do.

"All right. I'll see that he gets it, but I can't promise he'll be in touch. You know he's stubborn." She closes the door and I stare at my reflection in the frosted glass. A distorted, fuzzy image of myself resembling just how I feel on the inside.

I don't know what else to do. If I flew over to Sydney, where do I look? The idea of flying to the other side of the world while pregnant is ridiculous. If he doesn't want to see me again or be part of his child's life, his mum's right—I can't force him.

———————————

IN THE CHANGING ROOM, I take my red swimsuit from my bag. It's cute and one I bought for my holiday in Greece this Easter, although getting it on is a feat in itself. It's so tight. *Well yeah. You're six months pregnant. And you've been eating for two ever since you found out.* I thought lycra stretched, though.

After wrestling with the lycra for what seems like five minutes, I'm in. I have to adjust my breasts into the cup area, and I wonder if I made a mistake with this costume. It's rather low at the front. Great for lying on a beach working on your tan, but maybe not so good for doing aqua-aerobics. Oh well, I'm in a pool. Who's gonna see me? I should be okay.

I walk out in my red suit that has a small skirt attached to the waist to hide my arse and thick thighs. Although it doesn't even cover my arse fully, making the skirt totally pointless.

Holding onto the metal railing, I step into the rectangular pool, dipping my toe in the water first, and quickly retract. Oooh, it's cold. Remind me why I'm here again. *Just get in and do your warm-up*. Okay, bitch. Let's do this.

I'm a strong, independent woman. I'm a strong, independent woman. For frig's sake, I can handle the cold water. I climb down the ladder and lie back in the water, causing a mini tidal wave to ripple along the lanes.

Claire waves from the deep end as she does her breaststroke like a channel swimmer.

I do the backstroke while I wait for the aerobics instructor to start the session, but I'm basically just floating along the lane. Apparently, the more fat you have, the better you float— who knew? I don't think I could sink if I tried.

Claire's head bobs next to mine. "You made it."

"Just. After almost losing the battle with the swimsuit, you're lucky I'm not sitting in the leisure cafe right now."

She giggles. "How's the kids doing?"

"They're okay. They still hate me." I blow out my mouth, lifting my fringe up as I tread water, well float and waft my arms to keep my balance.

"They'll get used to it, especially when they realise they get double the number of Christmas gifts."

"I hadn't thought of that. Have I still got to buy Justin a gift? What's the protocol for ex-husbands? I mean, we're not even divorced yet."

"Just get him something from the kids, hun."

My baby bump sticks out of the water as I float on my back. "That could actually be his gift."

"What?"

"Divorce papers. He said he was going to sort it out. I'm not sure what's taking so long, although there's no rush is there. It's not like I have anyone else wanting to pick up the baton."

"Do you want another man? I thought you were happy re-inventing yourself as a new independent woman. I mean, look at you, here doing an aqua-aerobics class, of all things."

"I cooked a lasagna last night too. From scratch and the kids ate the lot. I even plated a portion up for Justin. You know, to rub it in his face. Not literally—although that's a good idea."

"Steady on, Nigella. Is Justin still all right with you?"

"Oh, he's living his best life. He's shagging Maxine on the side and out most weekends with the lads from the builder's yard. He thinks he's twenty again."

The music starts. A remix of 'Pump up the Jam' and the pint-sized slender instructor stands at the side of the pool in her lycra leggings and leotard, dancing like she's at a 90s disco on crack.

"Morning everyone." She jumps into a lunge. "Let's workout. We're going to start with a warm-up. Stand and stretch your arm."

Stand? I'm at the deep end. The bottom is out of my reach. I bob up and down a little and sway side to side, trying to follow her moves. The pointless frilled skirt rides up and fans out around me. I tug it back down while bobbing in the deep.

With each movement I swim to the right, moving further up the pool until my feet come into contact with solid ground. My breasts are half in and half out of the surface with a mind of their own.

"Okay, now move those legs. We're going to run on the spot." She bounces up and down in what she calls a run totally effortless. Every part of her body stays in place where it should be.

My feet move in the water, and it's like trying to jog on a trampoline. Everything is jiggling all over the place, and my breasts threaten to say hello at any moment. *Extroverts*. I tuck them in further, but they ride up again, bouncing on the surface like a pair of floats.

"Okay, make a circle, guys. You know what to do."

Everyone forms a circle, and I smile at an elderly lady who, to be fair, is twice my age, but probably in better shape.

"Now run in the circle."

Claire and the other women have clearly done this before —regulars. I follow their lead, although it's more like a jog in slow motion. We all get a momentum going and the current works in our favour, pushing us along. My heart races, and I can feel the burn in my thighs.

'Join aqua-aerobics,' the midwife said. 'It'll be good for you and the baby,' she said.

"And change." The instructor changes directions and runs on the spot.

"What?" Everyone turns around and starts running in the opposite direction. I'm forced to comply with the group, but it's like wading through treacle. The current works against us, making it hard to put one foot in front of the other. I wipe my brow, wetting my hair in the process, dammit.

The next song plays. 'Gonna Make You Sweat (Everybody Dance Now)'. *No kidding*.

The more we walk, the easier it gets. Several revolutions later, we're able to break into a jog again.

"Change."

Not again. I really am out of breath now. We just get a momentum going, then she wants us to change direction. I knew the midwife hated me. The way she took my blood, bruising my arm, was sinister enough. Then she recommended a pissin' aqua-aerobics class.

The instructor smiles like she's secretly laughing at us, all following her twisted commands. The sicko. Probably best mates with the sinister midwife.

My chest heaves. Gosh, I'm dying. I need water. *You're in a swimming pool.* I can't exactly drink this, can I? *Well, you drink everything else.* Oh, shut up. I'm not in the mood for you. *Haven't your endorphins kicked in yet?* Funny.

"Okay, guys. The warm-up's over."

Warm-up? I gasp. That was just the warm-up? Oh no. My stomach tightens at what else she has in store, and my heart thumps against my ribs as if to say, 'let me out'.

"Grab a couple of floats from the side of the pool."

I glance down at my out-of-control breasts. I don't think I need any more floats.

Claire bobs along to the side to get the foam woggles. "So, have you got in touch with him?"

"No. I even tried his friend Dean, who said he just gets a blank dial tone, but I left a letter with his mother. At least he'll know what's going on, even if he stays in Australia." I hold the float out in front of me, although I don't need it. I'm already floating. "Though I thought he might have contacted me by now. After all the conversations we had and how he was with his girls, I never thought he would just stay away. I mean, I never expected him to drop everything and come running, but I expected him to acknowledge he was having another child."

"Didn't he do this before? Do you think he's regressed to when he was a teenager?"

I stop moving, thinking back. He never wanted a child with me then. Maybe it's the same now. My limbs ache and not from the warmup. Every part of my body hurts, like being rejected all over again. Only this time he hasn't just rejected me, but our child as well.

CHAPTER *Fifteen*

CAL

"Beth, can you believe Harper is our cousin?" Livvie says in the back seat of the car.

"I don't know who she is." Bethy yawns.

"She's in my dance group."

"You'll meet her soon enough." I glance at Priya in the passenger seat as she rubs my arm. I told her she didn't have to come, but she's tagged along for moral support. For the girls mainly, it's daunting meeting family you don't know for the first time.

They were shy with Priya's parents, and they've met them several times and spoke on video calls. It's different with my mum, though. She's like a second home for the girls. Mum would always have them when we needed childcare.

"Take the next left and you will reach your destination." I follow the sat nav's instructions and arrive at a modest single-storey house surrounded by a large garden.

The warm air makes my skin sticky, and I tug at the shirt I'm wearing to fan me down. I'm still not used to this heat in the middle of November.

Priya takes hold of my vibrating hand. "You can do this," she whispers.

I swallow and inhale a deep breath before stepping out of the car.

The girls follow, and Bethy clutches my arm. Bending down, I scoop her up. Somehow, holding her in my arms gives me the extra confidence I need to keep moving forward. The twenty-minute journey here had me wanting to turn around every other mile.

Children run around the side of the house onto the front lawn. "Olivia's here." The girl runs around the side of the house before Helen appears waving us around the back.

I cling on to Bethy, her legs dangle around my waist as she rests on my side. Her spindly arms cling to my neck, and I kiss her cheek to reassure her that everything is all right, despite my trepidation.

I spot Danni's dark hair flowing over a yellow sundress as I round the house to an even larger garden, all perfectly landscaped and pruned. I never pictured Daddy dearest as an avid gardener. He never did shit when he lived with me and Mum, other than drink.

Helen calls out, "Callum, I'm so glad you made it." She wipes her hands on her apron and hugs Priya. "You must be Callum's wife. Welcome to our home."

Priya opens her mouth to correct her, but Danni follows and gives her a kiss on the cheek. "Hello, I'm Danni. We've actually met at dancing."

"Ah yes. I thought I recognised you."

"This must be your other daughter." Danni looks at Bethy.

"Yeah, this is Bethy-boo." She buries her head in my neck. "Do you want to play?"

"My son is running around somewhere. He's about your age."

Bill leaves the barbecue and gingerly steps closer. "I'm glad you made it, son."

"Sure. This is Priya. We're not married. Not even

together, but she's the closest family I have here. I hope you don't mind me bringing her."

"Of course not." Helen places an arm around Priya. "What would you like to drink? Would the girls like some lemonade?"

I whisper to Beth, "Do you wanna go with Mummy and get a drink?" I wipe the hair from her face, and she nods, biting her fingernail as I put her down.

"Can I get you a drink, Callum? I don't have any beer, I'm afraid. We're teetotal in this house, but I can offer you a ginger ale?"

"Fine. I'm driving anyway." I rock back on my heels and press my lips together while Dad pulls a bottle of ginger ale from the cooler. The women are all chatting amongst themselves.

Daddy dearest opens the bottle and hands it to me. "Cheers."

I take a swig, holding the drink in my mouth before I swallow hard with a gulp.

Dad looks around and points to the women. "I see they've all hit it off."

I nod and smirk. "Yeah."

"Helen can talk the hind legs off a kangaroo." He waves his bottle between us. "What are you doing here in Sydney?"

I shuffle on my feet and point to the women. "Priya moved back here to be with her family, and I followed so I could be near my girls. I'll introduce you to them soon."

"It's fine, son. Let them play. It's nice to see them enjoying themselves. Kids their age can make bonds for life."

"Yeah." My mind wanders back to Steph and I at their age. She was the only person I told about my dad's drinking. The last time I saw him, he was wasted. Mum started mouthing off and he shut her up with his fist. I jumped in the middle like He-Man, trying to defend Mum, but ended up face down on the glass coffee table.

The memory clouds my head like a thick black fog of fury taking over, making me want to plant my fist on his face just like I watched him do to Mum all those years ago. My fingers tense, stretching and clenching as if warming up for the act. My insides vibrate as I hold everything in.

Danni opens the cooler and pulls out another ginger ale, distracting me from my dark thoughts. "The children are getting along."

Her wide smile at Daddy dearest tells me she hasn't seen him at his worst. Although he was always kind when he was sober. Like Jekyll and Hyde. Pity he wasn't sober very often.

"It's nice for Harper and Jack to have cousins," Dad says, smiling as he watches them tag each other, running around the extensive garden like a pack of feral dogs.

"Doesn't your son have any kids?" I ask.

He pinches his eyebrows. "You're the only son I have."

It must have been someone else's kid. "I saw you about twenty years ago taking a kid to football."

"You were here? Why didn't you talk to me?"

I shrug and kick a stone edging next to the lawn. "You looked like you were playing happy families with your new son. I didn't think you'd want me around anymore."

"Cal, I always wanted you. I wanted to contact you so many times but…"

"I think that was me," Danni interrupts. "I used to play soccer, and Dad would always take me to my games."

I huff. "You're lucky, Daddy dearest never came to watch any of my games."

He hangs his head low. "I thought you hated football."

"Maybe if you'd taken me to a game, I might've felt differently." The stone edging I've been kicking loosens and rolls over, knocking into a plant pot that cracks open.

"Shit." I bend down and secure it back in place.

"Callum, don't worry about it."

Soil spills from the broken pot and the bedding plant hangs limp.

"Son. Leave it, please. It can be fixed."

Can it? Is he talking about the rockery or our relationship? "The pot's broken. You can't fix that."

"Leave it. I'll buy another." He growls.

"Is that what you did here? Bought yourself another family when you broke the first one, leaving us in tatters." I glance around the garden and home. He's done all right for himself. I scoop up the broken pieces of the pot.

"I don't care about the pot. Dammit."

I stand and meet his eyes head on with clenched fists. The broken pieces dig into the palm of my hand as old memories flash through my head.

"I care about you. I've always cared about you. When I got my life sorted out, your mother returned the money I sent. She wouldn't take anything from me."

"Can you blame her?"

"No. I felt ashamed at how I treated her and the longer time passed, the harder it became to make contact. I understand if it's too late for us, but maybe it's not too late for my grandchildren."

I have another swig from the bottle. With every breath, I want to get my girls and get the hell out of dodge, but looking into his sad eyes has my feet pinned to the ground.

Priya, Helen, and the girls join us. "Bill, this is Olivia and Bethany."

He bends down to their level. "You did great in the show, Olivia. How long have you been dancing?"

"Since I was three."

"Do you dance too, Bethany?"

"No, I like to kickbox with Daddy."

I smile. "She's a tiny thing, but she has a great kick."

"The food's almost ready. Help yourself to burgers, steak, salad, and potatoes," Helen says.

Bill asks the girls if they want a burger or sausage and takes them to the buffet table.

"Everything all right?" Priya rests her hand on my bicep, over my shirt.

"Yeah." I nod and give her a smile, grateful that she's here, although the one person I want to talk to about this is on the other side of the world. Steph was always there to listen. Not that I talked about Dad much, but I didn't need to. Growing up, she always seemed to know how I was feeling.

She'd be glad I was giving him a chance, I guess. She told me to look for him at uni. I never told her I took her advice all those years ago. Maybe I can tell her one day.

STEPH

"Eeeeek." Amy squeals, dancing on her toes as she steps towards me. Her heels click on the tarmac of the platform at Kings Cross Station. "I can't believe you're actually here. I've missed you so much." Her arms wrap around my shoulders, and she lunges in for a kiss on the cheek.

She goes in for another kiss after I pull away. "Oh, are we doing the double?"

"That's how they do it in Paris, sweetie."

"How is Paris?"

"Same. I'm determined to get you to visit me there again. We can do all the art galleries."

"Kinda difficult right now." I point to my ever-growing belly that looks like I have stuffed a lumpy cushion under my top. I'm at that weird stage where any slim person would have a perfectly round football shaped bump, but when you're a fat lass, it just looks like you're carrying extra holiday weight, and you've just eaten a large Sunday roast. "You're lucky I'm here in London."

"Speaking of art…I booked us into a painting class."

"What? I can't paint."

She waves a hand in the air. "Oh, hush. It'll be fun—there's wine."

I point to my large belly. "Er, I can't drink either."

"Spoil sport. It'll be like old times at uni. Remember those life drawing classes we took?" She giggles and takes the handle of my suitcase, wheeling it along the pavement as she links her arm through mine.

"How could I forget? Somehow, I was always positioned smack bang in the middle with the dangly thing in full view. I wouldn't have even minded if it was pleasant to look at. But it resembled a shrivelled prune."

Amy bursts into a fit of giggles. "You can't blame the poor bloke. It was chilly in that studio and he only had that tiny blow heater."

"I hope this one you've booked us on isn't nude male models. I've seen enough dick to last me a lifetime."

She glances at my enormous belly. "You've done more than see by the looks of things."

I swat her arm, and we both step outside the station. The autumn breeze blows her floral coat open, always dressed in the latest Parisian chic. We haven't seen each other in years, but it's always the same. We slip back into our younger silly selves.

She wheels my suitcase towards a black taxicab and the driver gets out to help load my case into the boot.

"The Grosvenor Hotel, please," Amy says as we climb into the back. "We can drop your case off before the class starts at eleven. They're providing a light lunch so we can eat there."

I tut and slump back in my seat. "And here's me, hoping for a relaxing weekend."

"No such thing with me, darling. Anyway, stop your whining. There's wine involved."

"Ahem." I point to my belly again.

She rolls her eyes. "You can have a few, can't you?"

"Yes, and hinder my baby's development."

"Why do you keep popping those wretched things out, anyhow?"

"This one wasn't planned, believe me."

"Oh?" She pulls out her mobile and starts texting.

I adjust my thin scarf with the Birth of Venus print, running the sheer fabric through my fingers. Wearing it always makes me feel a little closer to Callum, reminding me of the last time I was in London with him. Even if he is being a dickhead and ignoring me, I find it hard to be mad at him, especially with a part of him growing inside me.

With a tight grip on the scarf, I blurt out, "I left Justin."

Her head snaps up. "When?"

"A few months ago. It's a long story."

She puts the phone away, crosses her legs and rests her chin on her fist. "I'm all ears."

I tell her about the breakup but leave out certain parts. She doesn't need to know I'm a cheat, too.

WE DROP my case off at the room and freshen up. Another taxi ride and we arrive at an old building; part of the City & Guilds London Art School.

The brown leaves rustle in the wind, and I cling to my dress before it takes flight. "Have you been here before?"

"No. A friend told me about it. I thought it sounded fun."

I waddle through the door, following the temporary signs for the 'Life of Wine' workshop. My only request is they have a comfy seat, because there's no way I can stand all afternoon.

Amy opens a door to a studio full of easels and stools, and I thank the heavens for seats. Amy gives me an excitable glance as she walks in. The smell of paint is everywhere, and I inhale a deep breath, getting high on the scent.

"Good morning, ladies," a man says over the soft music playing in the background. He steps out from behind an easel where he was talking with another male.

"Morning, I'm Amy Bennet, and this is my friend Steph. We're booked in for the workshop."

"Amy. I thought I recognised the name." He grips her shoulders and goes in for an air kiss on the cheek...and another one doing the double.

Amy mouths to me, 'Who is this guy?'

Then it dawns on me. My body tenses and my eyes grow wide. I wipe my sweaty forehead, knowing I'm next for the double air kiss. Gosh, will he remember me? *Of course he will. He remembers Amy, and he never shagged her.* Oh no.

I glare at Amy, silently mouthing 'it's Mark', then fake smile as Mark releases her and steps towards me with open arms.

"Stephanie. It's so good to see you." He places his hands on my shoulders and goes in for an air kiss. I turn my face, not sure which side he's going, and end up with a peck on the lips. He pulls back and looks down at my stomach. "Congratulations. When's this bundle due?"

"20th January." I huff, still not over the coincidental date.

"What have you been up to since uni?"

"Not a lot, really. Not as much as this one who lives in Paris."

Amy strikes a pose as if someone's snapping a photo of her besides the Eiffel Tower.

"That's great. I lived there myself for a while until I married. What do you do, Amy?"

"I'm head of marketing for a cosmetic company."

"Nice. Your skin is so youthful. Do you use their products?"

"She doesn't have kids, Mark."

He chuckles. "Neither do I, but maybe I drink too much. Speaking of drink, we have non-alcoholic drinks as well. Please help yourself throughout the session. We'll be stopping for lunch around 1.30pm."

Mark takes hold of my hand. "It's really great to see you, Steph. I always wanted to apologise for my behaviour."

"It's fine. It was a long time ago."

"It's not fine. Cal was right to be pissed. Though I showed no one your drawing, it was stolen, but I should have stood up for you like Cal did. I just wanted to fit in."

"So did I."

"You? You always seemed to have your stuff together. I admired you for being so confident."

"I never felt confident, believe me. All I wanted was a boyfriend and to be loved and accepted."

"Me too, Steph. Me too."

A group arrives through the door. "I'll catch up later. Choose an easel, help yourself to drinks and nibbles."

"Thank you."

He greets the group, and I walk towards the easels with Amy, who whispers, "Shit pommel frites."

"Did you know?" I whisper.

"No. I can barely remember people I met last year, let alone some guy from twenty years ago."

I glance around at the art on the wall signed Mark Barnes. "This is his work, look." I stare at the London cityscape, then my eyes move to a painting of a naked man with a strong back and perfect arse, reminding me of Cal. My heart aches like it does each time I think of him. Will it always be this way? You'd think I'd be used to this pain by now.

"I wonder if that's who we're painting. It would certainly make the afternoon interesting, hmm?" Amy hands me a glass. "Do you want juice, water, or pop?"

"A glass of juice, please."

She fills a wine glass with cranberry juice. "Here, at least you can pretend you're drinking."

"Thanks." I pick up a chocolate from the table and bite into the truffle centre, hoping I have my antacids in my bag.

The room fills. I stand by my station with an easel in front of me, an adjustable stool, and a table I share with Amy for the paints and drinks. "It's quite a nice setup, actually."

Mark talks to the group and explains the day's events before introducing us to the life model. "This is Michael. He will be our model for today."

"Bloody-hell, he's an adonis." Amy's jaw drops. She glances behind her at the naked man's arse painting behind her. "It is him, isn't it? My prayers have been answered."

I giggle. "No wonder your friend told you to come here."

"Do you think he's single?"

I roll my eyes. "You wouldn't?"

"I bloody would. I didn't book us separate rooms for nothing. Do you know how long it's been since I had sex?" She says the word sex like a whisper and a mumble.

I wave my glass around while I chew down another chocolate. I'll definitely need the antacids at this rate. "Er, I don't know," I mumble. "Knowing you, a week?"

"If you're classing sex with my vibrator, then yes," she whispers. "Have you ever seen a sexier man?"

"Blondes aren't my type, and yes. I've seen sexier." I take

another chocolate. We're nearly out, and I wish I'd brought the full box to our table.

"Who?" She holds her hand up. "If you're going to say that prick Callum from uni, please spare me."

The model drops the robe and turns to face me. My jaw drops along with the half eaten chocolate in my hand. I glance at Amy, who's licking her lips, about to drop her knickers.

"I...I..." I can't get my words out.

"I know," Amy says.

"No... I actually know him."

"You're kidding? You haven't shagged him as well, have you?"

"He's gay." I glance back at Michael. I never knew his body was so defined when he was sitting in his suit at the work dinner. It really is a small world. "Oh my gosh, I just saw it."

Amy laughs. "That's so typical. All the guys I meet are gay or married or both." She picks up her wine and takes a big drink.

Michael sits on a chaise lounge draped in a red velvet blanket and lifts one leg, letting everything hang. I cover my eyes. "Why do I always get positioned full frontal? I thought taking these side easels would give us a side view."

"I didn't know the guy would sit sideways. At least this one doesn't look like a shrivelled prune." She snorts and gulps another mouthful of wine.

Michael catches my eyes. I hush Amy and elbow her across the table. He tilts his head and stares at me across the room.

I smile and wave. "Oh gosh. I think he recognises me." I whisper without moving my lips, still smiling and waving, trying not to let my eyes wander downwards. Stay focused. Keep looking at his face.

His eyebrows pull together as he concentrates on my face,

then he widens his eyes and shifts a little on the chaise, moving his hand to rest over his, er.

"Now look what you've done. You've made him go all shy. No fun." Amy pouts.

"He's gay." I'm still waving and smiling like a puppet.

"So what? A girl can appreciate the male anatomy, can't she?"

"All right, folks. We're going to use your pencils to sketch an outline before we apply paint to paper." Mark continues to speak, and Michael keeps looking at me as I sketch his body.

"Are you sure he's gay? He keeps looking at you. Maybe he's bi. I've always wanted a menagé."

"Well, the last time I spoke to him he was happily married to an art…" I drop my pencil.

"An art what?"

I lean over the small table between us and whisper, "Do you think Mark's his husband?"

She studies Mark. "It's hard to tell. I don't exactly have a gaydar. You should know, you're the one that slept with him."

I collect my pencil from the floor, glancing around to check no one can hear our whispers.

"Didn't you say it was a bad experience? Maybe you're the reason he's gay." She giggles.

"It was only a bad experience because he was a little overenthusiastic. He certainly wasn't gay when I slept with him. Was he? I mean, he seemed to enjoy himself."

"Sweetie, if he's gay, he was most likely born that way. I'm only teasing. Maybe he's bi. I don't understand why there has to be a label, anyway. People should be with whoever they fall in love with regardless of gender."

"Are you secretly hoping the Adonis will fall in love with you tonight?"

"Yes, but that's not going to happen when he hasn't taken his eyes off you."

He catches my eye again and smiles. I look away before I catch him smiling elsewhere. I daren't look.

Mark wanders around the room giving advice. "Hey Steph, that's looking good. Although you haven't quite got the proportions right."

"It's abstract."

"Then that's brilliant. We all have our own way of interpretation." He winks at me as he walks away, and I'm suddenly a teenager again. The way he made me feel was always so sweet, though I never got that stirring in my stomach from him. Apart from the time he bought me a hot dog at the cinema—the mustard sauce didn't agree with me—but he always made me feel comfortable, at least. If it wasn't for the way things went down, I think we could have been good friends.

"Looking good, Amy."

"Thanks." She flicks her blonde hair behind her shoulder.

"Are you still with that guy you were dating in uni?"

"Scott? He lives in the States, but we hook up when we're in the same place. Sometimes he visits Paris, or I go to New York and vice versa."

My eyes widen. "You didn't tell me you still hook up with Scott."

She shrugs her shoulders and continues to sketch. "It's no big deal. We both agreed that if we're still single at 45, we'll get married."

"You will actually get married?"

"Yes, but I told him I draw the line at kids."

My stomach grumbles. "I'm starving. Is it dinner time yet?"

"You never change. Have another chocolate."

The smell of cooked food travels through the window on

the autumn breeze, and I hope it's my dinner. I take a sip of the cranberry to satisfy me until then.

"Do you want another drink?"

"Yes, please… I just lurve cranberry," I say in my most sarcastic tone.

Amy snatches the glass and returns, looking smug with a glass of cranberry for me and a full-bodied red for her. I inhale the sweet aroma, and I'm practically drooling. Trust me to come to a pissin' art and wine workshop, and I can't even friggin' drink.

"You will get yourself up the duff. Haven't you ever heard of putting a sock on it?"

"I've heard of putting a sock *in* it. Do I sense a hint of jealousy because I've actually had sex in the last six months?"

"Do you think this is in proportion?" Amy shows me her picture of Michael with an oversized shlong.

"Is that wishful thinking on your part? Or are you seeing something from your angle that I'm not?"

She giggles and takes a drink. "It's the wine. Everything looks better with alcohol."

I shuffle on the stool. "My back is killing me. Do you think Mark will get me a cushion or something?"

"I'll go to the shop and buy you one if it will stop you whining. That's all you've done since we arrived."

"Well, it is an art and whine workshop."

We both giggle. Finally, the door swings open. Servers' wheel in two carts of pastries, sandwiches and cakes. The sweet pastries and sandwich fillings make my mouth water.

"Shall we break for lunch? Please help yourself to the buffet," Mark says.

I jump from the stool and dart to the cart, ready to tackle anyone who dares to get in front of a hungry pregnant woman.

After loading my plate, I turn around to see Michael, the Adonis, smiling behind me. At least he's robed now.

"Stephanie, isn't it?"

"Yes, how are you?"

Mark comes over. "Do you two know each other?"

"Yeah, we met at a work dinner, about this time last year, wasn't it?"

"It was in December."

"Mark, this is Stephanie. Stephanie, this is my husband, Mark."

Amy smiles. "Oh, Stephanie already knows Mark."

Michael's perfectly pruned eyebrows pull together. "How?"

Amy has a sinful smile playing on her lips. "Let's just say you're not the only one here she's seen naked."

Mark's cheeks flush, and he clears his throat.

"Amy," I scold, and glare at her. "You're terrible."

Michael looks at Mark and tilts his head. "Is this Steph who you told me about?"

Mark smiles and nods.

"The one you lost your virginity to?" he whispers.

Amy's eyes widen, and I cough up the mini sausage roll I almost choked on. My eyes water. I've never needed a wine more than I do right now. Amy hands me a glass of fresh juice, and I swallow to soothe my tonsils.

"Mark, is that true?" I say with a scratchy throat.

Michael runs a hand over his face. "Sorry, I thought you knew."

Looking between the two of them, my forehead wrinkles. "I never knew I was your first. I wish you'd told me."

Mark's cheeks are brighter than a tube of cadmium red. "It wasn't really something I wanted to advertise, Steph."

"But I would have given you a few pointers."

Michael laughs. "They would've been wasted on him. You're the only girl he ever slept with."

"Was I that bad?"

"Steph, no. I'm gay. I was just trying to fit in and be someone I'm not. I'm sorry."

"I wish you'd have told me. I would have supported you."

"It was a different time back then. I didn't feel comfortable coming out, but I always found you attractive. You know that, don't you? I never used you. I wanted so much to be one of the lads."

With tears pooling in my eyes, I wrap my arms around Mark. We all had struggles in our teens. I know what it's like to not fit in.

"What a small world, ay?" Michael says.

Amy passes me a napkin and points to my eyes. I dab under the lashes so I don't ruin my makeup.

"Hey Steph. Where's that handsome fella of yours? Cal was it?" Michael says, while filling his plate with mini sandwiches.

Mark smiles. "So you got back together? I never understood why he split up with you. It was obvious he was besotted with you."

"Wait. You knew Cal?" Michael asks Mark.

"Wait a minute." Amy buts in. "How do you know Cal?" she asks Michael.

"He was with Steph at a business dinner last year."

Amy glares at me.

Mark tells Michael about our history.

"I bet he's happy about being a daddy." Michael points to my belly.

I wince inwardly, but give him my best fake smile as a lump forms in the back of my throat.

Michael takes hold of Mark's hand and gazes into his eyes. "We've been wanting to adopt for some time."

Amy drags me back to our table. "You kept that quiet."

"Well, you never told me you hook up with Scott whenever you're in the same country."

"I assumed the baby was your husbands. Is this Cal's baby? Were you guys banging? Is he the real reason you and Justin split up?"

I stroke my stomach. Tears pour down my flustered cheeks. "You guessed correctly. Only he's in Australia. He doesn't want to know."

Amy hugs me, running her hand up and down my spine. "Are you still crying over him, after all this time?"

I sniffle. "Yes. That and the heartburn. I need my antacids."

She unzips my bag and rummages through all the crap I carry before pulling out a bottle of Gaviscon. "Here, get a swig of this and then tell me everything. And don't leave out any details this time."

I tell her the whole story. Her blue eyes fill up with sympathy for me. Now and then, she rubs my shoulder or hands me another napkin to dab my eyes.

"The worst thing is, I actually thought he'd grown up, but I guess some things never change."

Amy rolls her eyes. "The dickhead couldn't handle it the last time you thought you were pregnant. I don't know what's wrong with the bloke."

"You should see him with his girls. I honestly thought he'd be a man this time, and even if he didn't want to be with me, he could at least acknowledge his responsibilities. Like, why is a baby with me not worth his time?" My head fills with a collage of memories from our past. The moment I thought I was pregnant, things changed. He changed.

Amy pops her brush down and gives me a hug from across the small table. "Forget about him. This baby's probably better off without him, anyway. If he can't be bothered to get in touch, then he really isn't worth your tears."

I know she's right, but the ache in my heart intensifies with each passing day.

Towards the end of the session, Mark approaches. "I'm working near you next month, Steph. Would you let me paint you?"

Amy snorts. "Mark, you're not seriously going to go there again, are you?"

He rocks his shoulders, with puffs of laughter coming through his nostrils. "Tell Cal if he's jealous, I can paint him as well."

I roll my eyes with a smile. "I'm not even with Cal anymore. He's on another continent, so he won't be bothering you again. I'd actually love you to paint me pregnant."

His smile reaches his steely grey eyes. "Perfect." He hands me a card with his number on. "Call me and we'll arrange something."

CAL
Eight months later

"Mum, we're out of milk. Do you want anything else from the shop?"

"Yes, love, pick up some bread too."

"Can I come, Daddy?"

"No, Bethy. stay here with Nanny. You're still in your nightgown." I kiss her hair before walking out of the kitchen, grabbing the keys to Mum's little Peugeot car. I sold my Audi when I left for Australia, but Mum's insured me on hers for a fortnight while I'm visiting with the girls. She hardly drives it these days, everywhere she goes is in walking distance.

I asked her to come and live with me in Australia but she won't, besides she has my sister an hour's drive away, so she's not totally alone.

Turning on the stereo as I back out of the drive, the CD comes to life. A voice talks about the church. I roll my eyes and shake my head at my mum's bible CD or mindful self love shit or whatever this is. I turn a corner and pull up at the traffic lights, looking at the buttons on the radio just as he mentions his throbbing cock.

My hand hovers over the buttons, and I swallow, almost

choking on my saliva. He plunders into her wet heat and my eyes widen, feeling slightly uncomfortable but turned on at the same time with the way he's describing this woman; her curves, smell, taste.

Fuck, it's been so long since I had a woman. Danni set me up on a date in Oz, but I couldn't take it any further. I couldn't even kiss her. She just didn't compare to my Steph. Nobody does. I spent a lifetime trying to recreate the feeling she gave me when we were together in our teens.

Even when I had her in my bed again, I only got an essence of that feeling. Having her for the odd night wasn't enough to make me truly happy, like I was at uni when she was mine and only mine. If I could tell my twenty-year-old self what a selfish bastard he was, I would. I'd tell him to keep hold of that woman because you'll never be truly happy without her.

The guy on the CD has come into her now. I must have missed the bit where he went from licking her clit to burying his cock in her as I zoned out, thinking of Steph.

I only think of her occasionally now when something reminds me of her. At first everything reminded me of her, but time helps and memories fade. It's sad that someone you loved so deeply is now a stranger again.

The second time we parted was much worse. When I left at uni, I had the rest of my life ahead of me with no intention of settling down. I thought love like hers was abundant, and I was sure to find it again around every corner or every country I visited, but I couldn't have been more wrong. A love like hers is rare. Her entire being encompasses home and seeing her again at work was like being found when I never knew I was lost.

Now, a middle-aged man, I can only half live the rest of my life because the other half of my soul is with another. My only joy now is my girls, and I cling on to every moment I can with them.

Arriving at the store, I park up and skip the CD back to where it was, not wanting Mum to know I listened to her erotic fiction. I walk into the store and grab a basket. A hand touches mine, causing an electric shock to travel up my arm.

"Cal," a soft familiar voice says.

I turn to face her. "Kelly."

She crosses her arms over her chest. "I didn't know you were back. Are you back for good? Have you seen Steph? Why haven't you been in touch?"

I hand her a shopping basket. "Okay, one question at a time." I chuckle.

Her eyebrows pull inwards as she snatches the basket from me. Is she mad because I haven't been in touch with her? We're friends, but I didn't think she'd miss me that much.

"Well? What's your poor excuse for being an absolute bellend?" Her foot taps, waiting for me to speak, but I don't get why she's so pissed.

"I'm sorry I've not been in touch. I lost all my numbers."

The crease between her eyes deepens. "When did you last hear from Steph? You got her message, right?"

"I've not heard from Steph since the day I left for Sydney." What message? Blood rushes to my head, and the fruit and veg aisle fogs all around me. "Is she all right? Has something happened to her?"

Kelly sighs. "She's fine, Cal." She bites her lip and hesitates like she wants to say more.

"What is it?" I rub my middle finger over my eyebrow.

Kelly shakes her head. "You don't need to worry, but you should contact her now you're back."

I relax my shoulders, knowing she's all right. "I'm not

back for good. The girls are on holiday for a fortnight. I'm just visiting Mum."

"You still need to contact her."

My body tenses. "What for? Nothing's changed, has it?"

"Promise me you will get in touch with her while you're here. You owe her that."

I shake my head. Owe her? I don't owe her anything. It's her that wouldn't leave that husband of hers. "How is Steph?"

"She's—"

"Stop. Don't tell me anything." I don't know what I want to hear most, that she's happy or unhappy. I can't decide which would hurt the most. If she's unhappy, there's not a fucking thing I can do about it. Even if she left her husband, I live in Australia. If she's happy, then I'll know I did the right thing, but it will burn a hole in my chest because I'm not the one making her happy.

"She thought you'd blanked her." Kelly glares at me with eyes of steel.

My chest tightens as the rope that binds me to Steph pulls tighter around my heart. I never thought she would try to contact me. "I'll call into work while I'm here."

She smiles, and that seems to satisfy her.

"How is everyone? How are you?"

"Cal, so much has happened. I'm getting married." She waves a hand in front of my face, and I catch the glittering rock on her finger.

"Wow. That's great. I'm happy for you."

We both walk down the aisle and I grab a punnet of strawberries. "Who's your fiancé, then? Anyone I know?"

"It's Ryan," she says, like I should know the bloke.

"And?" I gesture with my hand for her to elaborate on who the fuck Ryan is.

"You know, the guy I was seeing. You must remember me telling you about him."

"Amsterdam guy?"

She giggles. "Bingo."

"He asked you to marry him, then?" She used to talk to Steph about him all the time, but I was too wrapped up in my own world with Steph. I never took much notice.

"Yes, in Amsterdam, would you believe?"

"He took you?"

"I told him I'd never been, after you and Steph painted such a wonderful picture of it, I thought I wanted to live a little. It was last year, and I had my first spiffy-thing."

I place my hand on my chest as the laughter takes over. "But you don't smoke."

"I know and I couldn't inhale, so he ordered me a cake, and then I felt ill. It wasn't for me." She giggles again.

"I'd love to have seen that."

"No, you wouldn't. I vomited in the canal. It wasn't pretty."

I shake my head and chuckle away to myself.

"Steph couldn't stop laughing when I told her either."

I take in a deep breath as her name leaves her lips. "How is everyone else?"

"Sarah and James are dating, and Jerry is going through a divorce. He's been knocking off Trish in finance."

"Fuck."

"Come to my wedding. You can catch up with everyone. It's on Sunday. I'd love for you to be there. Bring your girls too."

"No, I couldn't."

"Please Cal. I'd love for you to be there. Everyone would love to see you."

She pulls a notebook from her bag, tears out a page, and writes the details. "Here, I'm getting married at the village church on Sunnyside Green and the reception is at the Olde Bell Hotel."

I take the paper from her and shove it in my pocket. "I don't think it's a good idea."

"Just think about it. If you come, great and if you don't, I understand. It's been nice seeing you." She reaches out her arms for a hug.

I wrap my arms around her, pulling her close. "You too. Do me a favour."

"Anything." She looks up at me with eyes blue as the sunny sky.

"Don't tell anyone you saw me, especially Steph. I don't want to bring up any painful memories."

She folds her arms again and her eyes turn to a thundery storm with a flash of lightning as her words snap at me. "That's not fair, Cal. I won't keep that from her. I've had to work with her this whole time and…" She chews on her bottom lip. "And if you don't contact her before I leave for my honeymoon, I will tell her you're here."

"All right. Calm down." Why the fuck is she pushing this? Kelly of all people should know no good can come of me seeing Steph again. I'm so over this conversation. "I have to get going. Take care of yourself, and I hope everything goes well on Sunday."

"Thanks Cal, take care of yourself too."

I finish the grocery shop and head back to my car. Well, Mum's Peugeot. Years ago, I wouldn't have dared drive an old lady's car. It's funny how now I just couldn't give a shit.

"Everything all right?" Mum asks when I get back.

"Yeah, I bumped into Kelly, who I used to work with."

"Oh, I always liked her, dear. Why ever the two of you didn't get together, I'll never know."

"Mum, we're friends."

"But you went on those dates."

"It wasn't a date. She took me out twice when Priya and I split, nothing more."

"Anyway, she's a nice girl."

"She's getting married on Sunday."

"Oh, how lovely."

"She invited me."

"Wonderful, how nice. You can catch up with everyone."

I want to go more than anything. I want to see *her.* But I can't.

STEPH

CALEB FIDGETS as I sit in church, waiting for Kelly to walk down the aisle. Trust him to want a feed at this moment. Can I whip it out in church? Gosh, I can't have Kelly walk down the aisle while I'm sitting here with my boob out.

I knew I should have brought more milk. The thought of having a couple glasses of wine tonight was more tempting. So all my pumped milk is being used for tomorrow.

I bounce him on my knee and hold the dummy in place, watching him suck frantically on the teat, pulling his eyebrows together when he realises it's not the real thing. "Shh, hold on, little man."

The organ plays Wagner's Bridal Chorus, and I stand along with everyone else, shifting Caleb to rest on my cocked hip.

Kelly enters with her arm linked through her dad's. A tingle tickles my nose and tears prickle my eyes. She glides down the aisle, a heavenly vision in white. The incandescent fish-tail dress glitters as the light pours through the church stained glass windows, sending a spectrum of dazzling colours bouncing off her against the stone walls.

Caleb stops fidgeting. His eyes follow the dancing pattern, mesmerised by the pretty colours and the light raining down on her and Ryan as she approaches the altar like a gift from God himself, blessing this union.

As the vicar performs the ceremony, Caleb eats his own hand. The odd cough and clearing of the throat are the only sounds other than the vicar and Caleb's irritable cries. I'm left with no choice but to whip it out.

I drop the strap of my dress and pull my breast from my bra. James, the promotions manager, widens his eyes then darts them away, looking anywhere but in my direction.

Caleb latches on like a vacuum, sucking up a sock, and I relax my shoulders as my painfully hard breast deflates on one side like the air is being sucked from a balloon. At least he's quiet and not drawing any more attention. *No, everyone's just staring at your boob now.* James looks straight ahead, probably scarred for life after glimpsing my leaky teat that points to the floor.

I glance at Sarah's small perky handfuls. Although when I was young, they were never small, but my nipples did point in the right direction, at least.

After the service and photos, we make our way to the reception. Kelly has arranged for cars to take us to the venue. James is on hand to help grab the pushchair, and Sarah carries the changing bag for me.

As we enter the old stately home, now a hotel, we're greeted with a glass of champagne. The round tables display tall vase centres. Chairs are covered in turquoise bows to match her bridesmaids.

The whole affair reminds me of my wedding. I wanted a small event, but Mum couldn't have that. You'd have thought it was her day, not mine. 'You only get married once' were her words. I can still hear them now, ringing in my ears.

CAL

"I THINK you should attend this wedding. It will be nice to catch up with your old colleagues," Mum groans for the hundredth time.

"I can't. It started a few hours ago." I lift my feet up onto the sofa and lean back against the arm.

"You can go to the reception. Bring your clothes down. I'll iron them for you."

"Mum, I don't have any clothes. I only travelled light."

She gives me that look. The one where she knows I'm making excuses.

I jump off the sofa and storm upstairs. She's been going on about it all day. Maybe she knows I want to go more than anything. Fuck, I need to see her, but I don't want to see her. Fuck it, my desire to see her, along with my mother's nagging, has me looking through my clothes for something to wear. All I packed were jeans and joggers.

I find a pair of black jeans that aren't ripped, and by chance, a grey shirt was folded in my case. Mum is smiling in the doorway when I look up. "Give me those while you have a shower."

"Mum, I'm capable of ironing."

"So am I. Now don't argue with me and get yourself in the shower."

"Thanks, Mum."

The hot water washes the minty shower gel away, and I can't stop thinking of her. My stomach ties itself into knots. Will she be at the reception alone, or with *him*? What if she isn't even there, and I'm panicking about nothing?

Mum's laid my freshly pressed clothes on the bed and as I pull on my jeans, Bethy walks into the room. "Are you going out?"

"Yeah, you're staying with Nanny."

"Can I come?"

"Not tonight, boo."

Mum comes into the room as I button up the shirt. "We'll bake some cookies, shall we? We can have some fun of our own."

Bethy's frown turns to a bright smile, and she runs off, shouting at her sister. "Liv, we're gonna do some baking."

"I thought you would have had a shave." Mum says, as she inspects my face.

A puff of air leaves my lips. "Mum, this is me." Plus, Steph likes me this way—unshaven—and there's no way I'm gonna disappoint. Will she be glad to see me? Fuck, this is a bad idea. She won't be happy to see me. I should let sleeping dogs lie.

"Do you need a lift?"

"I've booked a taxi." I slip on my old Dr Martens that are the only shoes I brought. Mum wrinkles her brow when she sees them, but says nothing, as I don't have any other option.

AT THE HOTEL, the reception is already underway; the buffet is out. Everyone is merry. I have some catching up to do, but I'm thankful I've missed the speeches and shit. I walk by the large buffet table and shove a mini scotch egg in my mouth. Chewing it down, I scan the room, but don't recognise anyone. Fuck, am I at the right place?

There's a squeal behind me that makes me jump. Yep. I'm at the right place.

I turn around to a beautiful bride, throwing her arms around me. "I'm so glad you came. When you posted my card and gift, I thought you weren't coming."

"Yeah, I wasn't gonna come. I'm guessing you opened it then, if you know it was from me?"

"Yes, thank you."

"You look beautiful, Kelly. Congratulations." I kiss her cheek as she lets go of me.

"Let me introduce you to Ryan." She hooks her arm through mine and we walk to the bar.

"Ryan, this is my friend Cal, who I used to work with."

"Ay-up mate." He shakes my hand. "Good to meet you. What you drinking?"

The bartender places two drinks on the bar.

"I'll have a pint of Stella, cheers."

"A pint of Stella as well, mate," he says to the bartender.

"Cal." A gruff voice shouts. Jerry moves to the side of me, patting my back.

"I'll let you catch up with everyone," Kelly says before slipping away with Ryan to mingle with more guests.

"How you been?" Jerry asks, but he doesn't give me time to answer before pulling me over to James and Chris. I reach out my hand and collect my pint from the bar before being hauled to the other end.

"Good to see you, mate. How's things down under?" James asks.

"Yeah, everything's good." I take a big gulp of beer and scan the room again, but don't see her. "Anyway, James. You and Sarah?"

He smiles and looks down at his foot, tapping the bar stool in front of him. "Yeah, who knew, ay?"

"Is she here?"

"She's somewhere about. She was with Steph the last time I saw her."

My stomach hardens. Fuck, she's here.

"Have you been in touch with Steph?" he asks.

"No, why does everybody keep asking me that?"

He flinches his head back and flicks his eyes to Chris. "Just thought you would've got in touch with her, that's all."

I scan the room again, then spot Sarah walking into the function room. My stomach flips over when Steph follows behind. I try to swallow, but I can barely breathe. She's breathtaking. Literally. I almost didn't recognise her with blonde honey-toned highlights and even curvier than I remember, or maybe it's the figure-hugging dress that's accentuating all my favourite parts of her body.

The silky fabric clings to the round curve of her stomach, draping over her hips. My eyes wander to her tits spilling out over the top, looking even bigger than before, reminding me of Jessica Rabbit. Fuck, did I just compare her to a cartoon character? That comparison doesn't do her justice.

She's a goddess. Her fiery lipstick matches her dress, and the way she moves is graceful but sexy as hell. Her curls bounce as she tilts her head back and laughs with Sarah, full of life. She's Venus personified. My own Aphrodite. I pause. My own. I want her to be mine, and mine alone.

She saunters to a table and pours herself a glass of champagne.

"What do you think, Cal?"

I turn my head back to the guys. I haven't heard fuck all.

"We were saying it's about time James popped the question."

"Right? Yeah. Your turn next." I raise my glass to him before taking another big gulp.

"Give it a rest. We've only been together a year."

I need another drink before I talk to her. I order a double whiskey and another pint, needing to catch up with the guys plus calm my nerves. My heart hasn't stopped pounding since she walked into the room. I knock the whiskey back in two big swigs and relish the burn as it goes down.

"I don't know how you drink that shit straight." Chris shudders and sips his pint, wiping the froth from his lip with the back of his hand.

"I've got some catching up to do, haven't I?"

Jerry pats my back again. "When are you coming back to work for me?"

"I'm still in Oz. Just home for a few weeks." I realise I just said home. I guess England will always be my home. Or is it her? I've travelled all over the world, yet I always end up back here.

"You know there's a job for you when you want to come back, don't you?"

Jerry must be more pissed than I thought. "Cheers man." I scan the room for a fire engine dress. That colour always looked amazing on her, combined with her honey highlights. She's fucking electrifying tonight.

My eyes stop when they come to her standing next to a table with a group of women. Only now, she's holding someone's kid, resting him on her hip. His tiny legs dangle under her arm as she bounces him up and down.

The women are fawning over the little tyke as women do, and she beams with her sweet smile and those cute fucking dimples. I lean against the bar, taking her in, and watch her smile fade as our eyes meet from across the room.

She freezes. Blood drains from her face like she's seen a ghost.

STEPH

"Aren't you just adorable," Trish from finance coos as she pokes at Caleb's dimples. "He has the cheekiest smile and cutest dimples I ever saw." She pulls a face and tickles his tummy, causing another bout of giggles from him, making me laugh.

My body sways as I bounce Caleb on my hip to the music, and catch Cal in the corner of my eye. My hopeful imagination again, but I give him a second glance. Could it really be him?

With a gaping mouth, my knees weaken and my hand trembles along with my bottom lip. As I stare in wonder, he stares right back. A hint of a smile tugs at his lips, making my head dizzy. He's back.

"Are you all right, Steph? You've gone all pale." Trish breaks my gaze.

My hand holds my neck as I gasp for breath.

"Trish…I…can you take him? I need some air." My throat closes up as I speak.

"Give him to me." She holds out her hands. "Come on, sweetie, Mummy's been on the pop, hasn't she? Yes, she has." She bounces him on her lap and distracts him with a bottle of bubbles from the party favours.

Before my legs fail me, I dash towards the exit. The air is warm and muggy, even at dusk, and I still can't catch a breath. I walk by the outside tables, past the smoking area to the side of the building, and lean up against the stone wall, shutting my eyes. All this time. He's finally home.

Gravel crunches as footsteps close in on me. His voice whispers to me like the wind whispers through the trees. "Steph."

His hand grazes my neck, caressing my cheek with his thumb. "Breathe, baby. Just breathe. It's all right."

I turn my head away, but his words soothe my mind, and his touch calms my pounding heart. It's like a dream, and I almost don't want to open my eyes in fear he'll vanish, leaving me alone again.

"You look incredible tonight." His warm breath lands on my mouth, and I open my eyes to see him inches from my face. "I don't normally go for blondes, but for you, I'll make an exception."

I gaze into his blazing eyes; flecks of red and gold mirror the setting sun. Turning my head, I brush my lips against his palm and feel a shudder from his hand.

"Happiness looks good on you, baby. That and this dress." He moves his hand down, grazing my chin with his thumb, then my neck, following the curve of my breast until his hand rests in the valley, feeling the rise and fall of my chest.

He takes my hand with his other and places it over his pounding heart. What the hell does he think he's doing? He has me in some sort of trance.

I shake my head. Snap out of it. "Well, I have to be happy for my family. Seeing as you never cared to contact me. You think there hasn't been a day when I haven't thought about you? I wished for you to come back, but you never even bothered to get in touch." My voice trails to a croak.

He raises his brow. "You still think about me?"

I swallow. Is he for real? I'm raising our son. I think about him every time I look at my boy. "It's a little hard not to, Cal."

"Come here." He pulls me against his chest, wrapping his arms around me, and as shocked and mad as I am to see him again acting as though nothing's changed, it feels like home.

No, he can't do this. He can't show up here and expect me to welcome him back with open arms. All the tired nights, going it alone. I never expected him to come back and want to be with me, but I at least thought he would want a relationship with his son. At the very least he could have Face-Timed us occasionally.

CAL

I HOLD her as tight as I can, hoping this moment will sustain me for another year without her. Imprinting this into my memory, I inhale the banana and vanilla in her hair, the sweet aroma of wine on her breath, and the delicate scent of summer that lingers on her neck. Every inch of her is intoxicating, making me high.

"Where have you been, Cal? We missed you. I missed you."

My cock perks up at her words, and I have to get back inside, before I hike this dress up and take her against this stone wall. As the thought crosses my mind, I glance around, but we're not alone. Too many guests in the smoking area.

Besides, I can't start all this again. Getting over her this last year has been agonising. I'm still not over her. I doubt I ever will be, but it gets easier.

We've already said too much. I haven't spent the last twelve months trying to put some distance between us to ruin it now and go back to square one. I could easily steal a kiss or two, but I couldn't stop. One kiss is never enough, and I worry it will ruin us again. Or ruin me when she goes back to him.

Her chest vibrates with a buzz sound. She pulls her phone from her bra and turns off the alarm. "My taxi will be here soon. I have to go."

I still have my arm wrapped around her waist and can't move my feet. It takes all my strength to prize myself away from her and step back.

"Are you back for good?"

"Just a few weeks. Brought the girls' home during their school holidays to see my mum."

Her face drops, and she nods. "Will I see you again?"

"I doubt it. I'm going back next week."

She shoves against my chest. "You selfish bastard." Her eyes turn cold and dark like a hollow tree in a deep forest. She spins around and crosses the gravel path, pushing open the double doors to the entrance.

The music muffles as I walk back into the venue and watch her storm into the women's restroom. I'm selfish? She's the one that wants to have her cake and eat it. She wants me when it suits her.

Every muscle in my body tenses, screaming at me to hire one of these rooms and make love to her all night, but I wouldn't be strong enough to walk away again. It's better this way.

I head back to the bar to the guys, needing another whiskey. Sarah stands with James and the woman with the baby.

"Have you seen Steph?" Sarah asks.

"No, why?" I don't want to get her in trouble with Justin, or want anyone to think there's something going on with us again.

The woman with the baby widens her smile. "I didn't know you were back, Cal."

Jerry places a hand on her back. So this is who Jerry was having an affair with. I recognise her now, Trish, from finance. My head tilts, getting a good look at the kid wriggling in her arms.

"Here, he's a little irritable since his mummy disappeared." She thrusts him into my arms.

My throat grows thick. James gives Sarah a knowing look and then glances at Chris with wide eyes. Do they know about Jax, the son I lost? Can they tell I'm freaking out as my lungs won't function?

I glance down at the kid in my arms. His brown eyes gaze up at me through long dark lashes and he stops his fidgeting. The full head of thick black hair reminds me of my Jax, and the emptiness floods my chest.

His little hand touches my cheek as if he can sense the sadness in my heart. All I hear is the throb in my temple. Numbness creeps up my spine and all I feel is the pulse in my neck as thoughts of Jax blur my mind.

"Ah, she's here." Trish says, bringing me back to the present.

My eyes wander up to see Steph walking towards us with wide eyes. Her eyebrows squish together. She's still pissed with me. What the fuck have I done?

Trish rubs the kid's back. "Your mummy's here."

I turn to Trish. "Mummy?"

Steph snatches the kid from me. "You can't just waltz back here after all this time and play the doting dad." Her eyes are burning a fierce green.

The kid cries. Steph kisses his forehead and says, "Mummy's here."

"What the fuck?" Everyone's eyes turn to me, and I clear my throat.

Steph sucks in a breath. She spins around and walks away. I knock back my whiskey before following her.

"Steph." My fingers wrap around her arm, pulling her back to me. I take a good look at the dark-haired kid. He peers back up at me. "Is he yours?"

She swallows before she speaks, then chokes out her words. "Who else would he belong to?"

My fingers dig into my forehead as I rub the thrashing pain screaming in my head. "How old is he?" My hand squeezes her arm tight. "How old is he, Steph?" I growl, not caring who sees or hears.

"Five months, but you'd know that if you cared to contact me." Her voice wavers along with her trembling chin.

I pause. My mind scrambling to do the math, but I can't think straight. Fuck. I shouldn't have knocked back those whiskeys. I shake my head. "When was he born?"

"Five months ago."

"Fuck's sake Steph. What date?"

"Cal, please. Keep your voice down."

"Tell me what date my fucking son was born, Steph. Or shall I ask Justin?"

"February 3rd okay. And he isn't your son."

"Like hell he isn't. Fucking look at him, Steph." I can't stop staring at the kid. My kid. As soon as I saw him in Trish's arms, he reminded me of Jax. His thick black hair, brown eyes, just like all the pictures of me in my mum's photo albums.

There's an overwhelming pull towards him. I just know he's mine. I still haven't done the math, but I don't need to.

"You lost the right to him when you abandoned us. You

can't expect to show up after all this time, confuse him, then leave us again."

James appears behind Steph. "I think your taxi's out front, Steph."

I stammer back against a table. My entire body vibrates as my fists ball and my jaw clenches.

Steph's eyes fix on mine as she speaks to James. "Thank you. Can you help me with the pushchair and car seat?"

My stomach twists like the wringing out of a wet cloth.

"Outside. Now." I demand answers. After everything, how can she do this to me? She knows about Jax, and how hard that was. Now she has a son. Our son. Another son and doesn't tell me. It's like I've lost him all over again.

Sarah takes the kid. My kid. "I'll get him sorted. I'll bring him outside."

Steph walks towards the doors, and I follow, watching her movements. She's no longer the goddess in red, but the devil wrapped in lies and deceit.

The sun has set, and the darkness has swallowed the day, along with my soul. "What the fuck, Steph?" I shout, barging through the glass doors, letting them slam behind me.

She folds her arms over her chest. "You don't have to trouble yourself. I told you he isn't yours."

"Then whose the fuck is he? Because he sure as hell ain't bonny boy blues."

"What are you talking about?"

"Fucking golden boy wonder. Justin."

STEPH

MY BODY TREMBLES as Cal yells, hissing each word from his lips. I've never seen him this angry, not at me, anyway.

Usually I would kiss him to calm him down, but that's not an option right now.

"You can't come home and act like nothing's changed. When everything has changed."

"Who's fault is that?"

"You're not seriously blaming me. You're the one that swanned off to the other side of the globe without a trace and never bothered to get in touch."

"So you thought it was all right to have our kid and not tell me? Were you ever going to tell me we have a son?" He spits the words. His lips press into a thin, hard line, and his eyes pierce my heart as they throw daggers at me.

"I called you several times. You were unreachable. I even wrote you a letter, like you care. You couldn't handle it the last time I thought I was pregnant, so I wasn't holding out much hope this time around." I wrap my arms around my body as the suddenly chilled air swathes my bare arms. Or is it the chill from his icy gaze sending shivers through me? "Just because you're back now, you think you can act like you're father of the year. I told you, don't trouble yourself. He's not yours."

"Fuck off. He's mine. I knew he was mine as soon as I looked into his eyes. Anyone can see the resemblance." He waves a hand in the building's direction.

"Well, being the sperm donor doesn't mean you can claim him as your son when you feel like it. You should have been here. You've missed so much."

His hands grip his hair, pulling back from his face. "You could have called me. I would have come home, and we could have sorted something out."

Call him, he says. Who does he think I am, Mystic Meg? "I tried calling you several times. You changed your number. I'm not a pissin' psychic."

"Don't make excuses. There are plenty of ways you could have contacted me if you bothered to try."

"What like, my crystal ball, oh wait…maybe I could have consulted the tarot cards…wait…I got it, maybe I should have just held your journal and the number would have come to me. Stop being a dickhead."

"I'm the dickhead? You didn't want anything to ruin your perfect fucking life with golden balls. Just admit it."

"That's not true. I even—"

"Save your excuses."

He won't listen. How can he say this? He's the one that didn't answer my letter because he was in a relationship with Priya. I tried, I really did.

"Don't you think I wanted you to come home? I wanted it so badly. I prayed he was yours, so I would selfishly have a piece of you with me forever. A piece of you that would never leave me, that I could hold and love without fear of rejection." I hold my throat as a strangled sob escapes.

He glares at me, rubbing his fingers across his forehead.

"You were on the other side of the world rekindling things with your ex. I don't blame you. I want you to be happy, but don't you dare come back here and blame me for missing out on five months of his life, when you never acknowledged my letter."

"What fucking letter?" he shouts, pacing in circles, the gravel crunching beneath his boots.

"Are you saying you never received my letter?" My body trembles, but for different reasons this time. He's scaring me. Though I'm not afraid of him, I'm afraid of him hating me again.

"I never received a fucking thing from you. Don't you think I would have come back in a heartbeat if I'd known you were pregnant? Fuck's sake, Steph. It's like some nightmare or Jeremy Kyle shit." His words travel through the cool night air, wrapping around my body like a dense fog smothering my skin.

Cal drops on a bench, holding his head in his hands. I slide next to him. He's calm now, but the silence is deafening. I want him to talk, say anything, but we just sit in silence for a few minutes.

My body shivers under the dark veil of night. My teeth chatter as I sit here in my strappy dress, and he glances my way. He must really hate me or he would have wrapped an arm around me to warm me up.

He stares at me for a moment; the moon reflects in his shimmering eyes. "I don't even know his name."

"It's Caleb."

"With a K or C?"

"C. A. L.—"

"You called him Cal?"

All I can muster is a nod as I choke back a sob. "I have to go."

"Sure you do. You always have to go, don't you?"

CHAPTER Eighteen

CAL

I watch her leave the lawn, her arms wrapping tightly around her body as she shivers in the night air. She gets into a car waiting for her in the car park. James loads the pushchair into the boot and Sarah gives her a hug before she gets into the back seat. I don't see Justin. He must be at home with her eldest two.

The thought of my son calling that prick Daddy makes my chest ache. How much more can that man actually take from me? As if having my Steph all these years wasn't enough, now he has my boy.

I bury my face in my hands and let myself shed a single tear, but unsure who it's for; her, myself, my son, or the boy I lost. How did this get so fucked up?

The music echoes from the venue, a distant sound floating through the dark, but nothing can drown out the ringing in my ears or the thumping of my heart. Faint voices are in the distance with laughter, reminding me that despite all this chaos in my mind, there's a celebration going on.

I need another drink. No, I should go home. What I should do is order a fucking taxi and get my son. Fuck it. My palm runs over my face. I take in a breath and walk back to the entrance to drink myself into the middle of next week.

—————

SOMETHING SPRINGS UNDER ME, then again. "Daddy, wake up."

Aargh. I roll over, blinking my eyes. "Bethy." Her face is a blur. She's a silhouette against the blazing sun pouring through the window. How did I even get home? The night is hazy. I sit up, causing a pain in my head as the blood rushes there and glance down at myself still in last night's clothes.

"Daddy, are you getting up?" Beth bounces on the bed again. "We've been to church with Nanny. She's doing lunch now."

"Just gimmie a minute, boo." I glance around the room for my phone, then feel it in my jeans pocket. Fuck, it's dead. As I reach for the bedside table where the charger is, the events of last night resurface. I'd hoped it was all a bad dream.

Dropping back on the bed with a bounce, I pull Bethy down with me, needing a hug. Her slender frame hugs me back, her spindly arms wrapping around my neck.

"Did you like it at church?"

"We made crafts." She climbs to the edge of the double bed and runs off. My head pounds as I try to piece last night together.

"I made this for you, Daddy." Bethy jumps on the bed, holding a card with a hand-drawn cross and the words Daddy in bubble writing; each letter coloured in a different colour.

When I open it up, there's a picture. "Who are these?"

She points to her drawing. "That's me, Liv, you, Nanny and Mummy, Steve and Buddy."

I run my hand over my face. She'll be able to add her

brother to the picture once I sort something out. I'll be damned if Steph thinks I'm just gonna slip away back to Australia. What sort of person does she think I am? "This is beautiful, sweetheart." I kiss her cheek, and she hugs me again, giving me the motivation I need to get out of bed this morning.

The bright light shining through the window makes the pain in my head worse, and the smell of Mum's roast wafting up the stairway makes my stomach churn.

My mouth tastes like shit, so I stumble to the bathroom, holding my head to clean my teeth and shower, though it doesn't help much.

As I walk into the kitchen, Liv sits at the table with her headphones on, not even acknowledging me.

"Looks like you had a good night," Mum says, waving the knife in my direction before continuing to chop the carrots.

I huff. "It was nothing short of eventful. Put it that way." I sit at the table across from Liv, holding my head in my hands.

"I'll pop the kettle on." Mum makes a strong coffee. "How was everyone?"

"Yeah, same."

She continues preparing dinner while I stare into the coffee swirling around the cup just as my life has spiralled.

"Do you remember Stephanie?"

"Yes, dear."

I sigh, dragging a hand over my face. "She had a baby."

"That's nice, boy or girl?" She carries on chopping the veg.

"A boy, Caleb." Saying his name out loud causes a prickle in the back of my throat. "He's mine."

Mum drops the knife onto the glass chopping board. "You have another child?" She slowly bends into the seat at the table.

"Yep." I stare into the coffee, unable to take a drink with the nausea bubbling in my stomach.

"Oh, Cal. And you've only just found out?" Mum leans back in her chair, blinking rapidly and shaking her head. "Why didn't she tell you? Goodness, he must be what? Twenty years old by now."

"No, Mum. She had a baby five months ago."

Her face looks even more confused, and the gold and hazel hues of her eyes whirl. "You didn't go there again?"

I stay silent.

"I knew she was the reason you left your job, even though you said you wanted a new challenge. She wouldn't leave you alone when you were at university. When she came looking for you, wanting your number, I thought it was because she was harassing you like she did before. Wanting you back."

I grip the mug tight. "She was here?"

"Love, I told you I saw her. She called asking for your number, but I wanted to check with you before handing it over. I know how she was before, begging you to go back with her. You had enough on your plate moving to Australia. If I'd known she was having a child... but she never said a word." Mum holds my hand with worry etched on her face.

"He looks just like Jaxon."

"Oh, love." Mum gets off her chair and hugs me with tears in her eyes.

My eyes burn, and I pinch the bridge of my nose to stop myself from welling up.

"When can we meet him?" Mum takes off her glasses and dabs her eyes with her apron.

"I don't know. I'll have to visit her. We didn't leave things amicably last night." I realise I never even got her number. Fuck.

"She said I have no right to start playing dad when I haven't been around."

"You should get a paternity test. It will help if Steph is difficult. Plus, wasn't she married? You need to check he's yours."

"He's mine, Mum. I know he's mine. I don't need a paternity test."

She pats my shoulder. "Just get one, so you have some rights. Who's name is on the birth certificate?"

"Fuck knows. She probably put Justin's name on it knowing her. I'll go round to her house today."

<hr>

STEPH

CALEB IS ready for his afternoon nap that always coincides with the school run. I get him strapped into his car seat and just as I turn the engine, my phone rings.

Maxine's name flashes green on the screen. My stomach rolls. She rarely calls me. "Hi, everything all right?"

"Someone's here asking for you. He wants your address. Where are you?"

"I'm at home, just leaving to go to the shop before picking the kids up. Who is it?"

"I think it's Caleb's dad, with how Justin described him. Dark hair, tall, tattoos on his arms. Shall I get rid of him or what? He's waiting outside the house while I pretend I'm looking for your number. He's lucky Justin's at work."

My chest tightens as dread claws at my throat. "Put him on. It's okay."

"Steph. Have you moved?" His voice is gruff and angry, like it was last night.

"Yes. I'm on the other side of town." I give him the address.

"I'm on my way." He cancels the call.

I turn on the blowers to stop myself from sweating. Looking in the rearview mirror to apply lipstick, I wish I'd made more of an effort today before leaving the house.

My fingers tap against the steering wheel until I see a Peugeot park on the road in front of my car. As I step out of the car, the muggy air makes it difficult to breathe. The sun shines in my eyes, and it takes me a moment to adjust as a silhouette walks towards me.

Beads of moisture gather on my forehead as my heart races. My stomach churns my lunch as if mixing it in a blender. I breathe in the thick, hot air, and his cold eyes come into view. His lips press into a thin hard line, and he shoves his hands in his pockets and peers into my car, taking a good look at Caleb.

"He's sleeping."

"Yeah, I can see that." He glances up at me, then leans back against my car, letting out a sigh. "I've come to see him."

I run my hand under my fringe to stop it from sticking to my forehead. "I'm on my way out. You can't just show up demanding to see him when it suits you."

"I want to be part of his life."

"In what way?"

"In the way that fucking matters. In the way a father should be part of their kids' life. What other way is there? I'm sorry if that doesn't fit in with your plans." He waves a hand towards the house. "With your perfect fucking lifestyle. You should have thought about that before fucking me. I thought you were on the pill, anyway?"

"I was, but when Justin had a vasectomy, I stopped taking it."

"So, did you plan this?" He waves a hand towards Caleb in the car.

"Of course I didn't."

"You just forgot that you were fucking me unprotected?"

"It wasn't exactly my first thought, Cal, when you had me on the kitchen floor."

<hr>

CAL

MUM WAS RIGHT. She is being difficult. "Let me have him while you go out."

"He doesn't know you, Cal."

"He's never gonna fucking know me if you don't let me see him."

"He's right there. You can see him."

"You know what I mean. Why are you being so fucking difficult? Is it Justin?" Every time I think of him with my son, it's like a punch to the gut, knocking the wind out of me. "Please tell me he doesn't think he's the father."

She dabs the corner of her eye, barely looking at me. She knows she's in the fucking wrong here. "I'm not with Justin anymore."

My eyebrows pinch together. So this is why she's moved. I thought the house looked smaller. "Since when?"

She shrugs a shoulder. "About a year ago."

Standing straight, I crack my neck to the side. "You've been single this whole fucking time and never thought to tell me? All that bullshit about how much you wanted to be with me? Was it all lies?"

"I tried calling you, but you had changed your number and never thought to tell me, so don't blame me. How was I supposed to get hold of you?"

"Come on, not this again. There are plenty of ways of reaching someone."

"I called to your mum's house. I got the address from

work, but when she told me you were working things out with your ex… I get it, Cal, really, I do. You chose them over us. I just wanted you to be happy, Cal." Her voice wavers.

I stare wide eyed. Cogs turning in my brain as I piece everything together. I want to scream and break something. The frustration is explosive, but as I turn, the only thing to break is her car window, and my son is sleeping like an angel on the other side.

"I'm not with Priya. I never have been. She's marrying Steve the fucking dweeb, for fuck's sake." I don't know why I keep calling him that, I actually like the bloke.

Her hands cover her flushed cheeks. "I thought you were back together this whole time."

"Mum shouldn't have said that." My fingers run through my hair, pulling it from my face and balling it into my clenched fists. "I broke my phone. I lost your number." If I'd known what was going on, I'd have come back in a heartbeat. She should know that.

"Why did she say that if it wasn't true?" Steph stands with her hands on her hip as if calling me a liar.

"I don't know why. Probably wishful thinking. She always wanted us to work things out."

Her lip twitches and her eyes swell and darken, like moss in a damp forest.

I kick at the gravel driveway. "Do you want me to go?"

She shakes her head. "I want you to hold me like you did the other night."

I want to hold her. I also want to kick her to the curb. Her bottom lip trembles and I can't resist comforting her. "Come here." I console her without being overly affectionate. Her breathing relaxes along with her heartbeat.

She breathes in deeply and buries her face in my neck.

I pull away to look at her. "Do you feel better now?"

"I think so." She comes up to my face with her lips inches

from mine. She wants me to kiss her. I know her. She does this and I almost lean in out of habit, but I can't kiss her this time. I'm still furious with her.

She looks down and steps away. "I have to go. I can meet you somewhere tomorrow."

"I'll have my girls. We can take the kids to a park or something. Or is that gonna cramp your style?" I huff.

"No, that's fine. I have things to do tomorrow, but I can meet you after the school run at the cafe in the woods."

"Fine. I'll see you there." I take one last look at Caleb in the car, my heart aching to hold him before I go.

She slides into her Suzuki and starts the engine. With a heavy sigh, I watch her leave, taking my boy with her and the emptiness creeps into my heart. An icy chill shoots down my spine, making my body numb; the same numbness I had when Jax was taken from me. Nobody is going to stop me from being a father to my son. My kids mean everything to me. Steph should know this. I might not have always been there for her in our past, but I'd never abandon my kids.

CHAPTER *Nineteen*

STEPH

I haven't stopped sweating since I crawled out of bed this morning, knowing I'm meeting Cal. Although, I'll be glad when all this is over. I haven't slept since the wedding, and I'm just walking round like an extra from the Walking Dead.

When I have managed to get some shut-eye, I wake with hot flushes, and I itch all over. I wondered if it was the change, but I know it's Cal.

My hand trembles against the steering wheel. The closer I get to the cafe where I'm meeting Cal, the more my hand vibrates and the less oxygen there is in the car. The hot weather mixed with my anxiety has my fringe sticking to my forehead and my clothes sticking to my skin.

Maybe this shirt and leggings wasn't the best choice, but nothing else fits. I can't seem to shift this post pregnancy weight. It's my own fault. Justin said I wasn't just eating for two, I was eating for three. I told him to piss off. It was none of his business how much I ate, seeing as we weren't together, but now I'm paying the price.

"Are we nearly there yet?" Cairen asks.

"Nearly."

Caleb cries again.

"Cassie, just give him his dummy, please." She takes care of Caleb like a mother hen. He's been mardy all morning like he can sense my anxiety.

"Mum, can we have ice-cream when we get there?" Cassie asks.

"Of course." I think I need one as well to cool down.

I keep thinking, could I have done more? Hurting him wasn't my intention. Though I've actually been hurting since the day he left. I can understand why he's upset, but I'm also upset.

As I pull into the cafe car park, Callum is already here with his girls. They're waiting next to the car. I park next to them and wipe my brow, glancing in the rear-view mirror to check my hair and makeup is intact. My clothes may be drab and tight, but at least I can make sure my hair and makeup are on point.

Stepping out of the car, I take in a deep breath. "Hi."

"Hey." He bends over, peering through my car window, smiling at Caleb. "I thought we could go for a walk. There's a play area in the middle on the woodland trail."

"All right. The kids want ice-cream first."

I open the boot and Callum steps in front of me, pulling the pushchair out. He fumbles with the clip, unsure how to open the contraption.

"Fuck, how do you do this?" He chuckles, and it's the first time I've heard him laugh in a long time.

"Pull the clip and press the lever together."

"You'd think someone would invent an easier way to operate these things by now."

"Let me do it." My hand brushes his as I unclip the pushchair, unfolding it and clicking it into place with my foot. "You're obviously out of touch."

"Whose fault's that?"

The jibe stabs me in the chest.

"I'm sorry."

I get Caleb from the car seat and settle him in the pushchair, clipping his dummy to his jacket.

Cal squats down in front of him, takes the straps and straps him in. "Ay-up, mate. What you got there?"

Caleb waves a green dinosaur in his face and spits the dummy out, giving him a huge smile.

Cal takes the dinosaur and taps Caleb on the nose with it, making a gentle roar.

Caleb giggles and dribbles down his chin. It's the first time he's actually smiled today. I can't help but smile along at the two of them. Cassie and Cairen run towards the cafe to look at the ice cream board while I grab the changing bag from the back seat and hook it over the handlebars of the buggy.

"Shall we get an ice cream, then?" Callum says in a baby voice, giving Caleb his teddy back. He takes over pushing the pushchair. It suits him.

"Do you want to wait here? I'll sort the kids out. Do you want anything?"

"Yeah, get me a twirly one with a flake." He waits outside the bustling cafe and crouches down to play with Caleb again.

"Girls, do you want to come with me and choose an ice cream?"

When I return, I hand Cal his cornet, and we walk down the woodland trail. I suck on my ice lolly, savouring the cold ice, but wishing I could smear it all over my face to keep cool, or keep my cool. The kids walk in front, and Cal pushes the buggy with one hand.

"When do you go back?"

"I should have gone back today, but I've changed my flight to give me another two weeks."

"Then what?"

"The media company I work for will let me work from home or maybe do freelance, so I can split my time between here and there. I won't be an absent dad. I'll sort something out."

We arrive at a clearing, and the kids run to the climbing frame in the middle. Cal and I take a seat on a picnic bench.

"Do you want some ice cream, pal? Mummy didn't get you any, did she?" Cal holds his cone in front of Caleb's mouth, and he sucks on the cream, waving his arms with wide eyes.

"You shouldn't be giving him dairy."

He shakes his head. "Steph. I'm pretty sure Beth was licking ketchup from chips at his age."

"Well, if you're going to do that, you might want to put his bib on." I point to the changing bag on the buggy next to Cal.

He opens the bag and pulls out a large bib. "Is this for you or him?" He chuckles to himself, and I laugh along, thinking it's the first time I've laughed all week.

Cal pops the oversized bib over Caleb's head and lets him suck on the remaining ice cream that Cal saved in his cone.

I glance over at the kids. The girls are hanging out near the swings and Cairen is halfway up a tree. "Don't give him too much of that ice cream. He's not used to it."

"Chill, Steph. He's fine. Look at him. I have had kids before. Don't worry."

Huh, don't worry, he says, but I am worried. I'm worried about my son getting rejected when he decides he's had enough.

"So, what have you been up to?"

"Nothing, just work."

"How's Priya?"

"Fine. Apart from her dad passing, but she's okay."

I let go of my shirt and pick at my nails under the table. "I'm sorry."

"I met my dad." He rubs a finger over his eyebrow and gives me a pained look.

My head tilts, and I lean on the table with my elbow. "How was it?"

"Awkward at first, but I've been seeing him regularly with the girls. He's actually a decent bloke. Now he's teetotal, anyway." He huffs and turns his attention back to Caleb.

My chest fills with warmth. I remember how much he missed having his dad around, even if he was a waster. "I'm glad things worked out for you."

"I wouldn't exactly say that, would you?" He waves a hand in the air and looks down at Caleb covered in ice cream. "Oh, shit."

"Now you know why I have the bibs." I giggle and walk around to dig the baby wipes from the bag.

Cal takes the wipes from me and wipes him down, making it fun, causing a giggle from Caleb as he blows creamy bubbles from his mouth, gurgling away. Once Cal's cleaned him down, he unbuckles him and rests him on his knee, wrapping his large hands around him so he's propped up against Cal's chest.

The two of them look the spitting image of each other. I always knew he resembled him, but it's only now I see it properly when they're side by side. I don't want to deny him spending time with him, I just don't want him to let him down like has me.

"What will you tell Priya?"

He flinches his head back. "What about?"

I nod towards Caleb. "About all this."

"I've already told her. She knows why I'm keeping the girls here a few extra weeks."

"Is she okay about it?"

"Well yeah. Why wouldn't she be? What about Justin? He knows I'm the father right?"

"Of course he does."

"I know this isn't ideal for you, Steph, but it's not exactly ideal for me either."

I roll my eyes and put the wipes in a nearby bin, then take the bib from Caleb, fold it up and put it in the bag. He holds his arms out to me, opening and squeezing his hands so I take him from Cal and hold him in my lap

Cal gazes at the two of us with a smile on his face. "He has your dimples."

"I know. I think it's the only thing he has of mine."

"Do you remember the last time we were here?"

"I can't forget. You're still wearing your watch."

He looks at his wrist, then at my hands. "Yeah. You're not wearing your ring, though."

"Only because of Caleb. I haven't worn jewellery since he started pulling on my necklace and earrings."

<hr>

CAL

I RUB my face with my hand. Something else I've missed. It's a small thing, but I remember the first time my girls gripped my finger. "I still can't believe this is real. That I've missed out on so much already."

"I'm sorry." She looks down, kissing Caleb on the back of his head.

"I would have moved heaven and earth to get to you. Why didn't you try harder to find me?"

"Ugh, Cal, how many times do I have to tell you? I tried. I really did."

"You didn't try hard enough. You could have told mum

about Caleb. She said you never mentioned a baby. If you had, she would have told me and I'd have come home."

"And have her lecture me? I was already getting an earful from my own mother. I wasn't about to let your mum give me a lecture, too. She already treated me like I was something she scraped off the bottom of her shoe."

Every time I look at her, I just can't get past the hurt. It's like she's betrayed me. "There are other ways, Steph. My sister's on social media. So is Priya. You could have tried harder. Fuck, if it was me, I'd have got on a plane and done all I could to find you."

"If you're just going to keep going on. I'm leaving."

"I'm just saying."

"You expect me to travel halfway around the world to find you? While pregnant? The farthest I've ever travelled is the Mediterranean. What did you want me to do? Go door to door in Sydney? Be realistic, Cal." I chew on the inside of my mouth to stop myself from boiling over. "As far as I was concerned, your mother had spoken to you, so why would I feel the need to talk to anyone else? How was I to know she never passed on the message?"

Caleb cries out, breaking me from my rant. I stroke his hair and bounce him in my arms.

"I have to go soon. He's due his feed."

"Can I see him tomorrow?"

"Sure. I'm free in the evening. Come round to the house if you like."

"Fuck. I can't tomorrow. Liv's got tickets to watch her old dance school perform. I can't ask mum to take them. She's been a little under the weather lately."

"All right."

I don't want to leave it another day before I see him again. "I can take him tomorrow day."

"I'm helping out a friend. It's her son's first birthday

party. Besides, he may not settle with you. You need to get to know each other."

I ball my fists every time she says that. "I'm his dad, for fuck's sake."

Caleb cries again. He's getting ratty, just like me.

"I'm going to get going. I'll see you in a few days."

I take Caleb from her. He stops crying and pulls on my hair as he studies my face. "I'll see you soon, little dude." I strap him in his pushchair and round the kids up.

———

"How was the show?" Mum asks the girls as we walk into the house.

"Nanny, it was great. You would have liked it."

Mum strokes Livvie's cheek. "I know, darling. I'll come next time when I'm not all bunged up with cold."

"Are you feeling any better, Mum?"

"A little. My headache's gone."

"Can we stay up and watch telly, Dad?" Bethy asks.

I glance at my watch. "All right, get your pyjamas on and clean your teeth, though." I pat Bethy's bottom as she follows Livvie out of the room.

It's not too late. Maybe I can still drive over to Steph's. "Mum, will you watch the girls?"

"Of course, you don't even need to ask."

I snatch the car keys from the side before bolting out the door into the setting sun. The crisp air prickles my skin, but a warmth spreads through me at the thought of seeing my boy again.

The thirty-minute drive to her house seems to take forever. I can't stop thinking of all the things I've missed. All his firsts. I was there for every single fucking thing with my girls from the pregnancy test, the scans, the first time Priya felt them kick in her belly, not to mention their birth. Steph's taken all that away from me.

My throat prickles as I remember Jax. I spent all day putting furniture together. A wardrobe, cot, changing table, bookcase. We decorated his room with jungle animals in greens and blues.

The day after Rachel gave birth, and we came home empty-handed, I packed it all away. Neither of us wanted the reminder. We gave it all to a local children's charity, all except a few items that Rachel wanted to keep in a box with his scan pictures.

Seeing Caleb has resurfaced old memories that I thought I'd dealt with, but the pain never went away. It was just hidden. Does the emptiness ever go away?

I pull up on Steph's driveway. Her new home is different from her previous mansion. She's slumming it in comparison. I glance in the rearview mirror at my bloodshot eyes, but I really don't give a fuck.

Before knocking on her door, I take in a few deep breaths.

There's no answer, but her car's here, so she must be in. I knock again, harder this time, and a light flicks on in the hallway.

The door opens slowly. "Cal." She runs a hand over her messy hair and tightens the ponytail. "I wasn't expecting you. Everything all right?"

"Can I come in?"

She pulls her cardigan together, covering the stain on her top and stands to the side, allowing me to enter. Her hallway is smaller than mine in my old apartment. I stumble over a small shoe and a school bag that's dumped at the side.

Walking into her living room, it's simple but homely. She fluffs a cushion and waves her hand for me to sit. There's a glass of red on the coffee table and a half empty bottle along with a book. "Can I get you a drink or anything?"

I shake my head, dragging a hand over my face. She spins on her heel, but I catch her wrist, her breath hitches and her green eyes latch onto mine.

"Is he in bed? I want to see him." I was hoping I'd get to give him a bottle or tuck him in.

"He's at Justin's tonight."

"What? You wouldn't let me spend time alone with my son, but you let Jumped-up fucking Justin have him overnight?" My fist clenches, thinking of him with golden balls. I stand and pull my keys from my pocket as I walk towards the door.

"Where are you going?"

"To get my son."

"Cal, it's late. You can see him tomorrow."

"You've already stolen five months from me. I won't give up any more time. Don't ask me to." I swing open her front door.

"Wait. Please." She slips on her pumps in the small hallway. My chest grows tighter with every passing second my boy's with *him*.

I get into Mum's Peugeot. My leg shakes waiting for her to lock her door. Could she go any fucking slower?

She slips into the passenger seat, and I press on the accelerator before she buckles up, speeding off the drive. I can't get there quick enough. The sooner I get Caleb, the better. I can't think straight knowing he's with him.

"What the fuck is he doing at Justin's, anyway?"

"He came to pick the kids up and I wasn't feeling too well. He offered to have him for the night as he's off work tomorrow. Gives me a break."

"If anyone should have him for the night, it's me. I'm his fucking dad." I glance at her, taking my eyes off the darkening road for a second.

"Well, you haven't been here, Cal. Justin helps me out sometimes. How do you think it's been for me? Alone."

I take the corner too fast, accelerating with clenched fists wrapped around the steering wheel. "How the fuck do you think it's been for me, Steph? Don't you think this has destroyed me?"

"I'm sorry. I never meant to hurt anyone, least of all you, but Justin's been there for me."

"If boy fucking wonder is so perfect, why the hell did you keep turning up at my door? Did you even mean all that shit you wrote in that book?"

"You know I did."

The leather creaks under me as I shift in the seat. My chest burns thinking that he would hold on to Justin's finger and look upon him as his daddy with those big brown eyes.

It should have been me rubbing her back after a long day, running her a bath, holding her hair back when she had morning sickness. It should have been my hands on her belly, not his. I slam my palm against the leather on the steering wheel.

Steph flinches. "Let's go home, Cal. It's late. You can stay the night and we can stay up and talk like we used to."

Talking's the last thing I want to do. The whole time I was pining for her, and she was playing happy fucking families with my son. The one woman I love most has betrayed me in the worst possible way.

"I don't want to talk. All I want to do is hold my boy."

The brakes screech as I pull up outside her old house. "I take it he still lives here?"

She nods with a blotchy face, sniffling on her cardigan sleeve. "Please, Cal. He'll be asleep now." She wipes her eye, smearing the black streaks on her face across her cheek. "You don't even have a car seat."

"So? We'll get golden balls car seat. I can see it from here in his fucking Mercedes. He won't be needing it again."

"Cal, let's just go home. We can get him tomorrow. He's safe here. It's like a second home. Justin loves him. He treats him no different to Cassie or Cairen, even though he's not his."

"That will never be his home. His home is with me." I step out of the car and slam the door.

She follows, dragging me back down the drive, tugging on my t-shirt. "Cal, no. Please."

I ignore her and shrug her from me. "I can't believe you, Steph. He's mine. Mine. Not his."

"Please, Cal, don't do this, not here, not now."

It's no use however much she begs. I can't stand him being in this house. I won't be forced to spend any more time away from him. At the moment, I can barely look at her. I never thought I'd feel this way about her. Can't she see what this is doing to me?

My knuckles rasp on the door.

Keys jingle on the other side. Justin flings the door open. His face turns red, his eyes narrow to thin slits, and he speaks as if spitting venom. "You have some fucking nerve coming here, you fucking bastard!"

My head flings back as Justin's fist collides with my face. I stumble back on my heels, then I'm lifted off my feet and thrown against the wall. There's a ringing in my ears and everything is hazy.

"Please Justin, don't hurt him," Steph shrieks.

Justin slaps my cheek. "What's wrong, Steph? Don't you want me to ruin his pretty face? Don't worry, I won't hurt him…much."

I should have expected Justin to lamp me. I'll let him have that. It's what I would do. Fuck, if she'd been mine, and some bloke had her, I would have fucking lost my shit. He'd be on the floor, or in a hospital bed. I can't blame him for that.

Heat floods from my nose, filling my mouth with a metallic taste. Red drips onto my shirt. Fuck, my nose is bust. "I just want my son."

"Your son?" Justin's voice chokes.

The cool brick touches the bare of my back where my shirts rode up, causing an icy shiver.

Justin grips my t-shirt tighter, forcing me back against the wall. "That kid doesn't even fucking know you."

"Justin, let him go, please." Steph's voice cries out in the background. "Let's go inside. We can all talk about this."

Justin pushes me harder against the brick. "We're talking about it here, Steph. I don't want this prick's blood all over my cream carpets."

I lick my lips as more blood trickles down. "It's not my fault he doesn't know me. I only found out he existed four days ago."

"Serves you right for fucking with my wife. Were you fucking her the whole time you worked together?"

He wants answers, but it's not my place to say anything. Steph stares at me, her eyes pleading with me to stay silent. She wants me to keep my mouth shut and not make this scenario any worse than it is.

"I just want my son, then I'll go."

"What sort of man are you? Fucking with my wife and abandoning her when she needed you. It's the second time I've had to pick up the pieces after you. You piece of shit." He lets go of my shirt, but not before shoving me. "If you care for him, crawl back under that rock where you came from. He's doing just fine without you."

I stand up straight, wiping my nose. "I'm not crawling anywhere till I have my son." My fists tighten, ready to unleash all the hate I have for Justin.

CHAPTER Twenty

CAL

The redhead appears at Justin's side. "Caleb's sleeping. Why don't you come back in the morning, or we can drop him off?" Her voice is soft. A stark contrast to Justin.

I wipe my nose on my arm, smearing the blood across my skin. "I want to see him."

Justin deflates his chest and steps back, allowing me room to enter the house.

Walking into the hall, I take the stairs two steps at a time, using my top to wipe the blood from my nose. Once at the top of the stairs, it's obvious which room's his. The door is ajar with a soft glow shining through the gap. I creep inside the small room lit by a night light on the baby monitor.

He's sleeping in his cot like an angel. I fall to my knees as my legs give way and tears burn like acid in my eyes. I hold back the emotion and my throat prickles. Justin was right. I fucking hate him, but I won't wake my son from this peaceful sleep into this fucking nightmare of our reality.

I sit still, watching him suckle on his dummy. His eyelids flicker, his black hair is all mussed and wild. I never thought I'd have anything else in this world that I treasured like my girls, but I was wrong.

He's like a rare jewel that I held once before it was taken from me. Now God's given me another, and I'll be damned if anyone is gonna take this away from me.

As my blurry gaze floats upwards, Steph is hovering above me. She kneels, wrapping her arms around me.

I wipe my eyes. "I'm not gonna wake him." My voice is a whisper. She stands and holds her hand out to me, and I use it to pull myself up. We walk down the stairs to Justin in the hallway with a tense jaw and blue piercing eyes like shards of glass following my every move.

I stare back as I walk out the door, back to my car. Steph apologises to Justin and Maxine before getting into the passenger seat.

All I want to do is bring my son home, but I don't even have a fucking car seat, let alone anywhere for him to sleep. How fucking stupid. What was I thinking?

The drive is quiet. Steph glares out the window into the dark night, illuminated by street lamps as we drive through town. Thank fuck she's stopped crying. I just don't have the energy to deal with her at the moment.

I pull up at the traffic lights, and she turns to me. "How's your face?"

"Fine," I snap.

"Can I see?" She leans over and touches my cheek, causing me to flinch as if her touch stings, no longer igniting me like she used to. She's caused nothing but headaches these last few days.

"Your eye's cut." She reaches over again to touch the wound. Her words are like venom, and I swat her hand away, revving the engine once the lights turn green. I couldn't give a fuck about my eye or nose or anything. Nothing feels worse than the emptiness inside.

"Do you still love Justin?" I glance her way for a second, taking my eyes off the road.

Her eyebrows pinch. "No. Why would I?"

"Why not? You were desperate to stay with him before. Nothing I did would entice you away from him. What's changed?"

"I want to be with you. I've always wanted to be with you."

She says it so matter of fact, like I should already know, like she hasn't been pushing me away for the last two years. "Funny that, because you've had plenty of opportunities."

"I tried to contact you. We've been through this. When I saw you at the wedding, I thought you'd come home to me; that you wanted to be with us."

"I don't want to be with you." A wave of adrenaline shoots through me as I spit out the words.

"What?" She blinks rapidly and shakes her head. "After all the times you asked me to leave him? I thought you'd be happy?"

"Yeah. I'm fucking ecstatic. It's just a shame that now I know how selfish you are."

"Are you serious?" She stares at me in disbelief.

"I'm sorry, Steph, but I can't forgive you."

"You can't forgive me? You're the one at fault here, not me. I'm not the one that disappeared without a trace. And I've had to go it alone because you were too selfish."

"You've let me miss out on my son's life after everything I went through with Jax. If I hadn't gone to that wedding, would I have ever known?"

"I tried. How many times do I have to tell you?"

A puff of air escapes through my clenched jaw. "You didn't try hard enough. You probably didn't want me ruining your perfect fucking life."

"How can you say that? Nothing was perfect."

"Yeah, I know that, or you wouldn't have been fucking me. You just wanted people to think it was perfect. Just like your fucking mother. See if Justin will have you back, because I sure as hell won't."

"You heartless bastard."

"That's rich. I'm heartless? Says you, who used me for a good time, chewed me up and spat me out. You're probably only here because he doesn't want you now he's shacked up with that red-headed bird. I'm nobody's second, Steph."

I slow down as I come to another red light. She yanks the handle, and the door flies open.

"What are you doing?"

"Stop the car." Her words muffle through her sobs. She steps out before the car comes to a stop, and I slam on the brakes. She turns back to me before slamming the door. "You were always my first."

Fuck, I wish that were true. Every time she ran back to him. She always made it clear that he came first. Even now, letting him babysit when she knew how desperate I was to spend time with Caleb before I have to go back to Australia.

Her full figure gets smaller in the rear-view mirror as I drive away into the night. What the fuck am I doing? She means everything to me, even if I can barely look at her. Maybe she's right, I should have checked in, gave her my new number, anything. Anger squeezes my insides like an iron fist crumbling my stone heart. I'm mad at myself as much as I am at her. This fucked up situation has me acting like a crazy person, and I'm mad at the world.

Before Steph disappears into the distance, I make a sharp u-turn, and speed back down the road towards her. I might be mad, but I won't leave her alone again.

STEPH

I'VE MADE SUCH a mess of things. Now I'm stuck in the middle of nowhere with no car, watching Callum speed into the night without a care in the world.

The moon tucks behind a cloud, leaving me under a blanket of darkness. I take my phone from my pocket. Please have battery life. Please. I scroll my contacts, skipping past Mum. I can't deal with a lecture. My sister will come for me. If she answers.

"Steph?"

Hearing her voice makes my shoulders relax, and I let out a breath. "Sam." I choke back a sob as I say her name. "Can you come and pick me up?"

"Why, where are you?"

"I'm on the edge of town."

"Have you broken down?"

I huff. Emotionally, yeah. I feel like I'm having a mental breakdown right now, or feel like breaking his friggin' neck. "No. I'll tell you when you get here. I'm walking on the side of the road."

"Let me change from my pyjamas. See you soon."

"Thanks."

As I put the phone back in my pocket, Cal's car slows at the side of me, driving at the same pace as my steps. I glare at him through the window as he winds it down.

"Get back in the car."

"Piss off." I walk faster, though I don't know why. He's in a car for frig's sake.

"Steph. Get in the fucking car. Now."

I ignore him and pull my cardigan around my body to keep out the cool night air. As if shouting at me is going to make me comply.

"I'm sorry. Okay?"

I stop and face him. He slows the car to a halt.

"I'm not going anywhere with you. I'm not getting back in your car."

"What are you gonna do? Walk home? Let me take you home. I won't talk."

"There's no need. My sister's coming so you can fuck off."

"Fine. I'll wait until she gets here."

"You can wait, but I'm not getting in the car."

Sam pulls up, and I get in the passenger seat, glaring at Cal. As he spins his car around, I exhale and focus on my breathing, trying not to cry in front of my sister.

The radio plays late night love songs. That's all I friggin' need. I press the button for the next station. Rock radio. No, thank you. The next station tunes in to agony aunt Annie. I huff, thinking I should probably call her.

A poor bloke talks about his impotence and how his wife left him, and I'm comforted that someone has bigger problems than me, or not so big as it would seem. I should send him some of my spam emails. I must get three a day trying to flog me Viagra pills.

Next up is a woman struggling financially after her husband's passing. There's nothing like listening to other people's problems to put things into perspective.

"Are you going to tell me what's going on and who was in the car?" Sam parks outside my house, and I tell her everything.

When I walk into the living room, I kick off my pumps and drop like a lead weight into the sofa. I hug a cushion as my body curls into the foetal position, picturing Callum as he told me he didn't want me. I should be used to hearing those words by now.

The hurt in his eyes when he crumpled in front of Caleb's travel cot. I wouldn't hurt my worst enemy like that, let alone a man I love, even though I try so hard to hate him. He doesn't deserve this. I can't help thinking if only I'd have done more. Everything plays out in my head, thinking of what I could have done.

There was a moment when I saw him at the wedding, I thought, finally we can be together. How wrong was I. He'll never want me now. Reaching to the coffee table, I top my glass up with the remaining red wine… I need another bottle.

***

MY HEAD THROBS to the beat of knocking on the living room window. I sit up, wiping the drool from my mouth and open the curtain to a bright sun and Cal in his black attire, stuffing his hands in his pockets as he scowls at me through the glass.

I glance at the clock on the fireplace as I turn. How have I slept in so late? My leg bangs into the coffee table, causing the empty bottles of wine and gin to clink, and I realise the nightmare I had last night is my life.

I unlock the door and open it, bracing myself for another fight, although my head is delicate, and I don't have the energy.

His eyes move from my head to my toes, but not in his usual lustful way. "You look like shit. Do you realise it's the middle of the day?" He barges in before I offer an invitation.

"Nice to see you too," I say, closing the door.

He walks into my kitchen, eyeing the dirty dishes on the side. "Have you been drinking all night?"

"So, what do you care?" I fold my arms across my chest, then wince at the pressure on my full breasts like two water balloons ready to burst at any moment.

"Where's Caleb?"

I yawn and cover my mouth with my hand. "Justin hasn't brought them home yet."

He huffs. "Good. Look at the state of you. You're hungover."

I look down at the two ring stains around my nipples and pull the cardigan around my body, holding it in place.

He walks into the living room, inspecting the empty bottles. "You need to get yourself sorted out, Steph. This isn't like you."

"Piss off. You don't know me or what I'm like. You never stuck around long enough to pick up the pieces after ruining me the first time."

"If this is you, I think Caleb should come and stay with me. Permanently. You started drinking a lot when we were at uni. I've grown up in a house with a drunk parent. I don't want that for my kid."

"You don't have the right to take him away from me." Crescents imprint into my palms as I clench my fists.

"I have every right." He pulls his phone from his pocket and taps the screen, then holds it up to my face.

The words on the screen blur. "What's this?"

"My parental rights."

I snatch the phone from him to read the email properly. The screen shakes in my trembling hand. "You did a paternity test?" Water leaks from my eyes. I thought I was all cried out after last night. "You doubted he was yours?" My voice croaks out the words.

"I never doubted it. The first time I held him, I knew he was mine. I wanted to make sure you knew. You were being so fucking difficult. I won't have you tell me when and where I can see my son."

"When did you even do the test?" How can he do this behind my back?

"It was at the park when you went to get ice creams. I ordered a fast tracked test the day before. I had to make sure I could see him."

"What did you do? Did it hurt him?" My throat is sore and scratchy when I speak.

"No, it was just a mouth swab. He was fine. I wouldn't hurt my own kid. I was scared you'd make things difficult for me."

"I wasn't meaning to be difficult. I was trying to protect him."

"Protect him from what? I'm his fucking dad."

"And how do you think it's going to affect him each time you leave to go back to your other family? I was trying to shield him from abandonment. You said yourself you're going back next week. I never want him to feel what I felt each time you left me."

He rubs his middle finger over his eyebrow. "I'm sorry."

"You don't have to be sorry. I blame myself." I hate myself for allowing him to worm his way into my life. Every time I give him my heart, I know he won't take care of it properly, but I keep giving it to him, anyway. If I can shield my son from that, then I will.

The sour residue of alcohol lingers on my tongue. I stare into the living room mirror at yesterday's stained clothes, lifting my lank, greasy hair. My repulsive reflection contrasts the gold edged ornate mirror.

With anger spiking and shooting out into every limb, I grab the empty bottle of wine from the coffee table and throw it at the drab shadow of myself on the wall.

Glass shatters all around me from the bottle and mirror as it falls out of the frame. My legs cave. I drop to a heap on the floor, feeling the shards of glass beneath me. My shoulders rock as I sob uncontrollably, and I hide my face with my hands.

"Fucking hell, Steph, what the fuck are you doing?" Cal steps towards me, crunching the glass with his boots against the laminate flooring. Crouching, he wraps his arms around me, which only makes me worse.

I inhale the mint of his shampoo and the scent of his aftershave. The scruff on his jaw scratches my cheek, and I reminisce about all the things that will never be. I want to fight him, tell him to leave me alone and not touch me, but my body doesn't have the energy and my broken heart still thinks he holds the missing piece.

He hooks his arm under mine and lifts me to my feet. "Watch your step."

With bare feet, I lean on Cal as he helps me to the bedroom. I sit on the bed, and he kneels before me, picking the glass from my leggings.

"You've made a right fucking mess of your legs."

"I don't care." I cover my face with my arm so I don't have to face him.

"Steph, you're bleeding. Take these off." He steps out of the room, and I peel away yesterday's leggings. Blood trickles down my prickly legs, but I don't feel any pain. I'm numb, just going through the motions until I can sleep and leave the nightmare reality I'm living. Cal returns with a washcloth and a first-aid kit from my bathroom. He kneels in front of me, wiping my blood stained skin.

My legs shake as he runs the cloth over my knee, and I tug my cardigan down to cover my thighs.

"Not your brightest idea, was it?"

"Don't patronise me." I shove his hand from my knee, but he grips it firmly and holds a cotton pad from the first-aid kit against my shin.

"It's just the kids, Steph. What if one of the kids treads on a loose piece of glass? I have to clean that fucking room from top to bottom now. It's all over the fucking settee and everything."

"Just go. I'll clean it." I try to move my legs to the side, but he holds them firmly in place as he wraps a bandage around my foot.

"I'll fucking clean it," he growls, tying off the bandage. "What about the seven years' bad luck?"

My eyes flick to his. "It was the mirror or your face. Besides, the next seven years can't possibly be worse than how things are now." I wipe my sniffling nose with my hand. "Please stop going on. I'm so tired, Cal."

He stands and pulls the duvet down. "Sleep it off. I'll see to everything."

"I can't. The kids will be home soon. Justin."

"I can handle Justin."

"Like you handled him last night? He hurt you." The graze around his eye has almost disappeared, but there's a purple hue on his temple.

"I let him have that, but if he starts anything again, he'll fucking get it." Cal wipes my tear-stained cheeks. "Get some sleep."

Milk leaks from my painfully swollen breasts, and I open the cardigan to two wet patches. "I need my pump."

"Where is it?" He rests his palms on the bed on either side of me, caging me in as he pushes himself up and stands. I point to the dressing table, and he strides over, collecting my pump and handing it to me.

He watches me fumble with the bottle and connect the pump to the electric point behind the bedside table.

I glare at him. "Privacy? Or are you going to watch?" I already have my legs on display. He doesn't need to see any more.

He huffs, rolling his eyes but walks out of the room, leaving me alone to take my wet bra off and secure the pump under my t-shirt. The pain from my swelled breast eases as it drains into the bottle attached to the pump, though it sickens me to know I'll have to throw this milk away because of my alcohol consumption. What a waste.

The house phone rings. I lean over the bed, glimpsing the screen on my bedside table. It's my mother. I wondered how long before Sam or Justin updated her. I can't deal with her right now.

The ringing stops, and I relax listening to the sound of the pump, although she'll only ring again, or turn up at the house at some point.

A minute later, Cal enters the bedroom, holding another handset with my mother on speaker. "Put her on this instant."

I shake my head. My eyes plead with him to make an excuse for me.

"She isn't feeling well," he says into my handset, but narrows his eyes at me.

"I want to speak to her, not you." There's venom in her words. I always knew she disliked Callum, but I can really hear the hatred in her voice.

"She's asleep, Sue."

"Where is she?"

"In bed."

"Who's bed, hers or yours?"

He huffs. "She definitely isn't in mine, I can assure you."

"How dare you? You think you can turn her life upside down, then leave her like you always do. She's going to see your true colours one of these days."

"Bye Sue." He cancels the call. "Your mum hasn't changed then?"

It was actually refreshing to hear my mum in my corner. I didn't know she cared. Was she actually sticking up for me? For me and not because it's making her look bad at church or with her friends.

"There's a text from Justin, too." He hands me my mobile.

I snatch it from him and read the text.

'I'll pick the kids up from school, then drop off at yours.'

Cal's body stiffens. I can tell he's not happy, as he storms out of the room in a huff. A few minutes later, I hear the hoover downstairs. I swap the pump to the other side now I've deflated one boob. Justin will be here soon, and I really could do with a wash.

CAL

I HEAR THE DOOR. Cassie and Cairen run into the house, followed by Justin, carrying Caleb. I turn off the hoover. "Be careful in here. There's broken glass."

"What happened?" Justin focuses on the broken mirror, with half of the glass missing. The remaining glass could fall out at any moment. "Did you do this?"

"No." Who does this prick think he is?

He puffs his chest out and tenses his jaw. "You need to make sure there's no glass about before Caleb plays on the floor."

"Yeah, what's it look like I'm doing?" If he wasn't holding my son, I'd lamp the smug bastard.

"Where's Steph?"

"Bedroom."

The kids run upstairs, and I walk towards him to take Caleb. He reluctantly lets him go at the waist.

"Ay-up mate. Remember me?" I hold him in my arms, and his little hand touches my face, making everything seem right in the world.

The red-head appears at the side of Justin, stroking over the vein on his tensed forearm with a pained look on her face. "Let's go, Justin."

Justin glares at me and cracks his neck. I don't know what he's more upset about; sleeping with his wife or showing up at his house last night. If looks could kill, I'd be dead. I can't blame him.

"Maxine." Steph's voice is quiet as she steps into the room. "Justin."

Her eyes weep again, glistening as the afternoon sun shines through the window.

"Are you okay, Steph?" Maxine asks.

Justin tenses looking between Steph and I.

"I'm fine," Steph whispers, looking down at her legs covered in pink jogging bottoms. Her shoulders curl inwards, and she fiddles with the sleeve of a clean jumper she's now wearing.

"You know where we are if you need us." Maxine walks past Steph, followed by Justin.

The door slams behind them, sending a rattle through the house.

Steph shuffles on her feet. I've never seen her look so deflated. Even her tits have shrunk in size. Another tear rolls down her cheek, and even though I'm still furious with her, I can't bear to see her like this.

I step forward with Caleb in my arms, and lift her chin to look me in the eye. "I was gonna take Caleb to see my mum."

"I'm not really comfortable with you taking him. He doesn't really know you."

I grind my teeth and count to ten in my head. "How will he get to know me and my family if he doesn't spend time with us?"

The little lad pats my face, and I kiss his tiny hand, blowing raspberries on his fingers.

"I didn't mean to go behind your back with the paternity test." I sigh, not wanting to argue with her anymore. "An hour here and there isn't enough for me. I want to tuck him in at night, feed him, play with him, be there for him. Let me be his dad, Steph. I'm begging you. I'm not my father."

"Fine. There's frozen milk in the freezer. And some baby food in the cupboard."

"I don't have to go today. I can go tomorrow. You come with me if you like while your kids are at school."

"I'm starting back at work tomorrow. It's my first day back after being off for six months."

"I thought you got like a year for maternity these days?"

"That's nice for some, but I can't afford to take a year off."

"Who's looking after Caleb while you're at work?"

"Mum was going to have him. I'm only going back three days a week."

"I'll have him. I'll take him to see Mum and the girls tomorrow. Have an hour if you like. I'll watch the kids."

"Thank you."

She disappears back upstairs, and I strap Caleb in his highchair while I remove the mirror and hoover the rest of the living room, making sure there's no glass left.

STEPH

When I wake from my nap, I turn my phone on to check the time and have nine missed calls from my mother. Great. I've slept the day away, although it's still light out.

With heavy limbs, I walk downstairs past a laundry basket full of folded clothes. The fresh linen scent fills the hallway and the tidy kitchen. Is this my house?

The lounge door is ajar. I peer through to see him and the kids watching a movie while Caleb sleeps next to him on the sofa.

He laughs at something on the TV along with the kids. I imagine this is our life and I could curl up next to him and watch Netflix and chill. All that's missing from this picture are his girls. Guilt claws at my stomach when I think about how selfish I've been today. He could have been spending time with his mum and girls before he goes back to Australia, but he's been babysitting my kids.

"Hey." He notices me and leans forward. "How are you feeling?"

"Good." I nod. "Well, better."

"I made you some dinner. It's in the microwave. Are you hungry?"

"Starving." I hadn't even realised I haven't eaten since yesterday, but with the mention of food, my stomach has suddenly woken up.

"Cassie, will you watch Caleb for a minute?" He gets up from the sofa and follows me into the kitchen. I open the microwave expecting nuggets and chips or something. "You cooked a pasta bake?"

"Yeah, I wasn't gonna let your kids starve. Sit down, I'll warm it for you."

"Thank you." I sit at the kitchen table and he brings my warm plate over and sits next to me, watching me eat.

"Thank you for cleaning up my mess."

"It's fine. I feel I caused the mess, so the least I can do is clean your house."

"This is good." I scoop up a few more spirals in the tomato sauce.

He waves a hand towards the cupboards. "It was just a jar from your cupboard."

"When do you have to go?"

"Are you desperate to get rid of me?" He smiles and winks. "I'll stay longer if you want to take a bath."

"I meant, when do you return to Australia?" Was that his polite way of saying I need a wash?

He runs a hand over his face like he doesn't want to think about that. "I'm not sure. I should have gone back last week. The girls are missing school now. Priya wants them home. Obviously, she misses them, but she understands why I wanted to stay longer."

I nod and continue shovelling the pasta into my mouth before Caleb wakes up. My breasts are rock hard again. Caleb will want a feed soon.

"You really look like shit, you know."

"I feel it. I haven't cleaned my teeth in two days."

"I'll run you a bath." He leaves the kitchen and heads upstairs to the bathroom while I finish the plate.

I check on Caleb and the kids in the living room, watching a movie. "Everything all right?" Caleb is still asleep on the sofa, and Cassie is sitting next to him now.

"Mum, why is your friend here? Are you poorly?" Cassie asks.

"I haven't felt too good today. Has everything been all right with Callum?" They clearly don't know the truth yet about him being Caleb's dad.

"Yeah, he's kinda fun," Cairen says, making my shoulders relax.

"I'm just going in the bath. Will you be all right to watch Caleb until Cal comes down?"

Cassie nods.

The smell of coconuts gets stronger with each step I climb, and Cal walks out of the bathroom.

"Your bath's ready." He runs a hand through his hair, pulling it back from his face, and peers at me with his deep brown eyes. "Do you want me to take your bandage off?"

"It's fine. I can deal with it." Bubbles fill the bath like a snowy mountain landscape.

Cal stands in the doorway. "If it bleeds again, I'll redress your foot. In fact, try to keep your left leg out of the tub."

"Okay." I wait for him to go, but he just stands there in the doorway, biting his lip.

"Are you going to watch me get undressed or what?"

"Oh yeah, sorry." He turns around and closes the door behind him.

He's clearly feeling guilty for how he treated me last night. I like him this way when he's all attentive and kind. It's the Callum I fell in love with. I peel off the bloodstained cotton pad he attached to my shin, but leave the bandage on my left foot as I step into the tub with my right, trying to keep my other leg dry and let it dangle over the side.

Once my hair is washed, I lie back, closing my eyes, and sink further into the water until it touches my chin. Memories of us bathing together fill my mind, and I move the flannel over my hard breasts, wishing it was his hand washing me as he always would. I could get used to having him here. Usually, I can only do this when the kids are at Justin's. Or I have to bring Caleb in with me.

A knock at the door snaps my eyes open. "Yes?"

"Just checking you haven't fallen asleep and drowned or anything," Cal says.

"No, I'm still here." Even if I fell asleep, I couldn't drown. This bath is too small to lie down in, and I'm sort of wedged in at the hips.

"Caleb's woke up. Did you want to feed him or shall I defrost another tub from the freezer?"

"I'll get out." I walk into the bedroom with a towel wrapped around my body, barely meeting in the middle. Cal folds more clothes and places a pile on my bed.

"Hey, let me look at those legs."

I tug the towel over my body, gripping it in place as he kneels in front of me, inspecting my shin. His hand runs over my wet, prickly unshaven calf, making my skin break out in gooseflesh. Why didn't I shave?

"It looks all right. Best to let some air get to it. Leave the bandage on your foot until morning." He stands and heads back downstairs. I pop clean pyjamas on and a dressing gown.

I hear the TV in Cairen's room and poke my head around the door. "Are you getting into bed? Don't forget to clean your teeth."

He lets out a long breath as he speaks. "Yeeeeees, Mum."

"Night, night, sweetheart." I close his door and open

Cassie's. She nods her head to the music blurting out of her headphones. "Turn that down. I can hear that from here."

She tuts, taking the headphones off. "Mum, is your friend your boyfriend now?"

"No darling. He's…" I pause. I can't seem to tell them he's Caleb's dad. Not tonight. How can I explain it? "He's just helping me look after Caleb, that's all. Night, night. Don't stay up too late. It's school in the morning, and I'm back at work."

Thinking of work tomorrow, I need to tell Mum she doesn't need to babysit. I walk into the kitchen with my phone in my hand and make the dreaded call.

Mum picks up after one ring. "Stephanie? Huh. Where have you been? I've been calling you all day."

"Sorry, I wasn't feeling well."

"Yes, I heard…from *him*. What's going on? Don't tell me you're shacked up with *him* now?"

Each time she says the word him, it's like she daren't say his name, like Voldemort. "He has a name, Mum. And no. I'm not shacked up with him, but he is Caleb's dad." A lump fills my throat as I say the last line.

She hisses down the line. "Some father."

I close my eyes and hold the phone away from my head, ready for her rant.

"You should have worked things out with Justin. That man's been more of a father these past five months. You had the perfect husband, Stephanie, and you threw it all away for him. Now look where it's got you."

Justin could be an axe murderer, and she'd still think the sun shone out of his arse. She doesn't understand how he always made me feel. She makes me feel the same way, like I'm never good enough.

"Have you forgotten Justin was cheating on me, too?"

"Well, is there any wonder?"

"Mum, please. It's been a difficult few days. I don't need a lecture right now."

Cal walks into the kitchen, holding Caleb in his arms while he sucks on a rusk biscuit. I want to be the one in his arms. I need someone to hold me. His lips press into a thin line. I'm sure he can hear every word blurting out of my phone.

"You only have yourself to blame. I warned you about him. You should have stayed clear and kept your knickers on. Then you wouldn't be in this mess."

Cal steps forward and snatches the phone from me. "Sue. She doesn't need you going on at her."

I can hear Mum shouting down the handset. "Huh. She'll be needing me tomorrow though, won't she? Expecting me to babysit while she's at work. Put her on this instance."

He paces the kitchen, flaring his nostrils. "I can take care of my own son."

She screeches down the phone, but Cal cuts her off. "Bye, Sue." He cancels the call and drops my phone on the worktop. "Don't let her talk to you like that. She acts as though she's mother of the fucking year."

I wipe my cheeks, knowing I'll never own that title. Neither will my mother, but she thinks she does.

Caleb's finished the rusk and is now eating his own hand. "I need to feed him." I hold my arms out for Caleb, and he makes a gurgling noise, waving his arms like he's happy to be with me at least. *Because you're his dinner.* I carry him into the living room and get comfy on the sofa with a cushion under my arm.

He's over hungry and latches on as soon as I lift my top.

Cal sits next to me on the sofa. "I was thinking of staying the night."

"What?" My breath catches in my throat and a warmth

floods my chest that he actually wants to stay the night, or does he want to keep an eye on me?

He clears his throat. "If that's all right? I'll sleep on the couch."

"You think I'm going to have another episode while the kids are here, don't you? You think I'm a terrible mother that can't be trusted with her own kids?" I choke up and stare at Caleb. His tiny hand clings to my finger, giving me the strength I need to not cry again.

"You're a great mum." Cal's arm slides behind my neck, and he pulls me into his chest and kisses my wet hair. "But yes, I'm worried about you. Not that I think you'd hurt the kids."

I let Cal hold me close, never wanting him to let me go. I stay here for a long time, pressed against the side of his chest, listening to the beat of his heart.

Cal points to Caleb, still suckling. "He's really going to town on that, isn't he?"

A laugh rocks through me. "Did you feed him today?"

"Yeah, but he wasn't keen on that puréed jarred baby food."

"Which did you give him?"

"Cauliflower cheese, I think."

"Yeah, he's not too keen on that one."

"He kept spitting it out. I thought it was because I was feeding him."

Cal rubs his hand up and down my arm, reminding me of our days in the attic where he would hold me. All I ever wanted was to have a family with him, but I never thought it would be so friggin' complicated.

I swallow the lump in my throat and lift my head to look into his eyes. "I love you, Cal," I whisper, though it's barely audible.

He gazes back with eyes rich like my favourite chocolate. His fingers still stroking my arm. "I love you, Steph."

I gulp, shocked that he said the words back. My lips inch close to his. I want him to kiss me and make everything better. He must know I want to kiss him. I inch closer still, hoping he'll meet my lips.

He flinches his head back. "I just can't forgive you."

The words leave his mouth like flecks of glass prickling my skin as they did this morning. My heart sinks. I pull away and stand with Caleb in my arms. "I'm going to bed."

He grabs my hand. "I'm trying, Steph. I'm really fucking trying."

"So am I." I trudge upstairs. I'm trying to keep myself together. When the kids are around, I try to act normal and get out of bed every morning. Tomorrow, I'll need to focus at work and try not to lose my job along with everything else.

CAL

CALEB'S WHIMPER stirs me awake.

"Time to get up for school," Steph's voice travels down the stairs. I sit up from the sofa, pull the throw off and head towards the kitchen to boil the kettle.

Steph walks into the kitchen, carrying Caleb. "Morning."

"Morning." I yawn, taking her in. She has some colour to her cheeks and looks refreshed. Her blouse stretches around her breasts, and her skirt hugs her full-figure.

She follows my eyes as they rake her body, looking down at her nude tights that camouflage the cut on her leg. "Do I look okay? None of my work clothes fit like they used to. Everything's tight."

"You look fine." She looks more than fine. I always loved

her in clothes that gripped her big tits and ass. My head bobs towards her shoes. "How's your foot?"

"It's not bleeding anymore."

Caleb holds his arms out to me, opening and closing his fists. "He wants you," Steph says as she hands him to me.

My chest swells, and a warmth spreads through my body. "Hey, little dude." I hold him in my arms, gazing into his brown eyes.

"He's been fed. There's some fresh milk I pumped out this morning on the bedside table, and I'll feed him again when I get home." Steph wipes the drool from his chin with the small bib around his neck. "You're spending the day with Daddy, aren't you?" she says in her cute voice she uses when talking to Caleb.

Hearing the words 'Daddy' gives me an adrenaline rush, making me feel fully awake without the need for coffee. "We'll have a great time, won't we, mate? We'll see your sisters and Nanny, aye?"

The kids come into the kitchen in their school uniforms, and Steph pours them cereal as they sit at the table.

"I'll drop the kids at school on my way to work. Justin's picking them up as they're staying at his tonight. I'll leave the car seat in the hall for you. Do you want me to collect him from your mum's after work?" She stares at the clock on the kitchen wall.

"I'll drive back over and stay the night again if it's all right? I want to spend as much time with him as possible before I go back to Australia next week."

"What about your girls?" She bites on a nail with chipped pink varnish.

"They're okay. They're having the time of their life with their nanny. You know she lets them get away with murder, right?" A puff of laughter leaves my lips. "It'll be the same with this little munchkin." I tickle Caleb's tummy and he lets out the cutest giggle, showing those dimples of his that remind me of Steph.

"If I leave you my house key, will you be here when I come home?"

"Yeah, I'll make sure I'm here for five."

She walks into the hall and takes her key from the bunch and leaves it on the counter.

"Mum, where's my leotard for gymnastics?" Cassie asks.

Steph palms her forehead. "Oh no. I forgot about gymnastics. Is it not in your wardrobe?"

Cassie shrugs her shoulders while slipping on her shoes at the bottom of the stairs.

"Is it a light blue one?" I remember folding something yesterday.

"Yes, have you seen it?"

"Just check in the wash basket at the bottom of the stairs." I point towards the hall. Cairen places his empty bowl in the sink and turns around with milk stains on his school jumper.

Steph huffs and wipes it with a kitchen roll, glancing at the clock. "Get your book bag. I don't want to be late on my first day."

Cairen runs upstairs for his bag. Cassie walks to the car parked in the driveway, and Steph unlocks it with the key fob. "Right. If you need me for anything, just call work." She checks the time again.

"Steph. Don't worry. We'll be fine. I've kept two girls alive." I give her a wide grin, and she relaxes her shoulders.

"Have fun with Daddy," she says.

Cairen barges past me, knocking my legs with his Star Wars bag. "Daddy?" He scowls at me, as though I'm Darth Vader himself, before stomping to the car.

Steph sighs and closes her eyes, knowing she'll have to deal with him on the school run. I don't envy her, but they had to know sooner or later.

I squeeze her arm. "He'll get over it."

She gives me a half smile and pecks Caleb on the forehead, stroking his dark hair as I hold him in my arms. She locks eyes with me as if she was about to give me a goodbye kiss, too, but quickly turns away. "Bye."

"Steph." I grab her arm before she walks out the door.

She turns around and swallows. Her chest rises before me as her breathing quickens. "Yes?"

I'm torn between a betrayed heart and mind that won't forgive her for what she's done, but my soul's drawn to her. "Have a good day at work."

"Thanks." She gets into her car, and I stand in the doorway waving her off with our son in my arms. There was a time when I wanted us to be a family. I wanted to be her man and make her happy.

Now when I look at her, I get a sour taste in my mouth. If she'd told my mum about Caleb, things would have been different.

I want to forgive her. I wanted to pull her towards me and take her lips, smear that red lipstick across her cheek while she begs me to fuck her, but I can't. Something in me wants her to suffer like she's made me suffer. This whole time I've been pining for her, and she's been living her life without a single thought for me. Does she even care?

She tortured me each time she went back with that prick of a husband, and then she left him and never even thought to tell me, not to mention had our son. Is it her way of getting revenge for how I treated her at uni? I never thought she could hurt me like this.

STEPH

MY FIRST WEEK back at work went quick, despite Kelly still on her honeymoon. It's been so long since I had a holiday or a night out. Obviously, when Mark texted telling me he's back in the city for work, lecturing at the university, I jumped at the chance to go out. He's been up a few times since I met him on the art and wine course. I even let him paint me when I was pregnant. He still hasn't shown me the painting, though. Says he's still working on it.

"Who are you going out with tonight?" Cal asks, leaning against the bedroom doorjamb while Caleb plays on the bed, trying to get to the products in my clear makeup bag.

I pull a green dress from the hanger. "Just a friend." I daren't tell him about Mark. They hated each other at uni.

He stands straight. "Male or female?"

I turn around to face him. Is he jealous? "Male. Why?"

He shrugs a shoulder all nonchalant, but the tightening of his jaw doesn't go unnoticed. "You're not wearing that, are you?" He waves a hand towards the dress in my hand.

"Yes, so?"

"I think you should wear jeans."

"Piss off and let me pass. I don't want to be late."

"That black dress would look better."

"What black dress?" Is he actually being helpful now? His moods are giving me whiplash. If he's trying to help me now, that only makes me feel worse, knowing he's not affected by me going out with another man. Even if Mark is a friend.

Cal clears his throat and pulls out a black dress from my wardrobe.

"Are you kidding? That's something I'd wear for work."

"It suits you."

"Piss off. I'm not wearing that for a night out."

He looks through the rest of my clothes while I slip into the bathroom to change into the green dress.

"You don't want to give off the wrong impression," he shouts from the bedroom.

I step out of the bathroom, smoothing the dress down over my thighs. "What do you mean?"

He swallows and looks me up and down. "You look like you're desperate. Trying too hard."

"Don't be daft. I wore this dress for you before when we worked together, and you liked it." I spray my best perfume on my pulse points. The fruity scent fills the room.

He huffs. "You were desperate then."

I slam the bottle down on the dressing table. "How dare you? I don't remember you complaining."

"I wasn't. I just don't want you throwing yourself at the first guy who shows you any attention."

"I'll do whatever I like, and if you don't like it, piss off back to Australia."

He bites on the inside of his mouth, picks Caleb up from the bed, and walks downstairs just as the doorbell rings. "I'll get it," he shouts.

My chest tightens as panic sets in, and I scramble to find my matching shoes and clutch purse.

CAL

The hairs stiffen on the back of my neck as I open the door with Caleb in my arms. "What the fuck are you doing here?" I freeze, giving him an icy stare while breathing through my nostrils.

Mark smirks, pats the side of my arm. "Nice to see you too, Cal. I'm here to take Steph out. Is she ready?" He pokes his head around me, trying to get a glimpse of her.

I grind my teeth with a tense jaw, taking in what's happening. "Over my dead body."

Mark straightens the cuff of his shirt. "I can probably arrange that." He steps over the threshold, but I block him from entering further.

"I thought I got rid of you once."

He chuckles again, and with each laugh, I want to punch this fucker in the mouth. "If you took care of your woman, I wouldn't be back."

If I didn't have Caleb in my arms. I'd wipe that smirk off his face. "If you lay one finger on her, I'll fucking kill you."

"Are you jealous? Because if you wanna take her out tonight instead, I'll gladly step aside. I'll even babysit for you."

Steph appears behind me, and I look into her green eyes, filling with sadness at my silence.

Mark stuffs his hands in his pocket. "I didn't think so. Let's go, Steph."

Mark saunters back down the driveway, unlocking his BMW with a flick of his key.

"What the fuck are you doing going out with him?" I grip her arm.

She glances at my fist tight around her. I loosen a little, but don't let go.

"We're friends. He offered to take me out." She yanks her arm from my grasp. "I don't see anyone else offering. Am I not allowed to have a bit of fun?"

I huff. "Fun. With him? Seriously?"

"Who else is there, Cal? You haven't taken me on a date in years. Even when we were screwing, I don't remember you taking me on a date. Unless you class that trip to the cinema and Maccy's a date which, just so we're clear, it wasn't." A red hue creeps over her face, and her knuckles turn white as she grips her purse.

I lift my arm over her and lean on the wall, caging her in. "If you'd left that dickhead of a husband sooner, I'd have had the chance to take you out."

Caleb whimpers. His bottom lip wobbles.

"Have you finished? You're scaring our son." She spits the words.

"Shh, shh, shh. It's all right, mate." I bounce him in my arms while glaring at her.

"Can I go now?" She stares with a red face, ready to blow fire from her nostrils at any minute.

I step back, allowing her to pass and watch her ass sway from side to side as she stomps down the drive in her heels.

STEPH

SLIDING INTO THE PASSENGER SEAT, Mark turns the key, and his car comes to life. Cal's at the front door, scowling as we drive off.

"Is he still staring?" Mark asks.

"Yep."

"Oh, he's pissed." Mark chuckles.

"Do you think it's you or jealousy?"

"I think he'd be the same with anyone. It's obvious there's something there. I don't know if he still wants you, but he doesn't want anyone else to have you. Least of all me."

I let out a long breath and fiddle with the button on my bag. "I don't know how to get him back."

"Let him stew for a while. It won't hurt him. Maybe he'll realise what a good thing he's missing." Mark glances at me and winks.

"It's great to see you. Thanks for coming over. It's been so long since I actually had a date with a guy. Even if…well, it's still nice to go out."

He laughs. "Even if it's not a proper date because you're not getting laid at the end, you mean."

I giggle. "You know, at my age, I honestly can't think of anything worse. Other than Cal and my ex, I haven't slept with another man in over twenty years and, to be honest, I don't want to. The thought of getting naked in front of someone new turns my stomach in a bad way."

Mark glances at me before turning back to the road. "You got naked in front of me last year."

"That's different. You were painting me, and I'm pretty certain you weren't looking at my body in that way." I cover my mouth as another giggle bursts from my lips.

"You think you're safe with me because I'm queer?" He

flashes a smile. "I can still appreciate a woman's body and yours is an artist's dream, especially while you were pregnant. I can't wait to show you the painting."

"Have you finished it?"

"Yeah. I'll bring it next time I'm up this way. You can show it to Cal." He snorts with laughter.

"If you think he's pissed now, I hate to think what he'll do when he finds out I sat for you."

"You're right, maybe I'll keep hold of it for now."

We pull up at a nice restaurant on the outskirts of town, our usual spot where he took me before.

A server shows us to our table that Mark booked, and we corner the rustic country bar area with traditional wooden beams and a chalkboard on the wall.

Sitting in a cosy nook, the server lights a candle and hands us our menus. "Can I get you anything to drink, sir, madam?"

"Can I have a glass of sparkling water, please?"

"Yeah, I'll have a shandy, please," Mark says.

I giggle as the server leaves. "Right pair of lightweights, aren't we?" I'm breastfeeding, and he's driving. Not exactly hardcore party animals. I don't know what Cal thinks we're going to be getting up to.

"Do you think you and Cal can work things out?" Mark cocks an eyebrow, peering over the large A3 menu.

I slump against the table, resting my chin on the palm of my hand. "He's so difficult and stubborn. Not to mention annoying and moody." I stare at the flickering candle in a jam jar.

"But you still love him?" Mark smirks. He knows our history and how Cal would always defend me and I him. The love we have or had for each other was like no love I've ever had before or since.

"Why do I though? He's been a complete arsehole since he got back to the UK. He blames me for everything. Some days I wish he'd piss off back to Sydney, but when he goes I'll miss him."

The server returns with our drinks. "Are you ready to order?"

"The beef bourguignon, please," Mark says, handing the menu back.

"Hmm." I quickly scan the dishes. "I'll have the seabass risotto, please."

"When is he going back to Australia?"

"Next Wednesday. He delayed his flight, but the girls need to get back for school."

He squishes his eyebrows together, taking a sip of his shandy. "Isn't it the six weeks summer holidays next week?"

"Not in Australia. They have their summer holidays at Christmas." I shake my head. "I know it's weird, isn't it?"

"So, when's he coming back to the UK again?"

"He says next month. He reckons he can work freelance and spend a couple months in Australia and a couple months here."

"I don't envy the bloke. He's somewhere between a rock and a hard place."

"Ayers Rock." I giggle, sucking up my fizzy water with a straw.

After the meal, Mark drops me off at home around midnight.

"Thanks for everything. I've had a great night." I lean over to kiss his cheek, and Mark kisses me back on the forehead.

"Take care of yourself. I'll call you next time I'm free, and we can do it again."

I walk into the living room to see Cal watching reruns of

Game of Thrones. "I thought you would have been asleep by now."

He looks at the clock and turns the TV off. "I was getting worried about you. It's fucking late."

"Are you kidding? It's midnight."

"Yeah, and your son wanted feeding two hours ago."

"You know there's milk in the fridge that I pumped earlier. Did you feed him?"

"Of course I did, but he wouldn't settle. He wanted you and your tit. You could have texted me back."

"I didn't even get a text."

"Too busy being a slut, were you?"

"Screw you."

"No thanks, I don't do sloppy seconds."

"Cal, why are you being such a dick?"

He walks over to me and stands close, calmly saying, "If you wanted to get fucked, you only had to ask."

"I think you've fucked me over enough, don't you?" I spin around, and stomp up the stairs, unclipping my dress, ready to get my boob out for the night time feed.

The night light in Caleb's room gives off a beautiful glow, bathing his tiny body in a soft light as if an angel is watching over him. His little hand holds his dummy tight as he sleeps peacefully.

I tip toe from the room and freeze when the floor creaks, hoping I don't wake him as I creep to my room. Once changed into my fluffy pyjamas, I curl up on my bed and hug the spare pillow. The pillow that would be his if he shared a bed with me. *'Only have to ask,'* do I? He's changed his tune. Well, he can piss off. I'm not giving him the satisfaction.

———

CAL WALKS into the house with a bag of groceries in one hand and Caleb in the other, along with his backpack hanging from his shoulder. "They didn't have much blended baby food to choose from, and I wasn't getting him any more of that cauliflower cheese." He places the bags on the worktop.

"Hello sweetheart, have you had a nice day?" I take Caleb from Cal. He suckles on his dummy, and I lay him on his playmat on the living room floor where I can see him through the doorway.

"He's probably hungry. I haven't fed him since lunch." Cal empties the groceries he's picked up for me.

I run the iron over my blouse, ready for work again tomorrow. "I'll just finish this, and then I'll feed him."

"Leave the ironing board out when you've done. I need to iron a few things."

"I'll do it for you."

"It's cool. I can iron, you know? I'm a man of many talents." He smirks.

"I know, but I don't mind, really."

He opens his bag and places a few items on the back of the chair next to my ironing pile, then sits with Caleb on the floor, playing with his cars.

I lift up a black shirt. "Are you going out?"

"Yeah."

"Where to?" I drape the shirt over the ironing board and run the hot iron over the fabric.

"Just out for a few drinks."

"Oh, with Dean?"

"Natalie."

I hold the iron in front of my chest. "Who's that?"

"A girl I met today."

"Where?" Steam billows from the iron plate, clouding my vision along with a fog filling my mind.

"At the supermarket."

"So you just picked up some hooker at the supermarket?"

He smirks. "She's not a hooker. I don't think she is, unless she has another job. She works behind the checkout at Tesco's."

My eyes turn to thin slits, and I slam the iron down. "Do your own friggin' ironing."

He jumps to his feet, picking up the iron from the holder, almost smirking like he wanted this reaction from me.

I can't look at him. I feel sick at the thought of him going out tonight. My head pounds, and I can't think straight as a cloud of jealousy fills my mind.

I keep myself busy. Doing the washing and then ironing the kids' clothes while the ironing board is out. I know he must have been on dates in Australia. It's just getting too close to home, especially as he's been sleeping here this last week. I don't know why, but I just hoped he would want me back if he kept spending time with me, but even after I've got myself together, he still hasn't made a move.

He enters the living room looking hot as hell. His unruly hair feathers around his face, reaching the top of his collar. The minty smell of his aftershave catches in my nose, making me want to vomit, knowing he's got all dressed up for someone else.

He rolls the sleeves up to his elbows, showing off his ink. "I'm off then. Don't wait up."

I glare at him. "Don't bother coming back."

"What?" He chuckles like this is funny.

"If you're going to be out shagging all night, don't come back here."

"I have to be back here to watch Caleb when you go to work." He picks Caleb up and gives him a kiss on his cheek. "See you later, mate."

Cal places him back on his playmate and turns to me. "See you later, then. I have my key."

I wish I'd never let him get a key cut. What was I thinking? He acts like he lives here. It's worse than living with Justin. He'll be bringing girls back next. I freeze. He wouldn't, would he? I don't look at him. If I do, I'm afraid I'll either burst into tears or rip his friggin' head off.

As soon as he's out the door, I call Claire. Before she arrives, I pump more milk and feed Caleb and get him changed into his pyjamas. Car lights shine through the window. I look out into the dusky night to see Claire step out of a taxi loaded with wine, chocolate, and ice cream.

I run to the door and take the bottle of wine from her. "I'm so glad you could come at short notice." She hands me her jacket, and I hang it on the bannister. "I've been going out of my mind thinking about him out with another woman."

"That's what friends are for. To supply wine and ice cream in times of need." Claire works her way around my kitchen as I wipe my eyes and blow my nose. She hands me a spoon with a tub of Ben and Jerry's cookie dough.

"Thanks."

"Where are the kids?"

"Caleb's in his playgym in the living room, and Cassie and Cairen are at Justin's tonight."

I pour us both a glass of wine while she walks into the lounge.

"Where's my beautiful boy?" she coos, making me smile.

She has him on the floor with her when I enter, and she sits up, crossing her legs as I pass her a glass of red.

"Thanks, hun." She shakes a rattling teddy at Caleb. "Look, Caleb. Tiger." With a roar, she tickles his tummy using the toy, making him burst into giggles. "You're going to break some hearts when you're older. Just like your daddy."

I tut and sip my wine. "Let's hope he doesn't turn out like him."

Claire faces me. "Okay, what's happened now? I thought you were getting on."

I place the wine on the lamp table next to the sofa and bury my face in the palms of my hands. "He's met some girl called Natalia in Tesco, and he's taking her out tonight."

"Which Tesco?"

"What does that matter?"

"I might know her."

"Well, do you know a Natalia?"

"No, but I know a few staff at the little Tesco near me, if it's that one. I can text Louise. She might know her." She shrugs but has a sparkle in her eye when she gives me a mischievous grin.

"Okay, let's stalk the bitch. Call Louise." I scooch to the edge of my seat and sip my wine.

Claire calls her friend. "Hi, do you know a Natalia that works at your place?" Claire looks at me. "Is it Natalia or Natalie?"

"I mean, it could be Natalie?" I take another drink.

Claire continues talking into the handset. "She's going on a date tonight with my friend's baby daddy, if you must know."

Baby daddy? Who uses that term? Is that what he is now? Just my baby daddy. What does that make me, his baby mummy?

"Thanks, Lou. See ya." She cancels the call and goes straight onto her socials. "Nathalie Parkin. Age 34. Works at Tesco. Single. Oh my gosh, she's done a selfie," Claire squeals, waving her hand in the air. "All set for my date tonight."

"No friggin' way." I snatch the phone and stare at the girl out with my man. My body deflates. Every ounce of air in my lungs escapes as I sigh heavily. My arms curl around my belly and the nausea rises in my throat. It's like Emily—the girl he dated at uni—all over again. "She's pretty." I choke out.

"Pretty? What are you looking at?" Claire snatches the phone back. "She's got vinyl eyebrows stuck on for a start, and she's doing one of those trout pouts. I'm sure those boobs are fake, too. They look too big for her tiny frame."

Ugh. The wine bottle calls to me from the coffee table. I pour myself another, clinking the glass like music to my ears. Claire's just trying to make me feel better. The fact that this Natalia is tiny makes me feel worse. I imagine he can throw her around the bedroom. He could only just about lift me. Why did I look at her picture? I was hoping she'd be old or wrinkly. "I'm going to need therapy if I'm going to have to deal with him seeing other women around me."

Claire leans over and rubs my knee. "Tell him how you feel."

"He must know how I feel. My feelings haven't changed. I've never stopped loving him. He knows this."

"Does he though?"

"He says he can't forgive me."

"For what?"

I look at Caleb sucking on a crinkly ear of a tiger rattle. "He thinks I could have done more to contact him." I knock back the rest of the wine in my glass and top myself up.

"You're not serious?"

"Yep."

She points to the empty bottle. "I meant with the wine. I bought that for me. The ice cream was for you. Aren't you meant to be feeding this little monster?"

"Sorry. I have more wine in the cupboard. Help yourself. And I pumped his milk before you came."

She shudders. "I don't know how you do that. Don't you feel like a cow?"

"I don't need a milk pump to feel like that. Trust me."

"Your mummy's a silly mare, isn't she?" Claire ruffles Caleb's thick black hair, and he babbles to her.

"You were saying I was a cow a minute ago. Make up your mind. Am I a cow or a mare?"

"You're a unicorn. And don't let Cal or anyone else tell you otherwise."

A CRY HAS me sitting up in bed. My head is cloudy from the wine, and I'm in a carbohydrate slump from eating a full tub of ice cream. There's a throb in my temple, but I force myself to get out of bed as Caleb's cries become louder.

The crying stops, and I hear someone shushing him. His bedroom door is ajar, and the soft glow from the nightlight outlines Cal's masculine frame. He holds Caleb in his arms, his drowsy head rests on Cal's shoulder while his hand covers his small skull, soothing him from whatever was causing him distress. His eyes grow heavy as he suckles on his dummy.

Cal gently rocks and with each movement, the muscles in his back flex, highlighted by the nightlight. Black boxers cover his arse but cling to him, showing every outline. I love seeing him like this, our most intimate moments with our beautiful boy.

He turns, locking eyes with me as he continues to soothe Caleb.

I'm relieved that he's back. I may actually be able to shift this headache, knowing he isn't shagging some girl all night. Although he's probably already done that. The thought makes me nauseous, and I swallow to stop the bile rising in my throat.

He lays him down softly in his cot then creeps out of the room. I step back, letting him pass and close Caleb's door.

Cal stands in front of me and lifts my chin. "Have you been crying?" he whispers.

"No," I whisper sternly, turning my face to the side.

"Why are you upset?"

"I'm not."

"Yes, you are. Tell me what's wrong."

"Nothing's wrong," I whisper-yell.

"Is it because I went on a date tonight?"

"You arrogant arsehole. You think I've been sitting here crying over you while you've been out screwing some tart? I couldn't give a crap what you do."

He takes hold of my arm and pulls me into the bathroom across the hall, turning the light on so I can see my reflection in the mirror. Black streaks stain my puffy cheeks. I run a hand over my hair, trying to smooth out the bumps in my messy ponytail.

He stands behind me, looking into the mirror at my bloodshot eyes. "Tell me why you're upset."

I rub at the black marks on my face. "I'm not. I just had a drink, that's all."

"No shit. I saw the two empty bottles on the side."

I laugh, but only to stop from crying. "So, what are you, the wine police now?"

"When you're supposed to be looking after my son, yeah. You're a mess."

"Ugh, go back to your hooker and leave me alone."

"So you're allowed to shack up with fucking Picasso, but I'm not allowed to date?"

"Are you crazy? Mark's married."

"Well, it didn't stop you, did it?"

"To a man." I gently close my bedroom door, even though I wanted to slam it in his face. I curl up into a ball, facing the wall. The tears won't stop flooding out of me as my shoulder and chest shudders.

A few minutes later, the door creaks open. I freeze, not wanting him to see or hear me cry. He lifts the duvet and the mattress dips as he climbs into the bed.

A hand curls around my stomach, and he holds my hand that's tight against my chest.

"I didn't fuck her," he whispers.

"Liar." My voice is weak, and my throat is scratchy.

"I didn't even kiss her." His warm breath finds the back of my neck as he speaks against my hair.

"I don't care."

"I know you do, Steph."

His thumb strokes the back of my hand, causing a wave of goosebumps to travel up my arm. He would always tickle my skin. That's all he had to do to get me to melt for him. Is that what he's doing now? He squeezes me tight against his hard chest. Warmth radiates from him like an electric blanket, and I heat up next to him.

"I went to Dean's. I didn't even go on a date."

I turn my body, shuffling until I'm fully rotated to face him. His hand strokes my back. I lift my head inline with his and brush his nose with mine. "Kiss me," I beg.

"You're wasted."

"So, it's never stopped you before."

"I'm not kissing you in this state."

"Just because I've had a drink doesn't mean I don't know what I want. I want you. I've always wanted you, Cal. Kiss me, please."

"No, Steph. I won't."

"Well, if you're not going to kiss me, then get out of my bed." I push against his solid chest, but he holds me close.

I throw the duvet off and wriggle from his grasp and storm out of the bedroom. My feet stomp downstairs, my body craving another drink, hoping I can drink myself to sleep. The oxygen in the air grows thin, and the pounding in my head doesn't help the haziness clear.

Walking into the kitchen, I spot the remains of wine in a bottle. Deciding to finish it, I pour it into a glass.

Cal walks into the kitchen with his jeans on, but still shirtless. My heart pounds, matching the rhythm in my head. I lift the glass to my lips, but Cal snatches it from my hand and tips it into the sink.

"I think you've had enough, don't you?"

My mouth gapes. "Clearly not because I'm still awake."

I reach for the bottle, but he snatches that too before I can get a hold of it.

"I hate you."

He huffs. "You weren't saying that a minute ago when you were begging me to kiss you."

"I only fancied a shag. What's wrong with you? Can't you get it up these days?"

"Oh, I can get it up for someone who actually turns me on."

His words are like a knife stabbing and twisting in my heart.

"Well, if I'm so disgusting to you, stay out of my space. Oh, and you can find somewhere else to sleep tonight."

He huffs. "Fine. Pack Caleb's stuff up, and we'll go."

"Don't be ridiculous, you're not taking my son."

He steps forward, forcing me back. The edge of the kitchen table digs into the back of my thighs and he cages me in, resting his fists on the wooden surface behind me. "Our son, Steph. He's ours. And I'll be damned if I'm leaving him here with you in this state."

"Why do you have to be such a bastard?" I bang my fist against his hard chest, but he doesn't flinch.

His hand grips my wrist. "You think I'm a bastard because I won't kiss you while you're drunk?"

"I just want you to love me. Why won't you love me?"

"I do love you." He growls with a pulsing vein in his neck, and every muscle in his body tenses as he hovers above me.

"Then show me. Show me you love me."

He steps back but only to flip me over. Pressing his palm against my back, he pushes me flat against the table and leans over, growling in my ear, "Is this what you want?" His erection digs into the soft flesh of my behind.

Tears gather in the corners of my eyes as he tugs on my hair, lifting my head back to growl louder in my ear. "Is this what you want?" His voice deepens, like something from the depths of his soul has awoken.

I don't even know what I want anymore, but this isn't it. Memories of us flash through my mind. I've been here before, desperate for him to kiss me, and he refused. I tried to remind him how much he loved me by sleeping with him, but not kissing me just made me feel like a prostitute. He won't do that to me again. I won't be used for sex with no love or feeling. I can buy a vibrator for that.

"Not like this, Cal." I tilt my head to see his eyes as black as a starless sky.

"Then what?" he spits, bearing down on me so I can't move.

"Not like this, please. You're hurting me."

Immediately, he steps back. I rest against the table. My legs shake, and I cover my face with my hands as the tears pour out of me.

"Steph, I'm sorry. I never meant to hurt you. You know that, right?" He leans over to kiss my back. "Baby."

I elbow him in the face as I turn to push him off. "Get the fuck off me."

He steps away and leans against the wall, tilting his head back as he lets out a long sigh.

With tears still rolling down my cheek, I fill a glass of water with shaky hands. "You always hurt me, Cal. I won't let you anymore."

I don't look at him and carry my drink to bed, forcing each unsteady foot in front of the other. From his reaction, he must think I meant a physical hurt, but nothing he could ever do physically could hurt more than the twisting pain in my stomach and the tearing in my chest after he ripped my heart wide open…again.

CHAPTER
Twenty three

CAL

What the fuck is wrong with me? Fuck, I've messed things up good and proper now. She's never gonna talk to me again. All this because I arranged a date with some bird. I didn't even want to fucking go out. I just wanted to make her jealous, and it's backfired.

I creep up the stairs to check on Caleb, who's fast asleep in his cot. As I walk by her bedroom door, I hear her whimpers. I think about going in but don't know what to say or do. *Sorry would be a start.* Steph's voice in my head, she's right, but the words aren't gonna cut it this time.

My stomach feels like it's been through a laundry cycle on a high-speed spin, and my heart's shrivelled as if starved of love. I make my way downstairs and settle on the couch, staring at the ceiling. The last thing I want to do is hurt her.

I do love her, but every time I look at her, resentment bubbles under the surface. All the hours I've missed with my boy haunt me. I can't get past it. It's going to always be this thing between us. It's not entirely her fault—I know that—but if she'd told my mum about him, things would have been very different. I've done plenty of shit in the past and she's forgiven me for it. How or why I'll never know. I want to forgive her and move on, I really do.

<hr>

A WHISTLE JOLTS ME AWAKE, and I pull a cushion over my face, hoping I can get ten more minutes of shut-eye. I turn onto my side and fuck, my back is stiff. I don't know how many more nights of sleeping on Steph's sofa I can take. *Don't worry, I think that was your last night.* The memories of the evening come flooding back like a dream or nightmare.

There's a rustling coming from the kitchen. I force myself up and stretch my arms up with a yawn. I've no idea what happened to my shirt, but I have my jeans on. With a tight chest, I step into the kitchen, ready to face the music and grovel.

Steph is dressed for work in a pencil skirt and cream blouse. Her hair is curled, and she's done her makeup like she's made an effort, though no amount of makeup can conceal the bags under her eyes. I wouldn't be surprised if she hasn't slept all night. I know I haven't. She stands near the sink with a coffee in one hand and a slice of toast in the other. Her eyes move down my body, narrowing as they return to my face.

"Steph, I'm—"

"I want you gone while I'm at work. Pack up all your shit and go."

"But I—"

She holds a hand up, cutting me off. "You can take Caleb. I'll collect him from your mother's after work, and I can drop him off again each morning. You can have him in the day, and I'll have him in the evening. That way, we don't see each other."

Have things become that bad that we can't even see each other? "Steph, it doesn't have to be this way."

Her bottom lip quivers, and she pulls it between her teeth. "I have to go. I can't keep doing this with you. It's just too hard. I know you feel nothing for me, but as the mother of your child, please respect my wishes. That's all I ask." She throws the remaining coffee in the sink and tosses the crust from her toast in the bin. "Caleb's asleep still. There's milk in the freezer. Take what you need."

"I'm sorry, Steph."

"Save it. I just want you out of my house." She walks past me, collecting her bag from the hall, and then the door shuts. I bang the back of my head against the wall in frustration. How the fuck can I mess things up so badly? More importantly, how the fuck can I put this right?

"Hello, my darling. Have you come to see your nanny?" Mum's eyes are drawn to Caleb in my arms as I walk into her living room.

Caleb babbles to his nanny, waving his arms around. Drool dribbles from his mouth as he smiles and gurgles at her. Mum takes him from me along with the dinosaur teddy and truck under my arm.

"I'll be sleeping here until I go back to Australia. I think it's for the best." *Steph kicked you out, you mean.*

"Does that mean I get to spend all day with my gorgeous grandson?" She carries him through to the kitchen and sits him in the highchair she bought for when he visits. "Have you had lunch?"

"Not yet. Can you watch him while I get the rest of my stuff from the car?"

"Of course. Have you got some dinner for him?"

"Yeah, I'll grab it."

"Dad, is Caleb here?" Livvie shouts, running down the stairs.

"Hey, lollipop. Nanny has him in the kitchen."

Bethy follows bounding down the stairs after Livvie runs past me, and Bethy launches herself from the middle of the stairs into my arms. "Daddy."

"Hey, boo." I kiss her cheek, and she squeezes me tight, giving me the boost of energy I need to get through the day.

"Can I sleep at your friend's house tonight?"

"Did you miss me?"

"Not you Daddy. We miss Caleb."

"Cheers." I chuckle, carrying her into the kitchen.

"We want to have a sleepover at his house, can we?"

"Yeah, can we, Dad?" Livvie asks while fussing Caleb in my mum's arms.

"Not tonight, lollipop. He's going home later. I'm staying here." I can't even sleep over, kid. Give me a few days to get back in her good books. I have some grovelling to do.

"Aargghhh," she whines, sticking out her bottom lip.

"I've put the kettle on, love. Do you want a cuppa?"

"I'll make it, Mum. You see to Caleb." I hand her a jar of baby food from the bag and a bottle of Steph's milk that I took from the freezer this morning.

Mum studies my face and wrinkles her brow. "You look tired. Is everything all right?"

"Fine. I just don't sleep well on Steph's sofa."

"Get your head down. We'll take care of Caleb, won't we, girls?"

Bethy picks up her doll and strokes its long hair. "He can play with my dolls."

Liv places her hands on her hips. "He doesn't want to play with dolls, does he, Dad?"

I shrug my shoulders. "He might. You used to like to play with dinosaurs."

I ruffle Caleb's hair as I walk by his highchair and lean over Bethy, kissing her head. "I'm going for a lie down, then. Wake me if you need me."

Liv rolls her eyes when I blow her a kiss. I miss the days when she would blow me one back. I wouldn't mind, but she's not even a teenager yet.

Mum follows me into the hall. "Love, you're not still angry with her, are you? I know you blame her, but I think I'm to blame." Her voice quakes and her hand shakes as she walks to the chintzy sideboard in the hall where she keeps the girls' framed school photos.

"I don't blame anyone, Mum, least of all you." I'm not sure how much of that statement is true. The hurt still weighs heavily on my chest like a dull ache that won't go. If it had been anybody else, it wouldn't squeeze so tight around my lungs, but knowing Steph never cared enough to contact me or find me, that's the worst of all. Is this how she felt when I left her and I started dating someone else? I sometimes wonder if it's revenge.

Mum's wrinkled hand holds a letter. "I'm sorry, love. Liv found this yesterday while looking for a pen in the drawer. I'd forgotten about it with everything going on when I was in and out of hospital with the angina attacks."

I take the letter with my name on the front. "What is it?"

"Steph dropped it off for you. It slipped my mind until Olivia found it." Her voice wobbles. "The tablets I was on—"

"Mum, it's fine. You had a lot on. I don't blame you."

She pats my arm and dabs her eyes under her glasses with a tissue from her sleeve.

My legs are like lead weights as I force each foot up the stairs. The hairs on the back of my neck prick up and a shiver runs down my spine as I eye the white envelope.

Dropping to the bed, I tear it open and read with blurry eyes as guilt overwhelms me.

Cal,

I don't know how to start this letter. I've tried contacting you, but your number no longer works. The last thing I want to do is come between you and your family if you're working things out with Priya. Really, I'm happy for you.

But you said if I ever needed you, to get in touch. And I need you now. I need you to call me, text me, email me, anything. Not for me, but for our child.

Yes, I'm pregnant. I can't tell you how happy I am to have a piece of you, even if I can't have you.

I'm no longer with Justin, but for the first time in a long time, I feel like I can handle anything. I've even learnt to cook.

I don't expect you to come running back to me. Especially if you're settled over there with your family. I love you and I just want you to be happy, even if it's not with me.

Please don't freak out like you did before. I know this isn't ideal for you, but after everything we talked about recently, and how you are with your girls, I know you'll be a wonderful dad to our child. Of course, I'll meet you halfway and visit Australia when I can. We can make this work somehow.

We may not be together, but finally we have something that's ours, and something beautiful has come out of this. I have so many regrets, but this isn't one of them. I would do things differently for certain, but I don't regret being with you for a second if this is the result.

Your Steph x

I lie back on the bed, holding the letter against my chest. She did try. When she comes to pick Caleb up, I'll apologise for everything. I'll tell her I'm sorry. Fuck, I'll get on my hands and knees and beg her forgiveness if I have to.

Thinking of her going through this alone cracks my stone heart, but all the love I have for her that was hidden beneath the hard surface comes flooding out. She will forgive me. She has to.

———

"Love."

My shoulders shake.

"Love. Are you waking up? I've made supper."

"Supper?" I throw the covers off me and jolt up. "What time is it?"

"Around seven."

"Mum, you should have woken me."

"You looked so tired, love. I thought it would do you good to rest. Come down, I've made stew and dumplings. I've mashed some up for Caleb, too."

Caleb's cries travel up the stairs.

"I'm coming," Mum shouts. "He doesn't like you leaving him for even a minute, does he?"

"He's still here?" I reach for my phone on the bedside table and glance at the time on the locked screen. 6.52pm. "Is Steph here? Did she call?" I follow mum down the stairs.

"No dear. What time is she picking him up?"

"She was supposed to be here after work around 5pm." I check my phone for any messages or missed calls.

Walking into the living room, Caleb stops crying when he sees me, and I unclip him from his bouncy chair. "Are you hungry, mate?" I kiss his forehead and carry him to the highchair in the kitchen, smelling Mum's stew on the hob.

What the fuck is she playing at? I press the green button next to her name and pace the kitchen while Mum serves supper.

There's no answer. If she's gone to her mates to get pissed again, Caleb's staying with me tonight.

"I've mashed Caleb's stew up, love. It should have cooled by now."

"Thanks, Mum." I sit at the table and feed Caleb his blended veg and gravy. He pulls a face, spitting some out, but I scoop it up from his chin and feed him again. He gets used to the taste after a few spoonfuls.

"She's probably driving, do you think?" Mum places my plate in front of me. "Bethany, Olivia, dinner."

As hungry as I am, I just don't feel like eating as the fury of Steph burns up my insides. She could have at least text me to say she was running late. *Like the other night when she was out with Picasso.* I glance at Caleb's dimpled smile, reminding me of his mother. Rage burns my chest. It's one thing to be mad with me, but how could she not collect him?

She wouldn't do that. She might like a drink, but she's a good mum. Sick with worry as each minute passes and still no Steph. I force down each mouthful, not even tasting Mum's homemade stew that usually has me going back for seconds.

After clearing the plates, I try her mobile again for the third time.

"Hello." A man answers.

I clench my fist around the handset, ready to throw it at the wall, but remember what happened the last time I did that in Australia when I lost all my numbers, and I think better of it.

"Who the fuck are you? And where's Steph?"

"Callum. It's Justin. Is Caleb with you?" He speaks in a rush with a hoarse voice.

"Where else would he be?" I spit out, heat bubbling through my veins. I can't believe she's with him.

"Thank God." I hear a sigh in his breath as he says the words.

His tone tells me something's not quite right, making the hairs on my neck prickle. "Put Steph on."

He pauses. "I can't."

"Where is she?" I growl, getting more agitated by the second. Is she drunk again?

"She's here." His voice is low and quiet. Not his usual smug self.

"Then put her on. I need to talk to her." I clench my fist around my hair. Is she back with him now? Whatever it is, there's no way they can stop me from seeing my boy.

"Callum, listen." He chokes up with a waiver in his voice.

I sit back down and run a hand through my hair. "What is it?"

"There's been an accident."

I hold my breath. My hand moves from my hair to my throat as I try to breathe.

"She's alive, but she's in a bad way. A head injury and a broken arm and ribs."

I swallow, but the prickles in my throat grow as fear claws up my spine. "What happened?" I manage with a gravelly voice.

"She was on the by-pass. A witness said she just drifted to the side of the road and hit the central reservation. Nobody else was involved, thank God."

My eyes glaze over. There's an ache in my chest as if someone is squeezing the life out of me, making it difficult to breathe. "Where is she?"

"The city hospital. They've just given us her bag that was collected at the scene. I didn't know your number, or I would have called you sooner. Her mum was worried sick, wondering where Caleb was."

"I'm on my way." I stand and kiss Caleb on the forehead with tears blurring my vision.

"You don't need to come. There's not a lot you can do."

"Fuck that. I'm coming."

"She's in a coma."

Hearing the words coma, my body jerks like I've run into a brick wall. "I'll be there in half an hour." I hang up before he can tell me not to come again, and grab Mum's car keys.

Caleb cries, sensing my anxiety, and I walk back over and kiss his head again.

Mum stands. "What's happened?"

"Steph's been in an accident, Mum. I have to go. Can you watch him?"

Her silvery eyes glisten behind her glasses. "Of course. Call me when you get there."

I dart through the front door, into the drizzly rain. My fingers won't work and I drop the keys on the wet ground before unlocking the door. Jumping in the car, I shake the rain from my hair and turn the engine.

The dull sky mirrors the dullness in my heart. I back out of the drive, turning the wipers on to see through the windshield, though nothing can stop the spots in my vision. Flashes of her beautiful face fill my mind. All our memories and last night play over in my head, causing a bout of guilt to burn my throat like I've just swallowed battery acid.

A beep sounds from the car making me jolt back to the present and I remember to put on my seatbelt. Fuck. If she doesn't make it, what will I tell our son? That I killed his mother because I was so fucking selfish?

Seeing her happy with someone else made my insides twist. I wanted to make her jealous, because I could, not because I wanted her back. I do want her back though, and I've only just realised I can't live without that woman.

The setting sun blinds my eyes, and I pull the visor down. The dark clouds mixed with the raging red and yellow hues match the turmoil in my mind. Life isn't worth living if she's not in it. All I see now is red, as if the sky is set alight. A fiery furnace of hell that I must face without her.

My dry throat feels like I've swallowed a cactus. Prickling tears coat the lump that, no matter how hard I swallow, just will not budge.

I've never been one for prayers, but please, God, let her be all right. I'll do anything. Just let her be all right.

Entering the hospital, I follow the signs for the ICU. The smell of disinfectant catches in my nose, causing a shiver down my spine. The last time I was here was with Rachel and Jax. A cold numbness creeps over my skin, causing the hairs to prickle on my neck.

Walking into the waiting area, I choke up when I see Justin sitting on the plastic seating with his hands together as if in prayer.

I stand in front of him. "Can I see her?"

He looks up at me and rubs his hands on his work jeans. "Her parents have just gone in. They're only letting two in at a time."

I take a seat opposite him. My hand shakes as I run it through my hair, pulling the strands off my face. "Where's the car?" I don't even care about the fucking car. I don't even know why I asked that?

"It's a write-off." He points to her bag and a plastic carrier bag at the side. "They emptied the car. Here's all her belongings. I've taken the key for her house so I can get her some things and bring them to the hospital tomorrow."

"I can sort that out. I have a key."

He nods, pressing his lips together, looking around the waiting room at anything but me. "Where's Caleb?"

I clear my throat. "My Mum has him." Another long pause. The air is thick between us. My mouth contorts as the taste of disinfectant lodges in the back of my throat. "What about Cassie and Cairen?"

"Sam, her sister, has them."

Her mum, Sue, enters the small room holding on to her dad, John. I haven't seen them in years, but they haven't changed much, just older. She dabs a tissue under her eyes and sniffles. "You can see her now, Justin."

I stand and step in front of Justin. "If anyone's going to see her, it's me."

Her mum's teary eyes meet mine. She gasps and grips her husband's arm. "You've got a nerve showing your face here. Get out. You're not welcome here." Her usual fierce voice waivers, matching the wobble in her stance as she yells at me.

Justin stands. "Sue, he's Caleb's dad. He has a right to be here." Is this dude actually sticking up for me?

"Being a sperm donor doesn't make him a father." She scowls at me as though I chose this.

My body tenses, holding back every muscle to stay calm. "That's not fair, and you know it."

"You don't care about her. All you do is cause her grief. It's your fault she's in here." She wails and leans on Steph's dad.

"Sue, he wasn't driving the car. We don't know what happened," John, her dad, says.

If they knew the truth, they'd never let me near her again. I let out a long breath and rub my eyes.

John comforts Sue as she breaks down in tears.

A nurse comes over to us. "Visiting is closing in around thirty minutes. Only partners or next of kin allowed."

"Let's get home, Sue. The hospital will call if there's any

change. Nothing we can do here." John guides her out, nodding at Justin as he passes the nurse.

"Can I go in next?" I ask Justin.

"I'm sorry sir, only immediate family allowed," the nurse says.

"I am family." I glance at Justin, hoping he won't contradict me.

He nods, shoving his hands in his pockets. I follow the nurse, stepping into the ICU. Her room is the second on the right. Nothing could prepare me for the sight of her.

My breath stalls as my eyes follow the tubes and wires surrounding her. A purple bruise creeps out from under the bandage around her head. My hand takes hold of her puffy fingers that peek out of the cast, covering her arm.

Beeps from the machine match the thump in my temple, and I lean over and speak near her ear. "Steph." The word comes out choked as a lump grows and prickles the back of my throat. "Steph, baby. It's me."

Walking around the bed, I scrape the plastic chair closer and drop like a lead weight. My hands caress hers, and I stroke her free arm that's not in a sling while holding her cold fingers next to my mouth as I tenderly kiss her hand. "Baby, I'm sorry. I'm so fucking sorry."

My chest shudders as tears drip onto our hands. I wipe my nose on my sleeve and hold her palm against my cheek, feeling her icy hands. "I'll warm you up, baby." Needing to be as close to her as I can, I sit on the edge of the chair. I'd give anything to have her awake, just so she can shout at me, anything just to hear her voice and know she's well.

"Caleb's safe. You don't have to worry about him. He's happy and safe." I don't know if she can hear me or not, but I keep talking. "Cassie and Cairen are safe, too. Everything's okay. You concentrate on getting better, and I'll be here when you wake up. You hear me, baby? I'll be here waiting for you when you're better."

Footsteps squeak against the tiled floor. Justin clears his throat as he steps towards the bed. "I just wanted to see her before I go." His voice waivers as his eyes move from her head to the cast on her arm. He steps forward and stands at the foot of the bed. "I'm gonna head off, but I'll come back in the morning. I can call at her house and pick up some stuff if you have to get back to Caleb."

"I'm not going anywhere in case she wakes up. But I can get the stuff tomorrow when you get here."

The nurse pops her head in the door. "Visiting hours are almost over, guys."

Justin bobs his head. "I'll see you tomorrow then."

"Yeah."

With his head hanging low, Justin exits the room, leaving us alone.

My fingers interlace with hers again, and I bring her hand to my lips. "I'll be right outside, baby."

I head back to the waiting room and call Mum.

"How is she, love?"

"Not good. She's unconscious on a ventilator. She has a head injury, a broken arm, and ribs."

"Oh, love. I'm sorry."

"How's Caleb?"

"He's just had his bottle and gone down for the night. I borrowed a travel cot from a friend."

"I'm staying at the hospital in case anything happens. I want to be here when she wakes up."

"All right, love. Don't worry about Caleb, he's fine. I can go to the shop tomorrow and stock up on milk, baby food, nappies and what not."

"Thanks, Mum."

Leaning my head against the wall, I hang up and close my

eyes, thinking of all the things I want to say to Steph. Nothing from the past seems to matter anymore. All I care about is having her well to be a mum to our son. Even if she never speaks to me again, I want Caleb to know what a wonderful mum he has.

My eyes leak in the corners, and I pinch the bridge of my nose where the sting holds back the tears. I always said she'd be the ruin of me, but it's the other way around.

CAL

"Have you been here all night?" A voice rings in my head, snapping my eyes open. I blink to see Sue and Sam in front of me.

I run a hand over my face and yawn, looking out the window at the bright light. "Yeah. I wanted to be here when she wakes up." I glance at my watch to see it's almost 8am; visiting hours.

"Well, you'll have to wait. We're sitting with her for the next two hours. Come on, Sam." She pulls her daughter down the corridor. Sam gives me a half-hearted smile and a shrug as she leaves.

Knowing there's not a lot I can do here, I head back to her place with the belongings from her car. I'm not sure what she needs, and I wish I'd checked with the nurse before I left, but I pack her hairbrush and toothbrush, then open her drawer for clean underwear.

The stockings are here along with her sexy lace knickers, but I opt for the comfy cotton ones she likes to wear so much. I pack a few sets of short pyjamas and her slippers, wanting her to be comfortable when she wakes up. *If she wakes up.*

Her peach coloured bedroom closes in on me, and I drop

to the bed like a stone dropping to the ocean floor. Everything is murky, preventing me from seeing my hand in front of my eyes. She has to wake up. She has to. My fist crumples the garments in my hand as I take in deep, slow breaths. My heartbeat slows, and her room comes back into focus.

With a light head, I walk into the kitchen to get a drink of water. The pump she carries in her bag reminds me of the freezer draw full of expressed milk. I pack it up along with Caleb's pushchair and drop it off at Mum's, getting five minutes with my boy and the girls. I'll have to organise a way to get the girls back to Priya. There's no way I can go back to Australia now.

"Do you need the car, Mum?"

"No love, you take it. If I need anything, I'll ask the neighbour, and I can walk to the shop."

I kiss Caleb and the girls goodbye and head back to the hospital. Sue passes me in the sterile corridor with a scowl on her face. Sam follows.

"Dad's with her now, Cal," Sam confirms, before getting a pained look from Sue for even acknowledging me.

My stomach groans. I've eaten nothing since Mum's stew. I'm not sure I can stomach anything at the moment, but the emptiness in my belly is eating away at my insides, just like the emptiness in my heart has chewed away at my arteries.

Walking into the hospital shop, I grab a pre-packed sandwich and can of pop. A half-naked dude on a book cover catches my eye. He's the sort of tattooed prick Steph likes. *Like you, you mean?*

I've heard it's good for people to read to coma patients. Maybe this dude can bring her round, even if I can't. The guy behind the till raises an eyebrow and grins as he scans the barcode on the book cover. I smile inwardly and flash my credit card before grabbing my stuff.

The nurse from yesterday is outside the waiting room. "Hey, is there any change with Stephanie Bailey?"

"We've taken her off the ventilator, and she's breathing on her own, which is a really good sign." She smiles and squeezes my arm as I let out a sigh of relief.

My shoulders relax a little and my eyes flick to the heavens to thank God for answering my prayers. "Thanks. I have some things of hers here." I hand Steph's things over to the nurse before returning to the waiting room.

Justin sits on the plastic seating with Cairen. I slump into the uncomfortable chair opposite and shuffle in my seat.

"Hey. Cassie's in there with Steph's dad. The kids wanted to come and see her." He points to the door to the ICU.

"Haven't you been to school today?" Biting into the sandwich is like sandpaper on my tongue, but I swallow and force another bite.

Cairen glares at me as if my presence here is offensive enough. He hasn't been the same since overhearing Steph calling me Caleb's dad, and apparently he didn't take it well.

"It's the holidays now," Justin says.

Of course it is. With everything going on, I forgot about the summer holidays. There's an awkward silence, and it's clear the kid doesn't want to talk to me.

Each passing minute is like an hour, sitting here in awkward silence with Justin and Cairen, glaring at me like some kid from a Stephen King book, giving me a deadly stare. I actually like the lad, even if he is Justin's double.

Steph's dad appears with Cassie. "You can take over, Justin. I'll take Cassie back with us."

Justin stands. "Thanks John. Come on, Cairen." He places an arm around the kid.

I look up at him. "Will you give me a shout when I can go in?"

"Sure."

Two hours go by, and Justin pokes his head into the waiting area. "We're off. All yours."

"Thank you." I rush to the doors and press the buzzer. "I'm here to see Stephanie Bailey. Can I come in?"

"Not right now. The doctor is doing his assessments."

I check my watch. For fuck's sake, will I ever get to see her today? I trudge back to the waiting area and drop into the chair, burying my face in my hands.

The nurse from before approaches me. My heart races thinking the worst. "Is she all right?"

"There's no change, but I notice you've been sitting here all day and haven't actually had the chance to visit. She's free now if you want to go in. I know how difficult families can be."

"I appreciate that. Thank you."

I follow her to the room. The central station is a hive of activity and I pass various machines beeping and humming, but once I'm next to Steph, everything stills. The only sound is her own steady heart monitor.

I pull the chair close so I can take hold of her hand. "Baby, I'm here. I've been here all day." I kiss her fingers and hold her palm against my cheek. "Caleb says hi. He misses his mummy. I miss you, baby." I kiss her hand as I hold it against my face and scratch the bristles from my jaw against her palm.

"I bought you a book today. From a New York Times bestseller. You'd like the dude on the cover. He's got a few tat's, dark hair, brown eyes. A bit like me. Maybe you wouldn't like him as much as I like to think, but I'm gonna read you the story, anyway."

I pull the book out of the carrier bag with my drink and half-eaten sandwich. "You like to hear me read, don't you?" I kiss her palm and with one hand, rest the book on the bed, turn the page and read.

"Are you still here?" Sue's voice screeches as I was a quarter of the way through the book. I'd lost track of time.

"I'll be here until she wakes up." I fold the corner of the page and place it back in the carrier bag.

"She won't want you here when she wakes up. I know you had a falling out. She called me from work yesterday because she wanted me to have Caleb for a few hours so she could take a nap. She was tired and unwell because of you."

"If she doesn't want me around, she can tell me that when she wakes up. Until then, I'm staying." I know I'm to blame. I don't need Sue to keep reminding me. The guilt I feel has manifested itself in my stomach, giving me nausea and a throb in my temple that won't go.

Sue sticks her chin out and huffs, walking over to the bed. She brushes the side of Steph's cheek with her fingers. "You'll have to go because her dad's on his way up. He's just parking the car."

I stand and step away from the bed, but before leaving, I turn back to Sue. "I do love her, you know."

She tuts. "You've only ever disappointed her. If you loved her, you would have stayed away instead of getting her into this mess. She was happy before you came along." She breaks down and drops to the chair on the other side of the bed. I walk back to the waiting area with a wounded ego to go with my wounded heart.

Everything she said is true. Steph was happy. The woman I saw at Browns Media on her first day is not the woman she is now. I've zapped all the life out of her, drove her to drink, just like before. Why do I always hurt the woman I love the most? Did she fall asleep at the wheel, or did she do this on purpose? Either way, it's my fault she's here.

SEVERAL DAYS HAVE PASSED. I'm now on first-name terms with the hospital staff. Steph twitched her fingers the other day. Tracy, the nurse said it's just reflexes, but I'm sure she's trying to find a way home.

"It's only taken us three days to get through this book. I'll have to look for another one tomorrow." I place it on the table at the side of her bed. Then brush the hair from her face. I lean over and peck her lips, needing to feel the warmth of them against mine.

Dropping into the seat again, I interlace our fingers together. "Hurry and come back to us, baby. Caleb needs you. I need you." A tear forms in the corner of my eye, and I blink it away. "Come back to me. I'm gonna spend the rest of my life making it up to you. I'll never leave or hurt you again."

I stroke her arm with a smile on my face, thinking of when we were kids. Even then, I would hurt her, mainly to get her attention. We've known each other since we were five, but we weren't always friends.

"Baby, do you remember when the teacher made me sit next to you in year two?" I huff out a laugh, stroking her arm in the crease of her elbow. I was constantly causing trouble at the back of the class so the teacher sat me with little miss perfect.

"That became my seat for the rest of the year. I hated sitting next to a girl, especially one that was the teacher's pet. Your uniform was pristine and your long French plaits were done to perfection with little red bows on the end that matched your red uniform. I couldn't resist tugging on them. Even then, I liked to pull your hair, but for very different reasons."

A whimsical smile paints my face as my mind draws the picture of how we once were. I made her cry a few times, too. *Some things never change.* I'm sure she hated me back then.

"Even though I was a little shit, you still found it in your heart to show compassion." My lips press against the back of her cold hand and I hold it there against my mouth, my hot breath warming her skin.

"I was having a tough time at home, tried breaking up a fight between mum and dad and was knocked into the glass coffee table. I needed a few stitches on my cheek, near my ear. Had to miss a few days of school and I missed you. Even if it was only to torment you." A silent laugh rocks through me.

"When I returned to school, you studied my face. I kept my head down and said, 'what you looking at?' But you brought your hand to my cheek saying, 'let me make your poorly better.' Your lips were like an angel's kiss and all my troubles disappeared. I knew from that day you were more than just a girl I sat next to in class."

My eyes glaze over, blurring my vision, and I close them, holding her hand next to my cheek. I still tormented her, but she seemed to like it most of the time. She was my reading buddy.

"Baby, can you remember, we would share a beanbag and you would read to me? I used to stay in at playtime to listen to your stories. I was a better person when I was with you because I loved you."

My fingers stroke her arm just how she likes. "Let me love you again. Come back to me, Steph. I'm begging you, baby. Come back to me." My voice waivers as I drop my head against her arm, holding her hand in mine.

"I don't wanna do life without you." My shoulders shake as the emotion takes hold, and I let myself cry for the first time.

A chair scrapes along the floor. I turn around to Justin in his work clothes, clearing his throat. "I didn't mean to interrupt. How's she doing?"

"No change." I wipe my nose on my sleeve and run a

hand over my face. Justin probably knows I've been sitting here sobbing like a chick, but I couldn't give a fuck.

He places a hand on my shoulder. "You should go home, take some time off. Spend time with your boy. I've finished work for the day now. I can stay with her until Sue and John arrive."

"I want to be here if she wakes up. I need to be here."

"Mate, at least have a shower."

I lift my arm and know he's right. "Will you call me if there's any change?"

"Sure. Caleb must miss the both of you terribly. Bring him with you tomorrow. Having him close might help her wake up. The doctors said there's no brain damage, so we just need to pray she wakes up soon."

"I'll do that. Thanks, pal." I rub my hands over my face and stand to give her another peck on the lips before I go.

Justin places his hand on my shoulder again. "I'm glad she has you. I know we haven't always got on, but I can see how much you care for her."

I huff inwardly. If he knew the truth. The truth. Thinking about it brings the acid up from my stomach and coats the lump in my throat.

"Look, I'm no saint. But you're right about one thing. I care about her. I fucking love her with everything I have, and I'll spend the rest of my life showing her, if she'll let me."

GREY CLOUDS BILLOW above the church spire. Though even with the threat of thunder, everything is peaceful, like the calm before the storm. There's a stillness as if we're in the eye of the tornado, and everything around me whirls into oblivion.

Entering the church, you could hear a pin drop. The eerie

quietness deafens me. I walk down the aisle. All eyes are on me. I swallow, pushing down the prickling lump that's taken up residence in my throat. Caleb cries out. His screams pierce my ears, making my blood curdle. I bounce him in my arms. "Shh, shh. Daddy's here." But it's not me he wants. It's her.

A small ray of light pours through the stained glass window, shining down on the white open casket. The shiny gloss surface and silver handles remind me of Jax's funeral. Red roses surround her auburn hair as she lays peacefully still. I'd asked for her to wear her red dress and red lipstick. That's how I remember her. How I'll always remember my girl, my woman.

"Mammam," Caleb cries out, opening his hands to her. His body stiffens in my arms as he tries to get to his mother. The organ plays, though all I hear is a ringing in my ears, and Caleb's screams.

"Mummy's sleeping, mate." A tear drips from my lashes. Mum strokes my arm and takes Caleb from me with saddened eyes. Without Caleb in my arms to give me strength, I lean on the casket to hold myself up. A loose strand of hair covers her painted rosy cheek, and I sweep it back with my fingers. Her icy cold skin sends a chill down my spine.

"Baby, you're so cold." Another tear drips on her face as I lean over and take her hands in mine. "I'll warm you up."

Dean places his hand on my back. "Mate, come and sit down, yeah?"

"No, she's too cold. I need to keep her warm." I interlace our fingers, clasping us together.

"Mate," Dean whispers. "Everyone's watching."

I turn to the congregation, taking pity on me, but I couldn't give a fuck. "My Steph needs me."

"Mate. Come and hold your son. He needs you." Dean takes my hand, separating our fingers.

I let go. The emptiness grows inside me, making me

numb. The chill from her body spreads through every cell as if slowly turning my heart to stone. Stepping back, I stumble, but Dean holds me up, guiding me to the pew next to Mum.

The service is a blur. The vicar said some nice things about her, and so did Justin, but nobody knew her like I did. She was mine, and I wasn't there for her when she needed me. Our last words haunt my day and the emptiness of her haunts my night.

Before I know it, I'm in Dean's car with Mum and Caleb, stepping out at the cemetery. Rain beats down on the windshield, and Mum holds an umbrella over her and Caleb. I welcome the rain, holding my head to the heavens, feeling it on my face. A crack of white light flashes through a dark cloud, and I almost wish it will strike me down so I can be with her.

Caleb's cries jolt me back to reality. I have to live for him. Our son and my girls. I have to go on and be the best dad I can be. I couldn't be there for her, but I can do this. Another crack in the sky mimics Caleb's piercing screams. I'd hold him, but I can barely hold myself together.

The men in black coats lower the casket into the ground, and I drop to my knees. "She can't go in the ground. She'll be cold."

Dean kneels beside me. "She's not in there, mate."

"She never liked the dark," I shout over the thunder. My heart beats wildly like the hammering of rain on her coffin. I can't breathe as the crowd closes in on me. The coffin descends further into the ground.

"Noooooo," I yell with my last breath. Justin and Dean hold me back, but I claw myself away from them on the sodden ground, reaching out for the white casket disappearing into the soil.

"Love, she's not in the coffin." A voice says behind me.

My body convulses. The tornado swallows everything in

its path, whirling around me, getting closer and closer until it takes me. A welcoming darkness takes my breath and everything is still, black and quiet.

"Love, wake up." Mum's voice echoes through the void.

I jolt up in bed, sucking in a breath like a baby breathing life for the first time. A cool sticky sweat coats my skin, and my heart pumps adrenaline through my body as if I've been zapped with a new lease of life.

"Love, you were having a nightmare." Mum strokes my damp hair, pushing it from my eyes.

I run my hand over my face and let out a long breath. "She was dead." The memory crushes my chest, and I curl my shoulders, clutching my abdomen. "She was dead, Mum."

"Don't think about that. You have to stay strong for your boy. I've been praying for her. I'm sure everything will be fine. Stay positive. You'll be able to see her again in a few hours. Besides, the hospital would call if there was any change, wouldn't they?"

I reach for my phone on the bedside table and call the ward. I need to know she's all right.

STEPH

"Get the nurse, John. Her eyelashes are flickering."

"They did that the other day, Sue."

"She's stirring, her fingers are twitching, look. Press the buzzer thing."

My eyes slowly open to Mum's silhouette hovering above me, a bright light behind her like a glowing aura, as if she's an angel from the heavens awakening me. Only I want to go back to sleep where I wasn't in pain.

The pounding in my head along with mother's voice is almost unbearable, and when I breathe there's a stabbing in my ribs along with a dull constant ache in my arm. When I lift my hand, there's something weighing heavy, as if pulling it down. At least I can feel my toes. I wiggle them again to make sure and look at my dad.

"Hello, poppet. You gave us quite a scare." He kisses my forehead before the nurse ushers them out of the room.

A bright light blinds my eyes as the nurse checks me over, talking to me as if I'm a child.

"Mrs Bailey. You. Were. In. An. Accident." She repeats the words slowly.

Is that my name? Am I still Mrs Bailey? I must have

dreamt I was with Callum. Oh gosh, have I dreamt about my son, too? Was it all one big dream? I'm so dazed and confused I can't tell what's real anymore.

"You're at the city hospital. Where you've been for the last four days. You had a nasty bang to the head, causing a gash, so keep your bandage on. You've broken two ribs and fractured your radius and ulna, so you'll be out of action for a while. Do you understand?"

I nod, unable to speak. My throat is dry and scratchy. I'm so weak. My eyes grow heavy again and the darkness takes me.

"Water," I whisper.

"She wants a drink. John, pour a glass of that water, let her wet her lips." Mum takes the cup from Dad and brings it to my mouth, allowing me to take small sips.

With a weak, trembling hand, I take the plastic beaker from her, but she hovers, holding her hand underneath, ready to catch it in case I slip. I guzzle it down, quenching my dry throat like a desert soaking up the first rain.

"Where are my kids?"

"Everyone's fine. Don't you worry about them. You're being moved onto a ward. Justin will be here soon with Cassie and Cairen." Mum takes the cup from me and refills it.

Before I can ask anything else, Mum and Dad are ushered out of the room and I'm surrounded by several people. "We're moving you to a ward, Mrs Bailey. You'll be able to have more visitors. You're very popular."

I smile and my eyes drift again as everything goes blurry.

A voice shouts, "Mum." Startling me awake. Cairen runs towards me.

"Watch her arm. Be careful," Justin shouts.

"Are you better now, Mum?" Cairen says as he stops next to the bed.

I lift my arm with a wince as the pain shoots down my side, but I cover it with a smile and pull him in for a cuddle. "I'm getting better. I missed you."

"We stayed with auntie Sammy a few days when Dad had to go into work."

Cassie puts her arms around me and bursts into tears.

"Darling, what's wrong?"

"I thought you'd never wake up." Her small body shakes as she sobs into my shoulder.

I smile at Justin. Is he still my husband? I was certain we'd split up. I'm scared to ask.

"It's good to see you up. You had us all worried sick." He leans down and kisses my forehead.

Was it all a dream? Callum, Caleb? The walls close in on me, and I gasp for breath.

"Give her some space. Where's the nurse gone?" Mum shouts, but their faces spin in a blurry haze all around me.

The nurse comes into focus. "Breathe slowly. You're having an anxiety attack. Have you had them before?"

I can't take a deep breath as it hurts too much, so I just take small shallow pants. Slowly, everyone comes back into view. My kids are staring with worry written all over their faces, and Justin is on the phone.

"Do you want a cup of tea and a biscuit? Get your strength up?"

I nod at the nurse, and Mum passes me another water.

"Caleb?" I say, "Where's Caleb?"

"Callum has him," Justin says. "I've just called him. He's on his way."

I lean back and exhale. My eyes water as a wave of relief washes over me. The door opens. Adrenaline spikes through my heart, and I wince as my body jerks upright, expecting to see Callum and my boy.

"A nice cup of tea for you, Mrs Bailey." The nurse hands me a warm tea in a sippy cup.

I grip it with a shaky hand. "Am I that bad? I can't hold a proper mug?"

"You've been asleep for days, poppet."

"Mummy, we missed you."

"Drink your tea, dear. It'll make you feel better."

"It's one way to get out of doing the cooking and cleaning, aye, Steph?" Justin chuckles, but I don't see what there is to laugh about. Who's going to help me with the kids, the cleaning, cooking? Feeding Caleb? My breasts are tender but not bursting with milk like they should be.

The door opens again. My eyes move upwards and lock onto his. I freeze, sucking in a breath at the sight of Cal. It's only been a few days—I think—but it feels longer, like a lifetime since I've held my man and my boy.

"Hey, mate." Justin stands, making room for Cal and Caleb to come to my bedside.

He leans over, kissing my cheek. "How you feeling, baby?" he whispers, tickling my neck with his words. My hand shakes and tears pool in my eyes. He always has this effect on me.

"Now look what you've done." Sue takes the drink from my trembling hands. "I told you she doesn't want you here." She holds her arms up to Caleb. "Come to your Nanna."

Cal steps away from Mum and swallows. "Steph, do you want me here? If you want me to go, I will."

My eyebrows pull together as I look between the two of them. "Don't go," I whisper, still not able to speak fully.

"Mamama." Caleb holds his hands to me, but I'm not

strong enough to hold him, even though I want to more than anything.

"Yeah, Mummy. Clever boy." Cal perches Caleb on the bed next to my arm. I lift my hand and stroke his cheek and let the tears of joy roll down my face. It was real, it's all real. I just can't figure out what's going on with Mum and Callum. Why on earth would I want him to go? I love him.

Sam bursts through the door. "You're alive."

I laugh, then hold my breath and my side while the pain abates.

Sebastian follows. "Hey sis, good to see you're still here."

"Bloody-hell, I must be bad, if you're here."

He chuckles and walks towards Justin, patting him on the back. Looking around the room, everyone I hold dear is here. Even though I'm not in love with Justin, I do still care for him, and the fact that he's here shows he feels the same.

CAL

I MUST HAVE BEEN EXHAUSTED. Three nights sleeping in a waiting room has done my back in. I wanted to get here early today, but I didn't wake until late in the morning after tossing and turning all night and the nightmare playing over and over in my head. I was sure I set the alarm on my phone, but I must have turned it off.

The drink she's holding shakes in her hands, and I pause, worried she's trembling because of me. Because of the last time we were together. Our fight.

Her eyes glisten each time she looks at me, making the guilt fill my mouth.

Sam rambles on, and no one can get a word in. I take hold of her hand, needing to feel her close to me, and she gives me a warm smile. Has she forgiven me already? Can I forgive myself?

"I think Mrs Bailey needs some space." the nurse says, walking towards the bed.

"Callum, I think you should wait outside." Sue snarls.

I grip Steph's hand tighter. "I'm not going anywhere."

"Mum, can you give me a moment with Cal?" Steph says quietly.

Sue stands in a huff and juts her chin out as she exits the room.

"Kids, let's see what chocolate there is in the vending machine." Justin gives me a nod as he guides the kids out.

"Do you want me to take Caleb?" Sam holds her arms out to him, and I let her take him.

Once everyone is out of the room, I stroke her hair back from her forehead that hangs over the bandage. "How are you feeling?"

"Tired, but I'm glad you're here."

"Do you remember what happened?"

"No. I can't remember much. The last thing I remember is being out with Mark."

I stroke her fingers with my thumb. It's probably a good thing she doesn't remember our fight, but the guilt weighs heavily on my chest.

"I'm still trying to piece together what happened. Did I make it to work?"

"You fell asleep at the wheel on your way home Monday." My throat closes up. I can't look her in the eye. Instead, I study her hand as my thumb caresses her fingers, running my pad over her broken nail. "It's my fault, Steph. I kept you up all night."

She lets out a sigh. "Forgive me, I can't remember. Are we back together?"

My head snaps up. Her vibrant green eyes peer into mine. "You think I kept you up all night fucking?"

Her mouth hints at a smile on one side, showing her dimpled cheek. "It wouldn't be the first time."

"We had a row. I hurt you. I'll never be able to make it up to you."

She pulls her hand away from me; her smile turns to a frown. "You always hurt me." Her eyes dull, like the leaves turning brown in autumn.

"I'm sorry. I needed you to know. Steph, I need you to forgive me."

"How can I forgive something I don't even remember?" She turns away to look out the window at the city.

"I just want you to know I'm sorry for everything." I drop my head in my hands.

"I'm tired, Cal."

"I'll leave you to get some sleep." I stand. My fingers itch to caress her cheek as I would when she was sleeping, but I don't think she would appreciate that now.

"I'm tired of forgiving you." Her voice waivers, but she doesn't look at me and continues to look at the bustling city. A hive of activity, yet in here there's only silence.

After a long pause, I clear my throat. "I'll let you get some rest. I'll be outside."

I close the door behind me and slump to the waiting room with my head low and my hands in my pockets.

Her family discuss a rota of who's going to take care of her when she returns home.

"We have the room and I can take some time off work. She can move back in with me," Justin says.

My eyes widen. "Like hell she is."

Justin scratches the back of his neck. "I have the room. She's familiar with the house. She lived there for years. Plus, I can take time off work to help take care of her."

"She can move into her old bedroom back home," Sue says, clutching her handbag on her knee. "Her dad and I don't work. We can take care of her and Caleb."

"If anyone is taking care of Caleb, it's me." I press my lips together into a thin, hard line while they all discuss her fate, but they can leave my son out of it.

He sits on Sam's knee, sucking on a Milky Bar. White chocolate dribbles down his chin onto his clean clothes. "Sam, there's a bib in the changing bag." I smile inwardly. Living with Steph these past few weeks, I'm sounding like her.

She opens the bag that's between her feet. "I think we should ask Steph what she wants. Don't you think she'll want to return to her home comforts? I can sleep over at her place a couple of nights a week to help her out."

"I can do that too. We can take it in turns," her mum says.

"If anyone is staying over at her place, it's me. He's my son, and I'll take care of him and Steph." I pick Caleb from Sam and wipe his mouth.

Justin pipes up, "Aren't you meant to be going back to Australia?"

"I postponed my flight again. Wednesday, I should have left. My girls are going back soon, but I'm staying until Steph's better."

John stands, clearing his throat. It's not often he has anything to say, but when he does, everyone listens. "I think we should ask Steph what she wants when the time comes. It may be a while before she's ready to come home, so we're all arguing for nothing."

He walks over and places a hand on my shoulder. "If Steph agrees to have you take care of her, we'll all be here to help. You don't have to do this alone."

I drop my head, not wanting to look him in the eye. He doesn't know I need to do this. I need to take care of her. It's the only way I can atone for my actions. Maybe if I show her how much I care, she'll forgive me.

———

ONCE CALEB IS SETTLED in his cot, I walk into the lounge to find Steph fast asleep on the sofa. She's been desperate to come home since she woke a few weeks ago, and couldn't wait to be discharged today, but just getting dressed and getting in the car has zapped all her energy. Her brow furrows and her eyes move rapidly underneath her lids. I wish I could take away her pain, physical and emotional, but I'm the cause of both turmoils.

My ex was right when she said I've fucked up every relationship I've ever had and fucked over every woman I've ever known. None of the others seem to matter to me as much as Steph.

She stirs, letting out a murmur as I drape a blanket over her body. Her head tilts, leaning against a cushion, exposing the pulse below her ear. A strand of hair falls on her face from the loose ponytail. Grazing my thumb over her cheek, I stare at the smooth skin on her neck, and my breath hitches as I picture myself kissing and licking the spot that sends her wild.

If I could, I would suck her so hard, I'd mark her so everyone would know she's my woman. I wet my lips, swiping my tongue over my dry cracked skin, itching to suck on her neck like a fucking vampire needs his fix. My eyes roam to her soft, pursed lips. Lips I've kissed a thousand times, and it's still not enough to satisfy me. An eternity with her wouldn't be enough.

My head moves closer to her, and I hover over her face. It would be so easy to kiss her, brush my lips against hers, but I know she would reject me. I don't deserve her.

She's always forgiven me for anything, but not this time. I took things too far, but I swear to God, I'm gonna spend the rest of my life making things right. All I want is for her to be happy, whether that's with me or without me. Fuck, please let it be with me.

I've always taken her love for granted and whatever I did in the past she welcomed me back with open arms. Even after I broke her heart, crushed her dreams and told her I didn't love her, she still opened her heart to me. *And her legs*. And I took it all like the fucking bastard I was. I used her for my own selfish needs, knowing I wasn't gonna stick around. I hate that fucking prick that treated her that way. She deserved better.

Fuck, she had better when she had Justin, and I ruined that for her, too. How will I ever make it up to her? I can't offer that lifestyle; the fancy home with a white picket fence, European holidays. I'm sticking around this time, though. I'll make sure of it. Maybe one day she'll forgive me for treating her like shit and making her feel so low that she wants to end everything. After reading her book, I know that's how she felt the last time.

She's snoring now; a gentle purr. I pull the blanket over her body and around her neck, and she stirs a little more. I was going to put the TV on, but I don't want to wake her. Instead, I pull my phone out and read.

STEPH

A SHARP PAIN pounds in my head. I turn my body, and a dull ache throbs in my arm, causing me to blink open my eyes. Looking down, I see the cast resting in the sling and all my woes flood my mind as the anxiety fills my lungs.

I gasp for air, and with each intake, there's a stab in my ribs. As I turn to get a better position, Cal's face comes into view. He's sleeping beside me with the phone resting on his chest. Knowing he's here with me makes everything bearable.

I can get through anything as long as he's with me. Even though I know he'll never want to be with me again romantically, but having him here is better than nothing.

My meds must have worn off. I glance at the clock on the mantle. The soft light from the lamp gives off enough glow to see it's gone midnight.

I wince as I move towards the kitchen to reach my medication. I don't want to wake Cal. He looks so peaceful, and he deserves some peace after everything I've put him through.

Slumping into the kitchen, holding my side with my good arm, I pause for breath at the counter, trying to be as quiet as possible and breathe through the pain. A low groan leaves my lips as I reach for a glass. Moisture covers my face as my entire body tenses with the pain.

"Steph." His voice makes me jump, causing another shooting pain down my side. "I told you to let me know if you needed anything."

Turning around, I see the scowl on his face. "I didn't want to wake you." I swallow the tablets, gulping down the water.

"For fuck's sake, Steph. You shouldn't be moving around. You need to rest."

I'm panting through gritted teeth, doubled over. The pain in my side stabs me with each breath. I hear what he's saying, but it's sort of muffled.

"Look at the state of you."

Great. On top of being a burden and completely useless, I also look a complete mess.

He gently wraps an arm around my waist, and I hold on to him with my free arm. "Let's get you to bed."

I nod, unable to speak through the pain, hoping the tablets kick in soon.

Once in the bedroom, I sit on the bed, catching my breath.

"Do you want me to help you change?"

I glance at my leggings and t-shirt. "Leave these." I pant. "You've done too much."

Who would think walking from the sofa to the kitchen would be too much?

He pulls back the duvet, lowering me down. As he leans over to adjust my pillows, he hovers over my lips. His hair falls in front of his face, and without thinking, I tuck one side behind his ear. He stops in his tracks to look into my eyes.

His breath tickles my cheek, and I can almost taste his lips. He swallows hard, making his Adam's apple bob before me. His bicep bulges as he lowers my head to the pillow, darting his eyes from my mouth to my gaze, then back again. If only I had the strength to lift myself up to meet his lips. Before I have time to think, the moment is lost.

"Can I get you anything?"

"My water, please."

He disappears and returns with my drink.

"Thank you."

"Here, your phone too. I'll be in the living room. Just shout when you want something. Or call me on the phone. I'll get you anything you need. That's why I'm here, baby."

I suck in a breath through my teeth. Hearing the word escape his lips is like the sound of my favourite song. I reach for his hand. "Cal," I say, clasping his wrist.

"Yeah."

"Will you stay with me?"

"Don't worry, I'm not going anywhere."

"I mean, stay here with me. I don't want to be alone."

He nods. "I'll get some cushions for the floor."

"There's plenty of room in the bed." I sound pathetic, but

I'm too tired and fraught to care. Although, I should know he won't want to share a bed with me after everything that's happened, and I won't beg him or plead with him to take me back. Not after last time, when I threw myself at him daily.

He glances at the large king-sized bed and then back at me.

"You can put the pillows down the middle if you like." I gesture to the spare pillows in the blanket box. He places them on the spare side of the bed, then pulls his jeans off and slips under the duvet, turning to lie on his side. Unable to turn, I stay on my back, staring at the ceiling. Shapes dance above me like stars making love in the night sky, or are they fighting? It's hard to tell.

"Thank you, Cal." A tear rolls off the side of my face, disappearing into my hair.

"You don't have to thank me," he says, taking hold of my hand.

My eyelids grow heavy as the meds finally kick in. His thumb circles my palm, gently caressing my skin, and I fight to stay awake.

CHAPTER
Twenty six

STEPH

"Isn't your mum normally here by now?" Cal leans against the living room doorjamb with a coffee in his hands.

I yawn, then sip my coffee. "She's not coming today. She isn't feeling well."

He stands up straight. "Why didn't you say? I can help you shower."

"It's fine. I can go a day without a shower."

"What if she's ill tomorrow?"

"I'll ask Claire or my sister."

He slides into the seat next to me on the sofa. "But you don't need to. That's what I'm here for."

"Cal, you're not helping me shower."

"Why not?" His eyebrows pull together like washing me is the most natural thing in the world. Maybe it was once, but that was a lifetime ago.

"I'm not getting naked in front of you." I smile, but only to hide the embarrassment in my voice.

He laughs. "For fuck's sake, Steph. Is that what you're worried about?"

I squish my eyebrows together, tugging the hem of my pyjama top. "I don't want you seeing me naked."

He laughs harder. "I've seen you naked more times than I can even remember. Like a billion times."

"I think that's a little exaggerating. And besides, it's different now."

"Why have you grown a third nipple or something?" He leans back on the sofa, lifting his feet on the coffee table.

"No." I pull my fluffy pyjama sleeves over my hands and chew on the cuff.

"I can see you naked any time I like. Your body is engraved on my mind. I know every curve and every fucking freckle on your skin."

"It's still not happening." There's no way I could let him see me now. When he saw me naked before, he was in love with me, looking through a rose-tinted lens. He doesn't feel that way about me now. He would see every flaw. I may have gained some confidence and independence this last year, but that doesn't mean I want him ogling my extra rolls of fat and stretch marks.

He places his hands behind his head. "Suit yourself. Are you going to stay in those fluffy pyjamas all day?"

"May as well. Saves changing."

"Didn't you have those same sheep pyjamas at uni?"

"No, they had penguins on. The kids bought me these. They thought they were cute."

"They are cute, for a five-year-old." He snorts.

I throw a cushion at him and wince, holding my side. He flashes a cheesy grin, and even with the pain in my ribs, I can't help but smile along with him. I don't think I could look sexy if I tried, not with the plaster cast on my arm. Even if I wore a silk one-piece. Sexy is not in my power at the moment or on my mind. I can't even make it to the loo without breaking into a sweat.

"Did the kids get off to school all right?"

"Yeah, fine. Cairen's teacher wanted to talk to you. I told her to give Justin a call."

"What about?"

"He's probably been playing up in class again. She wouldn't tell me about it. I'm not his dad. They won't disclose any information to me."

"I don't know what to do, Cal."

"It's normal that he wants to let off steam after everything that's happened. I was the same when my dad left us. I watched that prick beat the shit out of my mum, but I missed him when he left. How fucked up's that?"

"I think your feelings were perfectly normal and valid. You were just a child. But Cairen's dad hasn't gone anywhere. He's still a big part of his life."

"Get Justin to talk to him about his behaviour. I can't say anything to him. The little dude hates my guts."

"He doesn't hate you."

Cal stares at me with an eyebrow raised. "Yeah, he does. I can see the anger in his eyes every time he looks at me. And me being here makes things worse for him."

"Perhaps I should enrol him in kickboxing lessons so he can get it all out of his system."

"Train him to kick my arse. Great idea."

I laugh, then wince at the pain in my ribs.

"Have you had your meds this morning?"

"Yes, first thing."

"I'm going to the library today to that parent toddler group you go to. I was gonna see if you wanted to come if you felt up to it. A change of scene might do you good."

"I can't, Cal. I can't face it, not yet. It takes all my strength getting to the bathroom."

He gives me a sympathetic smile. "I'll take Caleb. Do you want me to get you any books while I'm there?"

"I'd love that. You know what I like."

"Yeah. Do they have a smut section at the library?"

I throw another cushion at him with a wince, then wish I hadn't as it was propping my arm up.

He tosses the cushion to one side. "I have some in the car, actually."

"Have you been reading smut too? Is it because you're not getting any?" I giggle, then wince, and not just from the pain in my ribs, but the thought of him with another woman hurts more than any physical pain.

He stands and straightens the cushions on the sofa. "What do they do at this library gig, then?"

"Sing a few nursery rhymes, and the leader reads a story. The kids have a little play, and there's a cafe so you can get a drink."

"Sound. What do you want for lunch? I can bring you something back."

"A sandwich will be fine when you get back."

"All right. Can I get you anything before I go?"

"I'd like another coffee, but I daren't have one in case I need the loo again. I'm just going to veg in front of the TV. Unless you grab me those books from your car. I hope the pages aren't sticky." I smile as he narrows his eyes at me with a smirk.

"Hang on." He walks out of the living room, jingles his keys, and the front door opens and closes. He returns with two thick books in his hand. "Have you read them before?"

I take them from him, examining the front cover of one with a tattooed chest. "No, I haven't. Did you buy these for me?"

"I just got them a while ago."

"Thank you." I can tell they're used as the spines are creased and the pages are dog-eared, a bugbear Cal always does and it drives me mad. I wonder if these were his mum's. Either way, the fact he thought of me makes my heart melt.

"Right then, little dude, shall we have a sing song?"

Caleb looks up at his dad and smiles, displaying his perfectly placed dimples and his tiny milk teeth. Cal scoops him up in his arms and passes me the TV remote.

"Say bye-bye to Mummy." Cal bends down to me, bringing Caleb with him so I can give him a kiss. "Give Mummy kisses."

I kiss Caleb on his cheek and Cal's warm breath rests on my face as he holds Caleb close. Then his warm lips press against my skin. I suck in a breath. My eyes dart from Caleb to Cal, who looks away, swiftly shifting on his feet, and carries Caleb with him out of the room.

"See you in a bit," he shouts as he walks down the hall.

I let out a noise somewhere between a hum and a squeak. My head is light and my skin still tingles where his lips touched. Had he forgotten himself? Forgot he hates me or forgot we're not actually together? He did that once before in our teens; we were so used to hugging and then kissing. Weeks after we broke up, we gave each other a friendly hug and then accidentally kissed. Kissing him was just so natural, and it's given me a glimmer of hope. Maybe he can forgive me after all.

CAL

WHAT A FUCKING IDIOT. Why did I have to kiss her? Shit. It's gonna make things awkward. She already hates me.

I don't know what made me do it. She was just there and Caleb was getting all the action and… who am I kidding? I wanted to kiss her. Kissing her goodbye as she kissed my son —our son—was so natural.

I strap Caleb securely in his seat, in the new car I just

bought for Steph. One good thing to come of the accident was writing off that pile of crap she drove.

Even though I don't have any fucking money left with the flight from Australia taking up all my savings, I bought her an Audi Q7, hoping we'll get to use the seven seats at some point in the future. She thinks it's my car, but she can have it when she's better. It's sturdier than the last. I wanted to make sure I got her something more robust this time.

I tune the radio to planet rock, starting Caleb off early with a bit of Motley Crue.

Tapping my fingers against the steering wheel, I glance at Caleb before I start the car. "Your mother drives me crazy, kid. You know that, don't you?"

Caleb waves his hands and gurgles.

"What am I gonna do about her?"

He looks at me with his big brown eyes as I wait at the traffic lights. The cheekiest kid I ever saw. His thick black hair has a mind of its own, sticking up as though he's rubbed it with a balloon. He giggles, showing me those cute dimples on his soft chubby cheeks, and he reminds me so much of Steph when he smiles.

A horn beeps, startling me, and I see the lights are on green. I was mesmerised by our boy. Our perfect boy that we created. She's made me the happiest man alive. The only thing that would make me happier is making her my wife.

That and Priya moving back to the UK, which I'm working on. I miss my girls, but it made sense that they went back with Steve. He had to return to England for his brother's wedding, and he took the girls' back to Oz with him. They'd missed a few weeks of school, which Priya wasn't happy about, but it couldn't be helped.

After parking at the library, I make my way through the hoard of pushchairs and prams. I'm greeted by a cackle of mothers. Fuck. Not a bloke in sight.

They all look up from their seats or the carpet where some are sitting, and gaze at me as I walk towards the group with Caleb in my arms. They move, allowing me to step through. A woman removes a large changing bag from a chair and gestures for me to sit next to her.

Taking the seat, I nod and smile, settling Caleb on my knee while I wait for the story to start or sing-song or whatever the fuck it is they do here.

"I haven't seen you here before." The blonde next to me says.

"I haven't been here before."

"I'm Diane." She softly strokes her hand over her baby's head. "This is Henry. And who's this gorgeous one?"

"My names Callum."

She smiles, then presses her lips together.

"Oh, you meant this gorgeous one?" I laugh. "Sorry, I couldn't resist. This is Caleb." *Stop fucking flirting, dickhead.*

"Oh cute, Callum and Caleb. He's your double, after all." She flutters her eyelashes and I could take this further, but there's only one woman I want. Even if she is sitting at home in the most hideous pyjamas, vegging out all day and hasn't washed, brushed her hair, or her teeth. None of that matters because I fucking love that woman.

A lady from the library joins the group, sitting at the helm of the circle on a stool. Everyone sings 'The Wheels On The Bus' and oh… they're all doing the actions too. Thank fuck this kid is sitting on my knee, saving me from any hand signalling.

Caleb waves his hands around as if he wants to join in with the action. I wipe the drool from his chin with the tissue I keep in my pocket. That's a regular thing these days. If it's not needed for Caleb, you can guarantee Steph will be teary about something.

Next up is 'The farmer's In His Den' and as the song goes

on, I can't stop smiling to myself. Maybe it's just me and my dirty mind, but there's something very wrong about a bunch of women singing 'we all pat the bone'.

The librarian woman turns the page in her big book of rhymes and recites 'I Love Little Pussy'. It's the first time I've heard this one. I love playing and patting pussy, but I don't think it's appropriate. I can't seem to get the grin off my face, yet everyone seems oblivious to the lyrics.

Just when I thought it couldn't get any better…'Wee Willie Winkie' is on the next page of her colourful book, faced for all of us to see an old man peering into a kid's bedroom window. It's the stuff of nightmares. How is this rhyme still around?

Several songs and ditties later, thank fuck, that's over.

"Callum, we usually grab a drink in the cafe now." She points to a corner of the library where the coffee area is sectioned off. "The children can play in the small soft play area if you would like to join us."

"Sure, why not? Steph said Caleb likes to play in the soft play area."

Another woman holding a small baby approaches me. "Caleb, isn't it?"

"Yeah, you know him?"

"I do. How is Steph? I heard about the accident. I was praying for her."

"She's getting better. She's gonna be all right. It just takes time." It feels so good to say it out loud and know it's true.

The blonde turns to me as we make our way over to the cafe. "Are you and Steph together?"

I can't be arsed to get into details or have her flirt with me again, so I lie. "Yeah, we are." It feels good to say that too, and my chest stutters.

She looks surprised and the brunette smiles. "I'm glad

Steph's getting better. I was so worried about her. Do you have her number? I'd like to call her."

"Sure."

Caleb stretches out his arms and kicks his legs when he sees the bright colours of the soft padded cubes and toys next to the tables and chairs in the cafe. I place him over the padded barrier, wedging him between two soft cubes where there are some plastic shapes scattered around him.

The brunette with the baby sits at the table next to where I placed Caleb and the blonde has disappeared.

"Let me get you a tea. Then I'll get you her number."

"Thank you. That's really kind of you."

"Will you watch Caleb for me?"

"Yes, of course."

"Anything else?"

"No, a tea would be lovely. I'm watching my weight."

I smile. She sounds just like Steph used to. In the queue for the till, I wave at Caleb. He doesn't see me, but seems content enough. A homemade Victoria sponge with fresh cream catches my eye. Steph would love that. I order a slice to take away along with a coffee and a pot of tea.

Caleb's bottom lip quivers as he looks around. I make my way back to the table quickly. "Are you all right, mate? Daddy's here."

I ruffle his hair, and his frown turns to the brightest smile. He goes back to playing with the large plastic shapes scattered around the floor.

The brunette pours her tea. "Thank you."

"I'm sorry, I didn't get your name."

"It's Sally. I take it you're Justin?"

My eyes bulge. "Fuck no. Shit. Sorry for swearing." I glance around to check none of the mothers heard my bad language.

She waves it off. "Sorry, I just assumed you were Caleb's

dad. You look just like him. Steph said she'd split with her husband. I assumed—"

"I am Caleb's dad. My names Callum. Long story. I'm sure Steph will tell you all about it one day." Fuck, I'm getting myself into some right shit here. "Here, let me give you her number. She could use another friend."

I take out my phone and give Sally her number.

"Thanks. We always sit together in this group. She befriended me when I walked in. I was really nervous, being a new mum and all. She's a lovely woman."

"Yes, she is. She's the best."

"I'm glad she has you. I could tell she was struggling recently."

She was probably struggling because of me. I sip my drink and glance over at Caleb sucking on a ball. I shake my head. The things that kid puts in his mouth. Steph would take it off him, saying dirty, but he's already sucked it now. Knock yourself out, kid. I've had dirtier things in my mouth, and I'm still alive.

After finishing my coffee, it's lunchtime. I don't want to keep her waiting. She'll be due her meds now, and she needs to have them with food. "Sally, do you know where the dirty books are in this place?" I clear my throat. "For Steph."

Sally smiles. "She always disappears over in that corner." She points to a little nook behind the humorous section.

"Thanks. Nice to meet you."

"And you. Tell Steph I said hi."

I hold my hands out to Caleb. "Shall we choose some books?" I scoop him up and pry the ball from his fingers, then bounce him in my arms to distract him before he realises his new favourite suck toy has gone.

He wipes his wet chin on my t-shirt as I carry him to the dark corner of the erotic section. Two books stand out on top with shirtless dudes. She's not having them. If she's gonna be looking at anyone shirtless, it's me.

I opt for one with roses on the cover and another with a full-figured woman. She'll like that. She's always banging on about how larger women don't get enough representation.

"All right mate, we got Mummy's books. Shall we choose some for you, ay?"

He blows bubbles out of his mouth as he makes a noise and more drool drips down his chin before he wipes it on my top. In the children's section, Caleb's hands wave when he spots a multicoloured elephant. I grab a dinosaur book and 'The Tiger That Came to Tea.'

Once home, Steph is asleep on the sofa. I close the door to the living room gently so I don't wake her and settle Caleb in his highchair for his lunch and make Steph a sandwich for when she wakes.

Jerry has given me some freelance work to cover Steph's absence and give me a bit of extra cash while I'm over here, but I can catch up on that later when Caleb goes down for a nap.

"Cal," Steph calls from the living room.

"I'm here. One sec." I scoop the last of the butternut squash blend out of the bowl, one more aeroplane, and then wipe his mouth. After unclipping him from the highchair, I carry him into the lounge with his sippy cup and place him on the rug with his toys.

"How long have you been back?" She smiles at Caleb as she holds her side. I can tell she's in more pain than she's letting on.

"A while. Are you hungry? I'll get your sandwich and your pills." It pains me to see her like this. Each time she screws her beautiful face in discomfort, guilt roils in my stomach and I want to do everything I can to take care of her.

Twenty seven

STEPH

Caleb rolls on his play mat. Cal returns with a sandwich, a glass of milk, pills, and a clear container with a slice of sponge cake.

A smile spreads across my face. "What's this?"

"I saw it in the library. Thought you'd like it."

"I do. It looks delicious."

"Eat the sandwich first, though, so you can take your pills."

I take the milk from him, and he places a tablet on my tongue. I swallow along with a drink, and he gives me the second tablet. "Did you have fun at the library?"

Cal places the plate with the sandwich and plastic container on the armrest next to me with a chuckle.

"What's funny?"

"You didn't tell me it would be full of women."

"I thought you knew. Didn't you ever take your girls to anything like that?"

"No. I was always at work."

"They're a friendly bunch, though. Did they make you feel welcome?"

"Yeah, you could say that."

Oh no, I bet they did. I bite the cheese sandwich and chew, but the thought of him flirting with those women leaves a tangy taste in my mouth. I swallow it down with a drink of milk, knowing everyone would want a piece of him. No one can deny he's devilishly handsome and carrying our equally handsome boy would have made everyone swoon, no doubt.

"I saw Sally. She asked for your number. I hope it's all right, because I gave it to her."

"It's fine. She's really nice. We should have swapped numbers a long time ago."

"I got you some books, too. Hang on." He steps out of the room and returns with a tote bag full of books. "Have you read these?" He holds up two books.

"No, I started this one, though." I lift the book that he left me with earlier today with the tatted guy on the cover. "I've honestly never seen this book before, but it's odd, like I know or remember the story, and I knew what was going to happen before it did."

"Caleb, careful." Cal moves the coffee table to the side before Caleb bangs his head on the corner as he rolls around.

"Don't you think that's weird?" I'm not sure he was actually listening.

"Yeah, weird." He shrugs, avoiding my gaze, and pulls some children's books from the bag. "Do you wanna read a story, mate?"

Cal scoops Caleb up and sits next to me on the sofa. His legs nestle next to mine and Caleb's tiny feet rest on top of the both of our thighs as he leans into Cal's chest facing me.

Listening to Cal read 'The Tiger Who Came For Tea' soothes my soul. That man could read the phone book, and I would still get high from his voice.

Watching him with our son gives me a tingle in my

stomach. Plus, he sat right next to me when there's a full sofa and two chairs to choose from. He literally couldn't get any closer unless he sat on my knee. Hope bubbles in my chest, and tingles spread out through every limb. I hope he'll forgive me and learn to love me again.

Without his love, I'm like a flower with no sun. A rose bush cut back in winter, leaving only prickly thorns. I spent twenty years trying to live without his love, only half living. I didn't even realise until I found him again, and he made me feel complete.

Caleb looks like he may settle down. He sucks on the teat of his bottle, leaning back in Cal's muscular arm. His lids grow heavy and his eyelashes flicker as he gets milk drunk. Cal continues to read, and I rest my head against his shoulder, listening to his gravelly voice.

By the end of the story, Caleb's out for the count. Cal eases him onto the space on the sofa next to us and pulls the blanket from the footstool over his small frame.

I open the container and take a bite of the Victoria sponge.

"Give us a bite."

"I can't, it's too nice," I tease, licking the cream from my lips.

He grins. "I'd force you into submission if you weren't crippled."

I laugh, then wince as my meds haven't kicked in yet and the pain in my ribs jabs me with each rock of laughter. "Oh, how?"

He smirks, and I wonder what he's thinking. There are many ways he could easily get me to submit. Kissing me is one and probably the easiest. He could tickle me or lick my neck or just snatch it from me, which he could easily do now. I'm not in any position to fight, but I'd prefer a kiss.

"Give us a bite, and I'll tell you."

A smile pushes my cheeks. I'd spoon feed it to him if I could, or better still, rub this cream over his body and lick it off. "Here." I hold the wedge with my good arm, bringing it to his mouth.

He takes a big bite and wipes the cream from the corner of his mouth.

"Nice?"

"Yeah, I wish I'd got two slabs," he mumbles.

"Did you not get anything while you were there?"

"No, just had a coffee."

"They do nice cookies. Would you go again?"

"Sure."

Of course he would. I bet he loved all the attention, being the only bloke. "Do you want another bite?"

"No, baby. You have it."

I suck in a breath. The word baby caresses my skin, sending goosebumps along my arms like a domino effect.

I finish the cake and lick my fingers, savouring the fluffy cream taste and texture. My hand drops to my side, accidentally touching Callum's hand as it rests in the crevice of where our legs meet. His thumb circles my palm, causing my heart to pick up a pace and a tremble courses through my body.

"Are you cold, baby?"

Before I can answer, he pulls the blanket draped over the back of the sofa behind me and covers my legs. How can I tell him it's him? I smile and let him fuss with the cover. Then his hand goes back to resting next to mine and his thumb rubs circles on me again. With his other hand, he tugs his jeans near his groin.

"Was that a maintenance manoeuvre or a stiffy adjustment?" I joke.

He laughs, looking me up and down. "It's those fucking sheep pyjamas. They do it for me every time."

"Really?"

"No, Steph. Not really."

I knock his shoulder with my good arm. "I have some reindeer ones upstairs. Perhaps they'll get you going."

He laughs again. If only I could get him going. He looks into my eyes . His thumb still strokes my hand, and he pulls his bottom lips between his teeth. My breathing quickens.

"Can I get you anything?"

My head shakes from side to side. I don't want him to move or stop stroking my hand or looking into my eyes. I hope he can see how sorry I am and how much love I still have for him as he peers into my soul. .

"I'm gonna put the kettle on, then I have some work to do." He stands. "Want a drink?"

"I need the loo."

"Come on, then." He wraps an arm around my back, helping me off the sofa, and I hold my breath as the pain in my ribs spreads to my side and back.

"Thanks. I can manage now."

He lets me go, and I hobble to the bathroom.

CAL

FUCK, I wanted to kiss her. Would she have kissed me back? I'm such a dick, of course she wouldn't. She has more important things to think about now, like getting better. Kissing me is the last thing on her mind.

If I had kissed her, I wouldn't be able to stop at that. I need to have her, but she's not capable of letting me do the things I need to do to her. Just the touch of her hand in mine was enough to make my jeans uncomfortable, even in her sheep pyjamas.

I wonder if I can still make her feel the same. If her body would still react to mine like I do hers. I felt her breathing heavy, but she does that through the pain.

How could she feel anything for me after the misery I put her through? All this pain I've caused. I want it to be me. I want to take all this hurt. If I could have it inflicted on me instead, I'd gladly do that for her, just to see her smile again. To see her eyes sparkle and her infectious laugh that makes me laugh even when nothing's funny. She can't even giggle without it hurting her ribs.

With a coffee in hand, I sit at the kitchen table, waiting for the laptop to load. She passes me, her fingers graze my shoulder as she walks by, sending sparks of electricity down my spine.

"What are you working on?"

"Some freelance stuff Jerry sent through."

"It's kind of him to give you work."

"Yeah, he said I could have my old job back."

"My job, you mean."

"He said he'd make another position for me, and he'd be glad to have me back. When you're better and don't need me here, of course."

"Do you want to go back to work there?"

"I would if you wouldn't mind working with me again, but I left for a reason. I don't want to make things awkward or difficult for you."

She slumps over the back of my chair, holding her side.

I turn my head and see the pain carved into her face.

"Can I be honest, Cal?"

"Sure."

"I know this is really selfish of me, but I couldn't stand to work with you if you date other women."

"I—"

"Let me finish. I know it's going to happen eventually, and I have to get used to the idea. I just don't want to have it rubbed in my face every day."

I huff. "Like you did with Justin, you mean?"

"Cal, that's not fair."

"I'm sorry." I take her hand as it rests on the chair, her other arm clutching her side. Doesn't she realise she's the one I want? It's always been her. "What about when you meet someone?"

"Don't make me laugh. It hurts my side."

"What? You're gonna start dating again, eventually."

She looks at me like I've grown another head. "As if anyone is going to want to date me. A fat middle-aged woman with three kids to two different men. I can't even advertise that I'm a good cook."

"Now you're just fishing for compliments." I grin. She could have ten kids to ten different blokes, and I still wouldn't be put off by her non-existent culinary skills.

The size or shape of her body has never deterred me, either. It's her heart and mind I crave. Having her curves and something to hold on to is just a bonus.

She shuffles to the living room, and I hang my head low, carrying on with work. I want to tell her how much I want her. To take care of her and not just while she recovers from her accident. I want to take care of my woman in every way possible and be there for her emotionally, physically, and sexually.

But it's too soon. She might tell me to fuck off. I see it playing out in two ways. The latter or she would actually take me back, but only because she thinks no one else will want her. For too long, I've played second fiddle to Justin. I want her to choose me because she loves me. So I know she wants me for me and not because I'll be there to help with the kids and cook and shit. I'm not Justin. I'll be her roommate for now, but eventually I want more.

———

A FEW HOURS LATER, I walk into the living room to see Steph watching cartoons with Caleb.

"I'm gonna get the kids."

"Did you finish your work?"

"For now. I'll catch up later. Do you need anything while I'm out?"

"No, thanks."

"See you in about twenty minutes, then."

"Wave bye-bye to Daddy."

I fucking love it when she calls me that, and I look forward to the day when Caleb can say the words.

"See-ya, mate, back soon."

Steph holds her hand up and waves. Caleb copies, squeezing his hand closed and opening it again. I resist the urge to walk over and give him a kiss. After what happened earlier, I'd probably kiss her on the cheek again.

As I walk through the school gates into the playground, Cassie waves bye to her mates then scowls as she slumps over to me, lugging her backpack over her shoulder. Cairen glares at me from the other end and his teacher walks towards me.

"Fuck, what's he done now?" My muscles tense as I brace myself for whatever shit's gone down today.

"Not a good day, I'm afraid."

"Again? He's only been back a few days."

"Tell Mrs Bailey I'll schedule a meeting."

"Look, she's got enough on her plate after the accident. Can you schedule the meeting with his dad?"

"I'd like both parents to be involved. I'll call her next week." She pivots and heads back inside.

Cairen knocks my hip with his bag. "Can we go then? I don't want to see that dragon again." He stomps off towards the gate, and I follow in silence.

They both get in the back seat and slam the door.

"Good day, then?"

Neither kid acknowledges me. They hate my fucking guts.

"So what's been going on, Cairen?"

"Nothing to do with you."

"It is to do with me when it's upsetting your mum. She needs to concentrate on getting better. You can talk to me, you know."

"You're not my dad."

I wondered how long it would take for one of them to say the classic phrase. It's a good thing I'm not his dad as I wouldn't stand for his attitude lately. I clench my jaw and start the engine. The roar beneath me mimics the rage inside.

"Look, I'm not trying to be your dad. I care about your mum, and I care about you, believe it or not. If you want to talk, I'm here."

He looks out of the window, giving me the silent treatment. He reminds me of his mother, how she sticks her chin out when she has the face on. These kids may be Justin's double, but fucking-hell, they have their mother's personality. Steph can be stubborn, fierce and mardy as hell, not to mention spoilt.

I smile, thinking of her and despite it all, I fucking love her for it. Even when she's pissed off, she arouses something in me and her fiery temper dissolves at the touch of my lips. I snort, wishing I could resolve everything with one kiss. I'd kiss her until her pain stopped. Until she was happy again.

"You know, I love your mum. And I love you two kids even though you hate me." I laugh.

I glance at Cassie in the passenger seat and nudge her with my shoulder. "Is that a smile? Wait, let me take a picture to show your mum. I actually got a smile out of you."

She laughs, "I don't hate you."

"That's good to hear."

"I loathe you." She grins, and Cairen bursts out laughing. *Little shit.*

"That's the nicest thing you've ever said to me."

"We will like you if you buy us the new PlayStation," Cairen says.

I silently laugh. I have to hand it to them. They drive a hard bargain.

"Mate, if you can be nice to me and help me get back with your mum, I'll have a word with Santa. How about that?"

"Deal. If by Santa, you mean Mum."

"You don't believe?"

He smiles and looks out the window.

After pulling on the drive, the kids are first through the door and upstairs. I step over their bags and shoes in Steph's small hallway. Normally I would call them out on it and make them put them away, but not today.

It's easier to just put them away myself than to cause another row. I don't need another reason for these two to hate me any more than they already do.

STEPH

"YOUR MUM IS STILL POORLY, THEN?" Cal asks, dropping the groceries on the worktop.

"How do you know?"

"Because you've had those fluffy sheep pyjamas on for three days."

"I know. I really need a wash. Claire and Sam are working."

"I'll help you. It's no big deal." He puts the shopping away, and I think I can manage to take my bra and pants off if he helps me take my top off.

Caleb whizzes across the laminate floor in his baby walker. "Ay, mate, look what I got you." He empties a packet of milky buttons onto the tray and his eyes light up. They keep him occupied as he uses his fine motor skills to pick one up and bring it to his mouth.

"I'd love a bath. I can't remember the last time I had a soak."

"I'll run you one in a minute. Anything to get you out of those fucking pyjamas."

I follow Cal upstairs to the bathroom. He carries Caleb in one arm and places him in his cot with some toys to keep him occupied. The vanilla scent of the bubble bath billows around me as Cal pours it into the running water.

Standing in my fluffy pyjamas, I play with the drawstring of the bottoms. My skin tingles as a hot flush creeps up my neck.

"Are you getting in, then?" Cal mixes the hot and cold water as if he's getting the temperature right for a small child.

I pull my good arm through my top and tug at the other. Cal sees my struggle and lifts the pyjama top over my head, pulling the sleeve from the cast on my arm. My breasts sag against my belly, and I hold them up, partly covering them with my good arm.

Cal points to my bottoms. "Do you need me to take those off too?"

"I can manage now."

"I'll get the cling film for your cast?" He leaves me to undress alone. I tug at the waistband and shimmy my pyjamas down, wincing with every movement.

My knickers drop to the floor with my bottoms, and I grit my teeth as I lift my leg over the side of the tub. Clinging on to the edge of the bath, I lift my other leg in. Callum walks back into the bathroom with cling film just as I'm doubled over with my arse in the air.

"Here, let me wrap this around your arm. You don't want to get it wet."

"I'll be glad to get this pot off in a few days." I stand, covering myself with my hands and arm.

He doesn't look at me, his eyes don't rake my body like they used to with passion, want, and need. He just unravels the cling film, takes hold of my pot that was hiding my saggy breasts, and wraps the clear plastic over the cast until it's covered completely.

"Have you turned into a hardcore feminist?" He grins.

"What do you mean?"

He nods at my hairy legs.

"Oh piss off, this is why I didn't want you helping me into the bath." Heat spreads up my thighs as my body breaks out in gooseflesh. I've never felt so vulnerable.

"Calm down. I'm only joking." He chuckles. "Besides, I'm all for the European look."

I bend down to sit, using my good arm to lower myself. He quickly slips an arm around my back. "Lean onto me. I've got you." I lean back as he lowers me into the bath.

The bubbles cover my hairy legs, but nothing can hide the heat painting my face. My cheeks must be glowing.

I hold my hand out. "Pass me a razor."

"Razor? You're gonna need hair clippers, or maybe a hedge trimmer." He chuckles.

"Are you done? If you're just going to embarrass me—"

"You know I love teasing you. It makes no difference to me how hairy you are."

I sigh. He doesn't care. I mean, why would he? It's not

like he'll be kissing my legs and running his tongue up the inside of my thigh any time soon—if ever again.

"I want to shave. I feel scruffy."

He rummages through his wash bag on the windowsill and a box of condoms falls out. He stuffs them back in his bag and hands me a razor. "It's a new one and as you can tell, I hardly use it, so be careful. Do you want me to do it for you?"

"No way, it's bad enough you seeing me like this. I'm not having you shave my legs as well." My stomach twists thinking about the condoms. I can't bear to think of him with anyone else. Did he buy them recently? Has he been seeing someone?

CAL

"Do you need help washing your hair?" I unravel the bobble from her low ponytail.

"I can manage."

I was hoping she would say yes. "Shout me when you want to get out, yeah?"

"Hmm." She hums, leaning back in the bath with her cast resting over the side as she closes her eyes. I leave her to it, but prop the door open so I can listen out for her.

I couldn't look at her. If I looked at her, I wouldn't be able to help myself from getting naked and joining her in the bath. Even with her hairy legs, which don't bother me one bit, nothing could make me love her any less, or be any less attracted to her. Her vulnerability only makes me love her more, and I want her to know that things like hairy legs are superficial to me.

As if I love her because of how she looks. I couldn't give

a fuck how she looks. Her ass and those thick thighs turn me on like no other woman has, but that's because it's her. It's nothing else but her, and I love her, every last fucking detail of her. I love every one of those hairs on her body because they're hers.

I almost want her to stay poorly so I can stay here taking care of her, and I never have to leave.

The doorbell rings, and I open the front door. "Dean, come in."

"I can't stay." He nods towards the car with some blonde chick in the passenger seat. "I got that stuff you wanted. Thought Steph might need a toke to help with the pain." He pulls a small clear packet from his pocket and hands it to me.

"Cheers, mate. I appreciate that." I open the bag and inhale the delicious sweet aroma.

"How is she?" He runs a hand over his shaved head.

"She's getting better." I hear Caleb cry in the other room. "One sec." I unclip him from the highchair and carry him through to the hall. "Uncle Deanie's here, look."

Dean chuckles. "Fuck, he's the spit of you. Poor bastard."

My shoulders rock, and Caleb jiggles in my arms.

"Cal," Steph calls.

"I'll let you go." Dean squeezes my arm. "Take care of yourself too, mate. You look tired."

"I'm all right. Cheers, pal."

He pinches Caleb's cheek. "Be good for your old man, ay?"

I close the door behind him and walk up the stairs to Steph. "Everything all right?"

"I'm ready to get out." Her face distorts as she leans over the tub.

"Gimmie a minute." I put Caleb in his cot and return to the bathroom, grabbing a large bath towel from the cupboard.

"Hold on to me." My arm slips under hers as she pulls herself up.

Our eyes meet. Her lips part inches from mine. I hesitate for a moment, gazing into her green eyes like a wilting leaf. Once she's standing, I wrap the towel around her and help her step out of the bath.

"I got you something to smoke, to help with the pain." I hold the packet up, twisting it through my fingers.

She grips the towel tighter. Pain etched on her face as her lip contorts. "You haven't been in contact with *them,* have you? Please tell me you haven't got it from *her* or *him*?" She makes her way into the bedroom in a huff.

"Fuck no. I wouldn't deal with either of them again. Dean just dropped it off. He's been growing his own. It's good stuff."

She eases onto the bed, screwing her face up as she holds her side. "Callum, I can't."

"You can when the kids are in bed. It might help you relax and get a good night's sleep."

"The last time I smoked that shit, I was about twenty. The pain isn't as bad now, anyway."

"You could've fooled me." I stuff it in my pocket. "Suit yourself. I just thought it would help."

She looks up at me with heavy eyes. "How often do you smoke it?"

"I haven't smoked any in a long time. I only started when I left Browns Media, just to take the edge off, you know."

She shakes her head as if she's swallowed something vile. "I couldn't stand the thought of you and her together. It haunts me."

I huff. "It haunts me too, believe me."

Her brow wrinkles. "She must have meant something. You were sleeping with her."

"Yeah, I fucked her before you came back into my life.

We would hang out and fuck. It wasn't serious. It was never like us." I stop myself from saying any more.

Her mouth opens. A hint of life comes back into her eyes as she gazes at me from the bed in nothing but a towel.

My body tenses. It takes everything I have to not crash against her lips and rip the towel off. If she wasn't in so much pain, I'd be on top of her already. Would she kiss me back?

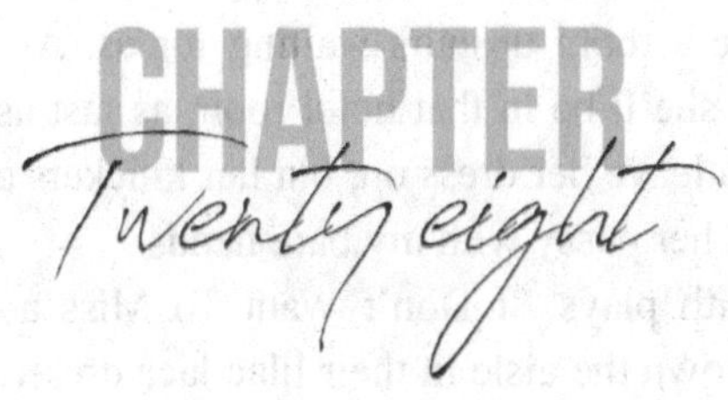

CAL

Sun pours through the large arched windows of the old manor hotel, casting a golden glow over the white roses lining the aisle. I straighten my suit and check my watch.

Dean places his hand on my back. "Mate. Stop fidgeting. She'll be here."

I let out a jagged breath. All our friends and family sit patiently waiting for her arrival. Mum holds Caleb in her arms, keeping him quiet with milky buttons. The white dribble runs down his chin onto his dapper suit. Steph would have a fit if she saw. I smile and wave at our boy in the front row.

Sue walks into the room and takes a seat. Her wide lemon hat covers her eyes, but her lips curl into a smile. *What's up with her?* I thought she would protest at this marriage, but so far she's been amiable.

"You have the rings, don't you?" I give Dean a sideways glance.

"Mate, just chill, yeah. Everything is under control."

Chill, he says. It's a little hard to chill, even if I am dressed up like a penguin. Fuck, this suit is so itchy. I scratch my chest over the white shirt. I'm sure it's given me a rash. When the service is over, I'll be happy.

We have a room upstairs waiting for us. As soon as she says 'I do', she'll be in that hotel room as fast as I can carry her. She can leave her dress on, but her knickers are gonna be ripped from her pussy with my bare hands.

Aerosmith plays, 'I Don't Want To Miss a Thing'. My girls walk down the aisle in their lilac lace dresses with white tulle. Bethy beams brighter than the sun's rays, and Livvie has that look where secretly she's happy, but she likes to pretend she's not.

Cassie and Cairen walk behind. The light bounces off their golden hair, and I know my Steph is next to walk through the door with her dad, John. I straighten my collar and smooth my sweaty palms over my jacket. Dean elbows me, giving me a grin as we face the doors at the back of the room, waiting for her to appear.

The wedding staff opens the double doors, and I hold my breath. Her dad, John, walks out in his black suit holding a white casket with silver handles, held up by Justin and several others. Chills course through my veins, and I look around me as the room is swept up into a tornado.

Caleb cries out, but I can't reach him. My girls have gone too, swept away with the whirlwind, and everything has turned to grey. Darkness closes in, suffocating me, and I reach for the coffin. Dean holds me back as I cry out. I claw my way free and throw open the lid to get to Steph. Her rosy cheeks have turned blue. She's so cold. "No, no, no…"

———

STEPH

A SHRILL SCREAM startles me awake. I throw the covers from me and rush downstairs to the living room, holding my side. Cal's head thrashes on the sofa.

"Cal." I kneel beside him, placing my arm over his drenched t-shirt and shake his shoulders to wake him. "Cal."

He jumps up head-butting my face, then fists my top and throws me to the ground.

"Cal, it's me." A sharp pain stabs me in my side, causing me to shield and protect my ribs.

His eyes are wide and his breathing stutters, like he's struggling for air. "Steph?"

He unclenches his fist from my pyjama top and holds his weight above me, resting his elbows on either side of my head. "Fuck Steph," he exhales, his breath tickling my cheek. "Did I hurt you?" His trembling hand caresses my face, almost scared to touch me, as if I'm a china doll.

"I'm fine." My face screws up as I say the words. The stabbing still piercing my side.

His fingers gently graze my skin, leaving tingles in their wake. "What are you doing?"

"You were having a nightmare." I move my hand over his damp hair, pulling it from his eyes so I can see his gorgeous face hovering above me. Our lips inch closer like magnets drawn to each other, but before he reaches me, he rolls onto his back on the living room rug.

His breathing steadies as his arm leans on his forehead.

I roll into his side and place my potted arm on his chest. "Are you all right?"

"Yeah."

"What were you dreaming about? I've never seen you like that before."

"I don't know."

The blanket from the sofa lays crumpled on the floor, and I pull it over the two of us. The pain in my ribs subsiding a little as I move and settle in next to him. His hand goes to my cheek. "Your lips bleeding."

I lick my lip and taste the metal. "It's nothing."

"Fuck, Steph. It's not nothing. I hurt you."

"Cal, it was an accident."

"Baby, I'm so sorry." His thumb runs along my lip, and I lick any traces of blood away.

"It's nothing, really. I can't even feel it." I lie. It stings, but the touch of his thumb there seems to make it all better. Even if it is only for a moment.

The soft light coming from the hall bounces off his watery eyes and when he blinks, I see a tear run to the side of his face. I place my hand on his cheek and wipe his tear with my thumb, as he has done with me many times. I've never seen him so vulnerable.

Was it the dream or the fact that he thinks he's physically hurt me? He could never physically hurt me. He's the gentlest person I know, unless he has me bent over, but that's different. His dad messed up his head. Watching him abuse his mother couldn't have been easy, it torments him, thinking he will turn out the same. He could never be like his dad. He just doesn't have it in him to hurt a woman.

"Talk to me, Cal. You can talk to me."

"I'm fine." He kisses my forehead. "You should go back to bed."

"I'm comfy here." I snuggle into him more. My cast rests on his chest, and I trace his ink with my fingers peeking out from under the plaster.

"It's the same nightmare I have most nights," he whispers.

"I've never known you have nightmares."

"It's since your accident."

"Oh." I freeze.

"You're dead." His body stiffens and his breathing stops for a moment.

I bring my lips to his cheek and kiss him there. "I'm not dead. I'm here, and I'm very much alive."

He closes his eyes and holds me close. "If anything had happened to you, Steph. If you hadn't made it—" His voice quivers.

"Shh. I made it. It's okay. Everything's okay."

CAL

WHEN I WAKE on the rug, she's gone. I walk into the kitchen to her making coffee.

"Mammamam." Caleb bangs a plastic cup against his high chair tray.

"Hey, mate." I ruffle his thick black hair and catch a glimpse of his dimples. "Steph, you shouldn't have carried him downstairs. Why didn't you wake me?"

She doesn't turn around, but shrugs a shoulder. "You needed your sleep. I'm much better. I can lift him with my good arm. Besides, I'm getting my pot off soon."

Standing behind Steph, my finger holds her chin, and I turn her to me so I can inspect her swollen lip. "Fuck, Steph."

She looks down. "Cal, it's fine."

"It's not fucking fine, Steph. I'm so sorry." Acid burns my chest, after what I did to her.

She steps closer to me. "It's nothing, really."

"How can you say that? Look at you. I can't believe I hit you." The words take my breath away. Are we really having this conversation?

Her eyebrows pinch together. "You didn't hit me, Cal. You could never hit me."

My head flinches back. "What the fuck did I do, then?"

"You jumped and your head knocked me. It was an accident."

I let out a sigh of relief. "Are you sure?"

She smiles, showing a hint of her cute dimples, then winces as her swollen lip stretches. "Yes, I'm sure."

I bring my hand to her face, my thumb grazing her lip, wanting to kiss it better, and take all her pain away.

"It doesn't hurt, I promise." She closes her eyes and kisses my thumb.

Watching her purse those lips against my pad, I want them to be on my lips. I remove my thumb and fuck it. I bring my lips to hers and gently peck the cut. She opens her eyes, parting her lips as she sucks in a breath.

I want to slide my tongue in and ravish her, suck her lip and lick the cut like an animal would lick their wounds. But my head instinctually goes to the side, and I wrap her in a tight embrace and tell her how sorry I am. I feel her lips press against my cheek.

"I know you're sorry, but you have nothing to be sorry about, Cal."

She doesn't know I mean for everything. I'm sorry for treating her like crap when I found out I had a son. I'm sorry for seducing her and ruining her marriage. But most of all, I'm sorry for pushing her away in our teens.

———

STEPH

WHILE CALEB IS NAPPING, I pick up my book with the tattooed guy on the cover. I know I've never read this book before because it's not listed on my Goodreads account where I rate every book I've read, but I can recall the storyline.

A knock on the front door breaks my concentration. I open the door. "Justin? Everything all right?"

"Yeah. Can I come in?"

I step aside, allowing him to walk through the hallway, then glance outside, looking for the kids. "Where are the kids?"

"Maxine's taken them to the cinema. I wanted to talk to you." He walks into the kitchen.

"Okay, do I need to put the kettle on, or is this a quick visit?"

"I think you better put the kettle on. Is Callum about?"

"He's grocery shopping."

Justin takes hold of my arm. "It's heeled nicely, not a scar in sight."

"It's the wrong arm." I show him my other arm. "It feels so nice to have the cast off."

"I bet. How's your ribs?"

"Much better. It only hurts when I take a really deep breath." I sit at the table opposite Justin with a pot of tea.

He unzips his hoodie and places some paperwork on the table. "I hope this isn't a bad time. I'm going to ask Maxine to move in with me, full time, but I want to finalise our divorce first."

I swallow. My voice comes out a little high. "That's great."

He smiles. "You just have to sign where the solicitor has added a sticky note. I'll pay for everything and deal with it all. Keep the paperwork and read through it if you like."

"I will, thank you." He's finally sorted everything out. I'm actually relieved more than anything. It'll be nice to be officially single again.

"I guess Callum will be pleased."

"What makes you say that?" I really don't think Cal cares about my marital status. I mean, the only thing to change will be my name from a mrs to miss, which doesn't really affect him.

"I just thought since he was living here with you, and you're back together, it frees you up for him to pop the question if he wants."

A puff of laughter escapes my lips. That's a joke if ever I heard one. "We're not together. He only moved in to be close to Caleb and to help out while I have my pot on my arm. He doesn't want me in that way."

Justin scratches his jaw. "Unbelievable. Has he said that?"

"Pretty much. A while ago." I pour us both a cup of tea.

"For someone who says he doesn't want you, he has a funny way of showing it." Justin shakes his head with a puzzled look on his face.

"What are you talking about?"

"Just how he was when you were in hospital." He sips his tea. "You still buy that Earl Grey for your mother?"

"I don't care about the tea. How was he?"

"He didn't leave your side. Day and night, he was there, sitting in the chair next to your bed, holding your hand, stroking your arm. He even read to you. He must have gone through a couple of books while you were unconscious."

I glance at my book on the counter and it all makes sense. No wonder I feel like I've read it.

"One night I called to drop some stuff off, and I could tell he'd been crying. I heard him talking to you, but he didn't see me. He was telling you if you woke up, he would love you till the day he dies. He kissed your lips, begging you to come back to him. I coughed as I walked in, and his eyes were red."

"But he wasn't there when I woke up?"

"He wouldn't leave unless someone was sitting with you and when visiting hours were over, he slept in the waiting room. The only reason he left the night before you woke was because I told him to go home and shower and spend some time with Caleb. He was a mess."

"So why hasn't he made a move on me? We've been living together all this time." I cover my mouth with my hands. "He feels guilty."

It all makes sense. He was so upset that he hurt me the other night. Even though a bust lip is nothing compared to what I've just been through. Realisation hits me in the stomach. Memories of him telling me the accident was all his fault resurface.

I rub my temples. "He blames himself for some argument we had, and I can't even recall it."

Every time he believes he's physically hurt me in the past, it brings up so many triggers for him, with his dad and the abuse he saw growing up when his dad was drunk. I know how his mind works. He'll be punishing himself, thinking he doesn't deserve me or something.

"He was in a bad way at the hospital. Your mum blamed him, too. Something about you calling her the day of the accident. You were upset over a row."

"I don't even care what it was about. I just want him to love me." My arms wrap around my body as if it's Cal's arms holding me. All this time, I thought he didn't want me. I need to tell him I forgive him.

The front door opens. Caleb stirs in his rocker.

"I'll leave the paperwork with you, then." Justin stands and gives Cal a nod on his way out.

"What did he want?" Cal places the shopping bags on the worktop and unpacks the food.

I unclip Caleb from his rocker and try to hush him back to sleep in my arms. "He dropped off the divorce papers."

Cal drops a tin of beans to the floor, causing Caleb to jump and cry out. He picks the tin up and strokes Caleb's head as it rests on my shoulder. "Hey. It's all right, mate."

I give him his dummy. He suckles with hooded eyes and settles back down with his head in the crook of my neck. "Will you help me read through the divorce papers?"

"Yeah, sure." Cal looks spaced out. "Give me him. It's not good for your arm to be holding him. Just because you've had the cast off doesn't mean it's fully healed." He gently lifts Caleb from me, and I help unload the shopping.

I lift a teddy out of a bag and smile. "Cute, but hasn't he got enough soft toys?"

"It's for Jax." Cal's eyes glaze over. He rubs Caleb's back and closes his eyes as if holding Caleb is filling the void from the loss of his son. "It's his birthday today."

I drop the teddy back in the bag. "Cal, why didn't you say?"

"You have enough on your plate. I'll nip to the cemetery after unpacking the shopping. I won't be long."

My shoulders tense, along with a tightening in my stomach. No wonder he's been having nightmares of death with the anniversary of his son's death weighing on his mind. "I'm coming with you."

"Steph. You don't have to do that. It's why I didn't tell you. I don't want to burden you."

My eyes water. Thinking of him going through this alone because he doesn't want to burden me with his problems breaks my heart. I step closer, place my hand on his cheek, feeling the bristles from his unshaven jaw against my palm.

"Cal. I'm coming with you. I'll always be there for you." Can't he see I love him? I've always loved him.

***

"CAN you call at the supermarket before we leave town?" I say, getting into Cal's new car. It's still an old model, but has that freshly valeted car smell.

He turns the ignition. "I just come from there. What do you need?"

"I just want to get something." I sit my hand on his leg as he drives, wanting to let him know I'm here for him. "How old would he have been?"

"Fourteen." Cal's voice is quiet. He places his hand over mine and gives me a half-hearted smile. Caleb babbles away to himself in the back seat, which makes us both widen our smiles.

Cal drives up to the doors of the supermarket and parks in a parent and toddler bay.

"I won't be long." I needed to do this for him. For Jax. I want to do something special.

Caleb's eyes bulge when I return, placing fourteen brightly coloured helium-filled balloons in the boot of the car.

"You didn't have to do that, Steph."

"I know, but I wanted to." I place my hand back on his leg and stroke over the denim fabric with my thumb.

His jeans buzz, sending a vibration up my arm. Cal lifts his arse and pulls his phone from his front pocket and hands it to me. "Just answer and tell my mum I'm on my way."

I swipe the green button right and press speaker.

"Hello."

"Mum. I'm on my way."

"Oh, love. I thought you'd got held up, so I drove myself. I'm here now. Rachel was here, but she's just left."

"I'll be about fifteen minutes," Cal says, speaking a little louder than usual.

"All right, love. No rush."

"Mum."

"Yes, love."

"Was Rachel all right? Was she well?" His voice quietens, and he gives me a sideways glance. His fists grip the steering wheel and I feel his body tense.

"She's doing great. Her husband and son were with her. She had a daughter, too. They must be doing all right because they've moved onto that posh estate near the private school."

Cal relaxes into his seat, nodding and smiling as his mum rambles on through the handset speakerphone.

"She asked about you, too. I told her you were doing well and have a baby boy and you're happy. You are happy, aren't you, love?"

Cal pauses, concentrating on the road. His Adam's apple moves in his throat as he swallows. He shifts gears as we come to a set of lights. His hand moves from the gear stick to my thigh and as the car comes to a stop, his eyes glance at the phone in my hand, then he gazes into my eyes. "Yeah. I'm happy, Mum."

With his fingers stroking my thigh over the black fabric of my leggings, I break out in gooseflesh. Suddenly the air in the car is stifling. Heat radiates from his hand, spreading across my body, rising to my face. Everything blurs and I'm weightless, like a hot-air balloon ascending to the clouds. His eyes are the fire, emitting the heat that's causing me to float on air as they peer into me, seeking my soul.

A hooter pips from behind, crashing me back down to reality with a jerk to my heart. Cal snaps his head away, pressing his foot on the accelerator. Who knows how long the lights were on green?

"Callum. Are you still there, love?" I'd forgot I was still holding his mother in the palm of my hand.

"Yeah, I'll see you soon." He chuckles, trying to put some distance between us, and the angry pipping driver behind who's been up his arse since we left the lights.

I cancel the call and relax back in my seat, but excitement bubbles through my veins at the way he looked at me. He needs my forgiveness, but I need his too. Can he? Is it possible that he could forgive me?

Cal parks at the cemetery. I hold on to the balloons while he unfolds the pushchair. He gently lifts Caleb's sleeping body from the car seat and lays him flat in the buggy, making sure he clips him in securely.

I cover him with the hood to keep off the fresh autumn breeze. Cal hangs the bag with the teddy hidden inside over the handlebars and pushes Caleb down the path, through the mass of headstones in all various shapes and sizes, until we reach the bottom where a smaller section of grass is carved out of the landscaped gardens. Several smaller plots line the area, covered in teddies, balloons, toys and flowers.

Holding the helium balloons in my hand, I feel so small. I can't imagine what he's been through. Although I have an idea from when I miscarried. My baby never lived beyond fourteen weeks. I never got to bury him or her or mourn the loss of my child.

"Hello, love." Cal's mum steps around a headstone onto the path and hugs Cal. Her hand rubs up and down his back. "How you doing? I know today is always difficult."

"I'm fine, Mum. Really." He reassures her with a smile.

She bends down, peeking under the hood of the pushchair, and lowers her voice. "Look at him, sleeping like an angel." She turns to me. "It's nice to see you're better."

"Thanks." I give her a fake smile. I'm still angry that she never passed my letter on to Cal and all this confusion and situation we're in may have been avoided.

"Well, I'll leave you to it. I have a doctor's appointment in thirty minutes."

Cal stops his mum's small, frail body. "Everything all right?"

"Oh, it's nothing, love. Just about changing my tablets."

Cal relaxes his face and gives her a peck on the cheek. "I'll bring Caleb round to see you tomorrow."

"That'll be lovely. Steph, you're welcome too if you feel

up to it." She smiles and walks along the path towards the car park.

Was that an olive branch? I guess seeing as I'm in a forgiving mood, I'll take it. If Cal wants me there. He might not want me to go. He probably goes to his mum's for a little respite from me.

Cal manoeuvres the pushchair onto the grass and, using his foot, he snaps the brake against the back wheel. His large hand engulfs mine, and he guides me a few spaces down to a grey headstone in the shape of a teddy with Jaxon engraved on the stone.

Fresh flowers cover the ground and a truck planter holds a small yellow rose bush. He lets go of my hand and pulls the teddy from the bag and places it in front of the stone underneath his name.

I drop the balloon weights next to it, in front of the truck planter, then take a step back and slide my arm around Cal's broad back, under his jacket. "You never have to do this alone. I'll always be here for you. And when Caleb's able to understand, you can tell him he has an older brother watching over him."

He kisses my forehead. "Thank you."

His arm slides around my shoulder, and we stand like this for a while, facing the small grave. The sun shines down on us, warming my face in the autumn breeze as if the heavens are smiling at us.

My arm tightens around Cal's waist, and my fist clings to the cotton fabric of his t-shirt. "I forgive you, for whatever it is you think you've done to me."

He clears his throat and stands a little taller, still looking straight ahead. "I've done many things, Steph. Many things that I regret every day."

"Let's not dwell on the past. I forgive you for everything. Can you forgive me?" I choke up on the last word and hold my breath. My heart throbs in my throat, hoping he will say the words I so desperately need to hear.

He turns to face me. His hands move to hold my waist. "Forgive you for what? Giving me the best gift a woman can give?"

Tears threaten my eyes, but a smile spreads across my face. "Are we talking about my book?" I giggle and look away as his gaze intensifies, making my heart almost burst from my chest.

He chuckles, glancing over my shoulder at Caleb sleeping in the pushchair. "The book was a good gift, but you know what I'm talking about."

I press my lips together as if in thought. "Hmm, it's the watch, isn't it?"

His fingers dig into the flesh around my waist. "Stop messing around. You know our son is the best gift you've ever given me."

My smile widens. "I thought he was a gift from you. You said you were going to give me a leaving gift I'll never forget."

A puff of laughter leaves his lips and tickles my cheek as he inches closer to my face. My breath hitches, and I lift my chin, ready to meet his lips.

A cry from behind makes me jump, and I remember to breathe again. Cal removes his hands from my waist and steps behind me towards our son.

He unclips him from the buggy and carries him the few paces back to Jax's grave. "Daddy's got you, little dude."

Caleb's bottom lip twitches as he comes around, rubbing his eyes.

"Look at the pretty balloons, Caleb." I point to the coloured balloons swaying in the breeze.

His eyes widen as they follow the movements of them dancing in the wind.

"Shall we watch them float up to the clouds?" I collect the strings and untangle them from the weight.

"Leave one on." Cal says.

I hand him the last one attached to the plastic weight in the shape of a star, and he hands it to Caleb.

"Here you go, mate. This one's for you, from your brother, Jax." Cal's eyes glisten under the sun's rays, shimmering like a smokey quartz jewel as he gazes at our boy. He glances at me, his smile reaches his eyes, making them sparkle once more.

Warmth spreads through my body, watching the two of them. "Are you ready?" I ask, holding the balloons out in front of me.

Cal's warm palm slips over my other hand, resting at my side, and our fingers entwine.

I release the biodegradable balloons, and we stay like this. Still. Holding hands while we watch the balloons spread out and fade into the heavenly blue sky.

STEPH

Stepping out of the bathroom after my morning shower, I hear Cal grumbling. The sound comes from Caleb's room. I throw on my dressing gown and stand in the doorway of his nursery, wondering what all the fuss is about.

"What's going on?" I smile as Cal wipes Caleb's bottom with more baby wipes than necessary and his t-shirt covers his nose.

"He's shit all up his back." Cal lifts his tiny legs on the changing table, and the smell hits my nose as he runs another handful of baby wipes down his back and bottom. A giggle escapes me, watching him screw up his face.

"Mammammam." Caleb babbles away. I don't actually know if he's trying to say mummy or if it's the only syllable he can actually say, which is why he says it all the time.

"Mummy, yeah. She wouldn't be laughing, mate, if she was the one wiping your arse." Cal throws the dirty wipes into the bin next to him, then pulls out a clean nappy from the box under the changing table.

Caleb wriggles, and Cal struggles to secure the nappy. Liquid sprays out like a fountain all over Cal's Motley Crue t-shirt.

"Ah, shit," Cal grumbles.

Caleb giggles, showing us those little dimples, and I can't stop laughing at Cal's sodden t-shirt. "I always said that band was a load of piss."

Cal secures the nappy. "Mummy's taking the piss now out of our favourite band. Shall we get her?"

"Mammamm."

Cal gently places our son in his cot and turns to me with a mischievous grin tugging at the corner of his lips. He pulls off the wet t-shirt, and my stomach clenches when I realise what he's about to do.

"No, Cal." I turn and run down the landing to the safety of my bedroom, but before I can close the door, his chest presses against me, pinning me between him and the wall. I hold his forearm away from me with the wee stained t-shirt crumpled in his hand.

"You're not laughing now, are you?" He smirks, threatening to rub the garment in my face. The ammonia hits my nostrils, making me gag a little.

"Cal, please. I've just showered."

"Take it back." He grins, getting closer to my face.

"Never." I giggle again.

"Then you're gonna get it."

I use all the strength of my good arm to hold him at bay as I wriggle to free myself. His warm body presses against my breasts, the hairs on his chest brush my skin, and I realise my dressing gown has come loose.

He looks down between us at my chest, rising and falling heavily against the flittering phoenix on his. "Baby."

The t-shirt drops from his hands. He crashes his lips to mine, tangling his fingers in my hair as he tilts my head to the angle he requires, taking full possession of my mouth.

A light burns through me just as the sunlight burns through the morning dew on the window. Every inch of my skin tingles with excitement. The headiness causes me to forget to breathe. If he wasn't pinning me against the wall, I would pool at his feet.

He tears the robe wide open and breaks the kiss, pulling back to rake my body with his ravenous eyes. The phoenix on his chest is in full flight as his breathing soars, matching my own heavy pants.

In another frenzy of passion, he collides with my lips once more, tugging the robe down off my shoulders. His hand cups the apex of my thighs, and I suck in a sharp breath, feeling his warm hand there. It's been so long since I've been touched. If this is a one off with him, I'll take it. He's the elixir I need, though I fear I'll become addicted, and he'll leave me cold turkey again.

A finger slips between my folds and finds my bundle of nerves. He moves lower, entering me and circles me with his thumb. With each flick of his pad, my body jerks at the unfamiliar sensation. It's been so long. His other hand squeezes my breast, grazing my nipple.

Tingles flutter across my skin as his hot mouth moves down my jaw and sucks on my neck. His fingers work their magic, like Jimi Hendrix strumming his guitar, creating a purple haze all around me.

Whines echo from Caleb's room, snapping me from this euphoria.

Cal pulls his erection from his joggers and rubs the dripping tip over my plump belly.

"Cal, Caleb is crying."

"He's fine. I put him in his cot." He continues to pepper my face with kisses as if he's deaf to his whimpers.

"But he's crying."

"I just need one minute." He spins us around, lifting my naked body to perch on the dressing table.

My makeup brushes and hair products topple over,

clattering against the glass top and fall to the floor as my arse takes up most of the space.

Cals's rough hands grip my thighs. "He'll be fine for one minute."

"One minute?" I gulp. "I need more than one minute."

"I don't." He parts my legs, wrapping them around his waist and rubs his length up and down my seam. "Fuck." He tilts his head back, closing his eyes as he lets out a low growl.

Caleb cries out again, as he does when he's left alone for more than a minute. The sound pierces my ears as only a mother knows, but I can't move. I don't want to move, afraid I won't get this chance again to feel him inside of me.

"Just let me have you. I need you, Steph. I need to be inside you. It's been too long." He sucks at my neck, nipping my skin. "Say you want me too, baby."

I cling to him, digging my nails into his back. "I want you, Cal."

He looks into my eyes as he feels between my legs, guiding his erection into me. I press my lips together as he pushes in slowly, feeling the pinch, and breathe out through my nostrils. Caleb's whines in the other room break my concentration, but I need to feel him fully seated; that delicious painful stretch when he fills me with ecstasy.

"Steph, baby. You're so tight." He pushes in further with a groan, and his eyes flicker. "Fuck, baby. I'm not hurting you, am I?"

I shake my head and bite hard on my lip. The burn as he stretches me is both pain and pleasure. Though I haven't been with anyone since him, everything feels different.

Cal digs his fingers into my fleshy behind, forcing me closer to him until he's fully seated inside me, and lets out another groan. "I won't take long." He pulls out slightly before pushing back in, making my eyes water with the burn. "Steph, baby. Let me know if your ribs hurt."

"I'm okay." I tense my legs around his waist while holding him tight against me so he doesn't see the painful pleasure etched on my face. A slight stab in my ribs with each heavy pant.

He grinds into me again and again, panting heavily into my neck as he races to the finish line. "I'm coming. Fuck." He cries out, drowning out his son's whimpers.

Resting his forehead against mine, he catches his breath. The burn rages where my opening is tightly gripping his length, but I don't want this closeness to go. I've missed him so much.

Taking my face in his hands, he kisses me again, softly and tenderly this time. With every feathery stroke of his tongue, I sense the love he has for me.

"You're gonna need another shower." He smirks as he pulls his head back, then looks between us as he pulls out of me. "You clean up. I'll get Caleb his breakfast." He pulls his joggers up and walks off without giving me a second look.

I lift my bottom off the dressing table, leaving an imprint of my arse on the mirrored glass. I collect my robe from the floor and wrap it around me before heading back to the bathroom.

After washing myself for the second time this morning, I walk into the kitchen. Caleb is in his highchair while Cal is doing the aeroplane, trying to get him to eat a fruity jar of baby food that resembles sick. I wouldn't want to eat that either.

"I made you a coffee." Cal nods to the pot on the counter.

"Thanks." I pour myself a drink and run my fingers through the ends of my damp hair.

He makes another aeroplane sound, waving the spoon in front of Caleb's face, but he spits it back out.

"Just give him a rusk." I pull the packet of biscuits from the cupboard and place one on his tray.

Cal rolls his eyes, but gives up with the fruity porridge and throws it in the bin.

I lean against the worktop, sipping my coffee.

His hand slides over the curve of my hip. "Are you all right? Tell me if I hurt you."

I shake my head. "It's fine. It pinched a little, but I'm fine."

"Do you need me to kiss it better later?"

I blow into my coffee. "I might take you up on that."

He drops his head, letting out a long breath. "I should have got you ready for me. I'll make it up to you, I promise."

That's all I needed to hear. Just knowing I'll be able to get my fix of him again is enough to satisfy me for now. "Go and shower. I'll take over here."

He pecks my forehead before he leaves, and I can't stop smiling. Even with the burn between my thighs, I smile with every biting sting as the ghost of him still lingers there.

The front door opens. I poke my head around the corner. "Did you enjoy the cinema?"

"Maxine bought us sweets and popcorn." Cassie drops her bag and shoes in the hall and runs up the stairs.

Cairen walks into the kitchen. "Where's my iPad?"

"Well, hello to you too."

"Hi, Mum." He huffs, then spots his tablet next to the fruit bowl where he left it a few days ago and walks towards the lounge.

Justin enters the kitchen and ruffles Caleb's hair as he sucks on his rusk. "All right, kiddo."

"Mammmmam."

"That's all he says lately." I shrug and smile at Justin.

"You look well." He smiles back at me.

"Do I?" My cheeks ache from smiling so much, but I can't stop.

"You're glowing."

My hands cover my cheeks. "Am I?"

"Yeah, something happened with…" He wiggles his eyebrows.

"It must be the divorce." I grab the paperwork from behind the fruit bowl and hand it to him. "All signed."

He chuckles. "Thanks, Steph. I guess this is a fresh start for both of us, ay?" He shuffles on his feet. "But I'll always be here if you need anything."

"Likewise."

"Great, well, I'll get these to the solicitors. What will you do, change your name back to Harrington?"

I slump against the worktop, thinking about all the paperwork. "If I'm honest, I don't know if I can be bothered. I have to change Caleb's name from Bailey to Richards, but I think I'll keep Bailey. At least I'll still have the same last name as Cassie and Cairen."

Cal appears in the kitchen wearing jeans and t-shirt, towelling off his wet hair. "Hey, Justin." He slips an arm around my waist as if claiming me in front of him and presses his lips to the side of my forehead, showing Justin I'm his and only his.

I didn't think my smile could get any bigger, but my cheeks push up even more, making my eyes squint.

"Hey." Justin rolls the paperwork up in his hands. "Right, I'd best be off."

"I'll see you out." I follow Justin to the door.

Justin turns to me before walking outside and whispers, "Maybe you'll be a Richards one day."

The thought fills me with warmth. That's all I've ever wanted, but I scared him off talking about marriage before in our teens. I'm not about to make the same mistake twice.

"Bye, Justin." Before I close the door, Cal passes me in the hall.

"Justin, wait up," Cal shouts, then closes the door behind

him. Caleb cries because he can't see us again. Ever since the accident, he's developed some sort of separation anxiety.

"Shh, shh. Mummy's here, sweetheart." I wipe the biscuit crumbs away and stand in the window watching Cal talk to Justin, wondering what it's about. It seems friendly enough. Cal pats Justin on his bicep, and Justin nods before getting in his work van.

I walk into the hall as he re-enters the house. "What was all that about?"

He smiles, walking towards me, lifts my chin with his fingers and pecks my lips. "Nothing for you to worry about. Just talking about changing Caleb's name."

———————

TODAY WAS A BUSY DAY. I tuck the kids in bed, letting them watch TV. Cal gives Caleb his bottle, then carries him to bed.

He returns to the living room, sitting next to me, then lies back on the sofa with the TV remote in hand, watching some viking series on Netflix.

My eyes flick to his, but he's fixed on the TV. "I'm going to bed." I shuffle to the edge of the sofa before lifting myself off.

"Night," he says like he does most nights.

"I'm going to bed, Cal." I stand above him, wondering if he understood what I said.

"Yeah, I heard you. Night."

I rest my hands on my hips. "Well, do you want to come with me?"

He sits up and looks around the room as if I could be talking to someone else. Pulling the hair back from his face, his eyes rake over me from head to toe, and he bites his lip. "Yeah. I'll be up soon, I'm just finishing watching this." He lies back down, staring at the TV.

My shoulders drop as I walk upstairs. I thought after this morning he would jump at the chance to spend the night with me. Once Caleb is settled, I check the kids, and turn their TV's off now they are sleeping, then rummage through my drawer for something sexy. The closest thing I have that fits is a short, strappy satin nightdress.

I climb into bed and read a book, hoping he'll join me after his program has finished. Some time passes, and I pull the covers back in a huff. Where the heck is he? I stomp downstairs, only to find him fast asleep on the couch.

Seeing him look so content, I can't be mad. He hasn't been sleeping well lately, so I don't want to disturb him. Instead, I pull a blanket over him and turn off the TV.

Though I worry this morning was a moment of weakness on his part, just a quickie, literally. Is that what we are now? Friends with benefits?

CHAPTER Thirty

STEPH

"**D**addy's here, look." I carry Caleb in my arms as we walk into the kitchen for his breakfast.

Cal's working on his laptop at the kitchen table and holds his hands out. "Ay-up, mate. You ready for your breakfast?"

"Mammammmam."

"Steph, why didn't you shout me to get him?" Cal secures him in the highchair next to the table. Then sits back down at his computer.

"My arm is much better now. I'm fine, really." I rummage through the cupboard for a jar of baby food that he likes.

After finding a jar of mango, I grab a spoon and stand between Cal and Caleb as I feed him the blended mango. His eyes widen, and he waves his hands in the air, excited for the next mouthful.

Large hands grab my arse over the tight denim leggings I'm wearing, then Cal holds on to my hips and pulls me down to sit on his lap. I welcome the interaction and turn to kiss him. He pecks my lips. Holding me around my waist, and I continue to spoon feed Caleb.

"I'm not squashing you, am I?"

"No, baby. Well, you're squashing my dick, but I like it."
He winks, then clears his throat as Cairen enters the kitchen.

"Mum, can I have pancakes?"

I jump up. "Yes, let me feed Caleb first."

Cal takes the spoon from me. "I'll do it."

I haven't had a moment alone with Cal since we were intimate the other morning. Hopefully, we can get some alone time tonight when the kids are at their dad's, and Caleb goes to sleep. We're both so exhausted at the end of the day, it's hard to find the time.

We need a night together to talk about where we're at. I'm so tired of walking on eggshells and not really knowing what this is. Do I let the kids see us together, like me sitting on his lap, or will it confuse them when he doesn't stick around long enough?

I want to kiss him whenever I please and not hesitate trying to second guess if it's the right thing to do or not. I want him to be mine. Mine forever.

CAL

AROUND MIDDAY, the kids are vegging out on the sofa with their tablets.

"Shall we go for a walk?" Steph asks, standing between the living room and kitchen doorway.

"I have work to do." I've been trying to catch up on the freelance work Jerry gave me; work that should be Steph's. Although she was due to go back to the office next week now her arm is healing nicely, but I told Jerry I don't want her driving just yet, so she has another two weeks off.

"That's so lame," Cassie says.

"We haven't even got a dog," Cairen grumbles.

"Well, at least play outside. The sun's out. Anything but sit on your tablets all day." She rolls her eyes and steps back into the kitchen, closing the door so I don't hear the TV. They're not even watching TV but like to have it on for some bizarre reason.

"What happened to that randy dog of yours?" I kick the baby walker, sending Caleb whizzing across the kitchen floor. I've been keeping him entertained like this for the last fifteen minutes while working. Who said men can't multitask?

"Cal, don't." She rolls her sleeves up and places a few empty cups in the dishwasher.

"Don't what? He was rampant. Did Justin get to keep the dog? I still can't believe he didn't let you keep the house." I huff and carry on typing.

She sighs, dropping her shoulders, and leans back against the counter. "He passed away last year, just before Caleb was born." Her voice chokes up, and her eyes water.

Fuck. Me and my big mouth. "Shit. Sorry." I stand from the chair and wrap my arms around her. She covers her face with her hands and her shoulders curl inwards.

"I loved that dog," she muffles and silently cries into my neck.

My hand smoothes down her back over the squishy rolls of her hips. I'm reminded of all the times I've dug my fingers into her flesh there and come inside of her, and my cock perks up. Down, boy. Fuck's sake, not now.

I remove my hand from her lower back and place it on her hair, reminding me again of all the times I've fisted her curls. Fuck. She was right when she said the dog took after me. I'm not much different.

I pull away before she notices my raging boner. "Are you okay? I'm sorry."

She wipes her cheeks. "I'm fine. I just miss him. He was

always there when things were tough. He would always lick my face when I was sad, and I just miss it."

"I can always lick your face if it will cheer you up." I chortle, hoping it will make her smile.

"You were usually the reason I was upset." A small laugh escapes through her tears. "I don't want you to lick my face."

I dip my head to look in her eyes. "You want me to lick something else?" I titter.

She smiles, pushing her wet tear-stained cheeks up, flashing her cute dimples. "Cal. Stop. You're as filthy as Teddy was."

"You said that before."

"It's true." She swats my chest.

I grab her hand and hold it against my heart. "He was pretty randy, though, wasn't he?"

She smiles "He was."

My thumb strokes her cheek, and she lifts her face, ready for my lips. The door from the lounge swings open. We both step away from each other like two teenagers that have been caught.

Cairen places his tablet on the worktop. "All right. I'll play outside. Can I have my water gun?"

Steph looks all flustered and shakes her head. "Just because the sun's out doesn't mean it's warm enough to be playing with water guns."

He stomps upstairs. Steph carries on tidying the kitchen, although it's already clean. I think she's just making up excuses to stay in the kitchen while I work. I love her being near me, but I'm not actually getting much done.

Cairen walks through the kitchen door holding something under his hoodie. He has a mischievous smirk on his face, and I know the little shit is up to something.

Steph notices too and spots the wet patches on his sleeves.

"Why are you all wet? What have you got under your hoodie?"

"Nothing." He walks past me towards the back door.

Steph tugs on his hoodie, pulling him back. "Show me. Have you got your water gun after I said no?"

He tuts and opens his hoodie, dangling a big pale pink oblong shaped balloon filled with water in front of us. "It's just a water balloon."

The tip resembles a nipple, and it's apparent that's no fucking water balloon. Steph's eyes dart to me as the colour drains from her face. "Where did you get that?"

"It was in a packet in the bathroom. I saw them on YouTube. Somebody put one over their head." The kid laughs like it's the funniest thing he ever saw.

Steph's eyes look between me and Cairen. "You can suffocate putting this over your head. Never do that, will you? Hand it over. These aren't toys."

"What are they then?"

"Cal?" Steph's eyes plead with me.

"Mate. You know they were my water balloons." I smile, so he knows I'm not mad. "Grab us the box."

He pulls the small box from his pocket. I'm thankful it's just my stash of johnny's he's found, and not my bag of weed. My brain ticks, trying to remember where I put the weed, probably still in my jean pocket. I tear open a packet and fill it up from the tap, making an even bigger one than Cairen's.

"What are you doing?" Steph says through clenched teeth.

"Water balloon fight. Want one?" I throw the balloon in the air and catch it. She folds her arms with a frown on her face.

"Come on, kid."

Cairen follows me outside into the back garden. "Come on then, throw it at me."

Using all his strength, he launches the johnny at my head.

It hits my stomach, bouncing off to the ground. I throw mine and miss the kid on purpose. Those fuckers come keen.

Steph stands in the doorway, holding Caleb with a smile.

Cairen laughs as he launches his balloon again, getting me in the privates this time. "Why won't they burst?"

I chuckle. "It's a good thing they're durable, trust me." Although they must be a couple of years old, the last time I used one was with Steph. They've been stuffed in my toiletry bag since I moved to Oz. They must have fallen out this morning.

Using all my strength, I aim mine at the wall. It splatters against the brick. "Yeah, I got one. Throw it at the brick, mate, see if you can bust it."

He grunts, using all his energy to launch it at the brick wall, but it bounces onto the floor, rolling along the grass.

"Have another go, mate. I'll get another one."

Steph follows me into the kitchen and watches me fill another johnny. "Make sure you save some. The kids are at Justin's tonight, remember?"

A smile spreads across my face. So she does want me. I was worried my one minute wonder the other day may have put her off. "I didn't think we needed to use these?" My eyebrows pull together. We didn't use one the other day.

She moves Caleb to the other side of her hip. "I haven't had a period since giving birth. You don't have them when breastfeeding, so I think we'll be okay, but I don't want to take another risk, do you? My milk dried up after the accident."

A red blush speckles her cheeks as she bites her lip and looks down. She's adorable like this, sending a warmth straight to my dick that matches the heat in her cheeks.

"It wouldn't be a risk. I'd have a dozen kids with you." My cock jerks to life like it's heard me and getting ready to perform the next sixty-second act.

"I'm not in the habit of having kids with people I'm not in a relationship with." Her wide green eyes stare blankly at me.

I tie off the water-filled balloon, staring back at her, trying to judge what she meant by that. Does she want a relationship? Fuck, if she doesn't, then my plans I made with Justin yesterday may be short-lived. "Neither am I." I step closer, hoping to sneak a kiss.

Cassie runs into the kitchen. "Can I have a water balloon?"

I hand her the one I just made and take another step towards Steph, brushing my fingers against her rosy cheeks.

"Cal, I did it." Cairen bursts into the kitchen with a huge smile on his face. "Can I have another?"

I pull the last one from the box and twist the clear wrapper between my fingers, staring into Steph's eyes. "Last one. Your call, Steph." I lean in and whisper in her ear, "But we're still doing that thing tonight, with or without this."

Her breath hitches, and the red glow in her cheeks deepens.

"Can I have it? Please. I need to get Cassie."

I wait for Steph to give the go ahead. She nods and looks away, getting Caleb's lunch ready.

"All right kid, this is the last one." I chuckle, filling up the balloon extra big. "Here, make sure you get your sister good."

"Thanks, Cal." He snatches it from my hand as soon as I've tied a knot at the top. I feel like we've made a little progress today and maybe the kid doesn't hate me after all.

And Steph, well, if she's willing to risk another kid with me, maybe she's in this for the long haul, because I sure as hell am not going anywhere.

STEPH

Cal sits back in front of the laptop while I spoon Caleb his warm butternut squash and broccoli blend. He spits it out and reaches for Cal.

"Mammamm." He holds his arms out, squeezing his hands closed and open again.

"Daddy? You want Daddy?"

"Mammamm." He jerks his body as if trying to get to Cal.

"He wants you, Daddy."

Cal sighs, rubbing his forehead. "I told Jerry I'd send this email an hour ago. The client's waiting, Steph. I can't even find the file on the server."

"What customer?"

"Some reiki shit. Just keep him busy for ten minutes while I try to sort this."

"I started that job. Let me find it and send the email while you feed him."

We swap seats, and I locate the file right away, remembering the guy and his third eye doing the Ago Doo dance. "Found it. Who am I emailing it to?"

"The sign company we use wants his logo. He's having a sign made for his workshop." Cal makes a train sound as he brings the spoon to Caleb's mouth, making him giggle out loud. No wonder he likes him feeding him. He even makes me smile, watching the two of them.

I open his emails. ancalagontheblack1@gmail glares at me. "Who is An Cal Agon the Black?"

"Ancalagon the Black is the greatest dragon in Middle-Earth."

"That's you?" Kelly was onto something. She said it was a character. I never thought to do the dragons. It makes sense now. It even included his name and the fact that he's always in black. I shake my head with a smile as I click the compose button.

A new email pops on the screen with a ding from Emily.

Hi, Cal. Hope things are going well, and you got everything resolved with the DNA test. I can't imagine what you must be going through.

There's more, but I can't read it as my vision blurs and everything turns red. "Who the heck is Emily?" It can't be the same Emily that he left me for all those years ago. My fingers prickle as they rest against the keyboard. Please, not again.

Cal scoops more food up from the bowl onto the spoon. "What?" He looks all nonchalant and continues to feed Caleb.

There are a load of emails back and forth in the thread, causing an uncomfortable itch all over my skin. "All these emails from Emily."

He shrugs his shoulders. "She's a friend."

I close the laptop before I spew up all over her name. "Cal, please, not her."

"What the fuck are you talking about?" His lips twitch as he stares at me.

Tears sting my eyes as my body trembles. "Please Callum, please tell me it's not her."

"We're friends Steph. What's the big deal?"

"How long have you two been emailing?"

"I've always emailed her. We stayed in touch when we broke up, and we email, so what?" He pinches his eyebrow where his silver ring used to be, reminding me of how he looked when he dumped me all those years ago, telling me he didn't love me while fiddling with the metal in his eyebrow.

My entire body tenses at the thought of him with her. "I don't want you emailing her."

He drops the bowl of baby food on the table with a clatter. "You can't tell me what to do."

"I don't like it." Every ounce of strength I have is being used to stop me from having a complete meltdown right now. I can't deal with this. It's such a trigger for me. "If you're going to continue emailing her, I can't do this with you. Whatever this is between us."

"What the fuck is wrong with you? You email people all the time."

"Not my ex-boyfriends, I don't." My neck pulses like my heart is in my throat, ready to explode. Can't he see how much she irks me?

"No, you just fuck them behind your husband's back." He huffs and wipes Caleb's mouth like he's just made a joke.

My nostrils flare and any threat of tears has evaporated, making my eyes burn with rage. "You didn't just go there. How dare you? You bastard."

"For fuck's sake, calm down." He flings the cupboard door open, pulling out a small packet of milky buttons for Caleb's dessert.

I stand too. My body vibrates against the table as I hold myself up. "Do you have any idea how I feel about her? She ruined my life. I know you left me for her."

"Don't be so dramatic. I never left you for her." He pours juice into Caleb's sippy cup and pours himself a glass as well.

"Yes, you did. I'll get your journal out to prove it. I could highlight a hundred times her name was mentioned."

He huffs out a laugh like this is funny. "I think you're exaggerating a bit there."

I mock his written words. "I saw Emily today at the bar. Emily has such a sweet smile. Emily is so kind. Emily is so innocent. Emily has a tight friggin' cunt."

He spits out his drink. "I never wrote that shit."

My fists dig into my hip. "I wouldn't know because you tore out several pages. So you probably did write that shit, and you didn't want me to see it."

He slams his empty cup on the counter. "Those pages I tore out because I was pissed off with you sending my stuff back to my mothers. They were all about you and how upset I was, and yeah, I called you a load of fucking names I didn't want you to read because I know you. I could write you a million love songs, and you'd still focus on the one bad line that was said in the heat of the moment. So forgive me for wanting to shield you from some fucking angry words I wrote once upon a time." He presses his lips into a thin line while breathing heavily through his nose.

Caleb cries out, sensing our distress. Cal soothes him by softly stroking his hair.

I hold up a milky button and hand it to him before turning back to Cal. "Was she a virgin?" I whisper-yell, trying not to upset Caleb again.

He strokes Caleb's head while whisper-yelling right back at me. "What the fuck has that got to do with anything?"

"Was she? Just tell me."

"Yes," he says through gritted teeth.

"So you were her first?" The tears flood out of me, knowing how you never forget your first. Even if your first was a quickie in the back of a van with some douche, I'll never forget it, no matter how much I try to erase that idiot from my memory.

"So what?" He stares and flinches his head as he says the words.

"I can't bear it. I can't stand you still talking to her. To know you have been doing it this whole time." I cover my face with my hands.

"It's only emailing, Steph. I haven't been shagging her, for fuck's sake. I haven't seen her in years. She lives in Hampshire."

"Why email her then? What's the big deal?"

"Because unlike you, she wanted to stay friends with me."

"You obviously didn't screw her over like you did me. Why would you want to stay in touch?"

"We're friends. Isn't that what friends do? Keep in touch."

"Well, get some male friggin' friends to email."

"Guys don't email."

"My point exactly. Why are you emailing her?"

"I'm not having this conversation with you. You're being so fucking unreasonable. Read through all my bastard emails if you're that bothered. Most of them are talking about you, anyway." He waves a hand to the laptop. "Go ahead, read them. Every fucking one. They're all on there."

"I don't want to read your *bastard* emails. The thought of it makes me sick to my stomach." I cringe, curling my hands around my belly as the acid in my stomach curdles and rises in my throat.

He shakes his head and pulls his bottom lip between his teeth. "You're bat-shit fucking crazy. What do you think I'm gonna do? She's fucking married."

"Well, that didn't stop you before. But God forbid you do anything to ruin miss prissy pants perfect friggin' life with her bastard emails."

A long sigh leaves his body, and he runs his fingers through his hair, pulling it back from his head. He stares into my eyes. "Is that what you think I did to you? You think I ruined you by sleeping with you?"

"I was happy."

He takes two steps towards me and quietly spits out the words. "Fucking liar." His orange flavoured breath from the juice lands on my face. "You were fucking begging for it. I only gave you what you wanted. You can't tell me you were happier with Justin."

He's right. I wasn't happy with Justin, but I'm not happy with him. Not if he's going to disregard my feelings. How can one person give me the highest of highs and the lowest of lows?

"I'm going." I spin on my heel, storm into the hall, and grab the car keys from the shelf.

He strides behind me. "Where do you think you're going?"

"Away from you." I push against his chest as he cages me between him and the door. "Let me go."

"You're not driving anywhere in this state. Give me those fucking keys."

"Let me go." I bang my fist against his chest.

His eyes narrow, making them appear darker with every heavy breath that leaves his lungs. "No fucking way are you driving like this. Not after what happened to you before."

He wraps both arms around me, holding me against his chest. I fight him, trying to squirm from his arms, but he doesn't falter and holds me tighter. Realising I can't win, I give in. The keys drop to the floor with a clunk, and I slump into his arms and sob.

He rubs my back with one hand and holds my head with the other, kissing my forehead. "I love you, you know. I fucking love you, Steph."

"Callum." I sniffle, shaking against him with every sob. "I love you. I just can't bear the thought of you leaving me for her again. She's everything I'm not."

"Exactly. She's not you. She's not the one I love." He lifts my chin and presses his warm lips to mine. "I won't email her again if it upsets you this much."

I open my eyes, staring into his glassy ones. "Really?" My voice wobbles.

"Yeah. Even though I think you're nuts, but I don't want you getting upset like this." He kisses away my tears and swipes his thumb over my cheek.

My shoulders relax. I run my hands over his t-shirt up to his chest. The beating of his heart beneath my palm soothes me, and I let out a sigh, knowing I'm being unreasonable. "I don't want you to stop emailing her."

He pulls back to get a good look at me and dips his head

to meet my eyes. "Are you serious?" He quirks a half smile. "You really do need medicating. Make your fucking mind up."

"Just limit it to maybe once a year," I say, smiling with my swollen lips.

"Baby, you can write the damn thing, because I never want to see you upset like this again. You hear?" He kisses me again, ravishing me against the door.

A knock vibrates against my back. "Hello."

CAL

I pull away as Justin knocks on the glass again. His shadow blocks out the sun through the frosted windowpane. "Are you all right?"

She nods, wiping her cheeks. Caleb cries out, letting us know he's still here like he does whenever we're out of his sight, even though he can hear us.

"I'll see to him," she says as I open the door and let Justin in.

"Are the kids ready?" He smiles, rocking back on his heels with his hands in his pockets.

"Come in. They're in the garden." I hold the door open, allowing him to walk into the small hallway. I close the door and follow him into the kitchen.

"Have you been crying?" he asks Steph.

She shakes her head. "I got an email from an old enemy." She lets out a sigh and waves her hand in the air. "It's nothing. I'm over it."

Cassie wanders into the kitchen like a drowned rat, dripping water all over the floor. Her giggles are followed by Cairen's laughs, who's also dripping wet. "Daddy."

"What's happened to the pair of you?" Justin laughs.

"Callum gave us his giant water balloons."

Justin glances over his shoulder at me. I hold my hands up.

"Kids, go upstairs and change. Your dad's waiting to go." Steph rolls her eyes as they both run up the stairs, leaving a puddle on the floor. "And leave your wet clothes in the bath," she shouts from the bottom of the hall.

"Giant water balloons?" Justin frowns, holding up an empty condom wrapper from the counter, looking between the two of us.

Steph puts her hand on her hip. "Cairen found Callum's stash in the bathroom and filled them with water, so Callum played along with it."

I pat Justin on the arm. "I figured you'd wanna be the one to have that chat with him. You know, man to man, when you're ready." I give him my best grin, and he shakes his head.

"You twat," he says with a smile tugging at his mouth. "You're lucky I like you."

"Wait. Did I hear that right? You like him?" Steph looks between the two of us, and I itch the back of my neck.

Justin shrugs a shoulder and leans against the worktop. "He's okay."

She laughs, causing me to laugh along. Would he feel the same if he knew how much I hurt Steph and upset her just minutes ago?

I gather Caleb's things together and pack up his changing bag with fresh nappies and bibs.

"Cal, what are you doing?" Steph asks.

"Oh, I forgot to tell you. Justin's having Caleb tonight." I flash her a grin and a wink.

She tilts her head, giving me a half smile. "Is this what you were cooking up between you yesterday on the driveway?"

Justin laughs. "Maybe. Anyway, I've missed this little man." He unclips Caleb from his highchair and picks him up in his large hands, bringing him to his face. "You can have a night with your uncle. We'll have some fun. Auntie Maxine's looking forward to spending time with you." He pulls a face at Caleb, making him giggle and babble.

"Are you okay with this?" Steph asks Justin.

"Yeah. We've been looking forward to it. We've missed having him."

I grip my fist around the bottle in my hand and count to five. It still riles me that I missed that time, but I choose to let go and drop the bottle in the changing bag along with the formula.

"I'll get him a change of clothes," Steph says, disappearing upstairs.

"Thanks for this, mate. I really appreciate it." I hand him the changing bag and he drapes it over his shoulder.

"Anytime."

"You have the car seat and everything still, don't you?"

"Yeah, everything's as it was. He still has his old bedroom. And as I said before, I'm happy to have him anytime."

Steph returns with a pile of clothes.

"Steph, he's staying one night, not a week," Justin chuckles, opening the bag with one arm so she can pop them inside.

"He's just had his dinner, so he'll just want his milk at supper with a rusk. He usually goes down around ten. That way, he doesn't get you up at the crack of dawn. And make sure he's not too hot in his cot. Do you still have the baby monitor?"

"Steph. He'll be fine. Just enjoy yourself wherever he's taking you."

"Taking me?" She smiles at me, forcing me to smile back as I always do when her cute dimples are on show.

"Oh shit. Right, on that note, I'll leave you to it." Justin walks to the bottom of the stairs. "Are you two ready or what? I'm going."

Cassie and Cairen come bounding down the stairs. Steph gives them all a kiss goodbye, and follows them to the car.

Re-entering the house, she closes the door behind her and leans back against the glass, tapping her fingernails on the wooden frame behind her back. "So, where are you taking me?"

I lean against the wall a few feet away. "You'll see. You'd best get ready. We have reservations at seven."

"How can I get ready if I don't know where I'm going?"

"Put that red dress on for me. The one you had on at Kelly's wedding." Ever since I saw her in that dress, I've wanted to peel it off. My mouth waters and my cock has the same idea as he nods in agreement.

She stares at me wide eyed with her mouth open.

I glance at my watch. "Time's ticking."

She smiles and runs upstairs. I could ravish her now. It's the first time we've actually been alone, but I want tonight to be special. I haven't avoided her for the last few days, to spoil it now with another quickie.

The other morning was over so quick it was like it never actually happened. I know she never came. She didn't go limp or tug on my hair or curl her toes and arch her back, as she always does. In my mind, tonight is going to be our first, and I'm gonna make it count.

"Wow. You look like Pretty Woman." My lady in red.

She turns around with her bright red smile. "Why are you always comparing me to hookers?"

"I'm not. Am I?"

"I recall you said I was like Ros in Game of Thrones before."

He chuckles. "Oh yeah. It's the hair. What I meant was you look beautiful. Fucking sexy as hell."

"You scrub up well yourself." She straightens the collar of my grey shirt and pecks my lips. I know better than to kiss her properly when she's just applied her lipstick, even though I want to, but if I did, she'd be bent over the bed in seconds, and we'd never make it out.

"Ready to go?"

She nods and grabs her purse.

———

STEPH

I SLIDE into the passenger side of his silvery-grey Audi, inhaling the fresh scent of polished leather. "How come your car still has that new fresh car smell?"

He turns the ignition and twists the tree shaped card hanging from the rear-view mirror. "It's this new car smell air freshener."

"It really smells like a new car."

Cal backs off the drive and turns onto the road. "How do you like your car?"

I squish my eyebrows together and turn sideways to watch him drive. "My car?"

He gives me a sideways glance. "I bought this for you. Figured you need a car for when you go back to work, and I wanted to get you a decent one instead of that poxy piece of crap you used to drive."

My mouth drops open. "You bought this car for me?"

"Technically, I'm still paying for it, but yeah. You can take it for a spin when you're up to it."

"I've never driven a big car like this before." I'm not sure why he felt I needed such a large vehicle, but my heart expands along with my chest that he would do that for me.

"I got a seven seater hoping when my girls are over, we can use it for all of us and make some memories." He glances at me again, flashing me a smile. His hand moves from the gear stick to my hand, and he interlaces my fingers with his, sending a wave of warmth through my body.

The car comes to a halt in the car park of one of the most prestigious hotels in the area. An old country manor turned into a luxurious hotel and spa. He smiles as he pulls the handbrake and turns off the ignition.

"Cal, I've never eaten here. It must be expensive."

"It's not London prices, but it is a little steep." He gets out of the car and runs around to my side to open the door.

"Can we afford it?" I whisper as my heels click on the concrete, getting out of the high seat.

"Don't worry about the cost. I'm taking my woman out. I think it's about time I treated you to a proper date after all this time, don't you?"

He closes the door and takes my hand as we walk into the hotel and through double doors into the swanky restaurant. "Mr Richards," he says to the young girl at the doors.

She checks her book and crosses our name off. "This way, sir, ma'am."

I follow Cal through the dazzling restaurant, lit by huge glistening chandeliers that send a rainbow of colours dancing across the white tablecloths. We meander past a large table full of men in suits and women dolled up to the nines. No wonder he told me to put my red dress on, although I do feel out of place.

Justin never brought me to places like this. *Justin rarely took you anywhere.* True. Gentle music plays in the background, and we arrive at a small table in the corner of the room.

She hands us two menus. "Can I get you some drinks?"

"Pint of Stella, please." Cal takes off his jacket and drapes it on the back of the chair. "Do you want a bottle of red, Steph?"

"Just a sparkling water for me, please."

Cal flinches his head back. "What's up with you?"

I shuffle uncomfortably in my seat while the server looks between the two of us. "I just want to keep a clear head tonight, that's all."

He quirks a grin and turns to the young girl. "Scratch that pint. I'll have a nonalcoholic beer, whatever you've got."

"Certainly, sir." She spins on her heel and heads towards the long bar at the far end of the room.

"You not drinking either?" I straighten the cutlery on the table and unfold my napkin.

He smirks, leaning back in his chair while gazing into my eyes. "I want a clear head for later."

His low, gravelly voice has my stomach clenching along with other parts of my body.

I shuffle in my seat again, feeling the heat there. "What's happening later?" My lips press together, knowing exactly what's happening later. *You hope.*

The server appears with our drinks. "Can I take your order?"

Cal scans the menu. "Soup for starters and steak for me, please."

I glance down at all the fancy dishes. "Oooh, are we having starters? Smoked salmon, please. And cheesy cauliflower bake for my main."

She nods and walks away.

"Cal, this is so lovely."

"So are you." He reaches over the table and takes hold of my fingers, sending a tingle straight to my core.

"I just need the loo. I'll be back in a minute." The chair scrapes on the polished floor as I stand and ask a waiter where the ladies' room is. I should have gone before leaving, but I was overwhelmed with how hot Cal looked in his grey fitted shirt I forgot I needed to go.

I walk back into the restaurant to see a woman standing next to Cal with her hand on his shoulder. Her brunette hair hangs in curls down her back over her flawless olive skin that's on show with her backless dress—if you can call that hanky she's wearing, a dress. He smiles and laughs at something she says. Cal turns his head. Our eyes meet as I approach, causing me to suck in a breath.

He stands and takes my hand. "Karla, this is my..." He glances at me.

I hold my breath, waiting for what he will say. What am I to him? His kid's mother? His friend or fuck buddy—if you can call that minute the other a day a fuck. I would say friend with benefits but there was no benefit for me, unless this place serves nice cake. I know he's brought me here as an apology.

"This is my Stephanie." He brings my hand to his lips and kisses my fingers that are entwined with his and a flutter flourishes in my centre. "Steph, this is Karla, an old friend."

Old flame, more like it.

"Nice to meet you," she says.

"And you." I smile, trying not to be the mad, possessive, jealous, crazy person I was earlier today.

"I'll leave you to it. Enjoy your meal. The chocolate mousse here is amazing." She disappears, swaying her tight little arse as she walks away.

I drop into the chair like a moody teenager. "Have you slept with her?"

"Steph, come on. Don't spoil tonight." He leans back in his seat, tapping his foot against the table leg.

"I want to know." I straighten my cutlery on the table, even though it was already straight.

"Why? So you can compare yourself to her?" He waves his hand in her direction.

"I don't do that."

He leans over the table and whisper-yells. "Yes, you fucking do. Come and sit next to me."

I shuffle in my seat. "I'm okay here."

"Steph, move your fucking arse and sit next to me. Now." He growls, making my eyes widen and every hair on my body pricks up.

"Please," he says painfully through his clenched jaw.

"What for?"

"So I can kiss that beautiful face of yours and reassure you that you're the only woman for me."

My breath hitches along with every other organ in my body and goosebumps pop up all over my skin, as if they're having a party. I do as he asks and move my chair next to him.

His hand goes to my knee, and he ruffles the silky fabric of my dress, using his fingers to pull it up inch by inch until he can feel my skin. I gaze into his eyes as his thumb draws circles on my inner thigh, making it hard to be jealous when I'm the one he's with and the only one he sees right at this moment.

"I dated her years ago. She could be the most attractive woman in the world, and it still wouldn't tempt me away from you."

My heart sinks. "You think she's the most attractive woman in the world?"

"For fuck's sake, Steph. No, not her. That's you." He lifts my chin to meet his gaze. "You're the only woman for me, Steph. And if I say you're beautiful, it's because you fucking are. I wish you could see yourself the way I do."

His lips inch closer and brush against the gloss I applied in the bathroom, and I wish I didn't have sticky lips right now.

He presses his mouth to mine and then licks his lips. "Cherry flavoured lipstick? I miss that about you. I miss kissing your lips. They always taste good."

I smile and grab the napkin from my old position on the table. "Miss legs over there didn't have flavour?"

He chuckles. "You know I love jealous Steph, even if she annoys the hell out of me." He kisses me again.

I'm not jealous, not really. Not when he has me like this, saying everything I need to hear.

"You're the only person I know that has scented or tasty lipstick. Do you still buy that strawberry chapstick? That was always my favourite at uni."

"I haven't had that in a while, but if you're going to be kissing me more often, I'll get some, just for you."

His thumb strokes my cheek as he leans in for another kiss and our starters arrive, breaking his concentration. It's probably the first time in my life I've been disappointed to receive food.

I place the napkin on my lap and cut the smoked salmon into bite-size pieces, like I'm cutting up a banana for Caleb, but I was lost in Cal, watching him lick the spoon after each mouthful of soup.

Cal wipes his mouth with his napkin. "I'm sorry about the other day."

I swallow a piece of salmon. "You don't have to be sorry."

He clears his throat. "Yeah, I do. I lost control with you."

"I like it when you lose control."

He leans close to me, brushing the shell of my ear with his lips. "I'm gonna make love to you tonight. If you want me to."

His breath tickles my neck and a shiver of excitement shoots down my spine.

"Are you going to last longer than a minute this time?"

He smiles, letting a puff of air out of his nostrils. "I can't promise that. My dick has a mind of its own, but my tongue can go all night."

My walls clench, like they can hear what he's saying, and I squeeze my thighs together. "Cal." I glance around to check no one heard him.

"Would you like that, Steph? My tongue on you all night?" He licks the spot below my ear that has me panting. I can't speak and let out a hum. His fingers trickle up my inner thigh and the server approaches.

"Everything all right with the starters?" He says in a chirpy voice as he places Cal's steak in front of him.

"Fine." Cal loosens the top button of his shirt, and I feel excessively hot. I'm practically panting like a dog to cool myself down.

The server places my cheesy bake in front of me and, as much as I love cheese, I want to go back home and have Cal's tongue between my thighs.

"I'm sorry it took me all this time to get my act together, Steph. I didn't think you would want me after how I treated you." He wraps his lips around the prongs of the fork and pulls the steak from the metal.

"I didn't think you would want me again."

He chews the steak and swallows. "I was just angry. Forgive me."

"You had every right to be angry. I never meant to hurt you, though. I loved you." My throat closes up, and I swallow the lump rising there. "I still love you," I whisper.

He cups my cheeks with both hands and kisses my forehead. "I love you, baby. More than you'll ever know. I'm gonna spend the rest of my life showing you."

A watery film covers my eyes, making everything blurry except him. His face is etched on my mind. He always has been, no matter how hard I tried to erase him. "Hurry with your food," I say before quenching my dry throat.

He grins, "Why, you desperate for my tongue? Or my dick?"

I almost choke on my fizzy water. "Both," I say with a dry, scratchy throat.

"You'll have to be patient, baby. This steak is expensive." He chuckles, and chews on more of his steak.

He's making me wait on purpose. He couldn't care how much the steak cost. With every mouthful, it's getting nearer to leaving, and the heat between my legs soars.

I wait patiently, watching him finish his meal, right down to the last pea, savouring every mouthful and teasing me by going so bloody slow.

He places his knife and fork together on his empty plate, leans back in his chair, and wipes his mouth with the napkin. "Shall we have dessert?" A cheeky grin spreads across his face, confirming that he's doing this to torment me.

"You can have your dessert when you get home. You promised me. Are you all talk and no substance?" I say quietly, running my hand up his thigh, hoping I can torture him a little too.

He chuckles and peruses the dessert menu. "Chocolate mousse, crème brûlée, salted caramel torte."

I snatch the menu from him when he mentions salted caramel. My hand reaches between his thighs, and I squeeze the bulge there, making him suck in a breath. He hardens beneath my palm as I glaze over the menu, not reading it, but staring as the words all jumble together.

"Steph," He pants as I continue to palm his throbbing dick.

"Hmm?" I pretend to be reading the menu, but all I can think about is getting him home.

"Let's go," he growls.

I snap my head up and smile. "I quite fancy a dessert now."

The server appears as if by magic, like he heard my words. "Are you ready to order desserts?"

"No," Cal groans.

"Yes, can I have the salted caramel torte, please?" I squeeze Cal again under the table, and he glares at me, shifting in his seat. "What did you say you wanted? Creme brûlée, was it?"

He gives the server an awkward smile as I have him by the balls. "We won't be needing desserts."

I squeeze his balls tighter and his voice goes a little high.

"All right."

I smile and relax my hand.

"Arrange for the desserts to be brought to our room."

The server nods. "Certainly, sir."

"Room?" I squish my eyebrows together.

"Yeah. You didn't think I brought you here just for a meal, did you?" Cal stands. The bulge in his tight trousers makes my eyes widen. He turns to the server. "We'll be ready for the desserts in two hours." He takes my hand, leading me to reception.

"Two hours?" I gulp as he drags me to the front desk.

"Mr Richards," Cal says, while tapping his foot impatiently. The man at reception hands him a keycard along with a load of pleasantries that Cal just doesn't have time for. He snatches the keycard from him and whisks me to the lift.

"Two hours, baby, then you can eat your salted caramel

dessert off my cock." He smirks, pushing me up against the lift wall as it ascends.

"Can you last that long?"

"I told you my tongue can go all night." He licks my neck, like flames licking my skin, and I'm about to combust.

STEPH

The lift dings as we reach the first floor, and I have to break into a sprint to keep up with Cal. He takes hold of my hand during the short walk, and fumbles with the keycard.

After opening the door to our room, we step inside and the lights come on automatically, illuminating the decadent space. The door closes, and he cages me against it.

Ragged breaths escape his lips. His chest presses against mine, squishing my breasts, and our hearts beat in rhythm. He moves his hand to my cheek, tangling his fingers in my hair as his thumb rubs along my cheekbone, sending goosebumps over my skin like a domino effect, trailing to every limb in waves of pleasure.

I press my lips against the palm of his hand as he runs his fingers along my jaw until they reach my chin. He lifts my head to meet his gaze. His head dips, and his lips crash against my mouth.

I'm no longer in the hotel room. I'm in the clouds. Everything is hazy like a wonderful dream that I never want to wake from.

His lips trail over my face, leaving kisses of love and admiration wherever they fall. "You're trembling."

"So are you." The palm of my hands rests against his chest, and I can tell he's just as affected as he takes possession of my mouth.

"I don't want to fuck-up. I want tonight to be perfect."

"Tonight is already perfect."

"This is the start of forever with us, Steph. It's me and you, baby. Whatever happens, it's me and you."

"I love you, Cal."

"Let's get you out of this dress, so I can show you just how much I love you."

I turn around, giving him access to the zip running down my spine. His lips press against my shoulder as the zipper reaches my lower back. The straps drop from my shoulders, and I shimmy the dress over my hips as the fabric falls to the floor.

He unclips the bra at the back and slides it off, tossing it to the ground. I cover the fresh stretch marks around my middle and hold my breasts up with the other arm.

Cal steps back. His eyes rake over my body in nothing but a pair of Spanx, holding my gut in. I want nothing to spoil this perfect evening. I want him to think of me as I was before. Plus, these Spanx aren't exactly a good look for me, but without them it's even worse.

"You don't have to hide anything from me, baby." He steps closer, takes both my wrists in his hands and pins them against the door as he dips his head and takes possession of my mouth again.

"Can we dim the lights at least?"

"No fucking way. I need to see you."

"You won't like what you see."

"Why, have you not shaved your legs again?" He chuckles and nibbles on my ear. Still pinning my wrists up against the door, he pulls away from my face and looks down at my body. "I must admit, I would have preferred the stockings, but you're still sexy as hell, even in these ridiculous things, whatever the fuck they are."

I smile. "Spanx."

"Whatever, they're getting ripped off." He spins me around and guides me to the bed. With his rough hands, he pushes me down, making me bounce on the comfy mattress.

Positioning himself between my legs, he hovers above me. His fingers swipe the curls from my face. "I fucking love you. No matter what you wear, or your dress size, or whether you've shaved or waxed or whatever. None of that matters to me."

"Cal." I can sense my eyes glaze as a watery film coats my pupils, and I blink it away.

He sits leaning back on his haunches while he unbuttons his shirt. "I'm gonna show you just what you mean to me, baby."

With his open shirt, he leans back over me, trailing his lips along my jaw, sucking at my skin. His love seeps into me with every touch of his lips.

CAL

HER HANDS GLIDE under my shirt, around my back. I need to be inside her, but tonight is all about her. I'm gonna make sure she's ready this time.

My lips trail down the valley of her breasts, caressing her curves with my tongue. Both hands manipulate her nipples while my mouth sucks her flesh over the top of her stomach, following the beautiful fresh silvery lines caused by our son.

She doesn't realise how beautiful her scars are to me. It was our love that created these.

My lips reach the hem of her cream coloured Spanx things and I tug at the waist, only they don't budge. Steph giggles, making her belly jiggle.

I dig my fingers under the tight fabric that clings to her like a second skin and try to yank them down.

She squirms. "You're tickling me."

"I will tickle you when I can get in. What the fuck are these things?"

She giggles again, louder this time.

I move back to kiss her face. "Baby, I've missed that laugh."

She moves the hair from my eyes. "I've missed you making me laugh."

"I'm gonna make you laugh every day. No more fucking around. You're stuck with me now. Forever." I brush my lips against her warm mouth.

"Promise?"

"I promise. Now help me get these fucking things off."

She giggles again and tugs at the fabric, lifting her bottom off the bed.

I grip the elastic, and using all my strength, I peel them from her. "Could you even breathe in these things?" I pull them down, and unhook them from her red sandals, then unclip the strap around her ankles.

Her legs tremble as my tongue licks up her inner thigh, getting a hint of vanilla from her buttery body cream. She tugs on my hair, making my dick harden.

"I'm gonna show you just how much I love you." My lips press against her pink little bud, and I drag my tongue between her seem, tasting her arousal. "Baby, you're so fucking sweet."

She fists the sheet and clenches my hair as I lick her

swelling bud repetitively before plunging a finger into her dripping pussy. Her hips buck. She pulls on my hair harder, rocking her hips as if riding me from the bottom like a racehorse, getting faster with every whip of my tongue.

She clamps down around my fingers and arches her back. The pull on my hair has my cock ready to explode. I need to be inside her, claim her as mine. I have her soul, but I want her body and mind and everything else she has. I want it all, for the rest of our lives.

Sliding up her body, my erection presses between her thighs, teasing its way into her slick opening. I lick my lips coated in her scent. "Tell me if it hurts, baby." I hold my weight above her as I inch in a little more. She's slick, but her pussy still wraps tight around my cock, making my eyes flicker each time I inch deeper inside.

"Do you need me to stop?" I gaze into her eyes, moving the hair from her face with my fingers.

With a pained expression on her face, she shakes her head. "I don't want you to stop."

I thrust my hips, seating myself deep inside her. "Ahhh baby, you feel so fucking good." Her eyebrows pinch, but she gives me a smile. "Does it feel good for you?" I swallow, then hold my breath, waiting for her to give me the green light.

"Yes, don't worry." Her palms rub against my unshaven jaw as she wraps her fingers around my neck to pull me to her lips. With every feathery stroke of her tongue, more blood rushes to my dick.

My stomach tenses, using every muscle I have not to explode. Fuck, I doubt I've been inside her for more than a minute. I need to last this time. I'll never hear the end of it.

Pulling away from her lips before my dick gets any ideas, I gaze into her eyes with ragged breaths. "Can I move?"

"Yes, don't hold back. I want you to take me like you would before."

"I don't want to hurt you."

"You won't. Now make love to me like you used to. Don't hold back Cal. I want you to fuck me like I'm the only woman you've ever wanted."

I slide out slow and push back in deep. "You are the only woman I've ever wanted. There's nobody else for me, Steph, only you. It's always been you."

Her nails dig into my back, and I clench my stomach before I blow.

"Steph, I'm not gonna last much longer. You feel fucking amazing." I pull out and push back in again.

Each time is easier, and I replace the pained expression on her face with one of pleasure as sweet moans escape her lips.

Her breathy whispers tickle my skin, sending pulses of ecstasy straight to my balls, making them tighten.

I groan out through gritted teeth, pushing into her heat again, determined not to come, but her sweet fucking moans are travelling straight to my dick like a siren's song. My heart beats against my ribs as if this is a live or die situation. "Baby, I love you so fucking much."

"I love you, Cal." Her words are like a symphony to my ears. Nails dig deeper into my flesh as she arches her back and her walls tighten and pulse around me. I push in again, hitting the spot I needed to make her weak.

She cries out, calling my name, and takes me over the edge with her, sending me straight to the heavens. I'm lost in a sea of stars dancing all around me as I float back to earth.

Opening my eyes, I gaze upon her beautiful face. A wet trail runs down her temples like a slug has left a shiny mark.

"Baby, what's wrong?"

Her lip quivers.

Fuck. I've hurt her. "Baby, I'm so sorry." My chest caves. I pull out and wipe her tears away with my trembling hand.

"Talk to me, baby." I roll to the side, sliding my arm underneath her neck to pull her close to me.

She shakes in my arm with every sob, and I hold her tight against my chest, stroking her hair and her back.

"You didn't hurt me, Cal." She cries and sniffles, holding onto me as tight as I am to her.

"Then why are you crying?" I lift her chin to pepper her face with kisses. "Was it that bad?" I grin, trying to make a joke. "Shit, did I come too soon? I'm sure I lasted longer that time." My stomach drops and my dick shrivels up with embarrassment. "I thought I felt you finish. Let me take care of you."

She holds me close, preventing me from going down on her again. "Cal, I finished."

"Then what's wrong?" I move the hair from her face and kiss her lips to reassure her of my love.

"I just love you so much, and it's been so long. I never want you to leave me, ever. I'm so afraid that this won't last."

"Baby, I'm not going anywhere. Not this time. Well, I am. I've got to go back to Australia and sort stuff out, but when I get back, you're never getting rid of me."

"Promise me, Cal. Promise you'll be mine, forever."

"I promise, baby. This is it now. I'm forever yours, and you're forever mine."

CAL

The following summer

"Daddy, Grandad's here," Bethy shouts, running up to my dad and Helen outside the church. Livvie follows. They've spent more time with him this last year in Australia than I ever did as a kid. Priya wanted to continue the relationship even without me there. I think having her own parents pass away made her treasure what grandparents the girls have left.

With Caleb in my arms, I follow the girls. "Dad. I'm glad you could make it. When did you get here?"

"Only yesterday." He smiles at Caleb and takes his small hand in his. "You must be Caleb. It's good to meet you."

Caleb smiles back, looking ridiculous in his cream shorts, white shirt and matching cream dickie-bow. Steph's idea obviously to dress him up like something from a period drama for this occasion.

Helen holds her hands out to him. "Well, aren't you just the cutest little ankle biter I've ever seen?" She takes him from me, pulling faces and chatting away, keeping him entertained.

"Why didn't you call me? I'd have picked you up from the airport."

"No need, son. You have enough on planning the Christening. We're just glad to be invited here, and to be in his life. Plus, we've missed seeing the girls since Priya moved back to England a few months ago, so we felt it was about time we came to visit."

It was bittersweet when Priya moved back to the UK after her mum passed away. She's had a tough time of late. I think Steve missed home too, so was glad to come back, mainly to stop my constant nagging.

"There you are. We're going inside soon." Steph slips her arm through mine, holding onto the white shirt she made me wear.

"Dad, Helen. This is my girlfriend, Steph."

She squints her eyes at me for some reason, then smiles at Dad and Helen. "Lovely to meet you."

Dad steps towards her and pecks her on the cheek, taking her by surprise as she hesitates which side to move.

When I turn back to Helen and Caleb, he's not in Helen's arms anymore, but nestled against a pair of... "Danni. I didn't know you were here as well."

"Hi, Cal, I wouldn't miss this one's Christening." She bounces him, making everything else bounce with her, drawing my eyes to the v of her dress.

"Your girls?" I force my head up. "I mean, your kids. Are they here?"

"Only Harper. She wanted to see Olivia. Their dad has Jack back home."

"This is my girlfriend, Steph."

Steph gives me another odd look, making me pinch my eyebrows.

"I've heard so much about you, Steph. Callum never stopped talking about you in Australia."

Steph smiles. "It's nice to meet you, too. We'd best get inside and take a seat." She takes Caleb from Danni and everyone enters the large wooden doors of the local church.

We hang back, letting everyone enter before us, and I put my arm around her. "What's wrong?"

Steph shrugs. "I haven't been anyone's girlfriend in a long time. It just sounded odd, like I'm a teenager again. I'm not introducing you as my boyfriend. We're too old for those titles."

I chuckle. "So call me your partner."

"Ew, no. That's not even halfway to how much you mean to me."

"So call me your lover, then," I whisper in her ear and feel her shiver next to me.

She giggles. "I'm not introducing you as my lover."

"I don't care what you introduce me as but you're my woman, and I want everyone here to know you're mine."

She flashes her dimples at me. "Your dad's kinda hot for an old man."

I pull her back before she enters the church. "Say my dad's hot again, and I'll have to kill him."

She laughs. "You have nothing to worry about. I have the newer model, don't I? While we're on the subject of killing people though…"

I smirk and kiss the side of her forehead. "Go on."

"Look at Danni's breasts again and I'll gouge your eyes out." She pecks me on the lips and, with a smile, walks in front of me down the two stone steps of the church.

Everyone we hold dear is here, gathered in the small church. The font sits in the middle of the aisle with the grey-haired vicar standing behind it in white robes, holding a hymn book between his palms. He nods and smiles as we enter and take our seats.

Once everyone is settled, the vicar gives his welcoming

speech. "We are gathered here today to baptise Caleb John Richards."

Hearing his full name fills my chest with pride. It took a while to get his name changed, but now that it's done, I couldn't be happier. There's just one more name change I need to sort. I squeeze Steph's hand as she sits next to me, and she smiles, gazing into my eyes.

The vicar's voice muffles as he continues with his speech. All I focus on is her radiant smile, with Caleb sitting on her lap. This kid has somehow made everything right in the world, and brought everyone together again.

Steph stands, snapping me out of my musings as all the Godparents are called to make a circle around the font. Steph hands Caleb to the vicar.

Priya takes a small candle and holds it proud in front of her lilac dress. The glow from the flame highlights her beaming face under her large hat like she's at a royal wedding.

Justin stands next to her, lighting his candle. His light blue tie matches his gleaming eyes as he smiles at our boy. Steph's siblings, Sam and Seb, gather round, along with my sister, Cheryl. It's only right to include Danni in the mix, rounding the Godparent's off to a nice, even number.

"Danni, would you come up here too," I say.

She looks behind her, then mouths 'me?' pointing at her chest.

"Yeah, you. You're practically a sister. Come up."

Steph glances at me, giving me a reassuring smile. Cheryl makes space for her to squeeze in between us and she takes a candle as the vicar proceeds with the baptism.

After the service, we all head back to our home. We were able to put a sizeable chunk of money down on a decent house after selling both our properties. Nothing massive, but the four bedrooms mean the girls can share the master room with an en suite, and Caleb and Cairen have a room each.

Justin and I set the gazebo and seating up in the garden yesterday, while Steph, her mum, Sam and Maxine prepared the food.

Walking into the house, Lady, our crazy Cocker Spaniel, jumps up at us. "Come on, girl, let's go outside." She follows me to the back French doors that open out onto the patio, and I let her out. The guests pile through. Lady jumps up one by one, excited to have fresh people to fuss over her.

Mum takes Caleb. "Hey, Mum."

"Hello, love. What a lovely service that was." She kisses my cheek, then places Caleb on the floor as he wriggles out of her arms.

"Doggy." He tugs on Lady's floppy spaniel ears, and she jumps on top of his back as if mounting him. Caleb giggles, crawling along the grass with her riding him.

I stare at Steph. "I thought you said girl dogs weren't randy?"

She laughs and pulls Lady from Caleb. "She's just excited to see everyone, that's all."

Lady runs around the small garden, jumping up at everyone. I whistle to get her attention, but she's having too much fun.

Mum waves her hand as she smiles at everyone fussing over her. "She's fine. Everyone loves her, look."

"Callum, great to see you again." George, Mum's neighbour, is here. He's been hanging around a lot lately, but I'm glad Mum has the company. "You never said you got a puppy."

"Someone Dean knew was breeding them and since

moving into the new house, I figured every family needs a dog, right?" I glance at Steph, and she gives me a peck on my cheek.

"It was a nice surprise, especially for Cairen's birthday. He's missed Teddy terribly since he passed. I think it's helped with his behaviour, too."

Mum pats Steph on the arm. "That's lovely, dear. Cal always wanted a dog when he was young, but I worked all the time, and it just wasn't feasible."

"We're so lucky that Cal works freelance now. He's able to take care of Caleb and Lady while working from home. I honestly don't know how he does it." Steph's smile reaches her eyes.

I shrug my shoulder and wink in her direction. "Best job I ever had."

Caleb tugs on Mum's long, floaty skirt. "Nan-nee."

She bends over slightly and takes hold of his small hand. "You want to go for a walk? Shall we look at the pretty flowers?"

Steph follows Mum up the garden path with Caleb, and my sister appears at my side.

She tucks her straight black hair behind her ears. "It's good to reconnect with Dad. Thanks for inviting him."

"Sure."

"I spoke to him on the phone recently. Did he tell you?" Her brown eyes look down towards the ground as she shuffles on her flat sandals. I know that look. The feeling guilty for wanting to forgive him after everything that's past.

"No, how did it go?" I grab a beer from the cooler.

"He asked if I wanted to visit him in Oz, said he'd pay for the flights and everything." Dad's way of trying to make up for everything.

"You should go. You'd get on with Danni. She's nice." Visions of that night in the theatre pop into my head. I take another drink to douse out the acid threatening to rise. "If Mum can forgive him, I'm sure you can put the past behind us." I place my hand on her shoulder, and she gives me a smile.

"You're still playing happy families then? After everything that happened between you two." She waves her hand towards Steph.

"I love her, sis." I take a swig of beer.

"You said that twenty-odd years ago and look what happened. You're insane."

"Maybe." She drives me insane, I know that.

"Cheryl, good to see you." Dean throws an arm over my sister's shoulders.

She rolls her eyes and wriggles from under him. "I see you haven't changed."

Dean chuckles as I hand him a beer from the cooler. Cheryl huffs and wanders towards Mum.

"Nice party." He smirks.

I know what he means by nice. "Fuck off. What did you expect, a rave?"

"You've got a decent sized garden for it, anyhow." His hand knocks my arm as he whistles. "Damn. Who's that?"

My shoulders rock as I silently laugh. "That's Steph's friend, Claire." I look around the party for Steph and see her holding our son, talking with my mother. She's smiling as my mum plays peek-a-boo with Caleb. He's giggling with those cute dimples on display. She sees Claire, and they both hug.

Dean knocks back a mouthful of beer. "Fuck, mate. This party just got a lot hotter. Who's that?"

I follow his gaze and smile as Amy approaches. Her heels dig into the grass as she walks, laden with bags.

"Callum." She gives me an air kiss on the cheek. "Where is she?"

I point to Steph, surrounded by several guests. More have arrived, including Kelly and Ryan.

Steph turns to us and waves us over. She's glowing as if emitting her own ray of light. The hot weather makes her cheeks shine, and a dusting of freckles across her nose is more prominent in the outdoor summer sun.

Amy gives her a kiss on both cheeks. "Sweetie, I brought gifts." She hands Steph a bottle of French champagne and a gift bag full of beauty products.

"You know he's only one, right?" I chuckle before taking another swig of beer.

She glares at me. "I can take the champagne back if you like."

"Amy, these gifts are wonderful. Thank you."

"I didn't know what to get the sprog, so there's a gift voucher in there for you to get whatever it is a one-year-old needs."

"A woman after my own heart," Dean whispers, nodding at Amy.

I shake my head. "You've no chance there, mate."

"Why not?"

"She lives in Paris."

Claire hands Caleb over to Amy, and she holds him at arm's length.

"Amy, he won't spew on your Versace dress. It's okay." Steph giggles.

"It's Dior, darling."

"Whatever. Give him here." Dean takes Caleb from her and starts chatting her up. That little dude's being passed around like pass the parcel, but he has a smile on his face.

I wrap my arm around Steph's waist, and she leans into me. Her cotton dress lifts slightly in the breeze as it swathes around her legs. A perfect summer dress that looks adorable on her, but I can't wait to take it off.

I'm going to unwrap her slowly, like the beautiful gift she is. I breathe in her familiar scent of banana and honey shampoo mixed with her signature perfume that I taste on my tongue when I kiss her neck.

She turns her head as I lick the spot below her ear, and our lips meet. My mum and everyone else are standing in front of us, but I couldn't give a fuck. I love this woman, and I'll kiss her when and wherever I please. I want the entire world to know she's mine.

"Dadda," Caleb says. Each time I hear those words from my boy's lips, my heart melts.

Mum beams at me when she hears the words. She knows how much it means to me to have another son, a second chance, just like I have a second chance with Steph, and I don't know what I've done to deserve either.

"Are you coming, mate?" I hold out my arms for him, and he waves his hands in excitement. Dean hands him over. Probably glad he's no longer cramping his style as he continues to try his luck with Amy.

STEPH

"STEPH," Mark shouts.

I turn to see him and Michael waving from the bottom of the garden, holding a large object wrapped in brown cardboard.

Cal waves back at them with a smile. "Look, Jackson Pillock and his partner are here."

I jab him in the ribs. "Be nice."

He mocks my voice as we walk towards them. "All right, I'll be nice."

"You're only jealous because they have the body of Michelangelo's David and a talent."

"I have a talent. You just said I was good at multitasking. And I don't hear any complaints about my skilled tongue." He smirks, and I smile along with him, thinking about just how skilled his tongue is.

We walk past our kids, throwing a ball to Lady. She's going to be worn out after all the excitement of today. I smile, hoping Caleb will be the same with a bit of luck.

"Michael, Mark, I'm so glad you came." I kiss them both, doing the double as they always do.

Mark spins me around. "You look amazing, Steph." He offers his hand to Cal, and I hold my breath, hoping he'll take it.

Cal not only grabs his hand, but he pulls him in for a chest bump of sorts before patting Michael on the shoulder and shaking his hand. "How's it going, fellas?"

"We brought you a gift. I know it's Caleb's day, and we placed his present on the table, but this one's for you, Steph." Mark offers the gift for me to take.

Michael interjects, waving his hand at Cal. "And you, too, Cal. Though you might want to open it inside."

"Maybe upstairs." Mark winks.

"Alone." Michael adds.

I beam at the both of them. "It's my painting, isn't it?"

"Painting?" Cal glares at the three of us.

"Thank you so much. Come inside, let's open it." I pick up the A2 sized gift and place it on the kitchen table.

Mark nods to a drawing pinned to the fridge. "Who's the artist in the family?" He removes the magnet that says 'a balanced diet is a cake in each hand' and holds up the coloured picture of us all.

"Cairen drew it, him and Bethy love to draw and colour." In the picture, Callum has Caleb in his arm with another arm around my waist that's a little on the long side, reminding me of Mr Tickle. A smile spreads across my face each time I look at it. I'm holding hands with Cairen, and Cassie is holding Lady. Olivia and Beth are in the picture and Justin and Maxine, like we're all one big happy family. I guess we are, in a way.

"It's really good. What is he now, nine?"

I nod before tearing away the wrapping to my gift.

My mouth drops open as I try to speak, but I can't find the right words. Cal's eyes widen, but he doesn't speak either.

The colours and light highlighting my enormous belly are breathtakingly beautiful. My hands caress our baby inside me, and my smile pushes my rosy cheeks up as I gaze at my baby bump.

My skin breaks out in gooseflesh as I'm overwhelmed with this masterpiece. I never imagined he would capture me so beautifully, or that I would ever see myself as this beautiful, even with my large belly, dimply thighs, and saggy breasts. My chest shudders, hoping Cal isn't mad that I sat for Mark like this. I know how possessive he is, but I hope he likes it.

Cal clears his throat. "You never told me you let Picasso here paint you. Again."

"I kept my knickers on. You can't see with my belly but…"

"Steph, it's stunning. I love it." He turns around to Mark. "I hate to say it, Mark, but you really are a Picasso. You have an amazing talent."

"Thanks, Cal. I'm glad you like it." Mark slips out of the room, leaving us alone.

"Right. As good as this is, I don't want anyone else seeing you naked." He picks up the canvas and carries it to the bedroom. I follow as he stands the painting on the dressing table, admiring the view.

He closes the door, and then his hands go up my dress. "You don't know how many times I've thought about having you today."

I smile at him. "Tell me."

"I thought about fucking you in the car. Bending you over that garden table, dragging you into the bathroom, sitting you on the garden swing—which we still need to christen." He nibbles my neck. "Have I told you how beautiful you are?"

"Not today." I smile.

His lips press against mine, and his hard tongue darts between my lips. His nimble fingers hook inside my knickers. "Fucking hell, Steph."

"What?"

"You're dripping, and I haven't even touched you yet."

"You only have to look at me to turn me on, you know that."

His fingers enter me, and I suck in a breath.

"Cal, we should go back down. People will wonder where we are."

"Soon." He continues to enter me, pushing in and drawing out slowly. While tasting me deeper as his tongue licks around my mouth. "I just need to have you, Steph." He unbuckles his belt and tugs his zipper down.

"This isn't going to be another one of those times where you only last a minute, is it?"

His lips turn upwards against my mouth. "Maybe, but I got you, baby. I'll take care of you too. I promise." He pulls me back with him as he walks backwards to the bed. I watch him sit on the edge and pull down his jeans and boxers enough to free his erection.

He lifts my floaty knee length dress, and I straddle his thighs. His hand pulls my knickers to the side, and he guides his erection into my slick opening.

"Cal," I gasp as I bury him under me. Rocking my hips, moaning his name.

The door opens. I jerk, but Cal holds me in place. I turn my head to see his mother.

"Oh, sorry, love." She shuts the door as quickly as she opened it.

I hide my face in the crevice of Cal's neck. "Oh my goodness, just kill me now."

He laughs, lifting my head up and kisses me again. "Fuck it."

"Okay, if there's ever a time when you're allowed to last a minute, it's now."

"Are you ever gonna stop going on about that?"

"Never." I giggle.

He eats my face, biting my lips. I rock against him again, losing myself to him, all worry vanquished for now as I just focus on my ravenous need for him and the need to come.

I really do feel like a teenager again. Every time I'm with him, I'm alive.

CAL

I FIND Mum in the garden playing with Caleb. "How is he?"

"He's been fine." She glares at me. "Cal, did you have to? Couldn't you wait till after the party? You're not teenagers anymore."

I smirk. "I love her, Mum."

"Clearly. You're both consumed by each other, just like you were before. I worry about you both. I worry it's going to end in tears."

"She loves me. She loves me more than any woman's ever

loved me. You don't need to worry about us." I pull another beer from the cooler. "Did you want me for something?"

"I was after a spare set of clothes for Caleb, before he ruined his Christening outfit. I sorted it."

"Thanks."

"There's the man of the hour," Sue calls as she waltzes over to us, practically singing.

"I'm here, Sue. What can I do for my favourite mother-in-law?" I give her my cheesiest grin. She laughs and swats my arm before scooping Caleb from the grass and showering him with kisses.

"Your daddy thinks he's funny."

"How have you been, Sue, after your knee operation?" Mum asks.

"Much better, thank you. Callum's been a godsend, chauffeuring me to the hospital while John and the girls have been at work. I really don't know what I would have done without him." She affectionately rubs my arm, giving me a warm smile.

I never thought I'd see the day when I actually felt kindness from her. She's not all bad. I smile inwardly, thinking if any of my girls brought home a fucking dick like me, he'd be kicked to the curb.

Justin and Maxine catch up with me. He clinks his bottle of beer against mine. "Are you all set for your trip next week?"

"Yeah, but Steph thinks we're going to the lakes for her birthday, so keep it all hush-hush."

"No worries. Who's having the dog?"

"Priya's looking after Lady for us."

"Ah, we don't mind having the dog as well."

"Nah, mate. I'm grateful that you're having Caleb. Besides, the girls wanted to take Lady."

As the day progresses, everyone seems to get along. Mum

and Dad even have a few civil words. Dusk descends and the guests leave. I'm totally whacked. Caleb's done in too, and I've just settled him in his cot for the night. The girls went home with Priya and Steve, and Cassie and Cairen went home with Justin and Maxine.

"Shall we watch Netflix?" Steph curls up on the sofa in shorts and t-shirt pj's with a slogan that reads 'Time to Wine Down'.

I flop on the sofa next to her. "Sure. You pick."

She chooses some soppy romcom. It doesn't matter. I'm knackered and will probably fall asleep, but not before nibbling her neck.

She bursts out laughing.

"What's tickled your fancy? I haven't got down there yet."

"I remember we could never get through a full film in our teens. There were so many films I missed the end of."

"I can't help it. It's not my fault you're irresistible." My tongue licks her sweet spot below her ear.

"Cal." She pulls back to look at me.

"What? I've been sitting here watching you watch the film."

She tilts her head and cocks her eyebrow. "You haven't been watching me watch the film as I've been watching you."

"So you haven't seen this film either. We'll watch it another day." I go back to nibbling her neck and slip my hand under her pyjama top, feeling her hard nipple beneath my palm.

She relaxes against me, moving her hand to feel the bristles on my jaw. "Or maybe not at all. It's obviously not gripping enough."

"Baby, nothing is as gripping as our own love story."

"I hate our love story. It's tragic."

My head lifts and I cup her face. "We have a happy ending, though."

Her emerald eyes sparkle like the precious jewel she is. "Is this the end?"

"No baby, this is just the beginning."

EPILOGUE
Part Two

CAL

As I open my eyes, her beautiful face sleeping beside me warms my soul. The Vienna sun lights up the room, bathing her in a sun-kissed glow. Her tousled hair splays across the pillow, and I fight the urge to press against her pouty, kissable lips.

Stirring, she opens her eyes, then hums as she snuggles into me, pressing her bare breasts against my chest. I already have my usual morning hard-on, but I'm sure the lad's just had a growth spurt as I felt him twitch when her nipples grazed my skin.

I kiss her forehead. "Happy birthday, baby." My lips wander to her ear, and I nibble on her neck, the spot that sends her wild.

Her hip rubs against my dick, and she kisses my jaw. "Hmm, Cal. This has to be the best birthday ever."

"We haven't even done anything yet, and I haven't even given you your present."

She pulls her head back to look into my eyes, pushing her hands against my chest as I hold her close to my body. "I thought this was my present?" Her hand waves around the luxurious hotel room. "This trip."

"It is, but I have something else to give you." I quirk a grin and roll her onto her back, pinning her beneath me, and grind my growing hard-on into the apex of her thighs.

"Oh, that present." She giggles.

I press my lips to hers, smothering her smile before she reads anything else on my face. Not wanting to give too much away.

"I did wonder if you were about to reveal another tattoo you've had done for me. I still can't believe you have me tattooed on your back."

I chuckle. "I was saving the middle of my back for something special." A mate of Dean's drew me up a design of the Birth of Venus but made her curvier with dark auburn hair to look like my Steph. He incorporated an 'S' wrapping around her body like a serpent to represent her initial and me, I guess claiming my woman.

I got the kids' names tattooed on my wrist, too. Caleb, Cassie, and Cairen to match my girls and Jax on the other arm. I think Steph was more emotional about that than the tattoo of her. But it only felt right to add her kids to my skin.

She's mine, and her kids are part of that package. It was what she needed to know how serious I am about her, and this is for life.

I wanted another kid, but she jokes it will unbalance the names on my wrists. Plus, we'd need a bigger car. I don't think we'd fit a minibus on the driveway.

My lips trail her jaw down to her neck while I rub myself against her opening that's growing slicker with every stroke of my dick.

"Stop teasing me and give me my present already." Her hips lift to feel more of me, and her legs wrap around my waist, holding me close.

"Don't you worry, baby. I'm gonna give it to you, all

right." I lift slightly to position myself, then slowly push into her sweet sex that's always dripping for me.

She gasps as she always does when I fill her, like each time is our first. "Cal," she pants and closes her eyes.

"Look at me, baby."

Her eyes flick open, and I gaze into those luscious evergreens that bring me home, reminding me of English fields. Her vitality and spirit have breathed a new lease of life into me that I thought had died. Nothing grew or flourished when she was gone.

Now everything is alive with her. Most of all, my cock. Especially now, looking into these deep eyes as dense as a field full of strawberries ready for the picking, and her red lips are just as sweet.

I pull out slow and push in again. The burn intensifies low in my belly, and I don't know how much longer I can last. "Come for me, baby."

"You know what to do to make me come, Cal."

"You want my finger in your ass?" I quirk a grin, wiggling my finger.

She slaps my chest with a giggle. "You know what I mean."

I dip my head and take her mouth, then pepper kisses over her face. "I love you, baby. It's always been you. Since we were kids, you've always had my heart, and now you have my body." That's what she likes. My gruff voice telling her she's the only one for me. She's mine, all mine.

"Cal," she pants as her fingernails dig into my bicep. Her channel squeezes my dick, and I know she's there.

"Baby." I let myself go. Flashes of white blur my vision, but I gaze into her eyes as everything else becomes a haze. My dick throbs inside of her as we climax together, like we always do.

STEPH

BEING on the big wheel with him reminds me of my nineteenth birthday on the big wheel at Blackpool. Only Vienna is a tad more romantic. Our large enclosed carriage stops at the top as people are loaded beneath.

I stand, looking through the open window. "You can see the entire city from up here."

Cal stands, looking at me, not the view. The setting sun casts a red hue over the skyline, reflected in Cal's eyes like a raging inferno.

"This is so romantic, Cal." I wrap my arms around his waist and his lips press against my forehead.

"Have I done good?" His chest rocks as he silently laughs.

I lift my head and kiss his lips. "So good."

He cups my face, angling my head so he can kiss me deeper. "Do you remember the last time we went on a big wheel?"

"I'll never forget my nineteenth birthday." I glance at my amethyst ring on my right hand. The jewels sparkle in the setting sun and a whimsical smile spreads across my face. "So far, this birthday has been the only one to top it."

"What, in the last twenty-three years, you've never had a better birthday than Blackpool?"

"No. Because I've never spent a birthday with you since that day."

Cal's fingers lift my chin. His tongue slips between my lips and his arms wrap tightly around my body. "I can't promise trips to Vienna every year, but I can promise we'll be together for every birthday from now on."

A hand slips under the fabric of my floaty dress and trembles against my thigh as he kisses me deeper.

"Are you okay?" I ask.

He pulls his bottom lip between his teeth. His hand delves into his Jean pocket. I press my hands against the cotton fabric on his chest, feeling the heavy rise and fall of his lungs, and pinch my eyebrows together, wondering what's weighing heavily on his mind.

He pulls his hand out from his pocket with a small red velvet box.

My mouth drops open. The surrounding cityscape spins around me as I take a step back. "Callum."

He steps forward, closing the gap. "Stephanie." His lip quivers, but curls in one corner, and his eyes sparkle. A trembling finger grazes my arm, sending goosebumps all over my flesh.

"This is your main present." He waves the box in the air and grins. "It's earrings." He chuckles, then places the box in the palm of my hand.

I stare into his brown eyes, burning with flecks of red and gold. My heart pounds. We've been here before. I can't figure out if he's teasing me or not.

"Aren't you gonna open it?"

"Aren't you going to get down on one knee?" I hold my breath. A tingle shoots down my spine and my limbs tremble.

He chuckles again. "I told you, it's earrings."

I smile. "You wouldn't be shaking if you were giving me earrings."

He pulls his jacket closed. "I'm chilly. Look, if you don't want the earrings, that's fine. I can take them back. Or give them to someone else." He shrugs a shoulder, acting all nonchalant.

I clutch the box tight and swat his chest. "I do want them. Stop teasing me."

He pecks my forehead. "You want me on my knees?"

"Always." I wrap my fingers around his neck and kiss his delicious lips while my other hand with the box rests against his heart.

He takes the box from me and breaks the kiss. "I'm gonna have to take these back. I'm afraid you're gonna be disappointed."

I hold on to his neck, gazing into his eyes with a smile stuck on my face. "You're such an adorable bastard."

He chuckles. "And you're such a lovable tease."

I giggle. "Is that your opener for asking me to marry you?"

"You're so confident, huh?"

I stare out at the coloured sky like a masterpiece painted by God himself just for us to see. "This scene is so beautiful."

Cal's gaze fixes on me. "Yes, it is." His fingers brush back my curls, blowing in the gentle breeze.

"A perfect setting for my gift?" I smile and hold out my hand, hoping he'll stop teasing me.

He quirks a grin. "All right. You can have your earrings now." He puts the box back in my hand but doesn't let go.

If this is earrings, I won't know whether to laugh or cry.

"You're right, it is a ring." His hand trembles again. "For your middle finger." He titters.

My cheeks ache from smiling. There's a flutter in my stomach as I pry open the box.

A multitude of colours dance on the surface of the glistening rock attached to a platinum band. My hand covers my gaping mouth, and my eyes must match the sparkling stone as I well up.

My hand quivers along with my voice. "Cal." The lump in my throat chokes my words. I can barely breathe, let alone speak.

He takes the box from me and removes the ring from the

cushion. With an adorable smile that reaches his eyes, his hand holds mine, and he slips the ring on my middle finger, stopping when it won't go past my knuckle. "Damn, it doesn't fit."

I giggle and swat his chest.

He removes the ring. "I guess you'll have to wear it on this finger." He slides it onto my ring finger with ease. "Until we can get it resized." He chuckles with a tremble in his voice.

I hold my hand up, gazing at the small dazzling solitaire diamond. "I'm never getting this resized."

He holds my hand, then gets down on one knee. "Does that mean you'll marry me, then?"

The light bouncing off the ring causes me to blink and with it the tears formed in the corner of my eyes drip down my cheek. I kneel in front of him as my legs weaken and feel his rough jaw beneath my palms. As I gaze into his eyes, our noses kiss.

"Yes. Yes. Yes."

Our lips collide, and our bodies press tight against each other as his strong arm pulls me close.

"It will always be yes, Cal. I should have said yes the last time you asked me."

"I should have asked you in Blackpool years ago." He kisses my cheeks, kissing away the tears. "At least I made you cry happy tears this time."

"It's a refreshing change." I tease.

We hold each other, gazing into each other's eyes, forgetting the magnificent view before us, until our carriage halts at the bottom and the attendant opens the door for us to get off. Like stepping off a cloud; a beautiful dreamy cloud, only it's not a dream. I pinch myself to make sure.

Cal interlaces his fingers with mine. "What do you want to do now?"

"I want to go back to the room and make love to my fiance."

He flinches his head back. "You have a fiance?"

I giggle. "Stop teasing me."

"I'm gonna have to kick his arse." He glances all around us. "Where is this dickhead?"

I grab his shirt and pull him closer to me. "He's right here." I kiss him again. "Take me back, Cal."

"Come on, then." He wraps an arm around my shoulder, and we walk to the hotel. Each time I look into his eyes, I know what he's thinking, and it's the same as me.

"You know, I had a speech planned." He kisses my ear and moves his hot lips to the spot on my neck that sends a tingle to my centre.

"You did?"

"Yeah."

My breathing accelerates as I turn my head to meet his lips. "Let's hear it then."

He chuckles. "All right. Steph, my lovable tease." He shakes his head. "I'm just kidding."

I jab him in the ribs with my elbow. "Tell me."

He stops walking and pulls me flush with his body. "Stephanie. You're my best friend. My rainbow on rainy days. My star on dark nights and my sun on wintry mornings. I want to marry you because you're the other half of my soul. You make life worth living, Steph."

Tears stream down my cheek, and he kisses them away.

Fairytales exist after all, along with happily ever afters. Home isn't a place or a destination, it's him. It's where I belong. Where I can be myself and where I'm loved unconditionally.

ENJOYED THE BOOK?

Your opinion matters, and reviews make an author's world go round!

Please leave me a review on Amazon, Goodreads & Bookbub.

Tag me in your social media posts. I love hearing from readers.

Thanks for reading!

Forever grateful,

Annie

Want more Cal and Steph? Would you like to see what their uni years were like?

For a limited time only, you can grab a free prequel novella, **Forever Young.**

https://sendfox.com/anniecharme

ACKNOWLEDGEMENTS

I have so many people to thank, but I will start with my readers. Without you, I wouldn't have carried on with this series. After some negativity (and a few tears), I thought nobody would like this book with the cheating aspect. But then I heard from my people. My readers. YOU. And I pulled up my big girl pants and decided to make this book the best it can be—for you. Because you deserve nothing less.

For everyone of you that turned the page, left me a review, joined my newsletter, followed me on social media, etc. etc. You will never know how much your words spurred me on and made me want to do better. You really are my light and motivation, and I can't thank you enough.

My family. Without my amazing husband, I wouldn't be able to write. He not only works full time, but takes care of everything in the home, keeping us all fed and watered, and supplies me with fresh coffee and biscuits.

I also want to mention my beloved Toby, our beautiful King Charles Cavalier, passed away in 2019. He is the inspiration for Teddy, the Cocker Spaniel and probably the randiest dog I've ever known, bless his heart.

My parents - Thank you for your support and for believing in me. Mum I'm sorry for making you listen to my story ideas, but I have many more to come.

My mother-in-law—my number one fan—who passes my work around the campsite each time she goes on holiday. Thank you for your continued support.

To my critique partners, you all know who you are, thank you from the bottom of my heart for taking the time to read my work. Jo, you are always my first port of call and give me the confidence boost I need to send it out into the world. A special mention to Michelle, Kat, Amie, Jenni, Elin, Amy, Rebecca Janete, Ash and Bonnie for your continued support.

ARC readers - I am grateful to all of you that read and reviewed my debut novel. I cannot express how much each review means to me and I read each and every one, saving screenshots for when I need a boost.

My Yorkshire Lasses. I think I speak to you guys more than my family. Without your support on a daily basis, I don't think I would be here today. You are there through the highs and lows. Thank you for keeping me sane.

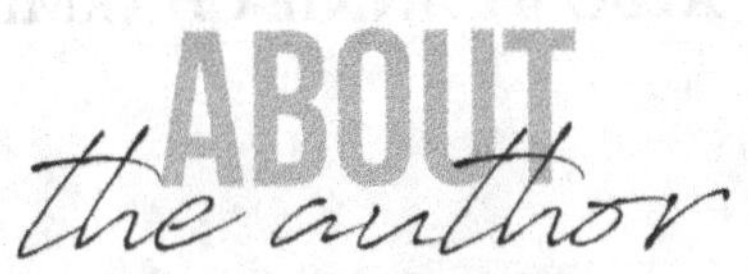

Annie Charme lives in the heart of England with her husband,
two children and a randy dog.
She is a graphic artist by day and author by night.
When she isn't working, you will find her enjoying time with
her family in the English countryside or curled up on the sofa
with a coffee, blanket, dog and a steamy book.

Being an avid reader of romance novels, Annie feels that the
larger woman is not represented enough, and books about
plus size women are very few and far between. This is
something that sparked her passion for writing and decided to
write about women who are perfectly imperfect.

www.anniecharme.com

ALSO BY ANNIE CHARME

The Temptation Series

Forever Young

A Prequel to the Temptation Series available as a FREE ebook when you sign up to my newsletter for a limited time only. Coming to paperback in August 2022.

www.anniecharme.com

Forever Yours

Book 1 of The Temptation Series

Standalone Books

When My Ship Comes In

A Naughty Nautical Romance